WINTERS HAVEN

THE TRANSFORMATION CHRONICLES BOOK ONE

WRITTEN AND ILLUSTRATED BY

E. S. SCRIVNER

Ebook ISBN: 979-8-89283-162-8
Paperback ISBN: 979-8-89283-163-5

Creative Writer, Independent Publishing

E. S. Scrivner:

teamentat@gmail.com

This book is dedicated to my dearest friend, Chad. You are gone, but never forgotten.

CONTENTS

ERLAN

KINDLEDCREST ISLES &
ATHENEUM TOWER

HARROWFELL

KEENING CLIFFS

SPIRELIGHT

ELDERIME RIVERS

FOOTFALL LAKES

WALL OF
HARROWFELL

MOONTHREAD RIVERS

UMBERWOOD

CHORALMOON CLIFFS

GRAY PEAK, TARN,
& RIVERS

EIGHTOWNS

OVERMOOR

HIGHMOOR ROADS

HARKEN ISLES

WINTERS HAVEN

SLIIPMOORS

N

MOONSONG SEA

20 MILES

THE ANCIENT GODS

ULLUMAIR   FERALZMOON

THE SLEEPING GODS

AURUM
(SUN)

ERLAN
(EARTH)

ORIZON
(SKY)

UMBRAL
(MOON)

THE NEW GODS

KINDRID
(PEACE & PROTECTION)

AWRUIN
(WAR & RUIN)

MERCIAL
(WATER & MERCY)

ILLINIR
(PHYSICAL AFFLICTION)

LAIFELL
(NATURE)

TROIN
(INDUSTRY & INVENTION)

AOVA
(LIFE)

OEVER
(DEATH)

AELINTH
(LIGHT & TRUTH)

FAID
(SHADOW & THE MIND)

HEARKEN
(MUSIC & EMOTION)

ULMAITH
(LOGIC & INFORMATION)

PROLOGUE

U llumair's existence was sacrifice, suffering, and assault. Black nails raked his flesh, rusted chains entangled him, and distorted screams filled his head. The odor of wild animal, the smell of the chaos-god Feralzmoon, overpowered his senses. For centuries he had held this chaos at bay, his embrace constantly moving—constantly shifting—and the shell formed by his body constantly regrowing.

But entropy could not be contained indefinitely, not even by the god of order. Ullumair had learned this much over the ages. Feralzmoon was gaining ground, breaking faster than Ullumair could build. Ullumair needed a plan. From within the moon where he held Feralzmoon in check, he scanned his beloved Erlan with his god-sight. Everywhere he saw points of light and darkness, the multitudinous natural and alien life dotting the surface and under-world of his realm.

But there was one which stood apart, one who was unique. This singular lifeform was a spiral of light and dark. He was drawn to it. It mirrored his existence: chaos and order intertwined. He focused on that spiral, and it gave him an idea.

CHAPTER 1

ILFAIR UNDER THE MOON

In the beginning the sleeping gods, Erlan the earth, Orizon the sky, and Umbral the moon, floated in the darkness of space. Ullumair, the god of creation and order, was the only wakeful of the quartet of gods. He ruled all of Erlan from his kingdom on the floor of the Moonsong Sea. He filled his kingdom, under the light and sound of his Flame and Song, with his children, the Moonsung.
—from the Athenomancer archives

I lfair paused his walk home from the caverns of the Fenrik Hills and looked up at the moon. The sky was cloudless, and the night air was crisp, uncharacteristic of the swampy lands below the hills. It was a full moon and marked the autumn high tide, just like the one he had been born under.

Ilfair reached up with his left hand and looked upon the moon through his outstretched fingers. The outline of his hand nearly covered the circumference of the moon, large in the night sky.

"Beautiful," he said, the fuzzy white light of the moon shining through his fingers.

The gravel of the road crunched under his feet as he shifted his weight. He watched the faint signs of his breath in the cool evening air pass between his eyes and the moon. Erlanlights, lanterns constructed by the engineer-priests of Iroin, the god of industry, flanked him. They flickered and hummed with energy mystically drawn from the earth.

He felt content standing on the road looking up at Umbral. The calm of the moment had been a rarity for him in recent months. In that contentment his hands went to his holy symbols of Illinir and Faid, the gods of affliction. He prayed to them for their continued protection of his mind and body, feeling their metal and leather in his hands.

Dealing with unsettling thoughts which came unbidden into his mind was something that he had dealt with off and on his entire life. There were periods of intense mental unrest and other times when the imagery was milder. Recently, for reasons he did not understand, the unrest was the worst it had ever been.

In the short reprieve of mental solace under the moon, he allowed his mind to wander, although he was careful to avoid any potentially disturbing thoughts. He felt connected to the world standing there: the feel and smell of the wet peat of the earth, the hum and sound of the myriad life, the soft glow of the moon. And so, his mind wandered down the path of connectedness.

He thought first of the two holy symbols. They were connected to each other and to him. Illinir was the god of discord, physical suffering, and afflictions of the body. Faid was the divine embodiment of shadows, dreams, nightmares, and afflictions of the mind. They were related to each other by that affliction: one of the mind and one of the body. And they were akin to him, who was afflicted in both mind and body.

He held the symbols on the road that linked the Fenrik Hills to his home in Fayrest, one in his left hand, the other in his right, just under his chin. He rubbed them between his thumb and index finger and felt their texture and shape as he prayed, eyes lifted toward the moon. The holy symbol of Faid was smooth against his chin, in contrast to the roughness of the spiral shape of Illinir.

"... and o' great gods of affliction, grant me your favor and be the guardians of my mind and body," he whispered, completing his prayer out loud. He was barely audible over the sounds of the night, which was his preference. He had the exclusive habit of praying in private.

He plucked a long thin auburn strand of hair from his head and blew it skyward toward the moon; a sacrifice to accompany and complete his prayer. He didn't know if either of the gods had ever helped him, but he didn't know they hadn't either. For, though he was afflicted with his shadowsight and dreadful images and whisperings in his mind, he was still alive and sane.

He had dealt with his odd eyes and these images and sounds, pressing against his eyes and ears, his entire twenty winters of life. And though he was practiced at calming the emotions that reliably called them forth, their mental assaults had worsened almost beyond his ability to control.

Despite all his maladies, his conditions were mostly concealable. *That's something at least, right?* he thought.

"Maybe that's a gift enough?" he asked the night, wanting the gods to believe him grateful, even if he perhaps was not.

Either way, he concealed his oddities, and many other things about himself, from everyone. Even his father.

"No one would understand," he said. "Of course, I hardly do." He added as if to convince himself.

Regardless, the contrast of the rough iron spiral of Illinir and the smooth nickel obelisks of Faid were calming to him and had allowed his mind to wander through more connections ... under his continued control, of course.

The light from the Erlanlights along the path back to his home in Fayrest flickered and shifted colors. The lights annoyed him, as they always did. The light interfered with his view of the night sky and agitated his eyes, causing his shadowsight to adjust continuously to their flickering and shifting colors.

But even with the annoyance of the lights, Ilfair continued to find connections. For the lights warned walkers on the roads of the lurking predations of the Leechkin. The lantern light would lose all its color and become intensely bright white when Leechkin approached, revealing their otherwise hidden presence in the murk of the Sliipmoors. For some reason the colors of the lights always softened in his presence, almost imperceptibly so. No one, save Ilfair, had ever noticed. A fact for which he was grateful.

These lights had been built throughout the region by the clergy of Iroin and had driven the Leechkin away. This permitted the flourishing of Overmoor. The founding of Fayrest and the other seven of the Eightowns to the north had followed quickly thereafter.

The connection here was that the Leechkin, while rarely seen anymore, bore an uncanny resemblance to the alien and eel-like creatures that often squirmed and whispered in his head. Ilfair had never seen one; he had only heard descriptions or seen poor sketches, but the similarity was clear.

Recently, a few travelers had claimed to have seen some on the Highmoor Road between the cities of Winters Haven and Overmoor, but many dismissed this as misidentification of species. There were many variants of Leechkin that resembled spiders, snakes, centipedes, and other putrid forms of life common to the Sliipmoors and Shadowfen Forest, so identification mistakes were understandable.

As he stood there on the lantern-lit road, ears filled by the insect songs of the Sliipmoors with the smell of red clay from his boots filling his nostrils, he felt his thoughts turn toward the dour as he considered his home. He wished, as he often did, that he had not been born in Fayrest.

It was not that he disliked Fayrest, but if he had been born in any of the other settlements of the Eightowns the water to the town would have come from the spiral pumps of Overmoor. That water could not have been infected with the black evil that infected their deep cistern which was fed from a stream high in the northern Fenrik Hills.

His mother would not have contracted the disease and passed it to him as a baby. That disease had taken her life, but he had survived. Somehow the severity of the pathogen, which had killed everyone else who had contracted it, had been dulled by his mother's milk.

The priests of Ulmaith and Iroin, who arrived quickly from Overmoor, were unable to help. Only the combined knowledge of water and light from the priests of Mercial and Aelinth could discern the origin and cure for the plague. The priests of Mercial had identified and isolated the pathogen in the water and the clerics of Aelinth had purified it with intense holy light.

But it had taken days for them to be contacted and to make the journey from Winters Haven. Many had perished in that time. He knew that it wasn't his fault of course, but he nonetheless felt something like guilt for surviving. He often shied away from making eye contact with those who had lost loved ones to the disease.

And, of course, there was the grief. Grief over the loss of his mother, even though he had never really known her. And, even though he still had his father, who was a good man, he missed her, and the memory was a painful one.

"It wasn't my fault. No," he sighed. He knew that was true, but it didn't really help.

Alas, Fayrest was too far away and too high in the hills for Overmoor's water pumps. And so, all those terrible things had happened. He sighed and more fog escaped into the night.

Besides the grief he felt at the memory, Ilfair also wondered if that disease had changed him somehow, if it had caused what was wrong with him. And that was the final connection. Was the infected water somehow connected to the Leechkin? This was where this kind of thinking always led.

"Why me?" he said with a single unconvincing laugh.

He shoved those mood-souring thoughts from his mind rapidly, so as not to provoke the whispering black eels. In that jarring moment, he was abruptly drawn out of his thoughts and noticed that, while lost in thought, the moon had seemed to grow larger. Ilfair looked down and furrowed his brow, and saw the ground was rapidly falling away from him.

At that moment, the realization struck him that the moon had not grown larger, rather he was floating up, quite rapidly actually. In response, he stared back up at Umbral, mouth open, his breath suddenly coming in irregular gasps. His thin red hair gently waving and his eyes, which were slightly watering in the cold night air. As he floated up unbidden toward the moon, he hoped he was dreaming. But, alas, he was not.

"No, this is no dream." Again, he spoke aloud, his voice uneven through his gasping breaths, as though to convince himself. *But if this is no dream, how can this be?* he thought. His heart began to quicken. He could feel his pulse throbbing in his neck and in his temples. As he approached near to the moon's surface, its massiveness, despite the beauty of its glowing fairness, made him feel small and exposed. Real, primal fear began to creep into his thoughts, with black eels threatening at the perimeter of his psyche. He focused all his thoughts on the moon, pressing all others out, to keep his fear and the lurking mind-eels at bay.

He approached the equatorial crater of Umbral, the largest of the thirteen craters of the moon. Though fantastic and unearthly in scope, all of what he saw was expected. What he heard, though, he could not have anticipated.

The faint sound of screaming filled his ears. Not just any screams but a cacophony, albeit distant and muffled, assaulted him. The sound was not unlike the upheaval often heard within the asylum-temples of Faid, the place he had always feared being sent because of the visions and voices in his head. He shuddered at the thought, as he always did, and his hands instinctively went to his ears. Anything to quiet the maddening sound.

The sound radiated from a cavern that opened at the bottom of the crater below him. Ilfair pressed his hands more forcefully against his ears as he entered the hollow, the sound there amplified by the cavity. For many moments he passed through the ghostly white passage, the echoing screams growing steadily louder. Eventually, for he knew not how long he had passed through the tunnel, he emerged into a mammoth black cavern within the heart of Umbral.

The screams, which had been growing more uncomfortable, were now deafening. He gritted his teeth and squinted his eyes. He pressed the palms of his hands to his ears so forcefully he feared the cartilage would break.

Forms the size of temples filled his vision. These gods, for they were so large they could be nothing else, struggled before him. The arms and head of an inky black creature were visible, bursting from an immense alabaster shell, a shell like one bleached by years of Aurum's sunlight. The arms, neck, and head of the emerging being were like those of a man, although skewed and disproportionate in an unsettling way. His wild eyes looked up and his mouth and hair were electric with chaos and screaming. Thick animal hair sprouted from around his impossibly long neck and the long taloned fingers of his free hand clawed at the alabaster shell that imprisoned him.

Despite his efforts to prevent their arrival, the slithering black eels were undulating and whispering in his head now. The scene before him was too much and his panic flared.

Ilfair floated in the inky blackness for many moments, eyes closed, hands to his ears, gasping for calmness against the chaos.

His mind was all distortion and static, worse than any episode he had ever experienced in his life.

Just before he lost consciousness, a wave of calmness washed over him. A halting voice penetrated the entropy.

"Ilfair Undermoon... help... me..." the voice filled his head. It was deep and rich, but muffled and echoing, like it was underwater.

Ilfair opened his eyes, his mind clear of eels, but still full of the static noise of the cracking shell and claws scraping against stone. In that moment, the wild-haired monstrosity of black-static made eye contact with him. It regarded Ilfair intently.

"... help me... help me..." the watery voice echoed in Ilfair's head. The ebon form grinned strangely, or grimaced perhaps, until a scream convulsed its body; it was an angry, bitter, yet somehow sympathetic scream. The shriek buffeted Ilfair, causing his ears, which were covered by his hands, to ring and his eyes to water and shut once again against its force. Despite his attempts to resist, Ilfair lost consciousness.

ILFAIR AWOKE at the bottom of a deep rift, in a land completely unknown to him, and noticed light snow collecting in his red hair. The moon shone down through the snowflakes which fell heavily from invisible clouds high in the night sky. He sat up, disoriented, a dim ringing still filled his fuzzy head.

He stretched his arms, rubbing them a little to warm himself. Some of the snow that had gathered on him while he slept melted and dripped from his thin hair. His wet bangs hung limply over his face, covering his light eyebrows and obscuring his view slightly. He smoothed it back away from his face and took in his surroundings. This cold, dark landscape was a far cry from his home in Fayrest.

The land around Fayrest was red and green hued from the oxidizing iron and nickel in the earth there, especially in the deepest mines of the Fenrik Hills created by the divine power of Iroin's Runeminers. But this place was black.

As he remembered the scene from within the moon and took stock of his surroundings, panic flared in his chest again and the familiar and terrifying images of dark, eel-like creatures whispered incoherently in his mind. He closed his eyes, looked down, and took eight deep breaths to calm his heart and thoughts.

"One... two... three... four..." Ilfair focused on his breathing, counting each breath carefully to avoid the slithering whispers.

"Five... six... seven... eight..." On the last exhale, he opened his eyes, the pupils and sky-blue irises reversed, as only his could, to allow him to see clearly in the darkness that had swallowed him. His shadowsight.

The mental assault persisted but was at least manageable enough for him to take in his surroundings. All around him were unearthly black structures. Sheer and tall black rift walls flanked him. Nearer to him, eight rune-covered standing stones rose up about him like dead trees from the shiny, wet, black ground.

An itching feeling on his arm took his eyes from the eldritch mystery of the scene. He looked down at the underside of his right arm, the source of the unpleasant sensation, and gasped at what he saw. Black runes spiraled and twisted on the pale underside of his exposed and lightly freckled forearm. Those runes had not been there when he left the caverns of the Fenrik Hills the evening before. He shook his head and furrowed his brow.

"How...?" he started to ask in a whisper, which escaped from barely parted lips like a sigh. But his question trailed off into the silence of his thoughts.

As he stared at the black spirals of runes that covered the length of his forearm, he again needed to calm the images and myriad whispers of the Leechkin that threatened his mind. He tried to think clearly, but the eels made it difficult. He mustered his willpower and determination and again counted to eight. He looked back down at his arm and ran his fingers over the runes. They glowed faintly at his touch. *Curious*, he thought.

"... help me... help me..." the watery-static voice echoed in his head. Ilfair squinted his eyes shut and shook his head.

"Why in godsname would I want to help that thing?" He looked up and regarded the visible sliver of moon, its fist-sized bulk mostly hidden by the rift opening. He continued to count as the undulating whispers subsided. "... 33... 34... 35." How he hated all this counting. "... 36... 37... 38." It made him feel weak... like a child.

CHAPTER 2

THE RIFT

Over time, the Aberiths, a writhing black horde of leech-like creatures,
descended to Erlan from space, fleeing some distant light. They
flourished under the dim glow of Umbral. Their ichor covered the whole
of Erlan, ocean and land alike. Ullumair reviled the suffocating Aberiths.
—from the Athenomancer archives

Tlfair Undermoon took a few moments to collect himself before he stood. Besides his memory and name, he took stock of what he had. He had his leather pack with various practical sundries, a half-full waterskin, and his leather working garb, sturdy and warm. Fortunate, for it was wet and cold at the bottom of the rift and his work attire was designed to keep the wearer warm and dry in the cold, dark, wet caverns of the Fenrik Hills. And it was thick and hard to tear, keeping the wearer's skin safe from the punctures of sharp rocks.

Handy, he thought as he looked around, eyeing the unkind and ill-intending features about him. Even though he thought he had at least an inkling of how he had come to be here, he had to admit he was more than a little unsettled. Owing to the images and voices in his head, he had navigated the unsettling his entire life. But nothing like this. He wondered if perhaps he finally understood how others felt in his presence.

Beyond the internal there were also the frequently disquieting circumstances associated with scouting the deep hollows of the Fenriks. Owing to his gift of shadowsight, small and lithe build, and general comfort with the deep places of the world, he had found his way when he was still young as a scout of the unknown caverns within the Fenriks. He knew how best to respond to circumstances like these and, even if this was quite extreme by comparison, he guessed—or hoped—that the same approach would prove effective.

He knew to take stock of his situation and focus on the immediate concerns first. He did have some basic items, but he was entirely without food and had but only the smallest amount of drinkable water. He would need to address this quickly, the water in particular. But more importantly, in the rift he was exposed, trapped, and cold. So Ilfair, in keeping with his experience in the caverns, put the bigger problem of why he was here out of his mind and focused on the immediate problems in front of him, one at a time. In this case, that was clearly determining a way out of the crevasse.

The most notable features down here were eight massive standing stone-like features. He stood at the center of the circle of stones and spun around in place. The circle could have fit two of his homes within it. The end of the moon shadow from one of the spires was touching the base of the one opposite. The stones looked like petrified branchless and gnarled trees with snow accumulating and melting on and dripping from various surfaces. As his eyes ascended the length of the angled obsidian structures, he decided the stones must be two or three times taller than the largest trees in the Shadowfen Forest southeast of his home.

Adding to the disturbing nature of the stones were the runes which covered the black structures. He noted that the writing came in spiraled groups. The twisting symbols reminded him of the mark on his arm, but the individual characters differed. The ones on the obelisks were more angular, sharp, and slanted, while his were distinctly more flowing, rounded, and symmetrical.

There was a dim white glow from the runes on each of the obelisks. Faint warmth therefrom melted some of the surrounding snow. Water dripped here and there from the columns and collected in pools at their base. He felt judgement pressing on him from the looming rock needles. It made him want to be outside of the circle.

At that moment, he brushed his hair from his eyes again, blew out a forceful sigh, and surveyed his situation beyond the ring. He was at what seemed to be the lowest point along the base of the fissure. In front of and behind him the steep walls rose, forming a jagged oblong opening which outlined the snowy sky above, blocking part of the moon. The top of the narrow, unnatural ravine was at least twice the height of the standing stones. Though simple in principle, this would not be an easy way out in practice, he realized, eyeing the wet, black glass-like rock, and imagining its slickness.

Lowering his vision again, he looked left and right. The gouge in the earth extended as far as he could see in both directions. He guessed, based on the stars he recognized in the night sky, that the opening in the earth ran east to west. Looking north, he saw a cave mouth on the side of the obsidian wall. It was a standing stone's length beyond the northern perimeter of the circle. Given the options, he opted for the cave. He was almost happy about it. He was comfortable enough with them after all. And the entrance looked man-made, which was paradoxically ominous in construction and encouraging with possibility. Regardless, it seemed reasonable that it may lead out.

So engrossed had he been that he had not, thus far, looked with much attention at his feet. As he made his way up and out of the circle of monoliths, he realized the ground looked like black glass. Cracks showed here or there on the ground, but nonetheless he could see deep into the bottomless earth below his feet. Startled, this hastened his exit from the circle in which he had awoken.

He scrambled up the surface and quickly reached the opening to the cavern. He climbed up the small rock lip leading up to the entrance and peered inside. His vision was briefly fuzzy as his shadowsight adjusted to the deeper dark. The Leechkin in his thoughts attempted to take advantage of the fear that blindness had created. Ilfair focused on the rock at his feet, his shadowsight now renewed, and used its firm reality to shake those thoughts from his head.

Stairs had been worked into the floor and led both up to his right and down to his left. The idea of going further into the earth seemed deranged, so Ilfair took the path leading up. Cautiously and carefully, he walked the wet stone path, encouraged by the signs of man-made structures. Everything down here, save the white fog of his breathing, was black and glistening: the snowy sky and the myriad forms earth.

Relying on his ability to see in the darkness, he followed the ascending passage quietly. He noted the presence of various runes on the walls, floor, and ceiling, similar to those on the standing stones at what seemed to be regular intervals. He noted that they were not dimly glowing or warm as they had been on the ominous monoliths. As such, he noted that the passageway was colder than from where he had come. As he climbed, he eyed the runes attentively and decided that, while very similar, the symbols here were decidedly not the same as those on the standing stones. These symbols were interlinked by an array of dots that were missing from the ones on the standing stones.

Shortly after this revelation, he stumbled upon an intersection. Judging by the rhythmic pulsing in his neck and his breath, which filled the dark with white fog, he guessed that he must have gained significant elevation.

"Halfway out...?" he said aloud. He had a sense of these things underground, owing to his experience running the Fenrik mine shafts.

"Yeah, halfway, at least," he said, answering the echoes of his question.

At his feet he saw a pair of iron rails and to his left a wooden rail cart, strengthened with iron bands here and there. This, along with veins of a strange multi-colored metal throughout the walls, revealed the purpose of the underground passageways. A purpose with which he was very familiar. This was a mine. To his left and right, the rails followed passageways hewn from the rock. His curiosity called him to explore the side passages, but his pragmatic discipline and empty stomach kept his attention forward to a large beckoning room: a massive cylindrical silo in front of him.

In particular, it was the spiral staircase at the center, and the moonlight and snowflakes leaking down into the room that brought a half-smile from him.

"Finally," he sighed, his voice resonating more loudly than he wanted in the cylindrical structure of the room. This brought a grimace to his face.

As he approached the staircase he noticed a large bucket of rotting black wood with a long black shackle attached. Flecks and small pieces of the multi-hued alloy were scattered in and about the container. The chain ran up along the back wall parallel to the stairwell, along which he saw more regularly spaced esoteric symbols.

As he ascended the black wooden steps, testing them for safety and grateful for his light weight as he went, he could now see the destination of the stairs and chain. They both met with two large portals in a thick wooden floor supported by thick iron beams that ran across the width of the floor, embedded into the rock sides of the hewn-out silo. Ilfair slowly crested the portal, some hundred or more feet from the floor below. He entered a large round room. Ilfair chose to place his feet on the wood he knew was supported by iron beams beneath.

Standing there on the floor, he could see the chain wrapped about an iron cylinder that stuck up from the floor, clearly attached to the iron cross beams beneath. About the room, the walls in most places were a few feet taller than he was and mostly obscured his view. He made his way across the floor, moving like a tightrope walker, to a set of double doors. The doors had naturally settled enough that he could slip between them and, at last, step outside. Looking around, he sighed.

"Just another hole."

CHAPTER 3

YET ANOTHER HOLE

Ullumair wished to rid Erlan of the ugly chaos and hateful consumption
of the Aberiths. His flame could create or destroy anything of Erlan. But
the Aberiths were not of Erlan and so they persisted, ignoring the will of
Ullumair and his flame.
—from the Athenomancer archives

Ilfair looked up and took a breath. It felt good to be out of the confinement of the rift and cavern. But the knitted brow that he had acquired in the rift below persisted, for things were no less strange here and only slightly less confined. As he looked around, his vision was blocked at odd intervals by towering masses of cracked blue ice.

So, after all his effort, he was just in another larger hollow. Except where he found himself now was also a maze of hill-sized chunks of glacial ice. The masses were tipped and leaning at odd angles, revealing, in their absence, flat, wet, black, grassless earth.

He felt forlorn at this and, for the first time since he had awoken, he truly felt the weight of his cold, wet fatigue. It was well past midnight at this point. But it wasn't the time that caused the feeling of fatigue. He missed home and the warmth of Aurum, the sun. He quickly pushed those thoughts from his mind, squeezing his eyes shut and shaking his head, chasing away the images and inane whispers of unearthly black eels that always accompanied such feelings. Besides, there was no time for such thoughts. Instead, he put his mind to figuring a way out... again.

"Think," he said to himself, his head still down and his eyes still closed, summoning his determination.

Based on the time of year and the location of Umbral, which he could see more clearly now behind the snow-dripping clouds, he was now standing just on the northern edge of the rift. He opened his eyes and turned around to regard the chasm. Its oblong perimeter continued for miles, disappearing under ice to his east and west. He moved around the round building to look down into the hole, just to see where he had been, and he shuddered. The gouge in the earth was deep and even his eyes struggled to penetrate its inky darkness to see the bottom.

"Glad to be out of there," he said quietly to himself, the sound of his own voice calming. He shuddered again, but this time due to the cold and not the unsettling scenery. He hastened to put the fissure again to his back. Motivated by the cold, Ilfair desperately looked for a way out. However, all around him, his view of the landscape was impeded by immense islands of ice, a maze of blue-white monoliths.

At first he wandered about, trying to remain calm as he searched for a better vantage point. Panic again began to rise in his chest as, around every ice wall he faced yet another and another. In response, his calm left him and his pace quickened. Just as he began to fear he would be trapped in the labyrinth of sheer ice walls, from around one of the masses, part of a large black structure came into view.

A black building protruded from an enormous wall of ice in the distance. The base of the building was roughly cubic. A cylindrical spire rose from the structure, its peak well above the top of the ice walls which entrapped Ilfair. A low black barrier formed a jagged and semicircular crescent in front of the construction before it too disappeared into the wall of rime. He could see two parallel ruts in the ground leading away from the wall to where he now stood. Here and there, the ruts would disappear under shorter patches of glacial ice.

The serrated black construction of the structure reminded him of the standing stones. It had the same ominous and threatening feel, but it remained his best next move. It would provide, at a minimum, shelter from the elements. If he was fortunate, the height of the structure would also provide him with a view from above the ice and, if he was skillful, a way to escape the glacier altogether.

"Hope springs eternal, even in the fall cold," he said, creating more white fog as he attempted to buoy his spirits with ironic humor. He sighed, failing.

He put his head down and began his walk, staying, where possible, between the ruts where the ground was a little drier to spare his feet from the wet and cold. He grabbed his arms tightly about his chest to keep warm and looked up and about, watching the snow fall. The scale and silence of this place was more disquieting than the rift had been, particularly the looming slabs of glacial ice which continuously wept water onto the ground as they thawed.

Being put off by circumstances was alien to him. He had grown accustomed to regularly processing odd images and sounds in his head unbidden, often at inopportune times, while maintaining his calm and composure. But this place and this situation were quite different from what he had experienced to date and the isolation of it made him uncomfortable and caused his heart to beat in his chest so hard that he could feel it in his neck. And it was bitterly cold. Cold enough that he was becoming concerned, feelings of numbness invading his extremities. He picked up his pace, passed the odd rock cairn here and there, and soon enough, thankfully, he reached the decaying rock wall.

Being near the structure, the visual obstruction of the wall calmed him a bit.

"Like blinders for a sliipmare," he said with a sarcastic scoff, trying unsuccessfully to amuse himself again.

He watched his breath for a moment as he calmed himself. He noticed in that moment that the longer he was out here completely alone, the more he enjoyed hearing the sound of his own voice. It was slightly disturbing, but understandable. It reminded him again of the need to get back to where people were. Not a normal thought for him, but a correct one.

As he walked toward the building, Ilfair hugged his chest and shivered.

He thought of the common hall he had frequented in Fayrest. He preferred this gathering place to his family's austere home. His home was nothing more than a single room attached to a larger adjoining building that served as his father's workshop. As Ilfair had gotten older, his father had set himself up with sleeping arrangements in the workshop. Ilfair had continued to sleep where he had grown up. This way they had some measure of privacy, which became more important as Ilfair grew.

One thing his home was without was a hearth. The common hall's hearth was what drew Ilfair. He imagined himself sitting in the alcove near the hall's large fireplace. He would go there and speak to no one, but he realized now that he did enjoy the company of the others, in his own way. He would avert his gaze, hiding his shadowsight eyes from the scrutiny of others and avoiding all but the most necessary of conversation. Still, it was pleasant. And warm. And dry.

Ilfair sighed as he was neither. He passed the wall through a now rusted and twisted gate made of the strange multi-hued ore. Spiralore. He decided on a name for it to help organize it among all the information in his head. He really did not need to pass through the gate, or any gate really, as the dusky stone wall was completely eroded in multiple places. Embedded in chunks of ice were bits of wood, metal, and black stone that had been carried away when the ice had separated from the main structure.

He could see now, clearly from this distance, that he was in the presence of an ancient temple. Runes and symbols and ornate construction characterized the rectangular prisms and massive central spire of the temple. The construction was a mix of spiralore, shiny black stone, and rough gray stone. Everywhere on the structure were decorations and details made of glass and a shiny metal with a coloring akin to a braised processing, much like the coloration of the ore he had seen in the rift mine. Only an edifice to a deity would warrant such attention. The temple, especially the parts made of stone and metal, had remained impressively intact; a testament to the sturdiness of the materials and construction.

As he approached, he stepped over a large symbol of stone and metal which had been laid into the ground just before the entryway to the temple. The symbol, which lay flush to the earth, looked like a gnarled tree with spiraling black roots. A large white circular moon created a stark backdrop for the obsidian-black tree. Looking up from the symbol, Ilfair regarded the temple proper.

The temple had three distinct steps in it. The first being the entryway and two adjacent buildings which he assumed must have been for metal forges or horse stables as the horse tracks from the mine terminated there with the rotting remnants of a wagon. Two more sections of the temple were visible above the entryway. At the topmost level, crowned by a twisting spire of obsidian and metal, he could see windows and the blue-white of the glacier's peak. This was, he hoped, his way out.

As he arrived in the entrance hall, he noticed the snow still fell on him. He looked up and saw it came through the roof, which had either been torn or rotted away. To his right, his earlier suspicions as to the function of the lower levels of the temple were partially confirmed as he could see into what was clearly a forge. He quickly and furtively stole over to that room.

As he entered, he could see the rotting wagon visible outside the room through an intentional opening amidst the far wall. At the back left corner of the room was the hearth, flanked to its left and right by anvils for working the metal. This furnace was notably different from the many others he had seen before. Most used shallow fire pits fed by wood or some other flammable substance. This one was deep, very deep. Looking down into it he could see the faintest orange light emanating from its depths.

Is that light below what fed the kiln?

As he pondered this, he noticed an odd tool amidst the rubble of rock and bits of alloy on the edge of the wall about the forge. The tool seemed to be made mostly from the strange braised-colored alloy, like the type he had seen in the mine, mixed with a dark stone. At one end of the implement was a spiral of metal with a flat surface that served as the hammer. On the opposing end was a pick. It seemed to be utilized as both a forging and a mining implement.

He hefted the spiralhammer in his hand. He felt the leather of the handle and thought of the stories of his mother that his father had told him. She had been a leatherworker before he was born. The item itself was lighter than it should have been. He smacked the wall with the hammer end and noted that it was no less hard than the iron hammers he had used. He thought it could prove useful for breaking or prying open doors or for climbing ice in the reasonably likely event that proved necessary. And, of course, for defense. Though he was quite skilled with hammers and picks as tools, he was no warrior and so he hoped it would not be.

Satisfied that he had found what was there to be found, and anxious to make the summit of the structure, he left the ancient forge. He hastened across the entry chamber to inspect the opposing room. Upon entry, he immediately recognized it as a stable. More than a score of stalls lined the walls of the windowless room. Snow and light seeped into the room from an opening at its northern end through which he could see the wall of the glacier in the near distance. He walked down the alley to the open doorway. As he walked, he looked left and right at the empty partitions; empty save one.

In the second to last stall lay a horse. Or rather, the remains of a horse. Judging by its eight legs it was similar to a sliipmare, but some northern and much larger variant. Its emaciated body had been mummified by the cold while chained there. The splendor it must have borne in life was replaced with a look of gaunt terror. It lay there on the ground, looking up at Ilfair with white eyes, its mouth open in a silent scream.

"Poor thing," Ilfair said, turning away from the horse. It was hard to look at, so Ilfair directed his vision out of the back wall. It was obvious this had once been a large stable door.

Ilfair considered inspecting these things further, but at that moment he heard a deep muted crack echo through the room coming from the glacier. The crack reminded him that the ice could shift and move more at any moment with any number of negative consequences. This hastened his exit from the stable and cast the image of the horse from his mind, shifting his focus back to getting to the top of the temple.

Standing once again in the ceilingless entry hall, Ilfair craned his neck skyward to regard the needlelike spire. It pointed up to Umbral, and, at this angle, the temple tower looked as though it would touch the moon.

CHAPTER 4

ABBY AND THE SPIRE

Ullumair, frustrated by the unmoving Aberiths, lamented. His melancholy song of failure filled the heavens. Aurum, a distant sun, was drawn to Erlan by the beauty of the song. Aurum's arrival brought light to Erlan. Pure and alien, the light banished the Aberiths where the light and heat of Ullumair's flame had failed.
—from the Athenomancer archives

Looking out from atop the tower of spiraling white stone on the high ridge of the Keening Cliffs, Abby's old childlike eyes came to rest on a black spire. The spike of obsidian rose above the blue-white bulk of the receding Elderime Glacier, gleaming beneath the light of a full moon far to the east of the tower. Abby sighed as the tower brought back centuries-old memories for her, and they were not good memories... not good at all.

"What a pity. It truly is beautiful," Abby's voice echoed out of the dark, a chorus of widely varying tones and pitches. Her voice sounded as though she was possessed of many vocal cords, for in fact she was.

She had spent decades watching, waiting for the spiral to

emerge, dreading the patterned recession of the Elderime. The rate of this recession was still near its peak even though the days were cooling and shortening as Erlan entered autumn. She watched as the inevitable cycling of Umbral and Aurum—moon after moon, sunrise after sunrise—caused the ice at the edge of the glacier to crack, creating fissures in the bulk. These smaller pieces of cracked ice with their increased surface area would melt to nothing in a few moons, ultimately feeding the Elderime and Moonthread Rivers and Footfall Lakes of the plateau and vale to the south.

Up until just a few days ago the glacier had still covered the Nihilin Spire. But finally, sometime during the last day, while Abby hid in the damp and shadowed spaces of her new home in the lighthouse tower, the ice had weakened and cracked in several new places. Now the spire, and in fact part of the Nihilin Temple from which it rose, were visible. Abby guessed that in a few months the ice would melt fully and the rift and standing stones at its base, along with the full splendor of the temple, would be revealed to her from the perch atop the lighthouse.

But, for now, they were not. Even from her high vantage point and with her shadowsight, which could bend the dark and flatten the horizon, she could not see the base of the temple. Colossal masses of cracked ice from the glacier persisted in the temple foreground, blocking the view thereof. She knew, though, that somewhere between those masses of blue-white ice just to the south of the temple lay a jagged oblong rift of great length and depth. And she knew that, at the bottom of that rift, eight gnarled standing stones reached up like old fingers toward the night sky. She could not see them, but she knew they were there.

And yes, she knew too of the young man there. She too had seen his divine message, even though it wasn't intended for her. She couldn't have avoided it if she had wanted to; it blasted through her mind from Umbral unbidden. The thoughts of others were something with which she was quite familiar, and she could walk within them with ease under the right circumstances. *But that was another matter*, she mused.

For now, though, she was more focused on the spire and the Feralrift at its base. The lack of visibility of the temple and foreground, even from her high perch and with her night-bending shadowsight, was not a problem for Abby. She remembered the details of that hole in the earth and its standing stones all too well, as if she had visited them that very day. Abby sighed again and smirked, looking down.

"That's the 50th smirk and 100th sigh just today. I really should be less dramatic," she said to her skittering pet, Ixognath. Ixo shuffled but did not reply. It was large, ancient, and possessed of unearthly power, but it was still just a bug really.

"And bugs don't speak, do they, Ixo?" Abby finished the thought aloud.

"Anyway..." she said, shaking her head slightly and looking back up.

The Nihilin reminded her of many things.

She remembered her parents, her home, and her childhood. And, yes, she remembered Feralzmoon, a long-forgotten god of shadows, darkness, madness, and chaos, for whom the Nihilin Temple was created. But the memory most poignant that had been kindled by the spire was the memory of the end of her life as an Ashfallen daughter of Harrowfell.

Abby turned from the window and made her way back to her favorite chair. The black wooden chair was covered in carvings of her own making and was positioned carefully near the western window overlooking the Moonsong Sea. It was shadowed by a pair of the many book-filled shelves that lined the circumference of the top room of the tower. Cold damp winds from the northern reaches of the sea leaked through the drafty window facing the chair. Most normal people would have been miserable in this spot in the room. But Abby was no normal creature of Erlan.

She sat there facing the dark sea, lost in her thoughts, remembering her spire-invoked past.

She had been one of the first generation of Ashfallen children, the name given to those born on Erlan. She was unlike her parents who had been born in Ullumair's kingdom under the Moonsong Sea. His kingdom was lighted by his Everflame and filled with the harmonious sounds of his song. Her parents' generation were known as the Moonsung, the first children of Ullumair, the god of the sea.

She remembered being told the tale of the Melancholy of the Moonsung by her mother many times.

She recalled it with perfect clarity there in the lighthouse that night.

"Shall I tell it?" she asked Ixo, who responded with a shuffle that made skittering noises on the stone floor.

"I will take that as a yes," Abby said with a forced smile.

Abby turned to the sea and spoke. "You see, the story begins with Ullumair, the god of life and order, sending his children to live on the land. It was his dream to bring the beauty of the life of his children, who lived under the Moonsong Sea, to the land." Abby made a flourish with her arms and looked back at Ixo.

Then her face turned serious and she continued. "The Moonsung walked the long dark of the seafloor with only the light of Ullumair's Flame that they carried with them, given to them by their father to bring to the land. But, as they ascended the land toward the surface, they found their way blocked by a mass of writhing blackness. Even the Flame of Ullumair could not breach the ichor. Thus began the melancholy, for the Aberiths, blights of alien life on the land, would not suffer the Moonsung to live upon Erlan. The Aberiths had filtered down from space, fleeing the light of some other sun, to a then sun-less Erlan. They eagerly devoured Erlan, covering the surfaces of its land and seas entirely with their writhing leech-like hordes. Their mass suffocated the land and sea so thoroughly that even the light of Ullumair's Flame could not banish them." Abby turned away from Ixo and again looked through the lighthouse window toward the sea, clasping her hands behind her back. She became wistful as she continued.

"Ullumair's failure filled the heavens with his melancholy song. Over time Aurum, an alien sun, heard and heeded the call of Ullumair from the far reaches of space. Aurum's pure and alien sunlight forced the unearthly Aberiths into hiding. Aurum silently joined the sleeping and eternal gods, Umbral, Erlan, and Orizon; the moon, the earth, and the sky."

She looked back to Ixo, who remained completely motionless.

"Most of the Aberiths escaped to the innards of Erlan through the caverns below the Godskeeps. Others hid under the muck of the swamps of the Sliipmoors south of the Godskeeps. Still others hid in the perpetual canopied darkness of the Shadowfen Forest. These creatures mutated over the years into the Leechkin, diminished and varied versions of the pure Aberiths under the Godskeeps."

"I suspect you are in fact one of those Leechkin, dear Ixo." She smiled and petted its carapace.

She gestured toward the Godskeeps and continued. "And, while the Aberiths and their kin remained hidden for many years, they would return to the surface of Erlan, many times in fact, in varying forms. They would attempt their revenge on Ullumair's beautiful Moonsung children, always by night, when Aurum's ever-returning protective light waned. And so, the Melancholy of the Moonsung and their offspring, the Ashfallen, continued for ages." Abby sighed in remembrance; she had seen it many times.

"But that is all in the past," she said to Ixo, completing her story.

Looking out upon the Ashfall Plateau, just south of the Elderime Glacier, Abby's mind raced through the events: the birth of the ancient chaos-god Feralzmoon, the emergence of Ullumair from the Moonsong Sea, Feralzmoon's capture and her subsequent death. Or, better to say, transformation into whatever she was now.

"Now we wouldn't want to skip over all the macabre little details, would we dearest?" she said, giving a creeping chorus of breaths to her thoughts.

Abby turned her head to look out of the south-facing window. She had been avoiding looking in that direction. From the lighthouse, which sat precariously on the edge of the Keening Cliffs, she could see the line of the cliffs moving gently southwest out to sea. The cliffs ended abruptly about ten or so miles south where the coastline turned southeast. At this cusp was a short stretch of land free of the cliff which started up again sharply just a few miles to the south of the reprieve.

That protrusion of land, the one she had shied away from, was the location of her home as a young Ashfallen girl. Her life there had been mostly acceptable. But it wasn't the bulk of the experience that she dreaded. It was but a short span of time which had changed everything.

She remembered looking from her bedroom window, just a child, out upon the land she now regarded from the lighthouse. She remembered she had spent many a day wandering thoroughly about the Umbervale, the Umberwood, and even the Ashfall Plateau, the land between the Godskeep Mountains to the south and the Elderime Glacier to the north. And, though she had lived as part of the city of Harrowfell on the cusp of land, this entire region had been her home and, even then, she had known it very well.

Back then, many centuries ago now, she had lived in a small agricultural enclave. The land was needed, being the only available rich land before the inland cold, rocks, or trees interfered. But her home lay outside of the wall around Harrowfell. The wall had been made by the Mythals, the priests of Ullumair to protect from Aberith raids coming from the Godskeeps just to the southeast.

Abby remembered hiding from the Aberiths when the long night winter raids were most common. She recalled running till her lungs burned, terrified, when they were awakened in the night by the bells of the wall guards.

The horrible look of the creatures and the hideous chorus of screeches they emitted during raids were still clear and real in her memory. The multi-toned screeches reminded her, with a combination of disgust and pleasure, of her own voice now.

She looked at Ixo.

"Your kind were certainly terrifying." Ixo was motionless.

Abby, and her parents, and indeed her people, had been proud and tough. Only with this land would the Moonsung population of Harrowfell have been sustained. She remembered she had wanted to be strong like her parents. It hadn't worked out exactly the way she had imagined, but she had been a very capable and brave girl.

"And just look at me now," Abby said to Ixo. All the tones of her voice were flat, her cynicism seeping out into her speech.

And so it was that the raids had been formative in her character and had filled her dreams with terror and wonder.

Returning to her reverie, she recalled that, at that time, she had looked up toward the plateau rather than down upon it as she did now. And it was, of course, day then, rather than night as now, for she had not the shadowsight then.

In the lighthouse, she turned her head slightly west, just beyond the coastline and into the Moonsong.

She could see the tips of the ruins of the larger structures of Harrowfell breaching the water. The remaining lower mass of Harrowfell, and the entirety of the peninsula, was now, and had been for ages, overwhelmed by the sea's encroachment.

Looking back to the drier inland, she could still see the glory of the Wall of Harrowfell, despite the cracks and vines.

She recalled that, on warm summer days, she and her mother

would walk down to the wall and watch the osprey dive for their meals.

Now, of course, her former home was gone, as were the rest of the buildings; victims to the ravages of the centuries. Only the remnants of the wall were durable enough to endure.

Agitated, Abby stood again and made her way back to the east-facing window. Her long, drab white dress, bereft of sleeves, dragged along the wood floor. The bottom dirty from years of neglect. She stopped just before the window to again regard the spire.

Abby shook her head and sighed, leaving white fog on the cold drooping glass. It masked the black spire in the distance, if but only for a moment. She realized she was delaying the most dreadful part of her memory.

"Back to the horror of it, dear." Abby's many voices bounced off the window, again leaving white fog thereupon. She wiped it away harshly with a rapid swipe of her small white hand.

CHAPTER 5

THE BIRTH OF FERALZMOON

The Aberiths fled the light of Aurum. They sought the solace of darkness in the muck of the Sliipmoors, the thick canopy of the Shadowfen Forest, or in the deep places under the Godskeep Mountains. There they mutated and changed as they awaited and planned their vengeance.
—from the Athenomancer archives

As the fog dissipated from the window, Abby's gaze once again fell upon the spire and the rekindled memory of the rift oozed back into her thoughts.

She remembered hearing the eight black tendrils, seeded by the hatred and arcane energies of the Aberiths, forcefully erupt from the earth. The roots rose, stark against the blue-white bulk of the Elderime. She remembered rushing to her window and looking for the cause of the sound. She remembered watching the black branches rise. They were covered in Aberithic runes that glowed white like stars sitting against the blackness of the roots.

She scrambled to the roof for a better view. Once they'd stopped their ascent, she saw a small dot floating delicately above the roots. It stuck out due to the stark contrast between itself and the cloudless blue afternoon.

At that time, she had not known what the dot was. Abby knew now, sitting atop the lighthouse, that the dot was the man Feral, the Most Imperfect. Feral was one of Ullumair's Moonsung, like her parents, but horribly afflicted in mind and body. For reasons known only to him, Feral had donned chains about his body and stitched a shirt of sliipmare hair to his own flesh and had wandered out onto the plateau unbidden. But the child Abby had not known that then. And so, from her perch within the lighthouse, the elder Abby hastened her thoughts forward and away from his ancient and lamentable origins.

The dot that was Feral simply floated there for a few seconds until something seemed to invade him. She would later learn that it was the stored arcane anger of generations of Aberiths. Fed from the dancing eldritch luminescence on the roots, pulses of ichorous inky-black matter enveloped and then coalesced within the dot. From her great distance, details of the event had been difficult to discern, even with her young sharp eyes.

Back in her home within the lighthouse, the elder Abby sighed. *What more would I have seen if I had had my shadowsight back then?*

Nonetheless, she had watched the dot grow to massive proportions rapidly and silently in the distance. And thus, within moments, the god Feralzmoon was born, emerging from the sphere of oozing pitch-black matter.

From that distance Feralzmoon had looked like a stick figure drawn by a child's dull black chalk on a white stone wall. He, like the roots, was now the breadth and height of many ancient trees of the Umberwood but had only seemed about the size of her hand at such a distance. Tatters of thick and coarse brown animal hair draped about his deformed shoulders. Chains spiraled about his twisted legs and waist as his massive gangling form descended to stand awkwardly upon the land.

At his now-massive size the roots could only manage to tangle and slither about his abnormally elongated and misshapen legs.

His body had shaken uncontrollably, like it was barely holding itself together; full of lightning, his chains rattled a terrible din. The roots about his legs had still pulsed with runic light and dripped with ichor. The chaos that pulsed within Feralzmoon caused him to struggle with the roots entangled about his legs.

As if in response to his struggles, the pulsing light had ceased. Feralzmoon drew three gasping breaths before a spasm shook his body. At that, he had doubled over at the chest and grasped the top of his head in his hands, his wild black hair erupting through the gaps between his misshapen fingers. It had been as if he were keeping himself from exploding from the Aberith's bitter, angry chaos.

Again, in his now doubled over posture, he had drawn in three more shuddering breaths. Then he stood straight up, arms spread wide and back arched. He seemed to have grown taller in that moment. He let out a scream, a primal screech that buffeted and shook the roof where Abby had stood, the force stealing the breath from her lungs.

At this moment, as if called from the sea by the scream, Ullumair emerged. He rose from the Moonsong Sea clad in armor covered in multi-hued veins of coral and took to the land. He set foot thereupon at the exact location where a lighthouse would one day be erected. The very lighthouse in which Abby, lost in her memory of the events, now stood.

The colossal form of Ullumair was crowned with a spiraling white shell that reached to the sky like a unicorn's horn. Ullumair's fire, the Everflame, burned at the point of the horn. His glistening form glided across the plateau to meet Feralzmoon, his footfalls and dragging spear leaving lakes, rivers, and chasms on the land.

Abby shook her head at the memory, for she was still amazed by the size and scope of it. She regarded the Footfall Lakes and Moonthread Rivers shining in the moonlight. The darkness of the two Whale's Echo Chasms that flanked the tower would have been disquieting to a normal person, but to Abby they were calming and beautiful.

Returning to the memory, Abby remembered the retinue of supple and glistening silver-bright eels of light that had accompanied Ullumair. They were his Ullumyths, his angels. At the time, Abby had been agape at the scene, turning her sight from the gliding form of Ullumair back to the frazzled figure of Feralzmoon.

Oozing black Aberiths, which had leeched up the roots from the bottom of the rift and undulated about Feralzmoon's warped legs and feet. They were tiny compared to Feralzmoon and only visible to Abby as a single mass. Mostly hidden from the sun by the walls of the rift, the roots, and Feralzmoon's bulk, the Aberiths were able to snake up Feralzmoon's legs, his unbidden and unwanted retainers. The memory of the bubbling black ichor and the Aberiths sent both a shudder of remembrance and teeth-grinding anger, undimmed by the passage of the ages, through Abby's tiny body.

Ullumair and his Ullumyths had arrived at the rift to face Feralzmoon and the seething Aberiths. Though the white shell cowl of Ullumair's crown hid his face, Abby recalled that she could almost see pity in Ullumair's posture. His subtle aquatic form, almost pitying of, or perhaps apologetic to, the suffering of one of his Moonsung.

At Ullumair's appearance, the Aberiths had begun to writhe and pull violently upon Feralzmoon. Some even suffered the searing light of the sleeping god Aurum. They crawled, smoking and screeching, from Aurum's light toward Ullumair. The collective mass of Aberiths had simply vibrated with anger and frustration at the return of Ullumair, the herald of their ancient banisher. They did not want to lose their champion, the god they had birthed at great cost to restore chaos to the world. He would bring their revenge upon Ullumair and his children. He would cast great masses of land into the sky. He would blot out the sun and permit their return to the surface of Erlan.

In response to the violence of the Aberiths, Ullumair had bowed his head and sheathed his spear. He extended his many-jointed arms and embraced Feralzmoon. Ullumair lifted Feralzmoon up from the land, dragging a horde of Aberiths with them. Many remained attached to Feralzmoon while others dropped back down into the pit below. Even from her home, Abby could hear the horrible, angry screeches of the Aberiths. She had heard it before, but never such a cacophonous din of so very many of them. It was chilling.

Even just the memory of it was enough to set her on edge, even all these years later.

Floating above the rift, the flame of Ullumair's crown flared. Its flames had snaked, lashed, and flared about the land with intelligent purpose. The flames had melted the land about Ullumair into an opaque white glass, like the shell of his crown, which he molded into a sphere. The shell-sphere enveloped them: Ullumair, Feralzmoon, Ullumyth, and Aberith alike. Or at least most of the Aberiths, as the sphere bisected the chain of Aberiths some distance below Feralzmoon's feet, sending the rest into the pit below. This chain of Aberiths had died, their bodies broken as they smashed against the walls and base of the rift.

Abby had watched the sphere ascend into the heavens. As the sphere ascended, she had witnessed the aftermath of Ullumair's flames. They'd washed over the land south of the rift, radiating east and west, reducing all the verdancy of the plateau to ash in an instant. Abby remembered watching the ash fall on what would henceforth be known as the Ashfall Plateau. The flames that had burned the plateau had also snaked about the now-named Umbervale before breaking against the granite base of the Godskeep Mountains like massive waves of water against a cliff. The flames had made the iron-rich soil of the valley turn permanently umber in color and made the trees of the Umberwood forever fall-colored.

The last of Ullumair's flames had sealed the rift, instantly turning the earth at the bottom of the rift to glass. The flame had shriveled the black roots down into the rift, petrifying them there. The tough hides of the Aberiths, hardened by the icy cold of space, could suffer the searing heat of flame, even Ullumair's.

So, even the smashed and dying bodies of the unearthly Aberiths littered about the base of the rift had been untouched by the heat and light of Ullumair's divine flame. Ullumair's holy flame was the creator and destroyer of any life or element on Erlan. But the Aberiths were not of Erlan. It was only the pure and other-worldly light of Aurum which they could not suffer. It was precisely the unearthly nature of it that seared their bodies, minds, and souls. In the shadow of the rift walls, the ichor of the Aberiths awaited Abby. She shuddered again at the thought of what was to come.

The ash had continued to fall like gray snowflakes to the plateau as Abby watched the sphere become a small dot in the sky, eventually disappearing silently into Umbral, the moon of the realm of Erlan. At that time, the moon, which was just visible in the early evening sky of that day's end, was a perfect white sphere, except for one large crater left by Ullumair's passage.

Abby looked up at the moon, now covered with many craters, through the lighthouse window. Ages later, for reasons unknown at the time, the new gods had emerged from Umbral. The twelve new gods, like shooting stars, rained down on Erlan from within Umbral.

"The Twelve Tears of Umbral." Abby gave a chorus of voice to her memory, naming the event.

The new gods landed on Erlan, scattered along the length of the Godskeeps, which was, in fact, how the mountains earned their name: the keeps of the new gods. After the event, twelve new craters were left on the surface of Umbral. Theoretically, such craters were within the Godskeeps as well, on the steep slopes of the high inner mountains, caused by the impact of the new gods.

Abby sat in the lighthouse, distracted for a moment by the numerous myths surrounding the hallowed sites of the mountain slopes: that each crater contained a temple-keep made of fragments of the moon. That they radiated divine energies which had created all manner of creatures, some as guards for the temples. Some said they were whale-sized versions of natural creatures, others mutated monsters. Some claimed that some of the creatures could assume the form of the Ashfallen and that they had been visited by them down from the mountains.

But none, not even Abby, had wandered deep into the cold peaks of the Godskeeps to verify the existence of the hallowed sites or the myths. The interior peaks of the mountains were not safe. But many, including Abby, had seen the outlines and hints of creatures, giant and otherwise, in the mists upon venturing into the mountain foothills. But still, no definitive proof of any of the new creatures existed. Abby looked from the moon to the mountains from her room in the lighthouse.

"So much still to do." She smiled to the Godskeeps as her eyes rose to the moon. Umbral, with her thirteen large craters, was full this night.

CHAPTER 6
A PECULIAR GIRL

Aurum, forever in vigilant silence, joined the sleeping gods. His light turned the sky, Orizon, a brilliant blue and illuminated the moon, Umbral, a brilliant white by night. His warmth forced back the great Elderime Glacier, revealing the beauty of Erlan north of the Godskeeps.
—from the Athenomancer archives

"Distracting, those myths of the Godskeeps. Don't you agree, Ixo?" Abby said, looking down toward the creature near her feet. Ixo shifted slightly. Abby sighed, looked back up to the moon, and returned to her memory.

In the aftermath of the birth of Feralzmoon and the emergence of Ullumair, all Harrowfell had understandably responded by looking inward, making safe their homes and their city. Many of those outside the wall left their homes and took refuge in the walled section of Harrowfell. But, being the peculiar and adventurous girl she was, strengthened by an austere life of labor and Aberith raids, Abby had set out to the rift that very night. She had been determined to be the first to see the unhallowed site of the birth of the god of chaos. She'd walked all night to get there.

For most, the way to the site would have been too dangerous to travel by only the light of Umbral, but Abby knew the land well and had always been able to see well enough by just the starlight. Before the sun had set on the next day, the western tip of the rift lay at her feet.

She had descended easily into the chasm from the western end, taking advantage of its gradual slope and her youthful nimbleness. As she'd made her way eastward, she saw sheer smooth walls rising about her. The width and height of the walls had grown as she'd progressed. After about a mile, the standing stones came into view and, shortly thereafter, the ground had turned a glassy texture. With excitement, she'd approached the immense standing stones; shriveled and diminished now compared to the heights to which she had seen them ascend. She was unfazed by the gravity of the otherworldly events of the day before. In fact, quite the contrary, she was driven by it, her curiosity piqued by the allure of the unearthly event she had observed.

During her exploration, Abby remembered standing just outside the still humming stones at the bottom of the rift. The runes still glowed and radiated warmth, even from her distance, but were fading fast. She'd knelt before the circle of black fingers. At the center, a seal of obsidian-like glass was visible over what used to be a massive hole. Ichor still bubbled and undulated on the surface of the glass as it slowly thickened. Like thick boiling black tallow, the Aberiths that had dripped from Feralzmoon lay dead or dying in a pool of black ichor formed from their smashed bodies.

The memory of what happened next brought a chuckle from Abby and a wry, black-toothed grin as she sat in the lighthouse, her breath again putting a fog on the cold window. She drew a face with a crooked smile and stringy hair on the window with her gnarled finger. She regarded it for a moment, noticing the likeness to Feralzmoon before wiping it away.

SHE STUDIED the black ichor that pooled on the glass-covered opening at the base of the rift. She'd seen Aberiths before and had seen the ichor of their inky black skin, but she had never seen so much of it, nor had she seen as many Aberiths as she had then. In fact, to be visible at all from her childhood home, there must have been scores that had dripped down from Feralzmoon's legs. Now, crouched by the black obelisks, she bore witness to proof of that number: a scene of broken bodies amidst a chorus of soft alien keening.

Abby dipped her tiny finger into the ichor. Encircled by the standing stones, she brought her finger up close to her face. She eyed it carefully, letting its acrid smell fill her nostrils, before bringing it to her mouth and dabbing it delicately on her tongue. She sat hunched there for a moment considering its alkali taste and waited.

She considered the sharpness in her mouth while staring out over the black pool, which gurgled and moaned as it continued to thicken and die. Being a child, and an odd one at that, she hadn't really thought very carefully about her choice of actions. Nonetheless, she was hoping for something... well, peculiar, to happen. When nothing did, she turned from the pool, shoulders slumped, pouting as only a child of her age could. She turned her back to the whole scene and carefully made her way up and out of the rift. She left the black burbling pool of ichorous death and the dimming root-like standing stones behind and walked home, strangely disappointed.

CHAPTER 7

THE TEMPLE

By Aurum's light, Ullumair was able to send forth his children, the Moonsung. They were to bring the beauty of his life from the sea to the surface of Erlan. Under the light of Aurum, free of the Aberiths, the Moonsung children of Ullumair thrived upon the land. And though they had left the Moonsong Sea behind, they still loved and worshipped Ullumair, their father.
—from the Athenomancer archives

Upon leaving the stable, Ilfair found himself back in the entry chamber to the temple. He eyed the wooden doors at the midpoint of the northern wall before him. The wooden structure of the doors was largely intact, though one was canted relative to the other. A large space spread toward the top of the ceilingless wall above the slumping door. Ilfair slipped his lithe form silently between the gap in the doors, deftly stepping around the bits of ceiling and wall scattered about the floor.

The room he entered was drier and warmer, but darker, as the ceiling was fully intact. As his shadowsight adjusted, he brushed snow from his shoulders, at least that which had not melted into his clothing. With a shiver, he pushed the hair back from over his eyes and looked about. This was clearly the worship area of the temple. The room was large with high ceilings. The construction here was like outside: granite and obsidian with inlays and decorative effects achieved with black wood and the strange alloy he had seen in the rift mine.

Numerous large wooden benches were arrayed in front of him. An aisle was open in between them, leading to a dais with a black figurine about the size of a small child atop. A massive black and white metal symbol was inlaid in the wall above and beyond the dais, matching the one on the ground outside. Ilfair thought that if he were ever to build a temple from the sentiments that often filled his mind, it might look an awful lot like this place. He imagined that if he succumbed to the thoughts in his head he would be comfortable here. That thought did not make him particularly happy.

He looked up at a massive mural, which stretched across the ceiling some thirty or so feet up. A thin man with long, over-exaggerated limbs and a distorted and concerning face stretched the full length of the ceiling. Thick black chains dangled about his waist. Over his shoulders were tatters of a thick tunic made from animal hair. He recognized it instantly, horsehair overgarments made from the manes of sliipmares were common in Fayrest. The same garments were sometimes also used as punishment. He wondered which was the case here. Since he could see no undergarments, he assumed the latter. Black eel-like creatures, all too familiar to Ilfair, and black roots spiraled about the figure.

As he slowly made his way between the wooden benches, he absently eyed the mural. He thought with some concern that these creatures looked very similar to the ones that often made their way into his thoughts. Of greater concern was the fact that the man himself looked like the creature he had seen within the moon just prior to his arrival in the rift.

He reached the dais and regarded the figurine there. Made from obsidian, it was clearly a depiction of the entity painted on the mural. Evidently, the people who had once used this temple worshiped this entity.

"And who exactly are you?" Ilfair said to himself, his quiet voice sounding small in the great room.

What was the connection between the black swarming creatures on the mural, his recent 'trip' to the moon, and this entity? And was there any connection to the thoughts that so often invaded his own? He continued to ponder this, which only served to increase his unrest, as he made his way over to the door to his left, just beyond the dais.

The door was stuck. Annoyed, he calmed himself and the black squirming whispers in his thoughts, again reminding himself to focus on the immediate issues. He managed to pry the door open with the pick end of his newfound spiralhammer. The room he entered was clearly meant to be a replica of the standing stones at the bottom of the rift in which he had earlier awoken. The stones were smaller in size but still massive, requiring the ceiling of this room to be even higher than the preceding worship chamber. He guessed it was nearly sixty feet high. This room, as was the temple hall previous, was completely without windows. It was truly pitch black here; truly like a cave. He imagined it would have been terrifying were he not possessed of shadowsight.

"Strange," Ilfair said out loud as he moved over to the stones in the middle of the expansive room.

Just as in the rift in which he awoke, at the center of the stones was a hole. Except this opening was not sealed with glass and appeared to have been dug rather than naturally occurring, as was also the case in the rift. Chains attached to the stones draped along the floor and down into the hole. Ilfair leaned over the precipice and peered down. He could not see the bottom, but he did see the same faint light he had seen in the forge, causing his brow to furrow and his eyes to adjust. He stepped back away from the hole. He appreciated the faint warmth, but everything else within the room made him uneasy. To his right, beyond the standing stones, came the sound of dripping water. He could not see water, but thought it was likely emanating from the other side of a door.

Leaving the hole behind, he made his way over to the door on the side wall and listened. When he was sure that it was, in fact, just dripping water that was making the noise, he pulled the door, which had been ajar, fully open. He quickly realized the room was a barracks of sorts. On the wall opposite him were dozens of alcoves dug into the stone wall. Chains dangled down from the ceiling to the floor, clearly used to climb up to the higher alcoves.

As his eyes followed the chains up and fell to rest on the details of one of the alcoves, Ilfair gasped quietly. The remains of a body were noticeable within. As he looked more carefully, he noticed many of the recesses housed similar desiccated corpses. Tatters of clothing, often coarse animal hair or chain-based, covered a few of the desiccated bodies. He wondered how long they had been dead. Clearly, some people decided to die here.

"Devout to the very end evidently, eh?" Ilfair asked the bodies in the alcoves.

At that, he looked down and noticed the floor was but a metal grating of some type. And below that grating was an array of tightly packed black cylindrical obelisks. The pillars had white runes scribed on them and holes embedded randomly along their length. The cylinders of rock descended as far as he could see. Some way down the obelisks, he could see water or, more accurately, solid ice coated with a thin layer of water.

Again, Ilfair gasped, more loudly this time, which startled him as he noticed countless skeletons dangling from the holes along the irregular columns. They were of some serpentine vertebrate. They looked like pictures he had seen of eels sticking out of their hole-homes in the wall of a reef. Each was about as long as he was tall.

They had long, spindly arms and hundreds of short legs along their perimeters. The arms ended with long curved talons on the eight thumbless fingers. The appendages were long and dangled down, pointing to the ice below. Ilfair noticed more of the snake-like skeletons now splayed out on the ice. Now that he looked more carefully, he could see they were everywhere below. Ilfair could even see them below the ice, frozen in various curious poses.

The skeletal faces were even more disturbing; something like a lamprey but flatter and filled with sharp teeth on a mouth on what must have been the underside of the creature. He then noticed that there were chains hanging along the left wall attached to the bottom of the grating upon which he stood. At that end, the openings in the grating were large. Easily large enough for him or one of those skeletons to fit through.

As had been the case in most of the rooms of the temple to this point, this room unsettled Ilfair. He searched for a way out. He hastened his way across the room to the staircase at its back corner, eyeing the masses below for movement as he made his way across the grating. He made his way up the spiral metal staircase. It was then that he finally found where the dripping sound was coming from; water was slowly dripping down the railing of the staircase. Upon reaching the top he realized the water was dripping down from above.

He reached the landing and carefully pushed open the door, which was leaning off its hinges. He stepped around the door and entered a much brighter area lit by the night sky. His eyes adjusted quickly to the change in illumination, allowing him to note the features of the chamber.

He was in another large space. It was colder here as one of the large windows to his left was broken. Ice slid in through the window from the north, like a frozen river, and was slowly melting. A small rivulet crossed the stone floor, hit the wall to his back left, and filtered over to the door and down the stairs. Based on the flow of the rivulet, it seemed as if the temple must have been tilting slightly toward the south.

Ilfair turned around and his eyes fell upon a large, ornate hearth, nestled in the corner where two walls met. He instinctively moved toward the fireplace and the beginnings of a smile managed its way onto his otherwise somber face. The lining of the hearth was inlaid with twisting symbols made from the spiralore. In the hearth there was another deep hole with a faint white light deep inside. A grating of spiralore covered the opening, a collection of ornate interlocking meandering shapes.

On all the remaining wall space in the room, save the hearth and windows, were shelves full of books. In the center of the room was a mostly intact table, long and sturdy, as well as eight chairs. On the opposite wall was one other door. The wood and books all showed, with the window to the room broken, the wear of being exposed to the elements. However, in the extreme cold they had maintained all their basic integrity.

There was no ceiling to the room, at least not in the typical sense. The top of the room stretched up into a conical steeple-like structure. The sides of the cone were black and decorated with spirals and dangling chains. He could not see the top. It disappeared into perfect blackness.

Despite the ominous ceiling, Ilfair breathed a sigh of relief. A path to the glacier's surface was now visible. But it was still dark. And worse, in the more exposed room, it was colder. He carefully walked over the ice flowing into the room. It was slick so he got down on one knee and moved carefully forward using the spiral-hammer for balance on purchase. He eventually made it outside onto the glacier. He looked about amidst forceful gusts of wind.

"Yes, very cold," he said to the moonlit ice. He thought it better to wait for the relative warmth of morning before leaving the structure and its protection from the elements.

He stepped back into the room. The blast of cold had brought his hunger, tiredness, and thirst back to the forefront of his mind. The hearth offered a solution to this if he could manage to get it lit. He set to work with the spiralhammer and dismantled two of the chairs. It was loud work, but he didn't suppose there was anyone, or anything, that would mind. At least, he hoped not.

He went back down into the room below and quickly recovered a few of the coarse hair tatters from the alcoves, being careful not to look down at the otherworldly skeletal creatures under the grate. He made his way back to the hearth, recovered his flint and steel from his own pack, and, with the tatters of clothing and wood from the chairs, quickly had a strong fire going.

The light and warmth from the fire immediately improved his mood. In fact, he had not realized how lonely he had gotten over the last few hours.

"Better," he said aloud to himself in between two deep sighs. The fire and the sound of his voice made him feel more hopeful.

He had not found a solution to his food issue, but the water problem was readily solvable if he could manage to find a stone or metal bowl. He considered making his way back to the forge but thought it better to check the other room first. He made his way across the room, watching his long shadow dance on the walls and books.

He pushed the door open with his spiralhammer and moved into the room. It was lit a ghostly blue as moonlight filtered through an ice-covered window to his left. A desk lay in front of the window. Again, books filled the walls except those immediately adjacent to the desk and along the wall opposite the door through which he had entered. To the left of the desk, the same spiraling tree, root, and moon symbol was inlaid into the stone wall. To the right, a long menacing chain, a sickle at one end and a sphere covered with sharp ridges at the other, hung by two hooks. At the opposite end of the room, behind him now, were alcoves like those one floor below, clearly for sleeping.

Collapsed over the desk was what had once been a man. The cold and dry air of this climate had reasonably well preserved his desiccated form. The warmth and wetness that was now entering the temple would surely rectify that soon. Ilfair inspected the man, carefully moving him with the pick end of the spiralhammer. The man wore a thick shirt of animal hair, which was stitched into his desiccated flesh. Ilfair made his way around to the other side of the desk and saw, as he suspected, the man had chains draped about his legs.

He assumed this was some type of sympathetic practice to emulate the god they worshiped. The priests of the god of malady, Illinir, often maimed themselves for that very reason. On the desk and under the man, Ilfair noticed a large map laid out on the table.

Returning to the purpose of his visit to the room, Ilfair searched the desk for useful items. He was hopeful as it was clear that this room was where the man had slept. A quick search of the desk and room revealed various potentially useful items, but he took only one of the metal bowls, a small knife, and a thick blanket. He then used the knife to carefully remove the intact sliipmare cloak from the man. It smelled a bit. Taking items from the dead made him very uncomfortable. But it was thick and, as he donned it, he knew it would be very effective against the wind and cold, as its intended design had most likely been.

He also carefully slid the map out from underneath the man. He winced as the body cracked like dry parchment with even the smallest necessary movement. He folded it up and put it in his pack for later consideration; he had more important things on his mind now. He looked sadly upon the man. He said a quick prayer to Oever, the god of the dead, and completed the prayer by drawing the symbol to Oever in the air, a horizontal figure eight, over the man.

Somber but satisfied, he went back into the main room, which he now realized was a library or study for the chambers he had just left. He chipped some ice from the large mass that flowed from the large broken window into the room. It was perfectly clear and most likely safe. He took the chunks of ice and put them into the bowl and took the bowl to the hearth.

He set the bowl near the flames and warmed himself as he waited for the water to melt. He rested contentedly, pleased with his current state.

"Better," he said again simply as he sat before the fire, feeling the warmth on his face. Yes, he was hungry, but he could go without food for days and he had solved his water problem and had gained a warm cloak and blanket to help with the cold. So, the imminent murderers, water and cold, had been put at bay for the moment.

He retrieved the metal bowl from the flames, using his shirt-sleeves to protect his hands. He allowed the bowl to cool just enough to drink. The warmth it brought was pure delight. He wished he had some tea leaves to make the drink more calming. Alas, having none, he unceremoniously downed the remaining liquid then set to work melting more ice to replenish his water skin. He sat now and rested his eyes, keeping his ear alert to sound, which he doubted very seriously he would hear. It was truly desolate.

He looked out the window, the intact one, which faced south. He could see moonlit mountains in the distance. He figured they were the Godskeeps. So, at least he knew where he was. Impossibly, he was on the Elderime Glacier, completely on the other side of the Godskeeps from his home near Overmoor. He had only heard of this place, for none had been north of the Godskeep Mountains for ages.

"What in godsname?" Ilfair asked quietly, raising his eyebrows, and shaking his head as he did so. He ran his hands through his short-cropped hair. He held his hands there for a moment, his locks sprouting from between his long fingers.

"Okay," he said, removing his hands abruptly, shaking himself out of his own confused thoughts before they could spawn whispering Leechkin.

He took out the map and spread it on the floor before the fire. The writing, always found in little spiraling clusters, he could not understand, but the drawings were more or less understandable. The map did not go farther south than the Godskeep Mountains. It showed the Elderime Glacier, though its southern edge was shown much further north than he had also been told. The map also showed the Moonsong Sea and the Ashfall Plateau and the totality of Umbervale and Umberwood.

The map showed as far east as the Umbervale Pass, as far south as the Godskeeps, and as far west as the Moonsong Sea. There were various black dots, cities or some other Ashfallen structure, labeled on the map in writing he could not read. One of the points, a city he guessed, was just south of the edge of the glacier. On the map at least, for it would have been covered by the glacier now, or so he assumed. The other mark on the map was on a small peninsula along the coastline a little north of the Godskeeps and south of the other glacial dot.

Two additional smaller marks near each of the cities were also evident and labeled. The northern one was near a feature that looked a lot like a small oblong rift. The other was just north of the larger coastal mark on a small triangle of land formed by two other larger chasms. A chain of rivers and lakes led to that inlet-bound dot.

Ilfair deduced with some confidence that he was near the more northern pair of points on the map. In fact, he thought it likely that the rift he had awoken in was shown on the map. He stood and walked over to the large, intact south-facing window and looked out over the lower part of the temple and the edge of the rift. He couldn't see the standing stones from here, so his gaze wandered up slightly as he looked out over the glacier. He could see the crumbled edge of the blue-white glacier, the dull-colored plateau and fall-colored valley, and the gray, snowcapped rise of the mountains in the far distance.

It was truly a beautiful sight to behold. He could have almost been happy here; the warm hearth and the beautiful view. Almost, but not quite. For his mind swam with questions. *Why am I here? Have I done something to cause this? Did I somehow invite or deserve this?*

Furthermore, and perhaps the more pertinent question, *what has done this to me?* His life had been odd enough up to this point, but now, with this new twist, he felt forlorn. He shook his head and sighed.

He walked over to one of the shelves of books near him and pulled one of the dusty tomes from it. The cover and spine were decorated with obsidian on thick animal hide. He thumbed through the books. Various maps and engravings, one even matching the mural he had seen earlier, were inside the tome along with more indecipherable writing in spiraled clusters.

"No answers here," he said, sighing to the book, completely unsurprised. He placed it back on the shelf and walked back over to the fire to sit. The ground was hard, but he did his best to get comfortable using the thick blanket as bedding.

As Ilfair lay there he tried to convince himself, unsuccessfully, that in the morning he would begin to uncover answers to some of his questions. He reminded himself to stay focused on what was in front of him.

"Yes, that's best," he whispered to himself.

In the morning, he would verify with his own eyes where he was and make his way toward the Godskeeps. He would move south and get off this glacier.

"Simple enough," he said to the fire.

For now, though, he would warm himself, rest, and wait for the sun.

CHAPTER 8

CHAINS IN THE NIGHT

Upon the arrival of the Moonsung, Umbral moved away from Erlan and
the Moonsong Sea receded, revealing a peninsula of land. The
Moonsung built Harrowfell, a city of shining blues and whites, in honor
of their father upon the peninsula between the Elderime Glacier and the
Godskeep Mountains.
—from the Athenomancer archives

S omewhere in the night, Ilfair awoke to the sounds of chains
rattling. It was a distinct sound and so he was certain of its
cause. He also had a very good idea as to the origin of the
din. The sound emanated from behind the doorway that led downstairs. He lay there for many moments, hoping it would stop.

It did not.

It was too cold to pick up and leave. He could hear the wind
whistling outside and just the sound of it made him shudder. He
simply could not brave the glacier in the cold of the night. So, he
picked up his spiralhammer and descended the stairs to investi-
gate. In the alcove-filled room, he detected no movement. The
serpentine skeletons had been his primary concern; the stillness
here calmed him slightly. He silently made his way over to the door

that led to the standing stone replica room. The rattling was louder from behind that door.

He cracked the door and peered into the room. His newborn fear was realized, and his heart jumped in his chest. He could see three of the four chains, which draped down into the hole in the center of the standing stones, jittering and spasming. This was the origin of the sound. He wondered now if all the noise he had made breaking the chairs had been a bad idea after all.

"Damn it," he said under his breath.

He quickly but furtively made his way into the room toward the hole. He gripped the spiralhammer in both hands and held it poised in his sweaty hands. He would need to improve the grip on the hammer, he realized at that inopportune moment. He held his breath and peered down the hole, keeping his fear and strange whispering thoughts at bay.

He looked over the edge down one of the jittering chains. His heart lurched in his chest. Slithering black creatures were moving up the chains steadily on hundreds of tiny legs. They moved like millipedes, their tiny legs undulating and rippling like water. Their white pupilless eyes seemed to be fixed upward, though that was most likely in his head as without pupils their direction could not be discerned. Water dripped from the end of their tails. And now he saw they were covered in sickly, slimy blue-black flesh, he realized they were the very same as those chained to the onyx columns beneath the grate in the other room.

While all of that was horrifying enough, what truly stopped his breath was the uncanny similarity these creatures had to the visions that often invaded his thoughts. In fact, it was this similarity that most disturbed him, for he had seen horrors such as these in his head his whole life.

All of this made him question whether this was a dream or not. This simply could not be. How could the things climbing out of this hole be the creatures that so often stirred in his thoughts? This thought drove Ilfair to panicked action. He took up the spiral-hammer in his right hand and repeatedly struck at one of the chains. The hammer shook his hand violently and the sound struck his ears painfully. He was used to the former, but the latter hurt as he was not wearing any mining gear to protect his ears as he would normally have done.

Over and over he struck. His ears rang and his hand grew numb, but the chain would not break. He paused a moment, breathing hard and squinting his eyes against the keening black eels in his head. He had to think, but it was so difficult. He centered himself and looked around.

With a thought, he rushed over to where the chains were attached to the stones. He switched hands, blessing Illinir for his ambidexterity, and struck the joint with furious blows. The joint fell quickly to the strikes, and the chain whipped away from the stone, rushing down the well under its massive weight. Its end grazed his leg as it rushed past, leaving a gash on the leather of his thick boots. *Lucky. And stupid*, he thought. He repeated this for the other shackles, being careful to stay clear of them when they rushed away from the stones.

As he worked at the last shackle, he hastened a glance over his shoulder. A glistening leathery black creature was just visible, cresting the edge of the well. Its legs rolled like a millipede and its white eyes, perched on the edge of its leechlike body, lolled abhorrently.

"Damn it," he gasped through labored breathing.

He could feel the creature bearing down on him. He swung again at the chain and the hammer twisted in his now sweaty grip.

"Godsname!" He regripped the hammer, with both hands this time, and swung again. With a crack the joint failed and the chain rushed away just as he felt the creature at his leg. The metallic restraint tore a long gash along the underside of the horrific eel-monster as it swiftly fell down the well, spilling black ichor on the ground. The piton at the end of the cable must have snagged the underbelly somewhere, for it was quickly yanked away from Ilfair. Two long arms on its underside scraped on the stone, and the round teeth-lined mouth, like a lamprey eel, let out an alien screech that sounded like many shrieks at once as it disappeared over the ledge.

He could hear a chorus of shrieking and keening, and he imagined it clawing with futility at the edges of the cavernous hole. The imagery of it was clear in his mind. He imagined them as they skittered down into the depths of the cavern with unearthly whimpers from their gaping lamprey-like mouths.

Ilfair stood at the edge of the hole for many minutes, gasping for air and wiping the sweat from his face and hands. He stared down to be sure nothing again stirred. The panic that had raised the black eels in his thoughts slowly passed, but it took him many moments to fully compose himself.

It took him longer than normal as the thought of the kinship between the creatures in the well and those in his mind kept interfering with his attempts to return himself to a sensical world where insane things were not happening. No matter how hard he tried—breathing and counting—he simply could not get the details of that creature's face out of his head. It had been so close that he could smell the fetid, earthy oil on its hide. Eventually, he abandoned reaching that state of quiet, and once the ringing in his ears subsided, he decided to make his way back up to the fire.

On his way up, he entangled and jammed the two sets of doors with bits of chain recovered from the breaking. He sat there staring at the fire, his heart still beating hard and his ears ringing from the sharp din of metal on metal and rock. He sat there for many minutes, staring at the hammer, thankful to have found it. He noticed just then that the pattern of spiraling colors on the hammer seemed to have changed. He couldn't be sure, though, so he stared at it for many minutes and, sure enough, he could see the colors on the hammer slowly sliding. It was almost hypnotic.

Watching it took his mind away from the insanity of the events at the well. He focused on the beauty of the shifting colors, the prismatic pattern breathing across the surface of the metal. He ignored the strangeness of it. There was no time for more confusion and disquieting possibilities. No. Just the beauty of it, for it was beautiful. At that moment, he felt his exhaustion begin to overtake him.

As he fell asleep, he said aloud to the night, "I guess it was no dream then."

CHAPTER 9

BACK HOME AGAIN

For many days, Aurum shone. And for many nights, Umbral glowed.
And thereunder were the seas calm and the land did provide. And so, for
many years the Moonsung flourished. Their thoughts were never
troubled, calm as the seas and steady as land.
—from the Athenomancer archives

Abby was still lost in her recollections, pacing about the lighthouse.

All those many centuries ago she had returned home from the rift in the dark of the early morning. When she had arrived, greater Harrowfell had been buzzing with distraction, which made her reentry go as unnoticed as her exit.

Her parents had noticed her absence, though they had not been as concerned as a typical parent who had misplaced an eleven-year-old would normally be. In the chaos of recent events, they had had more than enough duties to attend to and they had been confident that their daughter could look after herself. In addition, and in fairness to them, she'd had a habit of disappearing for bits of time, despite the dangerous nature of the surrounding region. And they had learned to accept her free-spirited nature.

In fact, they had often gone so far as to encourage it, knowing that her curiosity and independence were a strength of her character, particularly in the world of harsh and final consequences in which she had been brought up. She had an insuppressible adventurousness and had earned her independence from her parents over the years. Regardless, upon her return, her parents had not asked where she had been. They merely hugged their daughter, relieved to be safely reunited.

"Abby, stay in your room, please. There is much to do, and we don't want to find you lost again or to be hurt with the hurried work which needs to be done." Her father's tone had been kind but firm.

"Okay, father," Abby acquiesced.

She had disappeared to her room and into her books. For hours she read and wrote and drew in her books. She spent the time recording the events of the previous day and sketching every detail she could remember. When her eyes hurt too much to read more, she rose from her desk and walked to her east-facing window.

From there she had looked out into the streets, homes, and granges of the small agricultural enclave. She had watched the adults quietly for many hours. The main activity here, which had brought in all the men and woman of the little township, was to gather food stores for transport to Harrowfell. There was little in the way of talking but much in the way of activity. And her father had been right: a small child could easily be hurt by any number of the activities going on.

Growing bored of that particular show, she had moved across her room to peer out of the west-facing window, which looked toward Harrowfell. She could see the road meandering toward the city. It would soon be filled with carts bringing stores to the town proper.

She had seen the Wall of Harrowfell, a wall of amber stone that preceded the city that lay nestled between a small section of flat land and the sea. That land protruded into the Moonsong Sea between the rising walls of the southern Choralmoon and northern Keening Cliffs. Looming statues of sentries hewn from granite could be seen at the northern and southern tips of the wall as well as flanking the entrance to the city. The lure was simply too much for Abby.

"They won't mind as long as I stay out of their way in the township," she rationalized.

Satisfied with her logic, she had made her way out through the window and toward Harrowfell. Of course, she had waited for her mother and father to be distracted first. And, while she did have some residual fear from the events of the previous evening, it had not been enough to keep her in her room. She simply could be confined no longer. So, she had hopped out of her window and was off.

ABBY BLINKED her old eyes slowly before looking back out of the lighthouse window. She sighed. She still remembered that day all those centuries ago vividly. In some ways, it marked the beginning of the end of the little girl Abby.

THE YOUNG AND lithe Abby had covered the slightly downward sloping distance from her home to Harrowfell quickly. She'd followed the gentle curves of the flat, well-worn road to where the city lay. As she had approached the entryway, the color of the earth had changed from a fertile black to a less fertile composition of light gray and beige.

She had stopped, as she always did, to regard the two guards who flanked the opening in the wall through which the road passed. The guards, trained Mythals of Ullumair, had stood atop their gray stone perches next to the granite statues. They had been as silent and motionless as the statues and were clad head-to-toe in linked maille made of holy Amberglass with seafoam-green garments emblazoned with the holy symbol of Ullumair, a flame-tipped narwhal horn protruding from the sea with a sunrise backdrop. They had held their morning star bells, which had shone with a coating of Amberglass and served as both a weapon and an instrument of warning.

Abby had looked up to the Mythal on the right and then the one on the left. Then, having chosen her victim, she had looked back to the right and begun her rehearsed barrage of questions.

"Are those weapons heavy?" she had asked with her head tilted to the side and one eyebrow raised quizzically.

She'd waited, feigning interest in hearing a reply.

"Don't you get tired?" followed by a pause.

"Has a bird ever landed on you?" again, a pause.

She had turned to look in the direction the guard faced and shaded her eyes with her hand. "What do you see? Do you see anything? I don't."

She had turned back and looked up at the guard. His eyes had moved almost imperceptibly to regard her. His brow was knit with displeasure and his lips were pursed. Satisfied that she had gotten a reaction, Abby had smiled and giggled once before skipping into the city proper.

Just on the other side of the Wall of Harrowfell, Abby had seen a flurry of activity as adults of all types, both proper and practical, had moved to fortify the defenses of the city. This had seemed silly to her given the scale of what had happened. But she understood how doing something like this could give them feelings of control amidst the uncertainty. And they were adults, maybe they knew what they were doing. Regardless, she had always loved watching the adults move about in the city like ants in a colony. And this was no exception.

After some time watching the events just on the inside of the wall, she had moved down the main street to the center of the city. Her mind had continued to roil with questions. *How were the buildings made? Why are they different colors than mine?*

And then there was that big windowless building that looked like a big cube plopped down near the city center. She had heard that there was a furnace made of a giant ancient conch shell filled with whale oil and lit by Ullumair's Flame. And that the Mythals had trained around it and crafted wondrous items of Amberglass. *Maybe I could sneak in and find out?*

Distracted by her own mind's questions, she had soon found herself in the open town square, just to the seaside of the cube. Here again she had watched a new set of adults. They were clad much more seriously than the ones working the wall. They stood on a raised wooden platform. She watched them debate what the events had meant and their divine implications. That is to say, who to worship and how. She had heard the same sentiments in and around her home.

She had heard one man say, with sarcasm deep in his voice, "Who is the more proper of the two gods to worship? Should we worship Ullumair, as we have always done, and rely on his continued protection? Of course, we should!"

The man was met by a calmer toned man with the rebuttal, "We should entreat this new entity, this Feralzmoon. Does this poor Moonsung creature not warrant lamentation and appeasement? Did Ullumair not in fact *embrace* Feralzmoon? A sign clearly that we must embrace him as well! And we shall, with or without you."

"Neat... and clever," said Abby, a name for the creature. Feralzmoon, an amalgam of Feral and the word for his resting place.

Adults are clever, she had thought, *but boring*. She had heard more rebuttals and the throng droned on.

ABBY KNEW THAT THIS DIVISION, over the course of generations, would lead some Ashfallen to leave Harrowfell and build the Nihilin Temple and the city of Aberron. These Ashfallen would build great tunnels into the earth. Over many generations, their mingling with the deep earth, as well as the Aberiths and their ilk, darkened the hue of their skin, angled their features, and set them at odds with their kin at Harrowfell.

For some decades after the Nihilin was built, Abby had watched from afar as the raids from the Aberiths abated. Some thought the temple had pleased Feralzmoon and so left Harrowfell to join their kin at Aberron and the Nihilin Temple. However, soon after the raids from the Aberiths were replaced by raids from mounted Feraliths. The warrior-priests of Feralzmoon were convinced, by Aberiths and the barrenness of the northern lands, that they were owed some of the bounty of Ullumair's Harrowfell. And so, the divide deepened.

Abby sighed at this, relaxing her pursed lips and smoothing out the old parchment wrinkles on her face as she remembered the details of those mounted Feralith raids. They were, in fact, more frequent and no less terrifying than those of the Aberiths. Of course, she was long gone from Harrowfell by then, but still, they were inarguably awful.

"Oh, the trials and tribulations of the Ashfallen." She smiled and shook her head, looking out from the window of the lighthouse.

"Back to the horror show now, dearest Ixo," Abby said to the silent Ixo.

ABBY HAD SKIPPED AWAY from the town center of Harrowfell, her young legs carrying her toward the streets that ran to the pier.

She had possessed that gift which all children possess. No matter the terrors about in the adult world, children always managed to find other children with which to play. And soon Abby had found a group playing hide and seek.

She had waited for the group to end their current game and, when they were all gathered to start the next game, Abby had popped up and piped in over the din of the children.

She had known the eldest boy, Heron, so she had addressed him with a "Can I play too?"

"Sure," Heron had said.

"What is your name?" said one of the other children.

"Abby," she had said, smiling. She had almost forgotten the horrors of the previous days.

"Well, Abby," said yet another child, "Olive is the seeker, so you better get to hiding!" The young girl had pointed at another even younger girl, winked at Abby, and darted off.

Olive started counting and the children had scattered like roaches under lantern lights. And they all vanished just as quickly as well. Abby had found what she had believed to be an excellent hiding place behind a trio of water barrels. She could smell the pungent brine, but it had been tolerable given the quality of the hiding place. She had sat quietly, smiling, filled with self-satisfaction.

While she waited, her tongue had absently worked at one of her teeth. She hadn't noticed until then, but one of her lower left teeth had become loose. Quite to her surprise, it came free. Her mouth filled with a bitter taste, and she had spat the tooth into her hand.

"My gods," she had said. The spittle in her hand was black and slimy and the tooth had been riddled with black spots.

At that inopportune moment, Olive had come around the barrels, probably drawn by the noise of Abby's loud exclamation.

"What happened?" Olive had asked.

Abby had begun to reply, but when she opened her mouth, more black spittle had bubbled up, forcing her to close her mouth and clasp her other hand over her mouth. Abby had begun to breathe hard through her nose and her heart had begun to pound.

By this point a crowd of children had gathered.

"Gross," said one.

"What *is* that?" said another.

"What is wrong with her? That is *not* normal," said a third.

Abby had felt the judgement of the group grow quickly and, since she could not use her verbal wit for defense, she had done the only thing she could think of. She ran.

As she'd run away, she'd heard Heron leading the taunts of the children behind her. They had called after her, taunting her with the name Abby Abscess. In the coming days they would come up with a hateful little limerick that would stick with her for centuries:

> Little Abby Abscess,
> Always strays too far from home.
> Now your face is all a mess,
> And you'll surely die alone.

She had run all the way home, the insult ringing in her ears. Her lungs had burned. Tears ran down her cheeks and, as she sobbed, black spittle ran down her chin. She was hurt and she was scared. *What has happened to my mouth?* she thought. Somehow, she had known it was bad. Very bad.

When she had reached her home, she sped by her father, who

was working in the street in front of the house and went in the open front door of her home.

Her mother was inside the house, doing something she could not recall, for she had passed too quickly to notice, and her sight had been blurry with tears. She had run straight to her room and slammed and locked the door behind her. She'd gone to her bed and buried her face in her pillow, not caring the staining that would result. In moments her mother was at the door.

"Abby. What's the matter?" her mother spoke through the door.

Abby had only continued to cry.

"Abby, let me in. Abby!" Anxiety had risen in her voice as she jiggled the handle.

Abby continued to sob. Abby did not cry; she was not that type of girl. She felt ashamed on top of everything else.

"Abby. Let us in." Now Abby heard her father's voice. He had sounded determined, as he always did. That's probably where she got her unstoppable curiosity. In a moment he had the door open. How he did this she never knew.

In a moment, Abby's mother had her sitting upright in the bed. She had knelt before Abby.

"Abby dear. Abby, move your hand." Abby did not move her hand.

Abby's father sat next to her on the bed. He put his right arm around her shoulder and used his left to pull her hand away gently but forcefully. As he did so, a sob had racked Abby's small body.

Concern was knit on her mother's face. Her mother produced a cloth and cleaned her daughter's mouth. "We told you not to leave," her mother had said quietly, almost as though she were talking to herself.

"Abby, sweetheart, calm yourself," her mother said louder, quickly correcting her ill-timed criticism.

Her father gave her a moment and added, "Dear, what has happened?"

Abby finally regained enough composure to speak. She had looked up to her father and tried to force a smile. Then she looked down at her mother. She had been encouraged by the looks of calm and determination on their faces.

"I..." she had begun. But what issued forth was not her voice. At least it was not only her voice. An echo of multiple otherworldly voices filled the room. The look of calm on her parents' face had been replaced by shock. That look of shock matched the look on her own face. They had all sat alone in that room in silence for many minutes, not knowing what to do.

Over the next days, more changes had manifested and the disappointment she had felt leaving the rift changed to dismay. As the changes eventually became more pronounced, the dismay changed to horror and disgust. These feelings were mirrored by her mother and father as they also noticed something was utterly amiss with their daughter, something well beyond the oddities with which they had become comfortable and familiar.

The changes had been relatively mild at first, primarily visible in the discoloring of her skin and teeth. Then her changes had grown more systemic as her yellow hair had become black, like wet decaying seaweed; her lightly freckled skin thinned and wrinkled like delicate parchment, and her blue eyes filled with milky white spots.

The dots in her eyes strangely improved her vision, though she feared to tell anyone out of concern of some form of zealous reprisal. In fact, she barely spoke at all after that. She did not like the sound of it, for it sounded like she looked: awful and off-putting. And, while she could avoid looking at herself, she could not unhear her own words. She could not ignore the similarity of her voice to the sounds of an Aberith. She never spoke it out loud, but even then, she had known it was from the ichor she had tasted. Somehow, she just knew. She could feel it inside her.

"U<small>SELESS</small> A<small>BERITHS</small>. Y<small>OU</small> <small>RUINED</small> <small>EVERYTHING</small>," Abby said quietly within the lighthouse, intentionally using the language she would have used as a child. She let out a single audible sigh. The sigh echoed both of its own unearthly multiple chords from her throat and from the large room in which she stood.

I<small>N</small> <small>THE</small> <small>SILENCE</small> that had followed she'd seen her parents talking, lamenting. Sometimes they cried, sometimes they fought. Sometimes one would yell or cry; sometimes the other, sometimes both. They, along with other town elders, would try to talk to her, to ask her what she knew or what had happened to her to cause such horror. But Abby had been too ashamed and frightened to speak. She was ashamed of what she had done. She felt like a stupid girl. And, of course, she feared their reaction to what she sounded like and what they might do to her if they knew everything. That this had been caused by the ichor at the bottom of the rift. They would have neither understood nor forgiven.

Her silence had only fed her parents' frustrated impotence and despair over the situation. Over time, all was just silence and gloom within Abby's home. Her mother had even stopped singing to her, distant and weak as her voice had become as her demise worsened.

Eventually, her teeth blackened or fell out altogether. The neighbors used the now-cemented nickname, Abby Abscess, as well. Masking their fear and concern for themselves with cruelty.

The days after her teeth had fallen out seemed short, as she had spent most of her time sleeping. She did not eat and became gaunt in the body and hollow in the face. She did not get out of bed or go out of doors, for she had begun to dislike the brightness and warmth of the sun. She could remember her father's rough hands on her face and the occasional stroking of her hair by her mother. It was the last semblance of any contact between her and her parents. They had tried to project confidence, but she had known better.

As the months dragged on, eventually even the silent physical contact ended. Soon after her mother ceased lighting a candle when she came in. They did not know it, but she could still see them in the dark and she could see the looks on their faces. And it filled her with dread and regret. She could not stop regretting her decision to go to the rift, and she had become filled with a constant dread over what would become of her.

She had slept longer and longer in the following days until one day she did not wake. Those awful feelings of fear and regret were the last that she would have as Abigail, an Ashfallen daughter of Harrowfell.

ABBY SHIVERED, recalling the cold that she had felt as her young heart had weakened, it's beating becoming faint in her chest. Back in the lighthouse, Abby turned from the window and laughed out loud, a single cold scoff that sounded very much alone as she recalled what had happened next.

"If only I had died," she whispered to the lighthouse glass.

CHAPTER 10
IN THE GRAVE BUT NOT DEAD

One wicked evening, the peaceful existence of the Moonsung ended. Under the cover of thick clouds on the blackest of all nights, the first raid of Aberiths came to Harrowfell. From the caves below the Godskeep Mountains they came. The Moonsung keened and prayed to Ullumair in the grief that followed the raid.

—from the Athenomancer archives

Abby looked out of the lighthouse window, her gaze vacant. The fog on the window followed the rhythm of her shallow breathing. Her mind continued to wander through her past.

HER PARENTS, thinking she was dead, buried Abby. For why would they not? She looked truly dead, in fact, long dead, and that is what you did with the dead in Harrowfell. Her grave was in the high sands of the coast, just before the grass grew and the ground turned to the darker dirt of the plateau. The location of the burial in the Moonsung tradition was chosen to give the family time to grieve before the high tide of the next full moon of Umbral took the body out to sea to be returned to the Father, Ullumair.

Part of her had been glad to be buried. But that feeling was short-lived as she realized, over the next few days, that she was not ultimately going to die. At least, not like a normal person. In fact, while in her grave, she had found that, beyond not dying, she did not need food or water, and scarcely needed air.

She lay there quite passively face up, staring at the lid of her coffin. In the many hours of silence that had followed, a strange thing began to happen. At first it had been just an incoherent whisper here and there, impossibly so, for it was perfect silence in her grave.

Abby, came a disembodied voice in her head. Then random other whispers followed, hollow at first. Random words entered her mind: *lost, missed, love, why, the,* and then *Abby* again.

Over time, she knew not how long, the words became more substantial and less hollow. And sentences began to form. *We miss you, Abby*. And the sound of quiet sobbing had been followed by a deeper voice. *Oh, love. Oh wife. I'm sorry*. In a moment she knew. It was her mother and father. It was their thoughts just before they were spoken to one another. They were speaking to each other, and she could hear them. She lay there in the grave motionless save for her open, black-toothed mouth. Stunned.

And it was not only them she could hear. She could hear the thoughts of some of the other denizens of Harrowfell. Their thoughts were wide open to her, particularly at night when they slept and dreamed. At first, she could not understand why she could only hear some of the villagers. But Abby, being a clever girl, eventually surmised that they were the thoughts of those who had left tokens in her coffin. It was her parents she had heard first, for the connection there was strongest.

As she'd wandered in these thoughts and dreams, she had

learned something about the thoughts of the villagers that she would never forget.

Her neighbor, the father, was speaking to his eldest daughter.

It's a horrible thing, yes, but I am glad she is gone, he'd thought then said.

Father! the daughter had replied. *You should not say such things, the neighbors might hear.*

I am sorry, but it is true. You know it to be so, he had insisted.

Aye, she'd said. *It is true. I feel awful for saying it, but...* She trailed off without finishing the sentence, but she didn't have to. Abby knew how that sentence ended.

Soon she had discovered that the relief her neighbors had felt was shared by many, if not all, of the villagers who had attended her burial. She had been stunned and hurt by this, not understanding how such a thing could be possible. She had never felt such relief at the passing of any other villager, even in her short life. In the self-absorbance that had come with her grief, she'd ignored the fact that, while she had never felt relief at the passing of another life, nor had she really felt much of any grief either, she was but a child, and no one particularly close to her had ever passed away.

One evening, when she was floating about the thoughts of the villagers, she'd *heard* her parents. Or maybe she'd felt them. Regardless, she had been drawn into their conversation. She was offput at first. Her parents were happy. Well, at least they were not sad. Their thoughts had each been very complicated.

We miss you so much Abby. Her mother had said, her words echoing the thoughts perceptible to Abby.

The world is poorer without you. And our home is hollow. You were the life of this simple home. Her father had likewise thought and said.

She could see them in her mind. They must have been holding hands around the dinner table, as they often did. They had thought these things and spoken them, and she could tell they meant them.

But behind those spoken thoughts were hidden, unspoken ones. Thoughts like: *What could we have done? I am glad she is out of her misery. We all must move on, after all. It was all so difficult.* She could feel their relief in these unspoken thoughts.

Never minding that it was also riddled with guilt and despair, she had been crushed. She had been too young to understand the complexity of it all. She could scarcely comprehend the despair, helplessness, and frustration that her parents had endured, power-less to help their only daughter. No. She had only felt the pain of their relief at her passing.

That pain and grief had festered over the next weeks. Abby had watched as her grief-stricken parents visited her grave each day. By the end of the moon, they had learned to bury their grief, their faces reflecting a bewildered numbness. During this process her despondency had slowly become rage. And that rage was fueled unendingly by the strange unfairness of it all. She had found this rage a bottomless source and so she had thrashed and clawed for days from within her grave, losing flesh, tooth, and nail in the process, until finally she was free.

She had sat silently atop her grave covered in tears, dirt, sand, and blood. Hunched over, the shuddering of her slight form barely visible. She had considered taking revenge on all Harrowfell, but her rage had subsided slightly, owing to her fatigue, and had been replaced once again with despondent catharsis. And so, instead, she had fled Harrowfell for what she'd thought would be forever.

She'd fled north, bearing all the tokens... little lockets, bits of flower and clothing, heartfelt notes, drawings, pictures, a bird's feather... in and on her grave with her. She had run north along the beach until she could not run anymore. She'd squatted down on her haunches, the water from the Moonsong Sea washing over her feet, and experienced tearless grief. Eventually, she stood and walked further north to the beginning of the Keening cliffs. Using her now unnaturally enhanced agility, she'd scaled the cliffs for hours, buffeted by the hollowing winds. Finally, she found a cave. She crawled into the cold, wet hollow, and curled up into the fetal position on the hard stone. Her new home in the Keening Cliffs.

ABBY WALKED to the seaside of the lighthouse tower and looked south toward that old cavern in the Keening Cliffs. Abby noticed that at some point in her reverie it had started raining.

"How appropriate," she said to Ixo. It had rained the first night in the cave those many centuries ago.

As her legionvoice echoed in the room, she smiled at the sound of it. The effect was off putting to say the least and the Abby in the lighthouse loved the effect it had on the listener. She would often speak just to hear the sound of it. She had grown to love it over the years.

As she listened to her voice echo over the staccato of the rain on the windows, she recalled that everything about the caverns had been cold, wet, and hard, but she barely noticed at the time.

She'd sat silently in the cavern, eyes closed, hating the sound and look of herself and the world for that matter. Not like now; she had come to terms with what she had become.

For many days and nights, she had sat and wept, as the Aberithic ichor within her body finished its work. Soon it had filled not just her body, but her mind and soul, with its bitterness. She had been wholly corrupted by it.

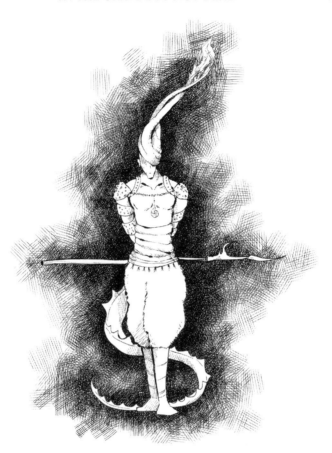

CHAPTER II

THE WITCH, ABBY ABSCESS

In response to their prayers to Ullumair, the Moonsung were gifted the knowledge to defend themselves. He gave them a vision of the Wall of Harrowfell. With the protection of the wall, the Moonsung's peace and prosperity returned.

—from the Athenomancer archives

The thing that had sat in the cold caverns those many ages ago looked much like the Abby who sat in the lighthouse this night. But the long-ago-Abby was young and hadn't the time-edified mind of the elder Abby.

She remembered having tried very hard to keep her rage and hate at bay in those early years in the cave. She had done what she always did when she became sad or scared: she disappeared into pages of words and pictures. She wrote and drew about everything she could remember. Everything that had happened, that she had seen or heard, and especially she wrote of the dreams and thoughts of the people of Harrowfell to whom she was linked.

They still filled her mind unbidden, day and night.

ABBY HAD KNOWN that she was now hideous, a mockery of a girl. She had seen herself in the reflections of the pools in the caverns. So, she stayed away from people, and she wrote until all the caverns of her new cliff-home, at least those that she wasn't too afraid to go down to, were covered.

Eventually, though, her loneliness had become too much to bear, even with the company provided by the minds of those to whom she was linked. So, she went back home.

THE ABBY in the lighthouse ground her teeth—at least, what was left of them—at the memory of all this weeping and loneliness. *All this... weakness*, she thought.

AT THE TIME she had been more, well, human and so she had succumbed to her human needs. Out of shame, she went only at night or dusk when she was very hard to see, owing to her new dark Aberithic gifts. Every evening, she would move closer to her home.

The child Abby, newly born of the Aberith's ichor, was easily able to scale the wall above the cave opening. The ichor had toughened her skin and strengthened her tiny bones and muscles, allowing her to pull her weight up the cliff with ease.

As she'd crested the top of the Keening Cliffs, she looked south toward her home, her shadowsight penetrating the dark. She descended the slope from the cliff's ridge, hopping carelessly through the intermittent ice-cold cascades that descended from the Ashfall plateau down toward the Umbervale and Umberwood. Her blood had been replaced with ichor and she was unphased by the cold. Her legs carried her with great speed over the land, owing to the same ichor-strength that permitted her to scale the cliff.

Eventually, she reached the farms that surrounded the township of her home. She moved to the wheat field just to the north of her home and sat a few rows back to avoid being seen.

She could see into her home from her position, and she watched silently, without breathing, for hours. She watched her parents move about in the lantern-lit home in which she had grown up. She listened to their thoughts and watched them intently.

Eventually, her mother sat in the chair in her old bedroom. Her mother held one of Abby's shirts and brought it to her face to smell it. She thought of Abby, Abby could hear it. Much about missing her, and frequent *"why has this happened?"* type thoughts, along with general confusion over the situation. But Abby could tell the intensity of it had softened.

Her father came in some moments later and bade her come to bed. He kissed her on the forehead and put his hand on her shoulder before leaving the room again. Abby's mother turned and looked out the window directly at her. *Abby?* She thought.

Terrified she had been seen, Abby stood and ran out of the field back home. She had heard her mother's thoughts filled with sadness and confusion. A soft sobbing followed Abby from her mother's home as she ran through the wheat.

She noticed as she ran that she made no noise. The wheat did not rustle, and her footfalls were silent. She noticed that she was able to call the moon shadows of the night to her. She could make it firm, solid, but soft and supple, using it to muffle all sound. She had used the shadows in their simplest form back then. Later she would learn to conceal herself within the thickened shadows and eventually walk *through* them. The moon shadows were the best, but she could accomplish similar feats with sun shadows too.

Eventually, she returned to her cave home and calmed herself.

She sat, staring out onto the Moonsong Sea, and thought of her newfound abilities for the rest of the evening. She decided she would visit more in the coming days and continue to experiment with her new self. She had hoped this might make her feel better. It did not.

Despite her intentions at the time, the visits only served to make her feel even lonelier, a reminder of a life now gone. And the experimentations only made her feel more like a solitary creature, like a witch from children's tales.

Weeks became months, which became years, and still she continued her clandestine visits. She had collected more tokens to attempt more thought connections to assuage her loneliness... but without success.

One terrible evening, one Abby would come to never forget, she came to the same hiding place near her parents' home that she had visited many hundreds of times before. This time she could see for certain something that she had been dreading might be true. Her mother was with child.

From that day forward, what had been a lonely sadness became an unbearable despondency. Night after night, for months she watched her father dote on her mother and her mother caress her growing belly. She knew logically that this was normal and that she should not be angry, but her mother was singing the very same songs that she had sung to her. Those songs belonged to her.

One day, a few weeks later, she stole away to the same hiding place where she would look into her old room to observe her parents. This time her mother sat in her room with a baby in her arms. She sang to the tiny creature in her arms.

Little Ahna dearest,
I will keep you safe and warm,
You are loved dearest one,
And you will never be alone.

All logic left Abby. The song reminded her of the ridicule from the children, the Abby Abscess taunt. She ran home just as she had those years ago. But this time her home was a cave. And this time she did not cry. She was filled with hate now.

Her feelings of general despondency changed to a very personal betrayal and forsakenness. And that was it. That was the moment that Abby felt she had truly died. Her parents had betrayed her, and she hated them for it. What Abby knew now, but did not understand then, was the influence the Aberith's ichor had played in the evolution and persistence of those feelings.

Irrespective, she hated her existence more deeply than she had before. She hated Harrowfell and the people there and their thoughts and dreams. And she hated her father. But most of all she hated her mother and she hated those mothering songs. In fact, she hated all music, anything that might make her feel something like grief or longing or might trigger a memory of her life before the darkness had overtaken her, was too much for her. Even bells and windchimes, once beautiful creations of metal, glass, and whale bone, made her angry.

"Hateful noises, those harmonies." Abby sneered in her echoey chorus of voices. She looked down at a broken windchime at her feet. She had destroyed all the beautiful musical creations that had filled the height of the lighthouse.

It was at that moment, watching her mother hold her new child, that Abby became Abby Abscess, the Witch of the Keening Cliffs. Nothing visible had changed about her, but now her soul and her intentions were as black and rotten as her teeth.

Everything had conspired to prevent her from any longer

resisting the bitter corruption of the Aberithic ichor that squirmed impatiently inside her. It had seeped and oozed into every part of her. When she had stopped resisting, she felt relief. It wanted her to be this way and, finally, she had given in.

IN THE LIGHTHOUSE the witch Abby sighed, and her shoulders dropped in a mirrored reflection of the memory of her capitulation to the Aberiths.

CHAPTER 12

A DREAM UNBIDDEN

For many years the Moonsung, the first born of Ullumair, prospered within and about the Wall of Harrowfell. But then Feral, the Moonsung child most imperfect, left the first home, Harrowfell. For what reason he left, none of the Moonsung ever knew.
—from the Athenomancer archives

The witch Abby patted Ixo's carapace as she continued her recollections.

It was but a blink of an eye in her now centuries-long existence, but the witch Abby had spent a score of decades after that night terrorizing Harrowfell, especially her mother and that child.

To this day she still refused to speak the child's name. She may have even killed it, she couldn't recall. Or, more precisely, would not permit herself to recall.

It would have been understandable, would it not? Not to kill of course, but to forget. It had been a very long time ago. She had written it down, the now dead child's name and story, and had it stored away in her now eclectic collection of writings and illustrations. She could have looked it up had she cared to. But she did not.

"Worthless," Abby sneered, but this time a slight shudder and moistening of the eyes accompanied the chorus of voices. Whether this was due to pity for the innocent child or just more resentment, she did not know.

She would not recall that tale. But she was happy to recall the tale of how she had terrorized the boy who had given her the Abby Abscess nickname. In fact, she thought of it often.

SHE STOLE BACK into Harrowfell for a few consecutive evenings and found the young boy's home with but a bit of patience. First, she had taken an item from his room silently while he slept. Over the next few days, now linked to the boy, she followed his thoughts and learned his habits. Then, one evening exactly eight days after linking to the boy, she went into his room and squeezed her index finger hard, drawing forth the ichor from her body: another "gift", her ichorink.

She wrote a little message on his wall.

Little Abby Abscess,
Can get inside your home,
Now your wall is all a mess,
And I will never leave you alone,

She waited until the boy awoke, enduring Aurum's light by hiding in his sun shadows. She could manipulate those as well, just not as easily or effectively. Eventually, the poor boy, Heron was his name, awoke. He screamed and cried. *That's right*, she thought, *you ruined my life and now I will ruin yours. I will never leave you alone.* And she did not.

In fact, she had harried the unfortunate man until he died. They had even come up with a story about it. The Harrowing of Heron they had called it. That had pleased her.

She spent the subsequent centuries terrorizing Harrowfell and gaining the name the Witch of the Keening Cliffs. In her mind she was a storyteller and so she had added "bard" to her title. Afterall, she was writing little stories everywhere was she not? She recalled one disgruntled Harrowfellian once saying something like: "Yeah, they're a regular poet, ain't they?"

And while the child Abby had certainly agreed, Harrowfell did not see it that way.

"They truly did hate and fear me. Didn't they, Ixo?" She chuckled a chorus of laughs, still delighted by the memory, and patted the chitinous shell of the creature at her side. Little millipede-like creatures shifted around on Ixo's shell, leaving little holes to find new ones on the insect's carapace.

She recalled reading the writings about her in the ancient libraries in Harrowfell. She'd learned from the writings that they hadn't even known it was her for many years. She had needed to start signing her writings to reveal her identity to them. She wondered what their faces had looked like when they learned that she was from the first generation of Ashfallen in Harrowfell.

How I wish I could have seen their faces when they first learned it was me, she thought.

Despite her efforts, most in Harrowfell did not think much about the bardic aspects of Abby. Mostly they thought of her as a witch and a terror, or just a killer. They used her stories, like the Harrowing of Heron, to terrify children and most adults as well. Mothers within and about Harrowfell would be sure to sing songs to their children quietly to not risk calling forth Abby.

As Abby aged, the excitement of spreading chaos and corruption—whether it be corporeal or literary—waned. With the allure of pure chaos diminished, her aims shifted and matured. Plus, she had become tired of the incessant and useless witch hunts. They would never catch her. How could they? She was like a god compared to them.

Abby smiled at this, her confidence ever overwhelming.

"They are but insects compared to me... no offense, Ixo," she paused and eyed the creature for a moment. It, as usual, did not react. She laughed out a single mirthless "Ha."

IN KEEPING with her new aims, she had begun to imagine more complex and insidious scenarios of revenge. And although she had hated the denizens of Harrowfell, over the years she realized that what she truly hated was Feralzmoon and the Aberiths for bringing the infection to Erlan and Ullumair and the Ullumyths for allowing it to happen.

Abby spent much of her time observing, reading, and thinking about the world, in search of some mechanism of revenge against the celestial beings. She would often sit and just look up at the moon in bitter impotence.

During the years of searching, she had seen many things. She had seen the formation of the holy city Aberron and the temple Nihilin to Feralzmoon. She had seen the Spirelight Tower, the very lighthouse she now called home, built in the first footprint of Ullumair just north of Harrowfell, isolated on a triangle of land made by the Whale's Echo Chasms from Ullumair's dragging spear and tail. She had watched the many conflicts over many generations of Ashfallen between the Mythals of Ullumair and the Feraliths of Feralzmoon. She had seen the simple faiths of order and chaos grow and strengthen and then fade and die, as only silence eventually met the priests' prayers to their gods within Umbral, the moon.

"If only I could rip you from the sky," Abby said to the moon as she leaned her face against the cold windows of the lighthouse. "Then maybe I could have the revenge due to me for all this suffering."

She'd watched over the ages as the cold of the north had

advanced southward. The Footfall Lakes and Elderime and Moon-thread rivers around the Nihilin Temple and the city of Aberron and even further out onto the Ashfall Plateau and Umbervale froze and never thawed, even when summer came.

Just as it had done for ages further north on the Elderime Glac-ier, the snow now fell further and further south and never melted. And so, the glacier advanced. Most of the denizens of Aberron and the Nihilin Temple fled. Only the most devout to Feralzmoon stayed behind as the glacier overtook Nihilin and Aberron.

I wonder if any Feraliths still remain, she thought, *dead... or better still, undead. Quite the welcoming party that would be, eh Ilfair?* She paused. *How is that place treating you, hm? Better than me, I bet.* She thought with a frown.

Decades passed, throughout which Abby had watched from the ridge above her cave home in the Keening Cliffs, as the glacier over-took the Spirelight. While this happened, the sea rose and slowly overwhelmed Harrowfell. The Mythals and other followers of Ullumair were eventually faced with the same dilemma as the followers of Feralzmoon. And so, left with no choice, they too aban-doned their homes in and around Harrowfell and the Spirelight.

Somewhere around this time Abby had found an entrance to the Spirelight lighthouse through the caverns of the Keening Cliffs below it. With the Mythals gone, she had delighted in desecrating the beauty within and had filled it with her varied creative collec-tions and her foul aesthetic. The eclectic items she had gathered from countless souls: dolls in various states of disuse, and books of all colors, sizes, and condition. All these items and others were mashed together haphazardly with an overlay of dust, cobwebs, and black mold. Except for the books. The books were kept clean, reasonably so at least. At the time she had enjoyed watching the snowfall about the tower and the ice creep up the sides of the Spirelight. She remembered the delight she had felt at ultimately snuffing out of the Everflame atop the tower.

As this had happened, she'd watched the life of Harrowfell and Aberron and the surrounding communities move south of the Godskeep Mountains. These refugees, at least the ones who survived the dangerous sojourn, settled in three cities.

Winters Haven on the coast was formed from the slow migration of old Harrowfell along the line just below the worst of the northern cold, in the shadow of Gray Peak. Iilhi had been formed earlier by the more rapid migration of the denizens of Aberron and the Nihilin Temple, who had come through the Umbervale Pass to the east. The city was formed about the protection of two crescent shaped ridges that rose in the desert above a deep cistern of water. Overmoor was later settled as a waypoint city between Iilhi and Winters Haven. That city sat atop a ridge engineered from out of the swamps of the Sliipmoors near the ore-rich Fenrik Hills of the Godskeeps.

She had seen the rise of the new gods, which had aligned with the appearance of twelve new circular marks on Umbral's surface. They had been formed by the emergence of the news gods from within Umbral; the Twelve Tears of Umbral. None, including Abby, knew why they had emerged, but it had occurred around the same time Ullumair and Feralzmoon had gone silent, assumed dead. Regardless, she had not much bothered with the new gods or their thralls, though she would harry them just as well as any of the ancient folk if the mood took her.

In fact, the dress she now wore in the lighthouse was decorated along the bottom with the symbols of the new gods. Abby had stolen it from a young girl of fifteen or so years in Winters Haven whom she had terrorized some years ago. She thought perhaps the girl's name was Samantha or Sandra or something like that.

She had loved the dress. It was off-white and too long for her, so it dragged along the ground. It had made her feel mature, some-thing she had, bitterly, never been able to attain. Plus, the symbols of the new gods were now covered in mud and dirt. The blasphemy of it suited her feelings on the matter of the gods quite well.

Although this Faid character – this god of shadows – intrigues me, she mused. *I shall need to look into you... someday, But not now.*

She had taken the dress from the young girl and then had made one of her many dolls, just as she had with Heron, using bits of thread from the dress. Having done so, she could visit the girl, or probably old woman by now, any time she pleased; either in person by shadowstepping or just in her thoughts or dreams by mindleeching.

"I will have to remember to do that again soon, to visit that is. Hopefully she isn't dead. Annoyingly short-lived, these Ashfallen." She shook her head and smirked as she walked over to her shelf and produced one of her many diaries. She opened the book and squeezed her index finger between her middle finger and thumb, producing a drop of ink. The ink dripped down a long nail she had manicured into a long sharp point. She scratched a note in her diary, closed the tome and replaced it on the shelf. The ichorink she could produce was another disgusting but useful trick she had acquired from the Aberiths. It was rather mundane compared to the shadowstepping, shadowsight, mindleeching, doll-linking, or her legionvoice, but she enjoyed its convenience nonetheless.

"Now where was I...?" She said, returning to the window.

SHE'D WATCHED THE PEOPLE, under the more nuanced faiths of these new gods, tire of and move beyond the constant conflict brought about by the raiding culture of Aberron. To their credit, these distant descendants of the old world had advanced far beyond what Aberron and Harrowfell had managed. It was as if the pause

of fleeing the cold had permitted the reconsideration of genera-
tions-long conflict. And, of course, they were farther from each
other now, separated by the inhospitable Sliipmoors and Shadowfen Forest. With this success, however, they risked losing some
of the important lessons of antiquity. But that was a separate issue.

Her reverie was nearing its end now, she knew.

Recently, the glacier had again receded, and even the sea level
had lowered a bit due to the movement of Umbral. The lines were
returning to their old-world positions, partially revealing the ruins
of Harrowfell and Nihilin as well as all of the Spirelight tower she
now resided in. This had drastically improved Abby's view and
allowed her to reignite the lighthouse beacon.

The flame was good, not because she liked the light or warmth,
for of course she hated it, but rather because she wanted it to be
seen. She wanted the moth to be drawn to the fire.

She remembered the joy she had felt when the Spirelight flame
had gone out so long ago, and she knew she would feel that joy
again soon, but for now she would suffer its burning.

Everything would work better if he came to her, and she did
love the drama of it as she played out the interaction with the boy
that she had anticipated in her mind. Of course, though, she was
practical and there was no way to be sure he would come to her. So,
she would send some of Ixo's children to recover a token from him
while he was on the plateau. One way or the other, she would be
linked to the boy. That was essential and she always got her way.

Abby sat back down and put her chin in her hands, thinking,
her hair falling in front of her face like a tattered curtain. She
thought back on all the things she had seen, all the things she had
recorded and even become involved in when it had proved necessary or at least entertaining. Of all these things, nothing was as
interesting or curious as what had happened last night. She had
heard a message, a message not meant for her. It came in the form
of a thought. Even though the mind was her realm, within which

she could wander with little effort if she was doll-linked, this thought was unlike any she had ever experienced.

It tore through her mind unbidden like an angry winter wind. It transmitted from the moon so loudly that she could not ignore it.

And it carried with it something else, something real. That *something real* was the young man to whom the message had been sent. That young man now lay at the bottom of the rift below the Nihilin. She could not see him, but she knew he was there. Through the moon's divine message, she had learned his name. Ilfair.

And most interesting of all was that the message had been sent by Ullumair, who, like Feralzmoon, was long-believed dead. The vision she had just experienced revealed that both of the ancient gods in fact still lived.

She was giddy at this new revelation. The message was very scattered, almost twisted. Nonetheless, she learned much from it, including why the forgotten gods had gone silent. But of all the things she learned, one thing in particular made her smile an intelligent and terrifying grin.

In all her centuries of life, despite her intellect and effort, she had never devised a way to interrogate the forgotten gods about her forsaken existence... until now. This message hinted of a way to obtain what had eluded her for her entire existence, answers to her questions. At the heart of this possibility was the young man, Ilfair, who now lay ignorant at the bottom of the rift.

Her thoughts returned to the ancient gods. "You will hear what I have to say. And I will have your explanation!" Abby spat at the moon through the window, her echoing voice shaking the glass and her small body with the force of her anger.

She relaxed, the intelligent malice returning to her voice. "Maybe I will pull the moon from the sky after all," her myriad voices mused.

"Maybe you both will be held to account for what you did to me. To my account," Abby continued, rolling her eyes toward the top of her head to focus her sinister gaze more intently on the moon, looking through her hair.

She knew now for certain that the moon still held the ancient gods Ullumair and Feralzmoon within it. This fact brought an unpleasant smile that ripped across her face. It matched the malice in Abby's eyes.

Her face was still plastered against the window of the Spire-light, and her unblinking eyes stayed fixed on the moon for hours. She stayed this way, the moisture from her mouth freezing on the glass, until the morning light of Aurum hid the moon and chased Abby back into the shadows.

CHAPTER 13

THE GLACIER

Feral, with a shirt of sliipmare hair stitched to his own flesh and dragging heavy chains of his own accord, fled toward the Elderime. By the waning light of the next day, Feral did come to rest on the plateau just south of the edge of that glacier.
—from the Athenomancer archives

A few hours later Ilfair woke within the glacier-encased temple. Embers crackled in the hearth, providing waning warmth against the brutal cold outside. After the events of the night before, he was settled somewhat by the relative brightness of the room. Gloriously, the sun had clearly risen. The night prior had been the longest in his memory.

Quickly, he rose and scrambled outside to get his bearings. He exited the room through the broken window, using the pick end of his spiralhammer for purchase on the ice as he climbed through. Once outside, he turned to his right. He relaxed a little as he squinted into the sun, low in the eastern sky. As he had hoped, he saw the granite grey of the Godskeeps curling around from the south to create a wall to the south and east. The sun was just breaking over their snow-covered peaks at their far eastern terminus.

He turned back toward the window, looking around the black temple. From his perch on the ice he saw the vale and plateau between himself and the Godskeeps. He had read about the Umbervale, Umberwood, and the Ashfall Plateau, but he had never seen them. He saw the iron-gray mountains give way to a wooded valley of perpetual reds, oranges, and yellows. Moving further north, the vale rose sharply at a moraine-covered ridge to a plateau of grays, blacks, and muted browns and greens, which ended just before him in a glacier of icy blue and white.

The ever-enflamed trees of the Umberwood filled much of the visible part of the valley. The trees dwindled as the valley rose and eventually died off completely at the ridge, preceding the muted colors of the Ashfall highland.

The Ashfall was dotted sparsely with gray and brown scrub and tall grasses that stretched far to the north and east. The flora there would occasionally turn greener near the Footfall Lakes and Moon-thread or Elderime Rivers, which dotted and lined its landscape.

The land under the plateau flora remained black and gray throughout. Its coloration earned it the ash in its moniker, much the same as the coloration earned the Umbervale and wood theirs. The Footfall Lakes of the tablelands were fed entirely by the Elderime Rivers. From there, the Moonthread Rivers cascaded down the Morraine Ridge into the Umbervale and Umberwood to the south.

He would follow the nearest of the Elderime Rivers to one of the Footfall Lakes. *That will be my destination for the day*, he decided. He turned then, to the west, and saw the coast in the distance. His long shadow stretched along the ice, pointing to the Moonsong Sea. Large ice floes floated everywhere in the far northern reaches of the Moonsong. The wind blew from that direction and was still cold, but not as bad as his last venture through the window the night before. Everything around him was consistent with the map he had found, at least approximately.

He stood there and thought for a moment. Not wanting to miss any opportunities the temple provided, he carefully slid back down into the room, dragging his pick in the ice to control his descent: a skill he had developed over the years working on the slick rocks of the Fenrik mines. He looked around at the books. Chains dangled everywhere, tethering most of the books to the wall. He opened a few of them and scanned through the ancient texts. As was the case the night before, he could not understand any of the writings. He decided after some consideration that he would not take any of the books. He did not want to carry any unnecessary weight and he already had the map, which was perhaps the most useful document he could have found.

He did decide, however, that he would again refill his water and leave now with the other useful items he had gathered here. As he began to walk out, he paused and broke the legs off a few more chairs for some wood for a fire in case there was none on the plateau. He shook his head, glad that he wouldn't be around tonight to see if the noise would bring forth more ichorous nightmares from the well.

Ilfair knew his smartest move was to get to the coast, but not along a directly western path this far north. He would get south, out of the worst of the cold first. He guessed he could get to the coast in a few days from here. He had water, but he was hungry, very hungry, and he had no food. That was his next biggest concern. He knew that he could go without food for about a week, but nearer the end of that period he would start to lose his senses and balance. And of course, the gnawing hunger just compounded his misery.

He doubted he would find any food on the glacier, and he didn't have anything to hunt with. But he was confident that if he made it to the plateau, he could find roots and flowers that, while not the greatest tasting, would get him by until he got to the coast. Once there the sea would provide plentiful options.

Over the next few hours, Ilfair navigated the glacial fissures and avoided unstable areas as best he could manage, which was well enough as it turned out. He steered wide of the jumble of ice about the rift and covered his head and arms with the cloak to protect his fair eyes and skin from the low sun in the cloudless sky. Even doing so, everything here was so bright, the sun reflecting from the ice and snow. He walked, squinting hard, parallel to the edge of the glacier for a few miles until, after some careful consideration, he finally found a narrow path off the glacier. It was still not without its dangers but was ultimately acceptably gradual and traversable. At this point, the temple was a few miles north and east of Ilfair. It felt good to be gone from there.

He moved a little south, as walking too close to the edge of the glacier was too muddy for easy passage and still very cold in the shadows of the icy ridge. Plus, further south he could see grasses and other flora growing up out of the black and gray dirt. The sight of green was encouraging. The grass, even though it was sparse, was tall and it made for difficult and annoying passage.

Keeping with his plan, he backtracked to the east a mile or so until he could see one of the still-frozen Elderime Rivers. With the Elderime guiding his bearings, using the easier path of its riverbank, he was able to make his way with less difficulty. Despite this success, he was exhausted, and he worried about the energy he had burned getting this far. The passage from here would be less arduous and it would be safer. There were better sight lines for any predators and the ground was easier to see so he could avoid injury from stepping in holes or on loose rocks.

He continued to follow the river south and after some walking, as he suspected, the icy river began to thaw. Though much of the river—now only a stream really—was icy, he knew soon it would thaw more fully. He was obviously still quite far north, even though he was at least a few miles south of the glacier ridge now.

Further south now, as he had hoped, there were ample edible burroot plants and clover flowers, which grew close to the running water. He was far from home, so he stuck to the burroot and clover, which he recognized as safe to eat. At least they *looked* like the ones he would forage around the Fenriks and Sliipmoors.

The growth near the rivers was greener and the earth softer in the warmer, though still very cold, winds. Walking on the softer land improved his mood as he followed the now westward running river. He would follow the water to the sea.

Soon he passed a patch of land that was dense with edible plants. Once he had collected many handfuls of root and flower, he paused a little longer to clean the roots and flower. He forced himself to chew slowly, for his hunger drove him to gorge himself. The food, while not tasty, gave him relief from the pain in his stomach. He realized, after consuming the root and flower, that the sun was vanishing on him. He had to get going again.

He continued to slowly nibble on the plants as he followed the river over the next few hours to the end of that day. Occasionally he would see a bird. Once or twice, particularly near the couple of partially frozen lakes he passed, he thought he might have seen a rabbit or similar small mammal. But they were expert at not being seen, and as such largely remained so.

A few times he even saw what he thought must have been black snakes. He was very familiar with the behavior of many types of snakes, being very common in the Sliipmoors, and so was unconcerned with the presence of this particular variety. He would catch the glint of their shiny black bodies and then they would be gone. He thought it odd, snakes this far north, but then again, he really had no idea what type of fauna were typical on the plateau. And, much like the other small mammals, these black creatures were good at remaining unseen. He knew, most likely, if he let them be they would return the favor.

Just before stopping for the day, Ilfair dug down into the earth with his pick. He found some worms among the burroot, but he wasn't that hungry.

"At least not yet," he mused aloud.

Despite the wry sentiment, his mood was much improved down here on the plateau. The sunlit granite of the Godskeep Mountains to his south were a beautiful golden-gray, reflecting the sunlight and the umber-colored trees and valley in its foreground. He had secured a source of water from glacial runoff which was so cold it was almost certainly safe to drink as well as some minimal food. Most mercifully, though it was still wet and windy, it was warmer.

Ilfair was unfamiliar with this region, so his movement was slower than it would normally have been, and he was not able to make it as far as he would have liked. Regardless, he would make it to the coast soon. Of this he was now confident as he could smell the sea, hear the soft sounds of the ocean, and occasionally see osprey that had strayed far from the coast. Moreover, his stomach was at least not empty and angry, so his urgency was lessened slightly.

Near the end of his first day, he noted that the grade had noticeably increased; his legs grew heavier and his heartbeat hard in his neck. He was climbing to the ridge formed by the edge of the Keening Cliffs that marked the edge of the sea. Ilfair was also walking against the wind, which made the hard incline all the worse. But he did have cover against the cold from his sliipmare cloak and his blanket.

That night he was able to make a small fire to keep warm. He was also able to warm the burroot which softened the strands on the insides and made it easier to chew and swallow. It was now more like eating than working. Things were far from perfect, but were much improved, and for that he was grateful.

CHAPTER 14

MOONFALL

Upon the plateau was Feral found by the bitter Aberiths. Black roots of Aberithic hatred erupted from below Erlan's surface to capture Feral. The roots lifted him high above the rift. With all the hoarded energy of their hatred and bitterness did they birth the chaos-god Feralzmoon from the man's flesh.

—from the Athenomancer archives

Ilfair got a late start to the next day. The day was overcast and the sunlight that would have woken him never came, blocked by thick low clouds. As he prepared to leave, he noticed that at some point during the previous day he had lost a button on his shirt. This fact along with the late start very much annoyed his meticulous nature.

As he began his walk toward the sea, a light snow began to fall, which softened the ground. And, though the wind was less, the muddy earth was slick and clung to his boots, which made for very slow going up the steep incline seaward. It seemed that his certainty of making it to the Moonsong this day was premature.

As he trudged along, he occasionally looked up toward his destination. He could see the vague outline of a white spire at the high point of the cliff ridge of the Moonsong Sea. He was reminded of the northernmost of the two coastal dots on the map.

The day prior, with the clear blue skies and the greater distance, the tower had not been clearly visible. Now, however, he was closer, and the gray clouds provided a darker backdrop for the lighthouse.

As he continued his arduous ascent, the river he was following split. He paused at the split and considered his options. The tower he was now aimed at sat in a triangle of land created by the Keening Cliffs and two chasms. In the distance he could see what looked like a bridge across the northern of two crevasses. So, he crossed the river to his right, avoiding getting wet by jumping on rocks. This burned energy and was riskier than it would have been a day ago. Here, the water was still cold, but it was also deeper and faster. A misstep and he would be completely drenched, or worse, injured. Either the cold or the injury would likely be the end of him out here. But he was careful and agile and managed to ford the stream.

The scenario on the northern side of the river was no different than on the southern side, and so the day of arduous climbing continued. Hours passed and the skies eventually darkened as the invisible sun began to set. He considered walking through the night to reach the tower, relying on his shadowsight. But there was a chasm bridge and slick, wet earth to navigate. He regretted now the time spent finding the path the day prior and all the time he had spent collecting food, wood, and water. But there was nothing that could be done.

And so, the day ended as it had begun, with gloom and drudgery: gray, wet, cold, and steep. He was exhausted, having slept poorly on the hard earth, but persisted on minimal food. His feet hurt and he was thoroughly cold, the kind of cold that only prolonged exposure to cold, wet winds could achieve. He had to be done with this exposure, and soon.

Ilfair gave up the march for the day and found a reasonably dry rock behind which he set camp. This night the weather would support no fire, so he sat and dejectedly ate root and flower.

As the dark fully set in, he regarded his destination in the distance with pensive interest. He could see the tall white tower was lit by a beacon of light that flickered at its pinnacle. He suspected this meant something like civilization was near, and this provided some hope for him. He needed that as he sat in the cold and wet under his sliipmare cloak and blanket. He thumbed the missing spot on his shirt where the button should have been, his annoyance bringing forth a hint of black eels in his thoughts.

"Godsname," he said. With that exclamation the fatigue hit him full force. Ilfair fell asleep seated, hunched under his blanket. He was awakened in the dark of the early morning hours by a pressure on his chest. He opened his eyes to see what at first appeared to be a small girl standing on him.

The girl was squatting down on his chest. She was heavy, even being so small, and her weight made it hard to draw breath. Her odd face was very close to his. She was speaking, but in his newly awakened mind he couldn't make out the words. He was stunned and confused and, as though suffering from sleep paralysis, was unable to act.

"Wake up," her voice echoed. It was an odd sounding voice, but in his groggy state he couldn't quite figure out why.

Before Ilfair could fully take in the whole of the girl, she hopped off him and said, "Look! Look there!"

She was looking up and pointing. She had enthusiasm in her posture and voice. She was up on her toes, almost bouncing on them, and the strange sound of her words issued urgently from her mouth.

Ilfair drew himself slowly up to stand next to her. For a moment he looked at her. She was the size of a girl, but her long faded dress, black hair, and white, oddly cracked and wrinkled skin, made her look old.

She looked back at him and repeated, "I said *look*. You need to see this." She jabbed her arm skyward again impatiently.

Ilfair looked up. "What am I looking at?" he said, seeing only the gibbous moon, the size of his fist, low in the sky.

"Umbral, the moon, silly. Look at her," she said, rolling her eyes with her voice as though it had been obvious. It was odd to Ilfair, her behavior. She had all the mannerisms of a normal young girl but was most decidedly not. It seemed to Ilfair to be an act, though he could not be certain. The whole scenario seemed totally unreal to him, like a dream.

Ilfair drew in a breath to say something again, but the small creature stopped him by saying "Just wait."

He looked down at her again, trying to figure out what was off about her voice, and then looked up as he heard a dull crack from the sky. At that, the small creature giggled and clapped.

"Isn't it wonderful?" she said, looking up at Ilfair with an unsettling black smile that split her face nearly from ear to ear. That smile instantly changed her bearing from an innocent child to a nightmarish creature.

Ilfair stood slack jawed. His heart raced and his mind began to sprout murmuring black Leechkin of anxiety as the pieces of Umbral moved strangely across the sky, some falling toward the earth, others floating as though weightless.

Some of the smaller pieces moved rapidly; the larger ones moved much more slowly. As he began to understand what was happening, a screech filled the air and a creature emerged slowly from within the heart of the bursting moon. A massive black hand reached up over the largest remaining fracture of the moon and a horrific face followed, revealing the origin of the scream. The visage was electric with insanity, the eyes wide, the mouth agape, and the hair like static. He had seen this face before. It was the same massive face he had seen on his *trip* to the moon a few nights hence.

"Oh, the Moonfall. Pure magic!" the little thing laughed. She almost jumped up and down with enthusiasm, little hands clasped in front of her chest. Ilfair was panicked, stunned back to silence and immobility.

Ilfair was startled out of the stunned silence by a roar from behind him.

"Here come the fishes!" the little creature said, looking up at him.

He whipped his head around to see a massive swell of water, truly a wall hundreds of feet high, slowly moving toward them. It eclipsed the Keening Cliffs and then engulfed the tower. Ilfair gasped; the little creature giggled.

At that, Ilfair snapped awake from his dream, just before the tidal wave hit him. He could still hear the little creature's giggle in his ears. He was sweating and gasping for breath, his thoughts overwrought with black writhing images, screeching by this point having been allowed to fester in his mind so long during the dreaming.

He was in fact still seated when he woke. For many minutes he just sat and stared at the tower in the distance. Maybe it was the lack of human contact, he couldn't be sure, but his mind was playing more tricks on him than usual. The dream had seemed so real. He could still feel the pressure on his chest.

He abandoned going back to sleep. He tried to light a fire but failed. He just sat there, shivering, clutching the symbols to Illinir and Faid in his hands, praying to the god Aurum for the sun to come up.

CHAPTER 15

THE LIGHTHOUSE

*Feralzmoon, suspended upon the black Aberithic roots, grew, and
deformed uncontrollably. His screams, amplified by the unearthly
Aberithic energies, filled the land. His Father heard the pain of one of his
children. It was then that Ullumair emerged from the sea and crossed
Erlan to save his child.*

—from the Athenomancer archives

Ilfair saw the sky lighten from black to amber as the sun rose
behind him. He had been staring for hours at the light atop
the tower in the distance. The beacon was now harder to see
against the lighter sky, but still he was grateful for the sunrise. He
could feel the warmth of the light on his back. His eyes adjusted to
the change and his mood improved almost immediately. He had
noticed the clouds dissipating in the night, but was glad to have
the confirmation provided by the sun that the day would most
likely be warmer and drier.

He recovered the wood from his failed attempt at a fire and
placed the salvaged wood back in his pack. The char on the wood
left black streaks on his hands. He took some more burroot from his
pocket to chew on, more out of habit and boredom than hunger,

and set off toward the tower in the distance. The ground was drier and less slick, which was good for the incline had increased.

He was still unsettled from the dream of the night before, so in keeping with his tendency, he focused on the lighthouse that lay before him. As unsettled as he was, he felt energized by the cold sea breeze and the prospects of civilization. That morning, despite his fatigue, he managed a light run, his impatience getting the better of him. To his left, the river was now gone, hidden down in the chasm, which deepened as he went.

He could see the bridge in the distance now and could make out more details of the tower. It was old, that much was clear, but beautiful. It had a smooth, white, spiraling length that reached high into the sky, set against the blue sky and green sea. A glass sphere with a massive flame within was gripped by four spiraling white fingers at the top of the tower. There were windows along the length here and there and around the entire circumference of the top, circling just below the glass-covered flame. At the bottom of the tower was a wide twisting base. Together it appeared as though the spiraling tower emerged from the center of a colossal nautilus shell.

As Ilfair drew closer, he could see that the tower sat very near to the edge of the Keening Cliffs, the land falling away abruptly behind it, the sea stretching out as a seafoam green backdrop. Just to the north and south were the two deep ravines, the Whale's Echo Chasms. As such, the tower sat on a triangle of land with steep cliffs on three sides.

Ilfair could see clearly now the northern bridge crossing the narrowest gap of the chasm. It was a rope bridge set to white stone columns on either side of the ravine. Ilfair eventually made the top of the ridge and carefully crossed the bridge looking down to one of the Moonthread Rivers many hundreds of feet below as it flowed out to sea. At its mouth the sun-bleached bones of a large whale could be seen on the inlet's beach. He could hear, but not see, the sea swells break against the Keening Cliffs just north and south of the chasm.

He stepped from the bridge onto the barren triangle of land and looked up at the tower with relief and awe. As he walked, he could see the black silhouette of a figure looking down from the window at the top. He kept his eyes on the figure as he walked across a bit of rocky land. When he entered the nautilus shell-shaped entryway, he lost sight of the shadowy figure.

The entryway had suffered some damage over the years. Light leaked in periodically as he made his way around the spiraling passage. Ilfair heard the structure trying to resonate with the sea breeze as it blew across the opening. Alas, the damage prevented a pure sound, but Ilfair could imagine the effect well enough. It was beautiful and sad even in its failure, like the sound, he imagined, of a dying whale. All along the length, the interior of the spiral was full of symbols. Or at least fragments of symbols, as the interior had suffered so much damage and aging that not a single symbol was entirely intact. He was reminded of the tunnel out of the rift, except where that had been black and angular, this was white and graceful.

The passage ended at an open landing with a west-facing vista of the sea. He looked over the cliff's edge. Iron rungs led down the cliff face to the beach below. The remains of another smaller whale shone in the sun at the mouth of the southern chasm. Water washed periodically over its bones, which were slowly sinking into the sand. He turned back to face the tower. A wooden door faced him, the perimeter arch of which was lined with images of whales and runes. Again, the symbols were unreadable, but in this case it appeared that they had been intentionally marred, like they had been clawed at and painted over with black ink. He wondered at such an act of destruction of beauty.

"Why?" he asked, shaking his head slowly.

He considered knocking on the door, but instead, out of an ill-timed awkwardness, he just pressed the door open and entered the room.

A staircase made purely of glass rose in front of him. It was dazzlingly high and impossibly unsupported for the full height of the tower. As he walked toward the staircase at the center of the tower, he noted a wooden hatch on the floor to his left. He dismissed the hatch, as he was still in awe of the staircase and was intent on finding the person he had seen in the window. He tested the structure with his weight on the first step. It was sturdy.

He even rapped at it with the flat of his spiralhammer. *Not even a chip*, he noted. He was eager to reach the top of the stairs, so began his climb. Only then did he notice what were likely once beautiful murals of aquatic beings and scenery lining the length of the tower's interior. These murals were marred by deep gouges and black marks. Still, the gist was clear, some reverence to the sea and sea life. A massive, beautiful gliding form, a man with various aquatic features and a flaming crown dominated the murals. Engraved chimes and bells made of whale bone, metal, and glass were draped everywhere along the height of the tower. All were broken and clunked and clinked mutely, nearly inaudible.

As he climbed, the steps glowed lightly with each step he took. Ilfair noted that the tower was darker than it should have been. Each window had been crudely painted black, allowing only small fingers of light to enter. It reminded him of the marred symbols in the entryway. The pattern of defacement concerned him.

The radius of the staircase increased as Ilfair ascended. At its top, the staircase fed the window-lined top floor of the tower along its outer eastern wall. Ilfair entered the room timidly, looking about furtively. He thought he saw something long and black, like a snake with many legs, dart behind one of the many bookshelves that lined the room. He was reminded of the black creatures he had thought he had seen on the plateaus. This increased the timorousness with which he entered the room. He even paused slightly and put his hand on his spiralhammer before continuing.

The room, windows blocked by numerous shelves and smears of black ink, was poorly lit, though that did not bother Ilfair. Only fingers of light from the noonday sun, riding low in the sky on the early fall day, leaked in. Light from the flame above filtered down through cracks in the ceiling, which were just the floorboards of the room above. The combination of the white sunlight and the yellow light of the lighthouse beacon was a beautiful combination. When combined with the dolls, dead animals, smears of black ink, and other ill-conceived and poorly arranged features of the room, it created an unsettling juxtaposition.

Chairs, tables, and bookshelves filled with books, dolls, trinkets, little insects pinned to boards, and other sundries were everywhere within the room. The dust in the air was revealed by the myriad beams of yellow and white light that entered the room at odd angles to one another.

A glass reservoir filled with a clear oil dominated the center of the room. A wick formed from the wrapping of numerous ropes floated in the oil. The walls were the same white stone as was the case throughout the tower. A small wooden stairwell twisted around the reservoir and led up out of the room onto what must have been the roof of the tower.

"Hello?" Ilfair called out sheepishly.

He paused at the landing at the top of the stairs for a few moments. Not seeing any motion, he made his way to one of the bookshelves. He pulled a book with a simple black cover, one of hundreds, down from the shelves and looked through its pages. It was written in the language he knew, but with an old-world cadence. The penmanship was truly beautiful. It looked like a journal of some sort. And one that was of importance to the author, as the spine showed signs of multiple reads and was hand-bound.

There was also a drawing of a little girl and her family on the cover, quite artfully done.

He tried to read some of the journal, but before he could, Ilfair heard a voice. It came from the far side of the room on the other side of the reservoir. Its origin was hidden by deep, flickering shadows cast by the tower flame. The voice came from the south-western part of the room and had an uncanny sound, like more than one person speaking. The people would have been old and young together by the sound of it.

The voice creeped about the room. "Put that back please."

Ilfair started at the sound of the voice. He turned and tried to determine the exact location of the voice. But he couldn't; it seemed to come from multiple places. Ilfair's mind began to race as he tried to get his bearings. He had expected to find someone up here; he had seen the shadow moving in the window. But there was something wrong here.

Fear crept into his mind, causing the whispering black eels to flare in his head. The voice was wrong but also familiar. He tried to place where he had heard it, but the damned whispering Leechkin made it so hard to recall things sometimes. He cursed them under his breath.

He needed more time to think, so he slowly walked backwards toward the stairs by which he had entered the room.

"Oh no, don't leave. It's just, you didn't ask. And my mother always said we shouldn't take things that aren't ours without asking." The voices bounced around the room in a very disquieting way. Ilfair could hear a sadistic joy in her statements. He didn't know why, but his finger went to the missing button and his thoughts to the small black creatures on the plateau.

CHAPTER 16

ILFAIR MEETS ABBY

*The passage of Ullumair from the sea to the capture of Feralzmoon left its
mark on Erlan. His footprints and dragging spear left chasms,
depressions, rivers, and lakes; the Whale's Echo Chasms, the Moonthread
Rivers, and the Footfall Lakes.*
—from the Athenomancer archives

The figure emerged into the golden-white light cast by the
sun and the lighthouse beacon. She looked up so that her
black hair did not shadow her face and squinted,
evidently annoyed by the brightness. It was clear that, despite her
discomfort, she wanted Ilfair to see her.

Ilfair took a step back at her presence. He had seen many
horrible things in his head, but this was real life, like the well in the
temple. She, and it was most definitely a *she*, was not exactly young
by the look of her, nor was she the physical size that would have
matched her apparent age.

She was about the size of an eleven or thirteen-year-old girl.
She resembled a child's doll left outside, too long uncared for,
white paint chipped, cracked, and flaked off. She had thin, long
black hair and creases in her thin skin. Milky white spots were

evident in her slightly too large eyes. But in every other way did she appear with the bearing and proportion of an adolescent girl.

Of all these features it was the dress that he recalled most clearly from the dream. It was simple enough, being long, white, and drab. But it was the symbols of the gods encircling the bottom, along with the fact that it looked slightly too big, that triggered his memory. He knew now why he thought he recognized the voice. She bore an uncanny resemblance to the young creature from his dream the night before, at least as best as he could recall. Perhaps he was wrong, but he thought he could feel the Leechkin squirming at the base of his skull.

"Please, just sit. Won't you, son? Certainly, one of these chairs is to your liking." The voice said quizzically with a hint of antagonism.

Ilfair let the question hang for many moments. He really wasn't sure what to say. He had never excelled in social situations, even under normal circumstances. And this was certainly far from normal.

"Um, well, no. They aren't... Not really." He spoke in a slow, halting way, giving himself time to think and consider his words. This was his way, and awkward as it might be, it had served him well, particularly when meeting people for the first time. That was when he always felt most uneasy.

"And... aren't you a bit, um, young... to call me son?" Ilfair responded after careful consideration of the apparent, though confusing, age and nature of her voice and appearance. He decided to interact with her under the assumption that she was a child. Though he really wasn't sure. He hoped this interaction etiquette might reveal something about the truth of her age and nature. As it turned out, it didn't.

Abby just stared at Ilfair silently. He felt the silence working on him and he became uncomfortable. It seemed to him that Abby was enjoying his unease.

"I'm twice your age at least, right?" He said, answering his own question with another question. He held a controlled breath and tone, trying not to reveal how unsettled he was. He belied his feelings by taking another step back and most assuredly not moving toward any of the chairs in the room.

The girl stepped forward and sat in the seat next to the glass reservoir. She seemed dissatisfied by her choice and disquieted mildly by the light and heat radiating from the glass. She folded her hands in her lap, and chuckled as she leaned forward and smiled a ghastly smile of black teeth, which split her very white face starkly.

"No, you aren't, in fact. And I know you much better than you think, Ilfair. I know things about you that you haven't even told your dear father. Mostly because you don't even know yourself. You think you do... but you don't," she said, the smirk dropping quickly from her face. She leaned back and allowed a small sigh to escape her slight frame. She stared intently at Ilfair, not blinking for many moments.

"Now sit... *please*," she said. Ilfair felt it a request only denotatively. The tone and its echoey childlike pitch conveyed a seriousness and a direction that he found compelling.

Ilfair ignored the outrageous claims of the creature but could not ignore her voice. It was chilling, and just hearing it set him on edge. The black whispering tentacles at the base of his skull climbed up the back of his skull to the top of his brain.

Again, he felt he detected her satisfaction at his discomfort. He managed to maintain his composure, taking some solace in the fact that she seemed discomforted as well, even if it wasn't due to his presence.

He chose a chair a few paces to his left and dragged it noisily and ungracefully across the floor right next to the landing of the stairs. It required him to move almost not at all from his original position at the top of the stairs. He sat in the chair, tucking his right leg under his left thigh and rested his weight on his left foot. It was an odd way to sit, but always felt safer to him.

"Oh, excellent," Abby said and laughed. He guessed that she was laughing at his abeyance to the exact letter of her request.

"I think I'm going to like you," she added, smiling a terrifying smile. He was certain now... she *was* enjoying herself.

CHAPTER 17

NOT SO SMALL TALK

With his retinue of Ullumyths, his angelic silver eels, Ullumair strode
over the home of the Moonsung to confront Feralzmoon and the Aberiths.
Ullumair embraced Feralzmoon and drew him away from the Aberiths.
And oh, did the Aberiths protest; a cacophony of violent screeches escaped
their vibrating hoards.
—from the Athenomancer archives

A smile broke the girl's face. The split, from ear to ear, transformed her from a little girl to a macabre creature in an instant. Ilfair was already struggling to process all the thoughts in his head, and her transformation was not helping. Eels stirred, whispers echoed, and he remained silent.

"Take your time, Ilfair," she said.

Ilfair closed his eyes and calmed himself. He had lost track of how many times he had done so in the last few days. He asked the simplest question, just to fill the silence with noise and to buy time.

"How... how do you know my name?" Ilfair asked eventually. Again, putting pauses in to give himself time to consider his words. He tried unsuccessfully to look relaxed. He waited some time for her response, shifting uncomfortably in his chair. The girl stood, stiffly at first, then shifted her weight from one leg to another, cocking a hip, and smiled. She shook her head slightly, looking down as if to say, *I've already been over this with you.*

"I'm... hungry," Ilfair said, realizing that she had no intention of responding to that question. He was overwhelmed by the array of questions in his head. His simpler needs rose above the deluge of other questions.

"Of course," she responded so quickly that it seemed that she had been waiting for that declaration, like it was an opportunity. She walked to a barrel, reached inside, and drew out some dried shellfish. She then reached into a box above her head, on a shelf near some books, and drew out some bread. She placed them on a wooden board and walked over to Ilfair. She extended the board, and Ilfair took it without standing but with measured hesitation. They were eye to eye, due to her small frame.

She paused for an uncomfortable moment. Ilfair noted how she extended the silence to heighten his discomfort. Eventually, she turned away and walked back over to her chair by the glass reservoir and sat down.

She watched him eat the food in silence. He looked up at her occasionally, but mostly averted his gaze. Looking at her made him worry about the wisdom of eating the food she had offered, but he was too hungry to resist. The salted fish was too salty, and the bread was dry. But he didn't care. It was the best food he had had in days. He drank the last of his remaining water to help wash it down.

The few minutes he had taken to eat had been cathartic, calming his nerves, and had allowed him a moment to collect his thoughts.

"Are you...?" Ilfair began.

"The creature, I assume you would call me, from your dream?" she finished. "Yes, I am."

"How is that...?" Ilfair began again.

"Possible?" Again, she read his mind. *Annoying*, Ilfair thought. "Dreams and feelings are my realm, and shadows too," she paused, interrupting herself, and interjected, "For how different are they, really?" She looked up quizzically before she continued.

"Anyway, they are to me like the waking world is to you. I walk about in them as you would in the world beneath the sun and the moon. I am Abby of the Keening Cliffs." She added an insincere flourish of her arms and a mocking bow of her head. Ilfair wondered if the Abby's dramatic presentation was intended to cover up some weakness in her abilities. He had seen this type of bravado before. But with Abby – she was *so* strange – he just could not be sure. *It could just as easily be to confuse me further*, he thought.

"Abby Abscess?" Ilfair asked. "But the Harrowing of Herod is just a Witch-Child fairy tale to scare children."

"Those are cruel names given by small people, long dead now. And it's Witch-*Bard*. But yes, I am her." She started to smile, but as it revealed her black and missing teeth, she stopped, looked down, and sighed. Ilfair noticed a self-consciousness at this. *From your appearance*, he thought. He almost felt pity at that moment.

"You are lucky. Long ago... with an insult like that... I would have killed you where you sat. And not quickly. But I have left most of that behind. That was for the ancient world and its people. I have nothing, for the most part, to do with the modern world south of the Godskeeps." She paused and looked over Ilfair's shoulder.

"I don't feel very lucky," Ilfair said flatly. And he didn't, all the more now, for he did fear her.

"Well, you are. And you are special. Like me," Abby said with a fake childlike uptick in her tone at the last two words.

"I am not like you," Ilfair said.

"I understand that you would believe, and want, that to be so. But you are, nonetheless. We are both corrupted by ancient creatures of the deep world. And the ancient gods, and the new, have let it be so," she shook her head and lines knitted her brow at this last comment.

"But, as I said, you are fortunate. The ichor that corrupted me was raw and unfiltered, ripe with the energy of gods. The Aberithic ichor in your body is older and dilute, filtered by your mother's love and weakened by the absence of the ancient gods and the presence of the sun. So, that ichor that killed so many in your village, including your mother, lives on in you, but is too weak to overcome your will. And some will you have, boy. But anyway, like I said, lucky... and loved." She gritted her teeth and narrowed her eyes carefully as the last comment.

"Aberiths?" Ilfair asked, for he had never heard of such a thing.

"Yes," Abby said. "Bitter creatures banished from the surface when Ullumair called forth the sun, so that our ancestors, yours and mine, might bring the beauty of life from the sea to the land." Abby said the word *beauty* like it was poison.

She continued, "The Aberiths have tried to return to the surface many times. But they have always failed. With you, and those in your village, they tried to pollute your water with their tiny young: their ichor. They are forever seeking revenge against the children of Ullumair. And they succeeded in some small way as some of your people fell ill or died. If they wished to find a way back to the surface? Well, again, it failed, for the most part. Though I suppose it remains to be seen what becomes of you." She paused for a moment. *For effect again*, Ilfair thought.

"But you are special," she continued. "For it did not kill you or make you sick. It lives on inside you and, when it can, it fills your thoughts with its bitter will. But you do have some will, don't you? Somehow you have kept their bitter chaos at bay within you. Like I said, you are lucky, and special—in fact, unique." She smiled at this, but kept her mouth closed this time. With her mouth closed, the smile made her look macabre rather than terrifying.

"I suppose you are right; things could be worse. I am alive." Ilfair paused. "But I don't know what has happened to me. I don't really know where I have been, where I am now, or what this is." Ilfair extended his arm and exposed the underside, revealing the long twisting and spiraling marks.

"And you seem to have all the answers, though I have no idea how. And I will admit, I am afraid of you," Ilfair continued, sighing for he was overwhelmed and frustrated.

He sat the plate down on the floor and shoved it away with his foot. He thought a moment. "I'm sorry," he said. He paused. "Thank you for the food."

Abby seemed to think for a moment too. "Don't apologize. And you are welcome. But you don't really need to thank me, everything, even things given freely, come with a price," she paused for effect.

"Nonetheless, everything you say is true and understandable. I didn't get spiral branded by a god and thrown across the land, far from home, to the birthplace of a long-forgotten god of madness. I have not lived a life fighting off bizarre images of bitter black Aberiths. I did not have to pretend to be normal so that I was not cast out, locked up, or worse," again she paused and sighed.

"No, that did not happen to me. But I too have gained the attention of the Aberiths and the disdain of the ancient gods. I was fully consumed by the Aberiths when I was eleven years old. I was buried alive and abandoned by my parents. I look like a fiendish, desiccated doll of a creature. I am reviled by all. And because of that I spare you because I understand you and don't despise you, even though I know the truth of you. A truth you have hidden from everyone. Haven't you?" She added the last comment with a sideways glance at Ilfair.

"Even now I use that connection with you to fight off an alien desire to rip out your throat and use your skin to make a doll of you." She was speaking more quickly, and water was glistening in her unblinking eyes; they were not tears, more like the glistening look of a predator.

Abby sighed. "Don't worry," she said, "the food was safe... to eat," she added. Ilfair looked down at the empty plate with concern. He sat stiffly, terrified.

"And even if it wasn't, you can't get sick like that. Haven't you noticed that by now? They won't let that happen." Evidently, she was referring to the Aberithic contagion in Ilfair's body.

"I am sorry. Truly," Ilfair said after that last comment. And he was. She was ghastly to behold, especially and cruelly, when she smiled. And now that he thought of it, if even some of what she had said was true, which it did appear to be, she had clearly suffered worse than he had. And she was different from what he had been told of Abby Abscess, the Witch-Child of the Keening Cliffs, by his father. Not less terrifying, but more complicated to be sure.

"And thank you for your... um..." he paused as he searched for the word to describe not being eaten, "help." Something about the look on Abby's face told Ilfair that help wasn't quite the correct word and that the tone of the conversation was about to change.

CHAPTER 18

ANSWERS, WITH LIES

To protect his deformed Moonsung child, Ullumair called forth his Everflame. With it he melted the rock of Erlan about them into liquid glass. He raised the molten earth and formed it into a sphere to surround them. As such, no more Aberiths were able to cling to Feralzmoon.
—from the Athenomancer archives

Abby shook her head.

"Here. We are sitting here, talking to each other like we are friends," Abby said. "We aren't. Why don't I just tell you what you need to know and be done with this? The sun is getting low in the sky, so you must be tired. Anyway, we will be able to talk again after you've left." Ilfair nodded slowly at that.

Halfway through his nodding, Ilfair's face screwed up in confusion. Abby knew what he was thinking. *How can she talk to me after I am gone?* But before he could question her, she continued.

"So, as I said," she began, "you have been chosen, marked by Feralzmoon, a long-forgotten and believed dead god. A god of chaos and madness. If I were to hazard a guess, he was drawn to you somewhat randomly, for he does nothing with pure intent, because you are infected with the essence of the beings that created him. Well, that and you don't despise him like I do. At least not yet." She paused for a breath. She had lied about a key aspect of this story: he had been marked by Ullumair, not Feralzmoon. But she knew that he would be more upset by the latter and was enjoying his fear. Beyond that, she knew much more than she was telling. But she had her reasons, and it was close enough to true. She had her own plans and had to be careful what she revealed so she did not reveal her own intentions. Also, she believed he was more likely to believe this version of the story from her, given what she looked like.

"And what of this mark?" Ilfair asked. "What is it?"

"It is a message. Written in the ancient language of the Feraliths, Feralzmoon's devout. I recognize the spiraling organization of the symbols. The followers of Feralzmoon hold the spiral as sacred. You have seen it now a few times, if you recall. I can distinguish the arrangement, but alas I do not know exactly what it says. But I guess that it is a dictate." Again, a bit of a lie, but laced with truth. The best kind of lie. She knew exactly what it said.

"There are some I know who could read it. Actually, I don't know them, but rather I knew their ancestors. Well, I didn't know them either, but rather knew of them. For almost everyone did. You should seek a member of the Graywater family who is a standing member of the priesthood of Ullumair. Oh, wait, I guess it wouldn't be Ullumair anymore, it's whoever the deity of water is these days."

"Mercial," Ilfair blurted out, a juvenile enthusiasm in his voice. He fell silent and looked down. To Abby's ancient and bitter eyes, his comment revealed his vulnerable youth and innocence.

"Of course," Abby smiled with condescending insincerity. "Anyway, that family has been in the city of Winters Haven from its beginning. They led the migration from Harrowfell ages ago. And they were still there the last time I checked, when I got this dress from what's-her-name." She stood and turned and said, "Do you like it?"

Ilfair looked on in stunned silence. Abby took delight in how unsettled he seemed at the rapidity with which she would change personas between child and adult, sincere and cynical, terrifying and sympathetic. It gave her delight to see the desired effect.

She scoffed and continued, "That was a couple of decades ago at least. It is likely still so. That the Graywaters are there, I mean. That family has a collection of ancient tomes that date all the way back to Harrowfell and the Age of the Ancients. Whether they know that or not, I do not know. One should never underestimate the stupidity of the Ashfallen," she paused. That last comment brought many specific instances to mind of her own stupidity as a living child. Not least of which being her own foolishness in consuming the ichor in the Feralrift.

She shook her head, smirked, and continued. "Anyway, Winters Haven is south of here, less than a week for you to cover by foot." Abby watched the young man work through the information she had provided. She could tell that he was trying to be sure it all made sense and was struggling to do so. She smiled without mirth.

Despite her tendency to partake in misdirection, she wanted the boy to succeed and did not want him to become lost. Sending the young man to the Graywater family was in his, and rather intentionally her, best interest. The current Graywater in the temple to the deity Mercial, as Ilfair had informed her, would most likely be a good and helpful man. Such had been the nature of that insipid family as far as she knew. And she knew quite far.

The Graywater family at least used to know much about the priests of water, including the ancient god Ullumair. The current Graywater in the temple may very well have no idea what he was looking at on the young man's arm, but he would be driven by conscience to figure it out one way or the other; to help the boy.

Abby's money was on "the other", given the ignorance of the modern Ashfallen. Regardless, she cared only about what, not how.

Ilfair spoke up with some hope at this. "I have heard of the Graywater family. I daresay almost everyone has, even those not from Winters Haven. And I am glad to hear that I am so close. I know that city, and though I have never been there, I know how to get home from there. And getting there is easy, I will just follow the coast south." Ilfair said unnecessarily.

Abby grinned. She could tell he was speaking mostly for his own benefit. It seemed to be making him happy. Ilfair was smiling now at the knowledge that he was close to real, friendly civilization and hearing the familiar and well-regarded name of the Graywater family seemed to be giving him confidence.

Abby decided she needed to do something about that, so she added, "I am glad I suppose, for you at least, but I don't suppose you will be going home very soon. But that is up to you." If necessary, Abby would make sure that Ilfair did not go home. Though she doubted it would be.

"Yes." Ilfair said simply. To which part of Abby's comment the affirmative declaration was directed was unclear, but Abby did not care. What she did care about was that her intentionally ominous comment had made him pause and think what she might have meant.

She saw the unease return to his posture and face and it prompted him to speak again. "What about the dream of last night? Was that even a dream?"

"It was not a dream. It was a thought, a thought of mine based on my understanding of the vision you received from the ancient gods. It is what I think will happen soon if you do not adhere in some way to your divine dictate." The sweeping tone of Abby's echoey voice became deeper and more solemn with the last statement.

"How could you possibly know that if you cannot read the

message?" Ilfair asked, his tone somewhat more frustrated and aggressive. *That's daring*, Abby thought, impressed that Ilfair would speak to her like that.

"I am very old. And I know all of what has befallen you. It is my supposition based on the information available to me. I can say no more than that." She, of course, could have said more, but Abby had decided. She was done revealing information.

CHAPTER 19

A FARE(UN)WELL EXCHANGE

Ullumair's flame of creation, upon creating the glass sphere that encircled Ullumair and Feralzmoon, scorched the verdant plateau above which they floated. When the ash settled thereupon, only a brown, gray, and black land remained, called thereafter the Ashfall Plateau. It was this event which also gave the descendants of the Moonsung their name: the Ashfallen.

—from the Athenomancer archives

"Allow me to present you with a token of my goodwill, such as it is."

Abby stood and grimaced; a strange sight to see a young girl struggle to stand. Then she moved rapidly across the intervening space, her feet moving as though she were walking quickly, but did not touch the ground and made not a sound. Likewise, she held her arms motionless behind her back as she moved. In a moment, she closed the space and stood in front of a startled Ilfair. It made him doubt everything about her. He suspected that was exactly the intent.

She slowly brought her hands from behind her back. She held

them out in front of her and slowly uncurled her tiny fingers to produce a necklace.

"This was from my mother. It is an amulet of the moon of the ancient world when it had but one crater. She made it for me from fragments that fell from the moon when the ancient gods entered. Wear it." She reached the necklace out in her small white hand. "This necklace has protective charms on it, some physical, yes, but particularly it protects against madness and maladies of the mind. The ancients believed that the Feralzmoon caused them and that the types of maladies were connected to the phases of the moon. In any event, I have no need for it anymore." Abby's face was covered by shadows as she looked down to her feet.

"Let us exchange necklaces given to us by our mothers. Yours is a charm against sickness and mine against the madness of the moon. It would be a nice way to remember our meeting, would it not?" She seemed somber and sincere.

Ilfair thought for a moment as he absently touched the necklace wrapped around his wrist. "How do you know of my necklace?"

"I told you already, I know more about you than you think, better than you think. Your thoughts and dreams are open to me," she said.

"And yours is just a necklace after all, where mine is truly valuable. Although maybe this Illinir will help me, I've never bothered to talk to the new gods for the old ones never answered. As for my necklace, it will truly help you, protecting you from madness. It would seem that you could use that, no? Graywater will verify this, rest assured. And after walking through Feralzmoon's ancient temple, I guess you can imagine the value of protection from his ideas."

Ilfair did not think that he would rest assured, but some of what she had said seemed reasonable. And again, that haunting echo of her many-toned voices was persuasive and confusing.

"That's what that was?" He spoke the question like a statement, mostly to himself. He thought it best to give her the necklace for he did fear her. So, he did, albeit with regret for it was dear to him. They exchanged necklaces. Ilfair donned her necklace and tucked the moon symbol on it under his shirt, next to the symbol of Faid. He rationalized, to calm his regret, that it made sense in some way to take this necklace. If the ancients thought the moon protected or caused psychopathy, then perhaps next to Faid is where it belonged.

She took his necklace and walked over to a shelf filled with an array of assorted dolls of varying sizes. She placed the necklace next to the dolls.

"Ok, this is good. This will work." With that Abby walked over to her chair, her back to Ilfair. She sounded old. Without turning she said, "There are places to sleep below the tower. You will feel safer there. I don't go down there, it smells of whalefall and I've never been able to get rid of the stench. Take food and water, as much as you like, I have no need of it."

She disappeared into the shadows of the room. From the shadows she made one last parting comment. "You may be asking yourself *why has this happened to me?* Take some advice: use that discipline of yours and be done with the hope of ever answering that mystery. I have pondered this for centuries and it has brought me nothing but pain and bitterness."

With that he heard something fall to the ground, a coin or the like. It made a tap-tap-tap sound on the floor. Then there was a strange skittering sound mixed with Abby's padded footfalls. He guessed she was gone, but to where he could not guess, although she had to be in the room still. Where else was there to go?

Ilfair moved only into the room far enough to get more food. As he did so, he saw something small and round on the ground next to the chair, obviously the coin Abby had dropped. He walked over and leaned down to pick it up. It was the missing button from his shirt.

"Abby?" Ilfair asked to the shadows. He waited for a response but received only silence.

He knew in that instant that it had been a mistake to give Abby the necklace. The necklace had been of the utmost value to him. Ilfair had lived an austere life, stripped of distraction by necessity, and the necklace was one of his few possessions of real sentimental value. Everything else he possessed was simple and practical to minimize the need for thought. He needed his mental energy to keep his calm, intentional, and emotionless demeanor intact. Emotion triggered the disturbing whispering black eels that invaded his mind.

The symbol-necklace to Illinir had been a gift, leather- and iron-worked for him by his mother and father to protect him from the plague that infected Fayrest when he was very young. He had worn it wrapped around his wrist so he could always see it and be reminded of everything that it meant to him. It was the only thing he had of his mother and now it was gone.

He gritted his teeth and pushed the feelings of sadness in his neck and chest down to his belly. He stood and walked over to the shelf with the dolls. The necklace was gone. She had the necklace now, but she had left the button. *But why?* he thought. Whatever the reason, he doubted it was good.

He felt defeated. Even though he had learned much, he wasn't sure how much was true. And he had lost his heirloom, his main connection to the mother he had never known.

"Why?" he wondered, running his fingers through his hair. His head felt fuzzy, as it had at the base of the rift.

"That voice," he said simply, his furrowed brow reflecting the impact it had on him.

He wondered further if their conversation had even been Abby's aim. As he walked down the stairs, he felt very sorry for himself. He focused on the small glow the stairs made under each of his footfalls. He took some small joy from the beauty of it.

He looked up over his shoulder to be sure he was not followed. Confident that he was not, he played a little with the stairs. He noticed how the glow brightened when he pressed hard with his foot. Or how the color changed if he struck it sharply with his toe or heel.

Quite without noticing, involved in his stair experiments, he reached the bottom of the stairs. He opened the hatch on the floor next to the stairs and peered into the hole. His eyes adjusted to the change in lighting. He climbed down into the hole, grabbing the iron handles that were pressed into the rock. He closed the hatch behind himself, which illogically made him feel safer. He knew he was not that far from the girl-creature known as Abby, but he did feel safer. Again, he thought of blinders on a sliipmare.

"So odd," he said aloud, referring to more than just the equine comparison.

He reached the bottom of the well-worked rock passage and turned to face a north-directed hall. He could see light barely leaking into the hall, though he couldn't see from where it originated. He could hear and smell the ocean. He walked some distance and reached a western turn. He could now see the end of the passage: he could now see the sun. It was setting over the Moonsong Sea. Again, his eyes adjusted.

This northwest-facing cavern stretched all the way to what he assumed was the edge of the Keening Cliffs. He noted all along the length of the cavern were whale bones embedded decoratively into the walls. And runes etched into the bones. It was beautiful really. And it smelled wonderful down here, it had the sweetness of aged ambergris, often used in perfumes. The walls had been worked down here to flow with the whale bone decoration. He only realized now how the entire tower, and especially Abby's flat at the top, had smelled off somehow; mildly stale and, well, rotten. He guessed it made sense that ambergris would smell terrible to her.

Along the length of the hall, to Ilfair's left and right, passages periodically bled off the main larger corridor, arches of whale bone marking each. Drawn to the light of the setting sun, Ilfair took to the right of the last hall. There he found a small alcove, clearly one of many sleeping quarters long ago vacated. He was still hungry and tired, so he took out his blanket and some of the bread and fish he had collected from Abby, lay the blanket down and rested upon it. He ate the food and drank his water while he listened to the sea and looked up to the ceiling.

He was warm and sated for the first time in almost a week. He eyed the runes on one of the whale bones that decorated his room. As he fell asleep, he noticed something. The runes on the whale bone looked very much like the markings on his arm. They were straight up and down on the bones. They did not spiral like his. As he thought of the spirals, he fell asleep wondering, *why has this happened to me?*

CHAPTER 20

ALONG THE MOONSONG

Ullumair's flame expanded outward, beyond the plateau. The holy fire reacted with the metal-rich valley before breaking against the Godskeep Mountains. That area before the mountains was left a combination of deep greens and rich reds, yellows, and oranges. The trees thereupon were also left forever the color of fall. These lands were henceforth called the Umbervale and Umberwood.

—from the Athenomancer archives

Ilfair woke to the sad sound of the wind and waves breaking on the cliffs. He had heard stories of how they sang a melancholy song to Erlan and to the moon. He nodded to himself in understanding. He could see now how the cliffs had come to be called the Keening Cliffs. It was a play on words, referring both to their sharp rocks and the wailing sound the wind made as it blew along them.

Despite this, he felt good. Still a bit fuzzy-headed from the insanity of it all, but nonetheless optimistic. The air was thick with a cool dampness, but he was warm with his blanket and his sliip-mare cloak. He stood in the alcove; he was just short enough to do so.

In the morning light, he noticed something he had not seen in the dim light of the night before. Something crumpled in the corner of the room. It looked like an amber-colored cloth. He kneeled and picked it up. He could almost see through the shirt. It looked and felt a bit like silk—gossamer- and diaphanous-like cobwebs—but stiffer and coarser. Closer inspection revealed what looked like woven translucent threads. They looked like glass, but that would have been impossible to achieve.

"Just like the staircase," Ilfair wondered aloud. Somehow the flight of steps in the tower were able to bear weight beyond normal glass and had no other noticeable supporting materials. And this glass-like fiber tunic was able to flex and stretch like cloth, but was tough and durable like glass.

He decided to keep the curious item and tied it around one of the straps of his pack. He left the alcove and walked to the end of the main hallway. From there he could see the northern Moonsong Sea spread out before him, ice floes visible in the northern distance. As he looked down, he could also make out a ladder worked into the cliff face. Hand and foot holes had been expertly dug into the wall and semicircular iron bands had been placed periodically down the ladder to prevent falling.

As Ilfair stood there pondering his situation, he remembered the single bridge across the Whale's Echo chasms on the patch of land with the tower. He had no interest in going back up there for he would have to pass through the tower. He feared crossing Abby again.

He thought it better judgment now to make his way down to the beach and look for an easier route south. With care, he descended, checking his footing and grip on the wet iron rungs as he went. He noted the beauty of the striations made by the stacks of thick rock that comprised the cliff. He also noted many caves. The wind blowing across their faces was likely the origin of the woeful sounding drone of the Keening Cliffs.

Eventually, when he put his feet on the sand of the Moonsong beach, he felt that he was far from Abby. He knew, of course, that he wasn't, and he looked up to the top of the tower, which clung to the sharp edge of the cliffs many hundreds of feet up. He wondered if she was looking down on him. He felt the answer was no. In fact, for some reason, he felt like she was no longer even in the tower, especially since the top of the tower was no longer lit. Who would stay in that cold tower without the flame burning for warmth?

"Well, she might," Ilfair said in response to his internal thoughts, remembering how Abby had reacted to warmth and light. Ilfair ran his fingers through his hair and shook his head. He was glad to be gone from her presence. He was glad to be out of sight of her. However, he was even more grateful to be out of earshot of that unearthly echoey chorus of voices. Even just the memory of it was enough to put him on edge, so he put it from his mind as forcefully as he could manage, along with a few tiny squirming eels.

At that thought, he turned abruptly away from the tower and looked south. The beach was small, not stretching very far west from the cliffs, north or south. Looking north, he could see the inlet formed by one of the many Moonthread Rivers at the northern Whale's Echo Chasm. The river he had crossed on the way to the lighthouse.

He made his way south, walking through the ribs of the whale skeleton he had seen the day before. He could see, at the south end of the beach, a small inlet cut into the cliff, another Moonthread River at the second of the two Whale's Echo Chasms. The slope on the southern cliff face where the river cut into the rock was shallow enough that he was confident he could scramble up to the plateau at its top.

Once in the chasm, he could see to his left the steep cliff face that formed the southern edge of the triangle of land that housed the tower. He splashed his way across the shallow water of one of the Moonthread Rivers to the other side of the chasm. Once on the other side, he paused to fill his water again. Most of it was gone from last night and this morning. He would boil it later to be sure it was safe to drink. Although, if what Abby said about his immunity to certain poisons was to be believed, he did not need to.

As he squatted there, he looked up at the shallower face on that side and worked out a path to the top. He scrambled up the shorter slope, only a few hundred feet in height on this lower southern side. As he climbed, the wet sand gave way to black mud and then to gray and green scrub, which covered the darkened earth. Abby's words were still in his head as he stood at the top. He furrowed his brow, trying to remember ever getting sick from anything he had consumed. He could not.

He was a bit short of breath, which he could see coming out in puffs in the frigid morning air. He could see the rising sun now, coming up low in the sky where the glacier met the Godskeeps to the northeast. The light felt warm on his face and helped warm the chill breeze from the sea.

He looked south from the plateau. The waves broke noisily against the Keening Cliffs to his right, the inlet being just a narrow respite from the sheer wall they formed against the sea.

He could see the far western end of the Godskeeps terminating at the sea in green tree-covered hills. The hills were maybe a day's walk from where he stood. The sight of the fall-colored Umberwood in the foreground of the Godskeeps made him feel better than he had in many days. This would be his goal. He had one quick look back to the lighthouse, beacon still unlit, reached into his pack for some bread, and set out for the Umberwood.

By late in the day, he had crossed many cascades and reached the end of the Keening Cliffs. The soft earth, a welcome relief for his aching feet, had changed from brown to green and he at last faced the edge of the Umberwood. To his right, the coastline turned southeast and rose again with more steep cliffs. A ruined stone wall lay just east of the coastline forming a miles-long semicircular line around a short cusp of cliffless land.

There was something about the wall that drew him in.

CHAPTER 21

THE WALL OF HARROWFELL

The milky-white glass sphere that hid away Ullumair, Feralzmoon, Ullumyth, and Aberith, rose into the heavens. As it rose, Ullumair formed his own body into a white, spiraling shell, as if from the Moonsong sea itself, to contain Feralzmoon. The rising sphere ultimately found its home within the hollow center of the moon. The only indication of its passage into the moon was a single large crater on Umbral's surface.

—from the Athenomancer archives

As he approached the northern tip of the wall, he noticed a ruined granite stump. Judging by the size of the greaves, this was the leg of what had once been a large statue five to ten times his size.

From there he followed the line of the wall south. He noted, periodically, markings on the wall. Very few of these markings were entirely intact. However, the ones that were looked like the symbols he had seen in the alcove in which he'd slept the night before. Curiously, the symbols retained a sharp white color against the gray granite construction of the wall, despite the erosion inflicted by the ages that had passed since its construction.

At about the halfway point, two tall metal posts protruded up from either side of a large gap in the eroded and vine-cracked wall. Metal bells hung from chains attached to the top of each post. The uprights marked an entrance through the wall. Ilfair could imagine guards standing alongside the metal uprights, serving as a watch atop the wall.

The shape of the time-blackened metal bells was unique, nothing like anything he had ever seen. Two massive whales entwined by great squids and octopi, whether in embrace or combat was unclear, formed the waist. Each bell had two openings, which housed clappers formed by the great open mouths of the whales. The cavity was formed by the body of the beasts. The tail and tentacles of the creatures wrapped about the chains attached to the crown. The dorsal fins of the whales protruded from the waist. They were sharp and pointed and hinted at a martial purpose. Deep engravings of letters he could not read were still visible. If he could have read them, it would have made the function clear, he speculated.

As he grew closer, a breeze picked up quite suddenly and the once-still bells swayed and clanged. The din from the bells and the howl of the sea's wind created a haunting feeling, especially here in the isolation of the coastal north.

As he passed the posts, the gusts from the sea abated and the bells calmed. As he neared the end of the wall, he noticed the remains of a statue, just as he had seen at the northern end. It was in better condition, but the statue seemed to have sunk into the earth up to the mid-thigh. It leaned back and to the side, gaining stability from a section of the wall behind it. The statues clearly marked the beginning and end of the wall at the points where the wall terminated at the coastline.

Ilfair's suspicions were confirmed from the remnants of the northern statue; even sunk into the earth it was clear that this statue would have been visible even from a great distance. He suspected that the head of the statue would have risen higher than the top of the wall. It looked like a soldier or guard of some kind. He suspected that it had been imposing, as even in its current state he was in awe of it.

He paused and looked up to the granite form. The sculpture depicted the soldier clothed in a doublet over his hauberk with a white horn protruding from the sea, tipped with white flame, and a rising sun in the background. The head was covered in a chain coif that draped down to the shoulders. Much of the complexity of the chain was ruined as the face was half gone, as was the entirety of the left arm. In the right arm was a spear, the butt end buried in the earth with the point tilted skyward. Bits of the statue littered the ground, some mostly buried. The most notable feature, though, was the Amberglass laced throughout the armor of the head, chest and spear.

It was the same color as the shirt he had found the night before. He reached up over his head to touch the glass. It had the same fibrous feel as the shirt. His hand slid to the granite of the doublet bearing the flaming crest. At that moment, a burst of wind came off the sea and set the bells to their uncanny din. He was frozen in that moment, hand touching the statue, as the black eels in his mind erupted, blackening his vision.

When his eyes cleared, he found himself in a changed place. It had only been a moment, one slow blink of his eyes to clear his head, but suddenly it was night. The ground around him was lit by moonlight. The statue, a ruin only seconds before, now stood complete before him. The wall also showed none of its previous signs of erosion or vine-growth cracks.

Agape, he stood for a moment. The sound of chanting caused him to snap his head around. Many scores of men stood in lines before the wall, chanting a low rhythmic song. Overlapping spheres of light surrounded each man. They were a wall of light in the night.

They were clad much as the statue was, facing the northeastern valley. All the men in the line aimed a spear at the valley, planting the base of the spear to the earth. Two men stood behind them atop the wall, bearing the chained bells he had seen before in their hands, their doublets bearing the flaming white horn symbol he had seen on the statue. Their eyes were trained east and slightly north, over the heads of the lines of men in front of them.

Ilfair followed their line of sight. For a moment, he saw nothing. Then he saw what the eyes of the watchers on the wall were trained on. He saw dozens of black-clad horsemen charging forcefully over the earth. But they made no sound. The hoof falls of the horses were muted and no din of chain or leather or breath emitted from the riders. They rushed toward the gleaming wall. The steeds had eight legs, like the sliipmares near Overmoor, but were much larger. The coursers and riders seemed to carry shadow and silence with them, the anti-image of the wall of light and chanting they bore down on.

Among their ranks flew a flag emblazoned with a gnarled tree set before a full moon. It whipped silently in the wind, born aloft by a bannerman hidden by the riders before him. Ilfair had seen this symbol before in the glacier temple. The armor was covered with black rivets throughout, and their faces were hidden under black cowls.

The horsemen bore down on the wall, hands free of the reins, bearing chained weapons. He had seen that type of weapon before as well, draped above the desk of the dead priest at the top of the black spire. One end of the chain ended in a sickle, the other in a spiked spiraling disc made of the same multi-hued metal as his spiralhammer and encrusted randomly with obsidian-like stone.

The horsemen silently closed the distance, splashing noiselessly through the cascades Ilfair had crossed only hours before. It was odd to watch the water splash silently. They grew closer, their collision with the lighted guards imminent, the breath of the horses visible in the cold night air. The chanting of the line of men increased and moments before the impact of the light and dark forces, the watchmen on the wall smashed their bells aggressively against the granite. They leapt down and ran past the lines of men, carrying their bells like morning stars. When the two wall guards passed the last line of men, the whole formation followed. In moments the distance was closed. Glass and wood shattered. Bone and metal cracked and crashed. The silence of the horsemen was broken by the encounter with the light and sound of the white-clad soldiers.

The clash of the men and the din of the bells made Ilfair jump involuntarily. His hand pulled free of the statue, and he was brought back from the dark scene into the bright sunlight. In the sunlit scene, the bells were still screaming on their chains and the wind was howling. The noise hurt Ilfair's ears. He fell back from the statue, hands to his ears.

The eels still squirmed in his vision, and he felt their anger more clearly than ever before. He scrambled to his feet and brought his spiralhammer at the loop of his belt to his hand. He ran from the ancient site, his initial awe replaced with foreboding and real terror. As he separated from the wall, the bells soon quieted. Soon after, he slowed his run, gasping for breath. He eventually caught his breath and summoned the courage to look back. It looked as it had before, ancient and ruined; silent and calm. But he saw it differently now. He saw it as something living and demanding of a respect he had not carried with him to the wall before.

He walked the remainder of the distance to the woods, turning a weather eye on the ruined wall periodically. Before he entered the forest, he turned and looked back one last time at the wall. He eyed it for many moments, waiting for something, though he did not know what. When nothing happened, he tilted his head slightly to the west. He could just make out the top of Abby's tower. He could see the steep rise of the Umbervale to the Ashfall Plateau. Dozens of waterfalls cascaded down that slope and the whites, blues, and grays of the Elderime Glacier and the Godskeeps provided a stark backdrop.

He could scarcely believe that he had been up there just a few days before. It was beautiful, the whole of the landscape—of that there was no doubt—but he was truly glad its unforgiving-ness was behind him. In a way, leaving the ancient wall ruins was like leaving the whole of the ancient world behind him; the glacier, the temple, the tower, the whole land north of the Godskeeps. Maybe that was what felt so odd. He looked back at the ruins one last time, furrowed his brow, confused by his feelings, and then turned and entered the Umberwood proper.

CHAPTER 22

EXTINGUISHING THE LIGHT

Within Umbral, the Chaos War silently raged between Ullumair and Feralzmoon. Since then, the seas have never been calm and lunacy afflicts the unfortunate descendants of the Moonsung. In their efforts to calm the land and heal the afflicted, the Moonsung and their descendants, the Ashfallen, directed their prayers to the moon; to the new home of the ancient gods.
—from the Athenomancer archives

Abby had gleefully extinguished the beacon the night after Ilfair's departure. It had served its purpose: the moth had come to the flame. She had not needed to seek Ilfair out, which had provided two benefits. First, she had not needed to bear the brutality of the lightness of the Ashfallen's world. And second, it had made Ilfair feel more in control, as if things were going according to his own agency, which had made him more receptive in general. Or at least she supposed.

"No matter," she hummed.

She had spent the remainder of the time since Ilfair's parting in the glorious darkness and the invigoration of the cold. When the sun rose, she moved her chair to stay in the shadows, having reverted the room to its previous state. She had arranged the bookshelves to block the windows as best she could. She wondered if she could produce enough ichorink to black out the unobstructed windows.

From her vantage point in the shadows, she watched Ilfair enter the northwestern woods of the Godskeeps foothills. As she watched him, her left hand absently patted Ixo's shiny black carapace. One of Ixo's children crawled over her hand. Ixo quietly fed, sitting next to her in the shadows, gorging on some small brown coated mammal of the Ashfall Plateau.

She had found Ixo deep in a wet cavern of the Keening Cliffs long ago. *Must have been centuries ago now*, she mused. Ixo was some type of ancient parasitic predator of the deep. She had fed it small mammals. While it fed, it had succumbed to her mindleeching and now was bent to her will.

The small mammal that Ixo fed on was a part of the ritual magic Abby had used to create her dolls. She would use the husk of the animal, imbued with the essence of Ixo's saliva, to craft the doll. She would need to make a new one now. As she thought of the doll, she held up the necklace she had taken from Ilfair in her right hand and eyed it carefully. It was well wrought; love had gone into its construction. It filled her with envy and bitterness. She squeezed it tightly in her little hand and that terrifying smile split her face.

"What do you think, Ixo? Will he manage this?" The echo of her eerie, tiny voice did not match the tone or sophisticated content of her words. Regardless of the content, Ixo did not answer, it just shifted slightly, feet clicking on the stone, and continued to desiccate the mammal.

"He's a remarkable young man, but this is a monumental task." She paused and shifted her closed mouth on her face.

She patted Ixo again and stood. "No need to worry. We will make sure that he does."

As Ilfair moved into the forest, the top of the unlit tower fell below the horizon behind him, unseen, for he did not look back again. He could feel the grade incline, and he set his thoughts to the work of the climb. He was just on the northern slope of the piedmont of the Godskeeps. The leaves of the white trees here were perpetually red, orange, and yellow, and they crunched under his footfalls as he made his way into the canopy of the forest.

It was getting dark, and so he quickly managed to find a thick area of trees with some rocks for coverage and for lighting a fire. Finding kindling and wood was easy here, and quickly, he had a fire lit. He was able to warm the bread and fish. The warmth made the unpleasant food go down easier. He boiled his water and sat with his thoughts, staring into the dancing flames.

Soon after eating, he bedded down. Things were looking better than they had in a while. There were still plenty of questions, but Ilfair knew where he was going now. Civilization was within walking distance, and he was glad for that.

He wanted a bath. It was not something he would have thought he would have missed so much. He missed the large metal drum in his simple home. He would spend all the time needed to get the water hot, almost uncomfortably so, and fill the drum half full. It was always a welcome feeling after a day in the dark, cold, and wet caves of the Fenrik mines. The thought of being completely submerged and letting the warmth seep into his bones brought a small smile to his face.

There was plenty to worry about; and but for the thought of the warmth of soaking in warm water, those worries would have kept him up. He was practiced at putting bad thoughts out of his mind. Even now, at this very moment, the strange creatures clawed and poked inside his skull, pushing their images to the backs of his eyes. That was the last thought he remembered before falling asleep near the fire, covered by his sliipmare cloak.

FROM THE SHADOWS of the tower, Abby used her shadowsight and peered into the shadows of the night forest. She watched Ilfair as he fell asleep. He was out of her view by the light of the sun, but not by the shadows of the night. Much of what Abby had become was horrific and a constant source of pain, but it was not without its perks.

CHAPTER 23
RAIN AND REBIRTH

The Moonsung and the first generation of Ashfallen saw the birth of Feralzmoon and his conflict with Ullumair as a sign. It split them, the denizens of Harrowfell, into those devoted to their Father, Ullumair, and those sympathetic to the suffering of Feralzmoon. The devout of Feralzmoon sought a new path, away from Harrowfell.
—from the Athenomancer archives

Ilfair woke the next morning to clear skies. He collected his things, ate some tough bread, and headed out. He wandered somewhat inland over the next few hours, moving away from the coast. The tree growth was becoming denser and, with the crisscrossing rolling hills, his sightlines were poor. He knew it would be easy to lose his bearings. He thought better of his current vector and made his way back to the coast.

"Impossible to get lost that way," he said, just to hear the company of his voice.

Ilfair found a stream and followed it to the cliff's edge. He watched the water fall into the sea. It was beautiful. Further out to sea he could see ruins of an old city. He could even see a bit of the land where the structures had once stood.

He took out the map he had taken from the Nihilin Temple of Feralzmoon and found the spot. Evidently, the sea level used to be lower and there was a city out there. He could hear Abby's words echoing in his head. Harrowfell, she had said, was the name of the city. He saw the text on the map; it didn't look like the word Harrowfell to him, but that was the way of language he knew. It was a bit north from where he now stood. And he could see that the cliffs were low there.

He could imagine a bridge out to the city or, if the water level were low enough, a road to the city. He could also imagine that the city would have been easy to defend, its approach surrounded by the wall he had seen the day prior. On the map, which looked somewhat military with arrows everywhere, he could imagine that Harrowfell and Aberron had had more than a few conflicts.

As his thoughts wandered and his legs rested, he heard a raindrop strike the map. Quickly, Ilfair folded the map up and put it away. He looked up; behind he could see storm clouds coming down off the Godskeeps. He could smell the yearning of the tree roots for the rain, and his heart sank. He immediately set off south, the smell of the coming rain and sea salt filling his head.

Within less than an hour of walking, the rain was falling steadily, and he was becoming drenched. He was freezing, especially his feet. As good as he had felt the day before, he now felt beaten. He searched for, and soon found, a rock outcropping under which to hide and wait out the downpour.

The outcropping did an adequate job of blocking the wind, but some water still leaked through and around. Not that it mattered much as he was already soaked through. It was as though all of what had happened to him hit him all at once. He was lonely. Usually, he was fine on his own, but not this alone and not for this long. He barely knew where he was, and he had even less of a clue as to what his branding and translocation could possibly mean. He knew Abby was right: he should put it from his head.

"Easier said than done," Ilfair grumbled the witticism to himself.

He was hungry and tired. He'd had some food and rest here or there, sure, but over a week with just enough to get by was wearing on him. And, of course, there were the constant thought eels, the Leechkin of his mind.

And then, on top of that, to find out that the black creature in his thoughts was not his own. He realized, shivering there under the rock, that he had never been a person of his own. He was a host, and honestly thinking back on it, that was what he had felt like. He constantly filtered and monitored himself carefully to keep the truth of what he had thought were his own thoughts from others.

He had never considered that it could have been something else. *Why would I?* he thought. But now that he had heard it out loud, he knew that it must be true. For his entire life, he had never thought he could tell anyone the truth. On that point, among others, Abby had been correct. He had feared they would lock him away in an asylum, or worse, try to purge the alien thoughts from him. He had seen people taken away to the asylums at Iilhi and he knew he did not want that. Either way, he knew it was best to be as silent on the matter as he could manage.

He also realized that he had never considered having a meaningful relationship with anyone; even his father, who he knew loved and cared for him. Many of the people in his village had been good to him, too. Even so, he would wander off as often as he could to avoid the difficult work of appearing the way he felt he had needed to.

His father had been good to him. But Ilfair had never let his guard down long enough to explore anything like returning that love. In that moment, he deeply regretted giving the Illinir necklace to Abby. Whether it had helped, he did not know, but it had been a gift from his parents and was dear to him. It had been made by his mother and father; he would often think of his mother when he held the leather bindings. His father had shared the story of its crafting with him more than once. He often imagined his mother's hands holding the necklace as she wound its leather straps. Now he imagined the love and care that she had put into the necklace.

He doubted that he could get it back from Abby. He wanted to vow that he would get it back, but he wasn't in the habit of lying to himself.

Suddenly, he felt as if he had betrayed her, and it made his heart hurt. As the emotions welled in him, he could feel those alien thoughts surge to rage in his head, as though they might burst from his eyes and ears. He sobbed once and quickly got his feelings under control.

He felt angry. He felt frustrated. But he was determined now. Surely, he could master these alien thoughts and still let his guard down enough to explore himself as a whole person and not just as the host to some alien species. He guessed it would be hard. As he leaned back against the rock and breathed deeply to get control of himself and the alien thoughts within him, he decided that starting tomorrow, he would begin that process.

He waited the rain out, sitting there shivering silently. He stared out over the sea. His face was impassive but serious. He thought of different ways that he might achieve the dichotomy. Nothing immediately came to mind. He wondered if he could find help. That wasn't something he had considered before. Perhaps that was key, to think in ways that he had not heretofore considered.

Maybe there is someone who will understand. The thought of finding that person calmed him, so he let that possibility fill him with hope.

Ilfair did not notice that he had removed the symbol to Faid from about his neck. He was holding the symbol pressed firmly between his thumb and forefinger, the leather strap dangling.

The symbol to Faid, the god of shadows and mental affliction, he had procured on his own when he was ten years old, about half the age he was now. He had worn it around his neck, the symbol tucked under his shirt, not wanting it to be seen to raise questions he did not want to answer. Faid was viewed suspiciously by some, especially in Overmoor and the surrounding Eightowns.

As a ten-year-old boy he had hoped it would help to ward off the dark murmurings of the black eels which so often infected his thoughts. He did not know to what extent, if any, it had worked, but he was unwilling to abandon it to find out.

He had lost the symbol of Illinir to Abby, so he would have to rely more on the symbol to Faid. Maybe this made more sense anyway. Sure, he had some strange physical abnormalities; his shadowsight eyes and his odd, patterned freckles, which fell under the domain of Illinir. But weren't the thoughts and ideas in his head the more affective issue? And wasn't that under the influence of Faid?

In any event, though he had not gone very far today, he was exhausted from the strain of his mental and emotional journey. As the rain abated, he decided that he would just stay under the rocks and rest for the night. He watched the sun set and absently ate and drank, because he knew he needed to, not because he wanted to. It was too wet for a fire, but honestly, he was happy to be morose. His mood matched the weather and it all felt somehow appropriate. It seemed fitting; he needed the catharsis to run its course.

Tomorrow will be a new day. He knew it would sound silly aloud, so he stayed silent. But in his head, he thought, *tomorrow will be a first day for me; a rebirth.*

He looked for a dry spot to lay down but couldn't find one. He took his pack off and inspected it and its contents for something dry to lay on. He noticed the shirt that he had taken from the caverns under the tower was dry. He could see the water bead on the shirt and slide off rapidly.

"Interesting," he said with a raised eyebrow.

He laid the shirt over his pack and put his head down. He carefully allowed the peculiarity of the shirt's properties to fill his thoughts and, with that as a distraction from the seriousness of his situation, he fell asleep quickly thereafter.

CHAPTER 24

THE WALL OF WINTERS HAVEN

*The followers of Feralzmoon abandoned Harrowfell and built the temple
of Nihilin at the edge of the rift where their god was born. Over time,
Feralzmoon's followers flourished and built the city of Aberron in the
shadow of the cold and barren Elderime Glacier.*
—from the Athenomancer archives

The morning began with more rain, which softened to a
light mist in the night. With the lessened rainfall and the
cover provided by the rocks, Ilfair began the day mostly
dry. As he reached his left hand down to press himself up from the
earth, he noticed he was holding the symbol to Faid. *Did I sleep all
night with it in my hand?*

He had often done this with the symbol to Illinir, held it while
he slept, that is. It was part of the reason he had kept it wrapped
about his wrist. With that thought, he decided to wrap the symbol
to Faid in a similar fashion. Not the same wrist, though. He opted
for the left hand instead.

As he wrapped the leather strap, a thought occurred to him. He
did not know as much about Faid as he did the deity Illinir, their
followers were more prevalent in Iilhi to the east. But now that he

knew more of the origins of the shadowy entities perverting his thoughts, he considered that he should seek to learn more. Perhaps the alienist-priests of Faid could provide some insights.

As he considered this further, he placed the Amberglass tunic over his head and shoulders and prepared to depart. The shirt, along with the sliipmare cloak, kept him mostly dry from the lighter rain of the morning. He could see the clouds were broken in the sky further ahead, to the south. He kept his eyes on that and his mood under control as he considered further the ideas in his head regarding the god Faid.

By keeping close to the coast, Ilfair had avoided the worst of the elevation gain of the Godskeeps. As such, by late morning he found himself on the descent of the southern foothills. Around high sun, he broke out of the thinning trees and into the sunlit fields of the side of the Godskeeps that he had been born on; albeit much farther to the east of the Sliipmoors. It felt good. It would have felt better under other circumstances.

The next day passed with a pleasant rhythm under rainless skies with high, thin, fast-moving clouds. He ate and drank while he walked, and he began to feel healthy enough that he would occasionally run on safer, flatter patches of land. He picked up light wood where he could find it. Pieces large enough to burn were sparse on the plains, but by evening he had enough for a fire. He walked along the coast, which had beautiful vistas in every direction. Massive mountains behind him, green fields to his left and the Moonsong Sea to his right.

That evening he stared out over the Choralmoon Cliffs to the Moonsong Sea. Like the Keening Cliffs, these cliffs were named with homonymic words describing the wind songs and colorful sea life that covered them. It was truly beautiful, and the light of Umbral, looking like a glowing-white sunflower in the sky, reflected in the black waters to make the scene even more magical.

Inspired by the calmness of the scene, he spent that evening practicing separating himself from the alien thoughts inside him. How successfully, he did not know. He tried to remember people and circumstances that he thought should have evoked emotion, whether positive or negative. He tried to remember them in as much detail as possible while trying to suppress the black tentacles in his thoughts. It was more like he was ignoring them than preventing them. But, as they did not dominate his thoughts, he considered that a success.

The two memories that were the most effective were of his parents. In one, he watched his father work leather into various items. When Ilfair was supposed to have been asleep, his father would go into the leather shop to work. Ilfair would creep to the doorway when he could not sleep, which was often, given the frequency of visits from Leechkin in his mind.

He would watch his father work by the lanternlight on his large workbench. His father had always radiated a calm and deliberate determination when he crafted. Everything he did in those moments was well considered and executed with the utmost care, always selecting the exact tool. It was appropriate to his current circumstances.

In the other memory, he imagined his mother holding him as a baby. He didn't really know what she looked like, nor did he remember being held, but he had stitched all of that together from what he had learned from his father. This too was calming and centering. It was visceral.

He realized in that moment that, while his upbringing and condition were far from perfect, he was rooted in his home. He did not feel any overwhelming sense of homesickness, rather just a sense of gratitude, calm, and identity. He decided that, when he did make it home, he would hug his father and tell him that he loved him; that he was grateful.

He stayed up very late that evening practicing his separation technique. He fell asleep that night and dreamt of the next day. In his dream, he continued the practice while he walked the way to Winters Haven. In his dream, many days were covered, and he noticed that he was able to make progress in the separation technique. It was a good dream, a rarity for him.

When he woke, he decided that he must try to do this practice of separation almost constantly. He would do it while he ate, while he walked. It would be like shadowing his face from the sun to keep from being burned; it would be constant. Except that it would be at night, too, before he went to sleep.

The thought of this made him feel better. It was just the idea of it, being separated from the alien, that made him feel better; better than focusing on the years lost being a host to it. It was hope.

With that in mind, he completed his morning preparations and continued south. As he walked, he kept his promise to himself and began more separation practice. He found that, with repetition, his mental training fell into the background of his mind.

With the catharsis that ensued, many thoughts occurred to him. One thought struck him, and he dwelled on it for many hours. He circled around the realization that his life hadn't been his. He had always known that life was difficult, but this was something else; something more.

Something his father had always told him rang in his head for reasons he couldn't quite put together yet, but he knew were relevant. His father had always said the challenge of life was doing two opposite things in exactly the right proportion at exactly the same time. It was a constant struggle, but his father had said that was what life was: a struggle. It was the terror and beauty of it.

Ilfair wondered if that was useful here. Could he manage to hold the alien thoughts at bay and genuinely be himself at the same time? Maybe not exactly opposites, but certainly very different things.

As he considered his father's words, he saw Gray Peak before him. He knew just beyond it was Winters Haven. He stopped and stared at it for a while, noting the small amount of snow on its granite dome. It looked large, standing alone on the flat land, rising up off the plains. Though it was small compared to even the foothills of the Godskeeps, it protected Winters Haven from the cold of the winter that came from the north, especially in the ages past when the glacier was further south and the winters were colder. The peak, combined with the curvature of the coastal cliffs, made Winters Haven easily defensible, which was key in the Leechkin Wars in the early years of Winters Haven.

He knew that soon, as he continued south, he would cross the Highmoor Road, which connected Overmoor to Winters Haven. A few hours later, just before reaching Gray Peak, he reached the road. It came in from his left, the east. Gray Peak was looming just beyond the road.

Ilfair entered the empty roadway, which was bent around the peak, following it as closely as possible while still taking full advantage of an isocline. This far out from Winters Haven the road was just worn earth. He could see the wagon ruts in the road and even some hoofprints from the sliipmares that pulled iron- and nickel-filled wagons from Overmoor or lumber-filled wagons from Winters Haven, among other things.

The walking was easier now; the rockier ground gave way to softer, flatter earth. He even lit into a light trot. He let his gaze wander off to the peak as he did not have to watch his footfalls so carefully. He was eager to get to the city. *Like the sliipmare to the stall,* he thought.

As Ilfair walked, the road improved from worn earth to cobblestone construction. Shortly thereafter, the road crossed a short arch-supported bridge that ran over the top of one of the two Gray Rivers that ran along a narrow gorge below. The river ran down the southwest side of the mountain and originated from Gray Tarn. He could not see the tarn, but he knew from stories the small glacier-fed lake was there. Another river, which he could see in the distance, ran down the southeast side of the mountain. It fell off a short cliff on the southeast side of the peak, crashing into a small lake. The two Gray Rivers ran to the northern and eastern sides of Winters Haven, following the gentle slope of the land.

His eyes followed the rivers and his gaze eventually fell upon the city wall of Winters Haven. It stopped him. He audibly exhaled from relief, it was almost a sob, it was such a profound sense of relief.

To his right, the nearest of the Gray Rivers followed the road. As he approached the city, the river snaked back under the road. He crossed a short bridge of wood and stone, which spanned the under-flowing river. It twisted to follow the curvature of the land toward the northern section of the city, where it disappeared under the city wall.

It was all quite beautiful, and while still quite cool, was warmer and less windy. Gray Peak did indeed shield Winters Haven from icier winds; Ilfair had heard this before, but now he could feel it. From the bridge onward to the city wall, wooden railing guarded the edge of the road, which was about two wagons wide. The wagons would be drawn by four sliipmares. Their mossy gray-green coats, which kept them safe from the biting insects of the Sliipmoors, kept them warm against the cooler winds from the Moonsong Sea. The railing was beautifully decorated with carvings of the symbols of powerful houses and deities that were key to the history of Winters Haven.

He recognized the upward turned crescent topped with a sinu-soidal curve on top as the symbol of Mercial, god of healing and water. This he knew was one of the key deities of Winters Haven. He also recognized the square with the straight line over the top as the symbol of Kindrid, god of protection and peace, and the arching branch of Laifell, god of nature. He believed the circle with the horizontal line extending through and beyond its radius, like a setting sun reflecting on the sea, was for Aelinth, goddess of light, beauty, and historical knowledge, but he wasn't sure. The other he knew for certain was for Hearken, god of music and harmony. The icon was comprised of two c-shaped symbols facing each other, capturing a precious open space.

Ilfair had now entered the final approach to the city. Large trees, the Oakgaard, flanked each side of the road. These trees had been planted just after the city's founding by followers of Laifell. The last two of these were just on the other side of the city wall.

The city wall was a combination of granite, sandstone, and black wood. Two large doors made entirely of the black wood made up the entryway. The wall was just a bit shorter than the trees; Ilfair could see spotters posted in man-made wooden structures at the top of the tree pair on the opposite side of the wall. The guards were named for the trees: the Oakgaard.

One of the gate doors was open and people were milling in and out of the city. Two additional guards stood to the left and right of the road, dressed in the white cloth and silver armor of the followers of Kindrid. Their tunics bore Kindrid's symbol, and their shields bore the symbol of the city of Winters Haven, a square inscribed with three different sized circles and a bold vertical line through the circles, breaking out of the square.

The guards were armed with spears, but remained silent and paid no attention to Ilfair as he came within speaking distance. Ilfair was not surprised by this as he was a rather slight young man and did not typically intimidate by his presence alone. *It's once you get to know me that folks get uncomfortable,* he thought, suppressing a wry smirk.

He was a bit surprised that the gates were open here. He wasn't used to that. In Overmoor, and even in his small village, the gates were kept closed, even during the day. He wondered if Winters Haven closed the gates at night, he guessed so. He guessed here that their more relaxed nature was due to better sightlines and natural protections provided by Gray Peak and the sea cliffs.

Plus, there was obviously less predatory life here. In fact, he had seen very little to be concerned about all the way here. The occasional hoofed creature, bird of prey, or burrowing mammal but little else. Nothing like the dangerous creatures that roamed the swampy mire of the Sliipmoors or Shadowfen Forest, which threatened the rock ridge Overmoor was built upon. The Leechkin creatures had been the chief threat of the Ashfallen long ago, but the amphibious creatures, which looked like a melding of millipede, man, and eel, had not been seen in numbers for many decades. Nonetheless, he shuddered at their memory, especially given how similar they were to the creatures that he had seen in the ancient Nihilin Temple and in his thoughts. Anyway, thankfully, nothing like that here.

Ilfair noticed that he was gawking and worried that he would appear suspicious or conspicuous to the guards. He set his head down and moved into the city.

CHAPTER 25

BEYOND THE WALL OF WINTERS HAVEN

The raids of the Aberiths ceased after the birth of Feralzmoon. They hid away in the deep earth below the Feralrift, praying to Feralzmoon and plotting their revenge. Their silence continued during the construction of the Nihilin Temple and the city of Aberron. Following the founding of Aberron, the Ashfallen at the Nihilin dug in search of the Aberiths and the secrets of the deep world, seeking the knowledge to worship Feralzmoon. It was then that the Aberiths saw their opportunity for revenge using these new devotees to their god-champion.
—from the Athenomancer archives

As he walked among the denizens of Winters Haven milling about the entrance to the city, Ilfair noted their general brightness. They wore cheerful clothing, smiled, and acknowledged his passing with pleasant nods or similar gestures. It was a stark contrast to the darker, more formal mood of Overmoor and the nearby Eightowns. He had heard about it, but seeing it was truly striking.

He turned to the symbol of Winters Haven on the doors to the city. Since the priests of Aelinth and Mercial, who had saved Fayrest from the recent plague, had come from Winters Haven, the city and its history were well known to many in Overmoor and almost all in Fayrest. The icon had been engraved in the wood and filled with white paint. It was large, fully as tall as a man. Smaller versions of the same icon adorned the city guards. The symbol was split down the middle, as the gate was open, but he could imagine the symbols together easily enough.

The city crest was a square, containing three inscribed circles and a thick vertical black line. The square, circles, and thick black line were the crests of the three main families of Winters Haven. These were houses Whitehaven, Graywater, and Blackstaff. The elders of these houses ran the city. The Graywater family was perhaps the most important, having built the key features of the city: all related to water and the rivers that fed the city with the guidance of the god of water. Most of the men in the Graywater family had been priests of Mercial or whomever the deity of water had been before for as far back as anyone could remember. This man, the current priest of Mercial, would be the one he sought.

From the other side of the wall, the city spread out before Ilfair. It was as graceful and natural to behold as Overmoor was practical and engineered. As a child of the mines, mills, and smiths of Fayrest and Overmoor, he was fascinated by the city's civil engineering. He saw the rivers enter the city through iron portcullises in the city walls: one to his left on the east side of the road and one to his right on the west side. In each case he could see that the rivers were split at the wall portcullises such that some of the water remained aboveground and some of the water flowed into a mound that likely fed into a cistern or into some underground waterways. Ilfair could not be sure, but those options seemed the most likely. In all cases, the earthworks, which marked the splitting of each river, were carefully hidden by well-placed trees, making the less pleasing mounds less visible, thereby not detracting from the natural splendor of the city.

As he moved his gaze radially inward from the Oakgaards and

the mounds, he saw the road and rivers move into housing and shops along the side of the main road. Most of the buildings were painted an off-white or were off-white owing to the color of the sun-bleached stone from which they were constructed. Adding to the beauty of the scene, the buildings had brightly colored doors and roofs. Earthy variants of reds and blues created a beautiful array of color before him.

Inside the wall, where still he stood stunned, the city was bustling. Winters Haven housed almost ten thousand people. Overmoor had less than half that. He had never seen so many people at once. He tried not to look overwhelmed. In fact, he was overwhelmed, and he could feel the anxiety draw Leechkin to the base of his skull. He calmed himself with the technique he had been practicing. It was easy, as the stress was relatively mild.

Ilfair stumbled and bumped his way through the busy street, turning completely around more than once. Over the next few minutes, homes and green spaces gave way to a marketplace. The city was clean, and the way the homes, shops, and roads flowed with the rivers as they meandered through the city was well conceived. His head swiveled back and forth as he walked, regarding the people and places that were Winters Haven. He again noticed the briskness of the people here. They seemed carefree and light: bright and ebullient, not weighed down by the work and weather of Overmoor.

Where the roads crossed the snaking river, ornate wooden bridges carried the roads forward. He crossed a few of these bridges and many people before he reached the town center, marked by a circular arrangement of shops around an open area. A massive stone orca whale rose from a fountain at the center of the scene.

Here, the major road, which ran largely parallel to the coast, met a crossroad. This offshoot likely led to a port, if Ilfair were forced to guess. The rivers also converged here, forming one larger river that flowed southward. Two large bridges crossed the wide, almost lake-sized convergence. The bridges met articulately in the middle, each supported by stone arches which rose out of the water. It was all wonderfully conceived in Ilfair's eyes.

Ilfair noticed in that moment that he was doing what he would do when scouting caves. It was critical to keep a sense of direction and surroundings when in the caverns. It could save your life. He had reverted to that mode of behavior in the larger, intimidating city. Here, he took additional advantage of the sky to stay oriented. He looked up at that moment. The sun was dropping lower to his right, setting on the Moonsong Sea, its orange light enhancing the autumn hue of the city.

He made his way to the crossbridge and paused at its nexus, admiring again the design. The wooden construction of this bridge was adorned, as was the bridge outside the city, with symbols of deities and houses. The nexus was slightly taller than the rest of the roads and afforded a bit of the panorama of the city. In fact, many citizens of the city were admiring various aspects of the city from points along the bridge. Others just leaned on the dark wooden railings of the bridge and looked down to the waters below, calming themselves, watching and listening to the water flowing rapidly over smooth many-colored rocks.

Ilfair's attention, though, was more focused on the vistas farther afield. To his left, eastward, he could see more homes and shops before the city wall. Straight ahead he saw only two large buildings, surrounded by flat open ground. One building was massive and nondescript, a white windowless cube of a structure. It was attractive in its monochromatic symmetry. Just beyond it and slightly east was a large white tower, windows dotting its vertical length and covering the entire circumference of what Ilfair guessed was the top floor of the tower. Above that the tower was crowned by a circular array of sixteen lights and some type of sophisticated clockwork structure that Ilfair could not quite figure out the purpose of.

Beyond that, farther west, rising above the homes and shops, and the line of the sea, was a massive statue, at least twice the height of a full-grown oak and much bigger around. It rose above the buildings just to the north of the main east-west road.

It was a statue of a man reaching up to the sky. Its back was mostly to Ilfair, facing southwest toward the sea. From his vantage point, only the top half of the construction was visible. The hands were holding a massive glass sphere wrapped in a network of wrought iron fingers. The massive sphere, which was the size of a large home, was more than three-quarters filled with water.

It was late in the day at this point and the sun was near to the sea horizon behind him. The sun backlit the sphere, almost eclipsed by the relative size of it at this distance. Somehow, seeing the orange sun low in the sky brought him back to himself and out of the distraction of the city around him. He was tired and dirty and, while he wasn't starving anymore, it had been over two weeks, he guessed, since he had eaten a proper warm meal.

He inspected his coin purse. He guessed he had enough moor-coin to stay at least a few nights in a simple inn. The moorcoin weren't as valuable here as the havencoin would have been, but with the trade between the cities being what it was, they would do well enough. Well, at least they would be accepted. He hoped.

He set about finding an inn. He saw one immediately that over-looked the rivers, but quickly concluded that would not be the most judicious use of his funds. The location of the inn was prob-ably enough for him to conclude that. But what he noticed was the ornate wrought iron metalwork of the windows. He knew how expensive that was for certain.

"Too clean for a cavern boy," he said under his breath.

He figured a better priced inn could be found closer to the harbor, probably off the main east-west road. His instincts were excellent. He made his way about halfway between the city center and the harbor. Then he veered off the main road to the northern side, away from any view of the cliffs, the sea, or the glass-sphere-bearing statue he had seen earlier.

Once in this vicinity, he wandered for many minutes, trying to find an inn. He wanted to be in a room before his eyes switched at full sunset and so, having failed to find it on his own, he had to rely on help from a local. He hated this, talking to total strangers. He wandered many minutes trying to find the right time and person to talk to. He wondered if others labored over such simple things. He doubted it.

Eventually, he held his breath, and approached an older man, a fisherman by the look of his clothing. The man had paused and knelt to adjust his shoe.

"Um, sir?" Ilfair approached the man and sheepishly looked slightly to the left of the man toward the ground.

"Aye... lad," the man said, looking up. He had a bright and forceful, but pleasant, voice.

"Sorry, uh, to bother you, but do you know where I might find a cheap place to sleep for the night?" He paused. "I have coin," he added. Immediately he regretted that. It was awkward and made him seem like he was a deceptive sort when he was anything but.

The man chuckled. "Aye, of course, son. You want the Osprey. It's that way," the man pointed. "You need to go one side street over though first, you see? And then up just a wee bit."

Ilfair thanked the man, who tipped his small cylindrical white hat and smiled in reply. He followed the man's simple instructions and quickly found the inn. A sign hung over the door with a hawk soaring skyward and the words The Diving Osprey over and under the white wooden hawk. Ilfair chuckled to himself at the cleverness of the name. A dive, indeed. At least the place knew what it was, and it had a bit of class about it, in its own way at least.

For one, the artwork on the sign over the main door was impeccable. Ilfair had some skill at drawing and realized this was no easy feat. The artist would have had to watch birds diving for hours and committed the images to memory to create such an iconograph. The narrow building was tall, at least four stories, and ran deep away from the road. It was hemmed in on both sides by shops and row-houses, mostly for the working class by the looks of it.

The shadows in the streets were getting long, and as he made his way into the building by the door under the sign, he saw men in white coats with the symbol of Aelinth, the goddess of light, lighting lanterns on the street. It reminded him of the road leading into Overmoor, lit by multicolored Erlanlight lanterns which warned of the presence of Leechkin.

He looked down the street at the row of lanterns and nodded to one of the lantern lighters as he stepped up the pair of steps to the doorway of *the Osprey*. He opened one of the dark wooden doors and walked inside. It was nice enough, and quiet. The layout was much as they were where he was from. A bar with stools just in front of him and a seating area with tables and seating alcoves along the walls to his left. To his right was the entrance to the kitchen. He heard noise coming from the kitchen of the type you would expect, otherwise it was quiet within *the Osprey*.

CHAPTER 26

THE DIVING OSPREY

The Aberiths gave those within the Nihilin temples the gift of
runemining with visions of Feric symbols scribed into the earth. In so
doing, the faithful of Feralzmoon were permitted the ability to channel a
chaos, which rendered the rock and earth as fog. With this gift, the deep
wells of the Nihilin were created and numerous secrets, hidden in the
great depths of Erlan, were discovered.
—from the Athenomancer archives

A young woman approached, emerging from another door
behind the bar of the Diving Osprey. She was, as were
many in Winters Haven, clad in warm bright colors. She
wore a blue shirt, layered over by a heavy green vest, for warmth he
assumed. A pleated green dress flowed from her waist, ending in
simple, but well cared for, brown leather shoes.

"Welcome, sir," she said. "You look like you could use a rest, if
you don't mind me saying."

"Um, yes. I mean, no, I don't mind you saying," he smiled
timidly and paused awkwardly. He decided to take a more direct
approach. "A table please, ma'am." He looked toward the dining
area. It was empty, being a bit late for dinner. He added, "Away

from the door, but close to the fire... if you don't mind." He added the last part with a hopeful tone, trying not to seem like an annoyance.

Ilfair never felt comfortable asking for anything extra, but he made an exception in this case, owing to his overwhelming desire to feel the warmth of the fire and to be undisturbed if anyone should come through the door. If he was lucky, he would continue to attract very little attention. This place, particularly with the hearth, reminded him of the common hall in Fayrest. It brought forth good feelings.

The young woman just smiled and headed into the dining area, looking over her shoulder and nodding wordlessly for him to follow. She led him to a seating area, a small alcove only fit for two. He sat on a bench with a worn purple cushion and set his pack on the other cushion across the table from him. It was nice enough. And it was dark and warm. Both of which suited him and made him feel at ease.

The young lady stood for a moment, and he realized she was waiting to see if he wanted anything further. She was just about to turn and Ilfair added, "Do you have stew? Something with meat? And hot, very hot. And tea? Oh, and how much?" He grimaced internally realizing he had just bombarded her with questions.

"Of course, sir." she replied, smiling and not seeming bothered by his numerous queries. "Extra hot. And three havencoin for everything" she added.

"That sounds good. I have only moorcoin, though. Will that do?" Ilfair asked hopefully.

"It will be four moorcoin, but yes that will do. You're from Overmoor?" She asked.

"Yes. Well, Eightowns, actually." He wondered why he offered the extra information. But then he thought, *why not? Is this not an opportunity to try to connect on a small scale with someone and keep my dark thoughts at bay?* Well, it was, but then he remembered that he would prefer to stay as anonymous as possible.

He realized at that moment that he had been doing much thinking and little talking.

"Four moorcoin will be fine," Ilfair said awkwardly and handed her the coin.

The young lady turned and walked away with a nod and a polite smile again. "Thank you," Ilfair added after her. She raised her left hand to her side and extended two fingers and her thumb in reply, a Winters Havian gesture of acknowledgement, he supposed.

Ilfair was left in the warm, dark, quiet. Just a single candle and the glow from the fireplace lit the dark wood table. He touched the table with his fingers. *Clean enough*, he thought. Overmoorians, and the denizens of Eightowns, were notably fastidious about cleanliness as a rule. A necessity when living around the more fetid climate of the Sliipmoors. The table passed his standards.

Regardless, he just breathed for a minute and thought. He needed to think about what to do. He knew he needed answers about the symbols on his arm. It was obvious that he couldn't be sure if Abby had been truthful. He suspected some, but not all, of what she said was true. He was pretty good at reading people, and though she was not really *people,* she was close enough to be read by him.

Ilfair had always been cautious. He had always been deliberate and thoughtful, and he felt the same would be necessary here. He did not think it wise to go in directly to some stranger, even a priest, and show them the mark on his arm. Or the spiralhammer... or the map from the temple... or the shirt from under the lighthouse. With that thought, he put the hammer in his pack, admonishing himself for not thinking to do so earlier. To the careful observer, the hammer was obviously strange and worth asking after, especially from a visitor. He hoped no one had noticed.

Anyway, he needed to think how to do this, how to ask after this mark. Showing that he was marked by it was obviously unwise. He did not want to end up in an asylum of Illinir, and he imagined that would be quite possible were he not careful.

The young lady returned with the food and drink. "Here you are," she said with a genuine smile.

"Oh," he said, startled out of his thoughts. She began to walk away when he added, "Thank you, ma'am."

Again, with the fingers and the raised hand, she responded with a chuckling "No problem."

At that moment, triggered by her laugh, he realized that he was adding more feeling to his matter-of-fact tone in a way that he did not typically bother with.

He liked the feeling. But it was a feeling and an attempt at a connection, and with that, he could feel the images in his head, again the black tentacled feelings and images just behind the eyes and ears. Uncomfortable, but not unbearable. More practice perhaps in small steps like this, just noticing the smallest connections, even with strangers. To think he had lived all these years and never noticed that he had never let feelings into even polite interactions with strangers. *Is the parasite jealous?* he wondered. *Or is it something else?*

He shook his head. Back to the matter at hand. His mind worked on a plan. This he was good at. First things first, he would need to make a drawing of the mark on his arm. This he could show someone. The next issue. Why? He needed a reason. He thought for some time. *The best lies are based on truths*, he thought. Why not say that someone in Overmoor was researching some old documents and came across the symbol and needed it translated? He didn't know about that yet. But maybe that would work.

He realized he had eaten most of the food and had but a little drink left. The young lady returned to take away the bowl and cup.

"How was it then?" she asked.

"Very good," he said simply, still in his careful, thoughtful brain. *She's nice*, he thought, *I will need to leave a coin on the table for her.*

"Oh," he added, "Is there a room available? Anything will do. Just a bed even".

"Yes, sir," she said pleasantly. "It's not much more than that though. On the top floor at the far end of the hall on the left. Two moorcoins a night, three if you want clean sheets each night."

"Yes. Okay. I will take it."

He handed her two more coins. *I don't need clean sheets.* Typically, he was fastidiously clean about his hygiene, but his monies were limited. *I can do without*, he thought. *Day-old sheets are by far cleaner than the dirt I have slept on the last few days, so at least there is that.* He smiled at his own thoughts.

She walked away and he stood to follow her. She took him over to the stairs up to the rooms. She stopped at the base of the stairs and gestured up, handing him the key. He nodded to her, took the wrought iron key, and started up the stairs.

He made his way up the stairs and took the proper turn to his left, noting the barrenness of the austere hallway. He inserted the key, looking to his right out the window at the end of the hall. The view was only of the wall of the adjacent row house.

He turned the key in the lock, pushed the door open, and entered his room. The room was simple, but his eyes were drawn to the bed. Upon sight of it, his exhaustion hit him. He dropped his pack, set the key on a small table, and collapsed into the bed, fully clothed.

As he lay his head on the pillow, he noted another window looking out onto the wall of the same row house just a few feet away. The monotony of it made him realize how tired he was. He directed his gaze to the ceiling and continued his thoughts about the mark on his arm.

He concluded that he should visit the market in the morning

for artists' tools. He had always been a good artist. As he lay there studying the ceiling, he thought again of his father's workshop.

He recalled standing in his nightclothes, hiding at the doorway, looking into his father's workshop. He had watched, as he often did, for many moments, as his father worked by the light of two table lanterns. In that instant, his father had only parchment and quill as his instruments. Suddenly, his father had turned and looked at him.

Ilfair feared he would be reprimanded. Instead, his father spoke.

"Can't sleep, huh?" he paused. Ilfair stood sheepishly at the doorway. "Come, sit with me, Ilfair," his father had said warmly as he pulled another stool up to the workbench.

Ilfair bounded across the room and onto the stool, his face beaming.

"Now, sit quietly please, son. So I can finish my work," his father had said with a gentle smile.

"Yes, father." Ilfair had watched his father work for many minutes. His father had been sketching some leather armbands for someone. This always preceded the work he knew. His father's work was detailed, careful, and gorgeous, at least in his eyes.

"Father?" Ilfair said meekly, eventually disobeying his father's request for quiet.

Patiently, his father had looked over at him without moving his hands from his work, eyebrows raised.

"Can I try?" Ilfair had desperately wanted to.

His father gave another knowing half smile and passed Ilfair a piece of the precious parchment and some black chalk.

Ilfair recalled spending many minutes attempting to imitate his father's work. This was the first time he had done this, but it would not be the last. That night though, at some point, he must have passed out on his sketch, for he awoke the next morning in his bed, the sketch laying on his chest.

The skill he had acquired over those years in his father's shop would prove useful here.

Ilfair smiled at the memory. As he studied his feelings, he noted the tingling of the Leechkin in his mind. He held them at bay, imaging he had two minds: one for himself and one for the Leechkin. He watched them from his other mind until exhaustion took him. Despite the Leechkin, he fell asleep in the bed at the Diving Osprey with a gentle smile on his face.

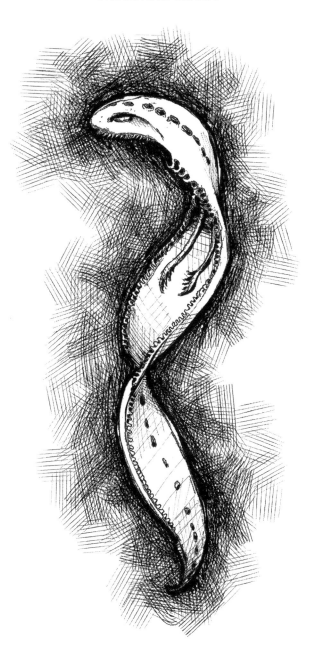

CHAPTER 27

AN ARTIST'S PREPARATION

Ullumair denied us, the Feraliths, the warrior-priests of Feralzmoon, the
fire of creation. But we have, in turn, rebuked him. We have dug deep
into the earth searching for the heat needed to forge, bade to do so by the
whispers of the Aberiths, the mothers of Feralzmoon. Here, within the
innards of the silent Erlan, we did find it. A molten earth created by
pressure and the Aberith's hatred with which to forge our weapons and
armor has been unearthed.
—from the Athenomancer archives

T he next morning Ilfair awoke to a gray day. The sky was
barely visible through his window. A gray, drizzly day to
seek Graywater.

"Fitting," he said to the sky at the top line of the windows.

He had slept in his clothes. He was glad of it, for when he cast
off the blankets of his bed, he realized it was a chill, damp morning,
even in his room. Rested, he now took full note of his room. There
was a basin, a spigot in the wall that he guessed would produce
water, a small wood-burning stove, a bin of wood, and a large
teapot. He hadn't really paid attention to all this the night before,
or at least he didn't remember doing so.

"Understandable though, right?" he said to the wall.

"I am going to need to stop talking to myself," he said, sighing at the empty space to his left.

He chuckled. In any event, he had plans for the basin, spigot, and stove this evening. He smelled terrible, as did his clothes. He decided that he would get some soap today and take care of that this evening.

It occurred to him to take off his tunic and replace it with the shirt that he found in the alcove under the lighthouse. The amber shirt was thin but warm, and though it was old, it did not smell. At least, not so badly. He put his sliipmare cloak on over the top of the shirt so that its oddness would not be so evident. He grabbed his money pouch, shoved it into his pants pocket, and left his heavy pack and the spiralhammer he had found in the temple forge. It would be nice to walk unencumbered by all that bulk.

He made his way down to the main floor. It was early and the dining area was much the way he had left it the night before. A few people were there eating; the air was dusty and the hearth was aflame. The main difference, aside from the few patrons, was that the room was a bit brighter than it had been the night before, despite the overcast day. He was anxious to get to the market, but his stomach had other ideas.

He made his way to the bar and exchanged more coin with the innkeeper, an older man with a familial resemblance to the young lady from the night previous.

"Tea and bread, please," Ilfair said simply.

The old man, clad almost entirely in simple white clothes, save for a bright blue apron with a white embroidered osprey, handed Ilfair bread and black tea. He simply nodded and smiled at Ilfair. *The quiet type*, Ilfair thought, *I can appreciate that, especially in the morning.*

The bread was moist and had a pleasant yeasty aftertaste. And the tea was strong, just the right amount of aromatic bitterness, and hot. He found a seat at the end of the bar nearest the door and finished his food and tea. Afterward, he stood and, getting the innkeeper's attention with a gesture, bought another slice of bread for the walk. He thanked the innkeeper, turned abruptly, and made his way through the door and down the stairs to the street level.

His mind worked as he made his way back to the town center. He tore a chunk out of the bread with his teeth. As he gnawed on the pleasant toughness, he was glad for the overcast skies, as they were easier on his fair skin. He made his way to the market center and realized that, in his anxiousness, he had arrived before anything had opened. In fact, he now realized, the city was just beginning to stir.

So, he sat on the edge of the white stone perimeter of the orca whale fountain he had seen from the bridge the day before. He had much to consider and so, as he watched the market open, he thought more on what he would say to Graywater. He allowed the white noise of the fountain water to calm him. He had decided for certain that he would not show the mark on his arm. That much was settled. So, he would get his paper, quill, and ink and remedy that later this day.

But he needed a story. The idea to use bits of truth recurred in his mind. He did not like lying as, besides being corrosive to one's integrity and character as he had learned from his father and in the mines, he wasn't particularly good at it. He could be silent well enough, but lying was more complex; one needed to exist in another fabricated reality, in which it was easy to become lost. Lying was no mean feat and the priest of Mercial would be no fool.

He thought for a moment and came up with a good story that required minimal fabrication. Something that, besides leveraging the truth, relied on things about which he knew a great deal. He thought it would pass as true. The drizzle was abating, and the sun was beginning to shine hazily through the thinning clouds in the morning sky of late fall. The salty wind was picking up and the leaves were casting about the open area of the market. As the market roused, the murmurings of morning routines and the varied smells of animals and food were, like the leaves, everywhere.

Ilfair knew, from experience in his father's shop, that the market tanner would be the best place to find parchment, as it was made in much the same way. He followed his nose to find the tanner in the market. The dead animal hide and chemicals used for tanning created a unique and frankly unpleasant smell that was hard to miss. As he suspected, vellum, parchment, ink, and quills were all available at the tanner's shop, along with clothes, shoes, and other leather and animal skin items. He quietly approached the shop owner.

The smell of the leather in the shop called forth feelings of home again along with unwanted alien thoughts. He controlled himself.

"Can I help you, sir?" A voice pulled him from his thoughts.

"Um, sorry. Yes... yes, sir, I mean," Ilfair finished, composing himself, remembering to be polite and sincere. He was practicing trying to be more heartfelt.

The shop owner waited a moment and added, "What can I get for you?" He seemed to have been waiting for Ilfair to offer this up on his own as there was a slightly ironic tone to the man's voice.

"Oh, yes. Sorry. Um, parchment please," he answered quickly.

The man nodded and disappeared, reappearing moments later with a cylinder of parchment tied with a red ribbon.

They completed the transaction. Before leaving, Ilfair decided to dare a compliment at the risk of conjuring Leechkin.

"I know how much work goes into making this," he said, gesturing to his hand with the parchment. "So, um, thank you, I guess." It came out awkwardly, but it made the shop owner smile. Ilfair gathered by the reaction of the shop owner that such specific gratitude was uncommon.

"You're most welcome, young sir."

The smile from the shop owner was encouraging to Ilfair. He felt buoyed by the interaction. Encouraged, he stopped just before exiting the shop and turned around to speak.

"Um… sir… do you know where I might find the temple of Mercial?" he asked, bowing his head slightly and holding his hands together in front of his belt, signifying formality and deference to the tanner due to him being Ilfair's elder.

"There are a few actually. Is there something you wish to do there?" he asked, raising his eyebrows.

"I wish to talk with a member of the Graywater family. I was told that I could find a member of that family there. That he would be a cleric," he said, hoping that that was not too odd a request.

Even if it was an odd request, it did not silence the shop owner's reply. "As long as it is for reasonable business, you will want to seek Elder Graywater within the Leviathan Temple. It's the large statue just west of here. You can't miss it. But I would recommend not wasting his time."

"I do not wish to. I mean, no, that is not my intent. Many thanks for your help, sir," he said.

"Of course," the tanner replied.

Ilfair smiled and nodded deferentially to the tanner as he turned to leave. The tanner nodded back and raised a hand after Ilfair as he departed.

Ilfair made his way back to his room. As he walked back, he beamed at the success with the tanner. Others would surely have felt nothing odd about the interaction, but to exchange sincere respects with the tanner while simultaneously ignoring the black Aberithic thoughts was a glorious feeling. Even now, the black thoughts, sensing his elation, tugged at the corner of his psyche.

Lost in the dichotomy of the black ichor and the white glow in his mind, he made his way back to the inn. Once inside, he stopped again at the bar and asked the innkeeper for soap and towels. In exchange for yet more coin from his rapidly dwindling purse, he was given two coarse towels and a cube of brown soap.

With everything he needed in hand, Ilfair made his way upstairs and set his plan for the day in motion. He opened the window to allow the cool breeze in but made sure to pull the shade closed to maintain his privacy. The room would do well with some circulation with the steam from the hot water, which would be forthcoming.

Ilfair opened the spigot on the wall and filled the adjacent iron bucket with water. He started a fire in the wood-burning stove and placed the iron container on top of it. He filled the washing basin about half full with cold water. By the time he had that finished, the water on the stove in the large container was already getting warm. The room was also starting to warm and the cool air from the window was creating a welcome draft.

Ilfair stripped bare. He had always been slight and lithe, but with the physical exertion of the last two weeks and the lack of food, he was all gaunt and gristle.

"I look like an overworked sliipmare," he said, simultaneously proud of his endurance but aghast at his appearance. He began the work of cleaning his clothes in the basin. Once cleaned he wrung them out and found various places about the room to drape them to dry; as close to the window as possible, even draping some over the windowsills. He emptied the basin from the drain at its bottom and watched the dirty water filter out of the room down the drain.

He felt a strange sense of accomplishment given the simplicity of the task of keeping himself clean. He realized now how much he took for granted. Eightowns did not have the amenities of Winters Haven, or even Overmoor, but running water was among them and he realized now how much he missed that simple convenience and how much more complicated and dangerous life was without it.

After the water was drained, he refilled the basin a quarter full of cold water. He then took the container from the stove, filled with scalding hot water, and added it to the basin. He tested the admixture for temperature. Finding the temperature acceptable, he climbed nimbly into the basin. He stood in the very warm water, which rose up to his chest, for many minutes. He leaned against the back of the basin and closed his eyes, taking many deep, relaxing breaths. He let the heat sink in, all the way to his bones. He felt relaxed for the first time in weeks, if only for a few moments.

"Unh," Ilfair let out a noise that was something between a sigh and a groan.

The room was very simple, but he felt like a king at that moment. It felt good, and even the black eel-like white-eyed creatures that squirmed behind his eyes, rising with his feelings, couldn't take the shine from his face. Eventually, he sighed and leaned forward and set to work with the soap.

When he was done, he got out of the water, ripe with froth from the soap. He used a towel to remove the remnants of soap from his body, primarily his legs. He then wrapped himself in two linen towels and again drained the basin. He sat by the wood-burning stove and watched the soapy water drain out of the basin as he finished drying.

Watching the water spiral down the drain brought his thoughts back to his arm, the spirals thereupon. He stood. He moved over to the table next to his bed and collected his parchment, ink, and quill. He sat back down in front of the fire. While his clothes dried, he unrolled the parchment and pinned it to a smooth part of the floor with the ink container and the key to the room. He studied the symbols on his arm again for a few moments before he set to work copying them onto the parchment.

He blessed Illinir again for his ambidexterity, drawing a quick spiral over his heart with his left hand, an homage to the symbol of the god. If he weren't, and the symbols had been on his dominant arm, the task of transcription would be more challenging to say the least.

Regardless, he returned his thoughts to the drain. He realized that each pair of symbols looked like two connected whirlpools that formed something like a figure eight. The writing was dense in the middle of each whirlpool, becoming less so as it spiraled out. He thought of whirlpools and octopi, and other things oceanic.

There were many symbols and he had to work carefully to get everything right. But, if Ilfair was anything, it was careful and meticulous. He worked the rest of the afternoon and into the evening. At which point he opened the furnace door to finish the details by firelight. It was difficult work, looking at the underside of his right arm and transcribing it with his left. And sitting on the floor was awkward and uncomfortable.

Eventually, Ilfair convinced himself that his work was done. He got up and eyed his work again from a different angle to ensure his satisfaction. Pleased, he tested his clothes. They were dry now, or at least dry enough.

Though he felt a little hungry, he was getting light on coin, so he decided to drink water from the spigot in his room and eat some more of the bread he still had left over from the morning, foregoing a formal meal for the evening.

"Clearly I need to be able to see more bones," he mumbled wryly through his shirt as he pulled it over his bony frame. He knew he needed to eat more, but his stomach was just not ready for more food given his anxiety and the duration of time it had spent near empty. He needed more time to be ready for more food.

Regardless, he continued to nibble on the bread as he dressed. As the evening cooled, he decided to close the window. As the room temperature rose, he doused the stove, and headed out of the room, locking the door behind him. It was early in the evening, so he decided he would go for a walk to get some fresh air and to stretch his muscles from the hours of being hunched uncomfortably over the parchment. He also decided that he would work out the route to the temple. The night air was brisk. He could definitely feel winter coming. He pulled the sliipmare cloak tight and walked. The colder months always found one running back and forth, annoyingly, between too hot and too cold.

After making his way out of the inn and onto the street, he only needed to walk a few minutes south before he could see the Leviathan Temple to the southwest. It was quite large and hard to miss, looming on the other side of a river. Ilfair was able to snake his way through the streets to the temple.

He passed shops, which had been put away for the night, and could see into the homes above many of them. He looked through the windows as the denizens of Winters Haven lived their lives by lantern light. He saw more than one of the guards as he had seen at the gate, clad in their symbolic garb in honor of Kindrid. They were serious figures, but not threatening, and contributed to an overall sense of safety and security along the nighttime streets of Winters Haven.

Soon, he found himself standing on the road just east of the temple. A river lay between Ilfair and the temple. The temple was surrounded by large, green open spaces and, as such, was lit only by the moon; the lamp light from the roads lit the path to the temple, but not the temple itself. From his vantage point he could see lights on in the temple and two groves of oak in the open spaces to the left and right of the temple.

He walked to the bridge that crossed the river that interceded his path to the temple. He found a bench there and sat. He looked up at the temple. The construction was from some type of aged white stone. It was a man fully formed from the knees up. Below the knees he was buried in the earth, or at least that is how it appeared. It gave the appearance of the man down on both knees. The man was looking skyward at the massive water-filled glass sphere that he held over his head. The head of the statue was adorned with a five-pointed crown, with lights topping each point of the crown. There was a door on each leg, roughly at the position of the outer thigh.

Two pathways split off from where the bridge made landfall on the other side of the river and meandered through the two opposing circles of trees to doors on the statue's legs. It was dark but there was light visible behind the doors and up higher on the statue through shuttered windows along the height of the statue. The light would flutter when figures passed between whatever lit the room and the window.

He considered going to knock on the door, to be done with the waiting, but decided against it. He was not ready yet. He looked a little longer at the statue. Starting from the top in the water filled sphere, he noticed tiny holes, probably to capture the rain.

"Clever," he said quietly to the temple.

He noticed iron tubing coming down off the sphere and spiraling down the arms, body, and legs of the statue. The iron cylinders terminated in the groves.

"Pressure for the room water and to water the grove?" he wondered aloud.

He stood then, with that thought, and made his way back to the Diving Osprey. He went up to his room and lay on the bed. He knew he would have to work to find sleep this night, and so he lay down and set to the labor of the evening.

CHAPTER 28

A WALK UNDER THE MOON

The Feraliths created the greatest forges on Erlan, deep below the Nihilin Temple. In these forges they made masterpieces from spiralore. This holy ore, made of metals and obsidian, was formed by the divine energies that had radiated from the birth of Feralzmoon and his initial conflict with Ullumair. The Feraliths fashioned arms and armor from the ore. The items were stronger than metal and lighter than obsidian and, when used by the Feraliths, were silent, as if covered by thick cloth and perfect oil.

—from the Athenomancer archives

S leep evaded Ilfair. He sat up in his bed for a long while thinking about the lie—*no, story*—he had created for Graywater. He would have to tell this story tomorrow. He lay there, staring at the ceiling with his shadowsight in his now dark room.

Ilfair closed his eyes and tried to rest, but he could not. The anxiety of it was conjuring the black eels, their alien white eyes glistening and rolling asynchronously.

He needed to distract himself. First, he lit a candle and watched the flame flicker and felt its warmth with his hand. When that failed, he used the candlelight to look at his parchment whereupon he had transcribed the symbols from his arm. And, while it was well done, it did not distract or calm him.

At that moment he recalled his thoughts regarding the god Faid. He closed his eyes and held the symbol to Faid in the palm of his left hand. He held it to his chest and thought of the symbol.

The symbol was a tall obelisk casting a long shadow from a shining bright moon behind. He imagined the obelisk in his mind. He visualized it casting a shadow over the eel-like creatures. In his mind he imagined his shadowsight did not work and that the creatures were hidden by the dark. The problem was that he could still imagine them squirming and writhing in the shadows. It was almost worse that way. And, with that thought, they emerged, terrifying, from the shadows. He sighed and opened his eyes. Their incessant harassment was fatiguing and had made his eyes blurry.

Frustrated, he abandoned his room, hoping the cool outside air and a walk would calm his jangled nerves. He wandered around a bit garnering the attention of some of the lamp lighters and city guards in their white regalia, one functionary and simple in nature, the other ornate and militaristic. He gave each deferential a nod and that seemed to be enough to quell any concerns they may have had. He realized, quite without trying to, that he had made his way back to the bench on the bridge by the Leviathan Temple.

There was someone else sitting on the bench opposite him: small and thin, covered in brown blankets. He took the bench opposite and sat. *A homeless one*, he thought. So sad, and surprising, as he had seen none up to this point. Two lamps lit the benches and cast long shadows. The clouds had broken, and the gibbous moon was waxing and beautiful in the sky, most of its thirteen craters visible. He looked up at it for a long while.

Suddenly but slowly, the moon began to come apart. A heartbeat later, he heard a dull crack and saw black gnarled fingers grip a moon fragment. His heart raced. He looked down and across the bridge, hopefully, at the other person on the bench. As though they could do something about it.

The other person looked up at the moon. And with motion that belied panic, rushed across the bridge to Ilfair. The short frail form looked up at him, her face a paper-white mask of smiling black-toothed evil.

"Beautiful, isn't it, Ilfair? It's time for you to get moving, don't you think? Now." Abby said as she reached up to grab the necklace, her necklace, that hung from his neck.

Ilfair awoke with a start. It was still dark. He was holding the parchment in one hand, tightly, and the symbol of Faid equally tightly in the other. He spent the rest of the night staring at the ceiling in the dark. Restless, he shed his blankets, unable to wait for the morning light to leave his bed.

He was still scared and beyond anxious. He milled about his small room, his heart racing; he felt like an agitated sliipmare thrashing and shaking in her stall. He checked the lock of the door, sighing as he realized that would do nothing to either Leechkin or Abby. He lit three candles in his room, knowing that neither liked light. It wasn't much but was better than nothing and made him feel a little less useless.

Calming a little, he said a prayer to Illinir and Faid, again holding the symbol to Faid.

"Faid, call forth your opposite, the light of Aurum. Let his revealing light cast your shadows across Erlan. For you are the shadow and the shadowcaster," he said under his breath.

He repeated this a few times. The mantra helped further settle his nerves and heart. Surely the morning light would come soon. He would feel better then, certainly, but the waiting was unpleasant to say the least.

Eventually, he sat back on his bed. As he did so he realized he was still wearing the necklace Abby had given him. Reflexively he tried to remove it. He yanked at it but it would not come free. It was heavy and would not be lifted over his head. He tried and failed to cut it loose with a small knife.

Frustrated and desperate, he grabbed the lit candle on his bedside table. He managed to pull the cord away from his neck enough to get the flame to it. It was hot and the wax dripped on his hand.

"Godsname," he pulled the flame away. He went over to the mirror in the room to inspect the strands. His efforts had done nothing to the necklace. It would not be removed. *Damn her*, he thought.

"And to think, I actually pitied her," he said with uncharacteristic disdain.

With that, it was settled. He would go to the temple today. Now, in fact. He grimaced as he realized that was exactly what Abby had instructed him to do in the dream. Regardless, the fear of Abby's visions and the necklace that clung to him overwhelmed the anxiety of talking to Graywater.

He would make his way down to the dining room of the Diving Osprey soon. He needed, at the very least, to clear his mind of the Leechkin. Perhaps some food and drink and the company of strangers would help him prepare himself mentally to lie to Graywater. *Gods help me*, he thought.

CHAPTER 29

THE LEVIATHAN

The Feraliths, warrior-priests of Feralzmoon, wielded their secrets against their brethren in Harrowfell. The Feraliths, in the unyielding and barren north, believed they were due some of the spoils of Harrowfell. This idea was insinuated to them, without their knowledge, by the Aberiths. Thus influenced, the marauding of Harrowfell resumed; this time at the hands of the Feraliths who, without fully understanding, did the bidding of the Aberiths.
—from the Athenomancer archives

I lfair sat on the bed, steeling himself to go down and leave his room at the inn. As light entered the room with the morning sun, it prompted him to rise. He heated some water and used a linen cloth to wipe his face, chest, and arms. The warm water felt good. He would have liked to stay in the room longer and just look out the window, but there was nothing to see but the gray wall of the adjacent building and he knew he would only be delaying with no real purpose. So instead, he went downstairs to the dining area for black tea. He was hungrier this morning than the last, so he went for some inexpensive dried fish and bread. *Lots of things here are fish*, he thought. *Not like the cabbage, potatoes, erlanroot, and game meat back home.*

Despite his hunger, he found it hard to eat. He was anxious and the anxiety was interfering with his appetite and causing images to scratch and claw around in his head. It gave him a headache at times. This was one of those times. He had to force himself to eat. The tea was good, though, and the warm, bitter liquid calmed him some. It amazed him that knowing the images in his head were from the Aberiths and not because his mind was broken was somehow comforting. But it was.

He eventually summoned the needed courage and, with a deep breath, stood resolutely and left quickly from the dining area.

"Sir, you forgot to pay," the young barkeep said, stepping after him.

Ilfair stopped and turned, embarrassed, so distracted was he by what was to come that he had forgotten to pay. He reached into his lightening purse and produced a coin.

"I'm sorry," he said, grimacing and trying not to make eye contact.

"Um... Sorry, but it's two if you're using moorcoins, sir," she said, seemingly genuinely apologetic.

"Er, uh..." he fished around a bit and produced another,

"Here," Ilfair said. He was already flustered, and that awkward interaction served only to make him more scattered in his thoughts. Unwanted images flared in his head. He rushed away as quickly as he could. His heart rate would have calmed as he got away from the situation, but he was no less anxious about where he was going than where he had been. In fact, he was more anxious. He stood just beyond the stairs, which fed from the inn down onto the street. He could see the osprey-shaped shadow at his feet.

Ilfair stood there for many moments, head down, studying the shadow for no real reason. Eventually, somewhat calmed, he began his walk. He could walk there, to the temple that is, without really looking up. Ilfair was talented in that way. Once he had been somewhere he could get back quite easily, even with the images pressing into his consciousness getting worse as he approached the temple. He opened his eyes as he crossed the bridge, sighing and shaking his head as he eyed the bench where Abby had sat in his dream.

When he reached the footpath on the other side of the bridge, he looked up. The temple was majestic and brought forth thoughts of reverence. It was mostly white stone construction with open windows that dotted the height. The dark wrought iron that encircled the glass sphere and height of the temple added a dark character to the statue. Orange, yellow, and red leaves, fallen from the two circles of trees that flanked the statue, settled in flat places here and there on the statue, a colorful contrast to the stark austerity of the sculpture.

Ilfair took the path to his right. It led him through a circle of trees to a short stone staircase. He took the three steps up to a brown wooden door. The door was windowless, rectangular, and arched at the top. It had clearly been worked into the original construction of the statue, indicated by the interlocking stones around the door's perimeter.

Ilfair knocked on the door, using the circular metal knocker in the middle of the door. He stood for a moment and waited. He could hear footsteps approaching. The door opened inward, and a pleasant but plain young woman stood in front of him. She was dressed in a simple white dress with the symbols of Mercial embroidered in blue along the shoulders.

"Good morning," she said simply. She paused and bowed slightly before looking up to meet his gaze with her brown eyes, which sat below the edge of her short brown hair.

"My name is Embrey, a temple acolyte. Can I help you?"

"I... I.... need to talk to... I've been sent to find a cleric of Mercial by the name of Graywater. Have I come to the right place?" he eventually asked.

"You have indeed, sir. He is the archpriest here." she seemed to expect Ilfair to respond. When he did not, she added, "So, as you have found him, do you need to meet with him?"

"Um, yes," he paused. "Can that... is that possible?" Ilfair asked sheepishly with raised brows.

"Can I have your name, young sir?" she asked simply.

"Oh, yes. It's Ilfair Undermoon."

"Wait here a moment, sir." She walked away, leaving the door open, and disappeared down a stairwell behind her.

Ilfair stood on the top step and waited. He turned his back to the door. He looked up at the trees in the grove next to the Leviathan. He crossed his arms across his chest, pulling his cloak close against the chill morning air of late fall. He took a few deep breaths to try to calm himself. He was very nervous and fighting back eel-ridden thoughts in his head.

Quickly lost in thought, he was startled to feel the young woman's hand on his shoulder.

"... young sir?" she said, but it was clear that it wasn't the first time she had said it.

"Oh, sorry, yes... I was just admiring the trees. It's um... the trees, in the grove, are very beautiful. I guess my thoughts floated off. Like the leaves." He smiled.

"They are beautiful. The trees. You wouldn't be the first to find peace of mind there," she smiled back. "Elder Graywater is occupied at this exact moment, but he asked me to find out what you were inquiring after... and that, if he deemed it appropriate, he could see you after high sun today. Will that be okay?" she asked.

"Oh, yes. Of course." Ilfair was a bit disappointed. He had hoped to be done with this. He looked down.

"And what would you be inquiring after?" the young lady prodded after him, tilting her head to the side and slightly forward.

"Oh, yes, sorry. Hold on." Ilfair took his pack from his back and set it on the stairs in front of him. He kneeled and searched through the contents and retrieved his parchment. "This." he said, handing the parchment to the young lady.

The young priestess took the parchment and unrolled it. "What is it?" she asked, with a furrowed brow and a hint of concern in her voice.

"It's a symbol we found in a chamber unearthed in a mine north of Overmoor. In the iron mines of the Fenrik Hills near Fayrest." he began the lie. It was all the harder for, as he lied, he grew more nervous, which made his head swim with images. He wondered if she could hear his heartbeat in his voice as he continued.

"I found it. In the mine. Along with other things. Concerning things. Our Elders of Iroin thought the priests of Mercial would be the best from whom to seek help. And the Graywater lineage is famous all over Erlan for their knowledge, wisdom, and grace. Or so I was told. I'm just the messenger." He cringed internally at the last two sentences, feeling they were a bit unnatural sounding.

"Well, I can certainly agree with you on all of that," she smiled. "It is concerning, and the Graywater family is everything you have been told. I am sure Elder Graywater will be most engaged by this. Come back after high sun and he will help you, I'm sure." She bowed again gently.

"Okay. Thank you."

They nodded to each other and exchanged smiles. Then the young lady turned and closed the door.

"Damn." Ilfair said under his breath after the footfalls had receded. Not because he was disappointed in his lie. He felt it recoverable enough, but the true test would be with the elder. Rather, he was frustrated to have to wait. The only thing worse than the moment was sitting on the edge of the moment, waiting. Better to have it over with.

He decided it was pointless to try to busy himself. Instead, he decided to find a place to wait in the grove. He put his back to the sea breeze and the sun to protect his skin and to stay warm, and he sat quietly for hours in that grove, listening to the wind in the trees. He watched the colored leaves fall. It was peaceful. It almost radiated calm. He felt here as he had felt in the basin of warm water in his room.

He sat quietly and looked around. Only then did he notice, to his left, just beyond the grove was a small abbey or chapel. The door to the chapel was adorned with the symbol of Laifell, the god of nature. The abbey was melded with the grove in such a way as to not stand out. It was narrow and tall and sat in the space just between and beyond two trees. It had a steep pitched roof that went halfway up one of the large trees at its top and almost touched the ground at the bottom. The roof was covered with fallen leaves. It was constructed entirely of wood and blended well with its surroundings, almost looking like a shorter, stouter tree.

Ilfair let the scene calm him. He had practiced doing this. Sitting quietly to calm himself, sort of like a meditation, but the type of meditation that a child would come up with. It was not a stillness of mind but an imaginative wandering of the mind. So, he was not surprised that it did not feel like long had passed before he felt the sun on his face. He knew this meant they were just past high sun.

With enthusiasm and trepidation, he rose and crossed the grove to the door. He stood a moment to steel himself and knocked. The door opened quickly. This time he noticed that Embrey had symbols of Laifell in green embroidery on the back of her shoulders, not just the symbols of Mercial he had noticed before.

"Come. Come in, please. I would ask you your name again, young man, I'm afraid I have already forgotten. My apologies," she said, reaching out to touch his shoulder. She was taller than him, being one step higher up inside the temple.

"Ilfair." The question, along with her humble demeanor, calmed him. He had just a moment before he felt very self-conscious, as though he was being an imposition. But her demeanor belied an interest and enthusiasm in his presence now, rather than the formal politeness of their prior interaction.

"Lovely. Well then, come in, Ilfair. Elder Graywater is eager to meet you." She smiled, ushered him in, and closed the door behind them.

The space they entered was plain, a cylindrical room that functioned as a landing for two stairwells: one leading up, the other down. There was a ledger on a simple wooden table with a chair. The young priestess wrote something therein, he guessed his name and the date perhaps. He eyed the book, quill, and ink jealously. He knew how much they were worth.

She finished writing and stood back up, facing him. "Follow me, please." she said and again turned around and went down the stairs. Ilfair followed.

They descended the granite stairs. As they descended into the earth, Ilfair noted the stairwell was windowless, lit instead by sconces. They flamed with smokeless fire. Green vines snaked up the walls. Impossibly, numerous blooms of colorful flowers adorned the vines.

He did not know how deep they were now, but they eventually reached a door. He guessed they were at the foot of the statue, as deep in the earth as the head was above the earth. The door before them was identical to the one at the entrance to the temple.

The young priestess rapped but once softly on the door. Ilfair and Embrey waited in silence as the knock echoed up the stairwell.

CHAPTER 30

HALLOCH

*To combat the marauding of Aberron and the Nihilin, Harrowfell built
the Spirelight Temple north of Harrowfell in the first footprint of
Ullumair, to honor their Father. A mighty glass sphere with flame fed by
whale oil burned atop the watchtower by day and night. This permitted
those of Harrowfell to see far out onto the plateau between Harrowfell
and Aberron and, by so doing, anticipate the raids of the Feraliths.*
—from the Athenomancer archives

"Enter," came the resonant baritone of a man's voice from the
other side of the door.

Ilfair watched as Embrey pushed the door open. She
stood next to the door and bade him enter. Ilfair took the wordless
direction. He paused and looked at her. She smiled and nodded to
him. Encouraged by the warmth of her gesture, he entered the
room proper.

"Thank you, Embrey," Elder Graywater said with the famil-
iarity of a father to a daughter. The young lady bowed slightly
again, this time to the Elder. She snuck a glance and a smile to Ilfair
as she turned and left, quietly pulling the door closed behind her.

The Elder, a broad-shouldered man of medium height, had not

turned to face him yet, distracted by something he faced on the back wall of his quarters. Ilfair scanned the room quickly. To his left and right were bookshelves from the floor to the high ceiling. Behind him to his left and right were more sconces and flowering vines. It smelled nice: of moss and flower blooms. In front of him were two chairs on Ilfair's side of a large desk. The desk was covered with scattered parchments and unlit candles with melted wax pooled about them. The Elder's lower body was partially obscured by an ornate chair on the other side of the desk. The fabric of the chair was a deep velvet blue, and the dark wood was marked everywhere by images of water, sea-life, and symbols Ilfair could not read. *What is it with people and all these symbols I can't read?* Ilfair thought.

Ilfair saw next the object that had the Elder's attention: a map of the city embedded into the wall. The map was three dimensional with buildings protruding from the wall. Ilfair could see the temple, the city wall, the rivers, the bridge, and the cube and tower he had seen when he had arrived. What's more, azure water flowed on the wall. Above and below ground waterways were represented as different hues of blue. The below ground water was so dark as to be almost black.

At the corners of the map were holes in the walls. In fact, what drew his attention to these holes was a small creature made of water, which suddenly emerged therefrom. The creature was the size and shape of a squirrel, chipmunk or the like, and moved as quickly. The little creature held parchment in its hands. It rushed over and put the parchment rolled up and sealed with a red ribbon into a cubby in the wall and disappeared rapidly into another hole. There were several parchments in the wall on each side of the map, one in a red ribbon, the others in blue or yellow ribbons.

The man moved over to the cubby on the wall and retrieved the red-ribboned parchment. He turned around, removed the ribbon, and took his seat behind the desk. As if he had forgotten Ilfair was even there, he glanced up from the parchment and regarded Ilfair and said, "Have a seat, son. Ilfair isn't it?" He was already looking back down at the parchment, which he was now rolling out on the desk in front of him.

Ilfair shyly took a seat with his hands on his lap. He felt hot in his sliipmare cloak. "Yes... sir." he said sheepishly and deferentially.

"Call me Halloch."

The Elder looked up again briefly with a calmness radiating from his face and posture. The man had black hair speckled with gray and a close-cropped beard similarly colored. His eyes were a metallic gray, sharp but kind. He was dressed in the formal regalia of an elder of a priesthood: plain brown pants and a sky-blue tunic draped with a white surcoat and cloak with symbols of Mercial embroidered in deep blue. At the center of the surcoat were two large orcas entwined with one another, head to tail. It reminded Ilfair of the bells he had seen back at the Wall of Harrowfell.

Halloch took a fresh piece of paper and scribbled on it with a bold practiced hand. He rolled the parchment up and sealed it with the same red ribbon. He stood again and walked over to the cubby, placing it back where he had taken the other from. He made an intricate gesture with his fingers in front of the hole where the little water creature had come from as he walked back to the desk. As he walked, he said, "I looked at the symbols Embrey passed to me this morning. They are curious, yes?"

Ilfair realized that he expected a response. "Um, yes." he said quickly.

"Did you do the transcription of the symbols to the parchment?" Hallock asked.

"Yes sir... I mean, Halloch." It felt awkward to call his senior by the familiar moniker.

Halloch laughed. "Relax son. You are as safe as you could possibly be," he paused and added, "Your parchment work is remarkable. Have you considered studying to become a scribe?"

Ilfair had not ever considered that. He answered flatly and plainly. "Well, my father is an iron and leather worker. Near Overmoor. I have always known I would work with the metals in the earth when I first smelled the deep earth on my father's clothes. I have never considered anything else. And, of course, I am good in deep, dark places. It is there that I am most useful, bless Illinir, bless Faid," he noticed the confidence and pride with which he referred to his work. He hadn't ever noticed that before. It reminded him of his father. He did miss him... and his home.

"That is laudable, young Ilfair," Halloch said with kind seriousness.

"Thank you. And I mean no offense to Mercial." He found it easier to just drop the formal sir, rather than say his familiar name. They did not talk like that in Overmoor.

Halloch seemed to notice as he smiled. "No offense taken, son," he paused and smiled, setting his shoulder back, before he continued. "Why don't you tell me about these symbols?"

Ilfair told him the story that he had rehearsed in his head, and even once out loud in his room in the Diving Osprey.

"Well, I am a deep runner in one of the iron mines, the one mined by Fayrest, the First of the Eightowns, north of Overmoor. The Runeminers of Erlan had recently opened a new tunnel for mining. I was asked to deep run the tunnel, and I passed by a small side passage, which had been intersected accidentally." Ilfair looked up from his hands toward Halloch. He was looking straight at Ilfair with his full attention.

Ilfair continued. "This kind of side passage is not uncommon to come across and it is standard practice for the runners to scout them out... to make sure everything is safe." he paused and looked up to see if the Elder was buying his story. It seemed he was.

"That sounds dangerous," Halloch said with sincerity.

"It is. But I am very careful. I'm good at deep running. I seem to have a way of knowing when things are safe and when they aren't.

And where I am. At least so far." Ilfair added, not wishing to tempt the fate of the gods or to come across as egotistical.

"I see. Please continue," Halloch bade.

"Yes, okay," he paused a second to regain his place in his lie.

"So, I followed the side passage to be sure that it would not make the main tunnel unstable. It led to a chamber full of many curios: a dais with a statue and a circle of stones chief among them. On the pulpit, a black slate rock was covered with the spiraling symbols I gave you. I brought it back to the Runeminer captain. He had the side passage sealed and sent the slate to his superiors, the Thirteen of the Circle of Eights in Overmoor. They said that this knowledge was of the ancients and, as it was not of numbers or engineering, they had no hope of deciphering or understanding it. They instructed that the information be sent to Winters Haven where knowledge of the ancients was still understood. Specifically, the instructions were to find the Elder Graywater priest of Mercial in Winters Haven for help in translation. It seems your family is known for this." Ilfair took a breath.

"As the deep runner, and the one who had found and investigated the chamber, that duty fell to me as I would be best able to answer any questions that could not be anticipated. So..." Ilfair took another, deeper, breath, "I made my transcription and bore it hence." Ilfair was proud of his delivery. He was calm and didn't rush through it. There was enough detail for it to be believable, he guessed.

Halloch had leaned back in his chair during Ilfair's telling and had placed one arm across his lap and rested his chin in the hand of his other arm. He placed his chin in his hand, chewed on the inside of his cheek, and furrowed his brow. *Like a statue of contemplation*, Ilfair thought.

"I see," he said eventually.

He looked up and rubbed his chin then looked back down, leaned forward, and considered the symbol on the parchment.

"Well, very curious indeed. And your captain was right. The Graywaters have an extensive library of ancient texts, especially as they pertain to ancient religions. In fact, we have a whole floor in the Winters Haven tower library." As he said that he turned around and pointed with the feather on his quill to the tower on the map next to the cube building.

Halloch continued. "I will need to visit my family's wing within the Aelinth Tower," he paused, seeming distracted for a moment. He looked up and said,

"Maybe I will see my old friend at the Aelinth Tower, Lady Starscribe." He smiled.

Suddenly, he shook the smile from his face and said, "There I can begin my research. It will take a couple of days I suspect to figure out what we have here." He turned back around and rested his quill on Ilfair's drawing.

He looked at Ilfair. "But first, I think we should start at the beginning of the story again, so that I can be sure I have all the facts straight." He paused and leaned forward again, raising his eyebrows.

He continued. "But maybe this time you could try telling me what really happened. If it's dire enough to be worth being deceptive about, it would be a pity to lose time chasing lies."

Ilfair's disappointment at the thought of more days of waiting was rapidly replaced with a rush of panic. He was struck by it so quickly that he momentarily considered running. In fact, he felt himself jerk involuntarily in his chair. Obviously, that wouldn't work, so he stayed still.

"But..." he began.

"Son, you have no need to lie here. As I already said. You are in the temple of Mercial. You could not be safer." He stood as he said this, and somehow managed to be both imposing and gracious.

"I can't tell you what happened. It's not safe," he tried a modified lie on the fly.

"Safe for whom? Rest assured I can take care of myself and my wards," he said, turning his head slightly with a curious side glance.

Ilfair almost sobbed, but held it in. *Safe for me, you old fool!* he thought. He felt bad for the negative thought and the Leechkin punished him for it. He was terrified and the images in his head weren't helping. His eyes watered and he locked gaze with Halloch.

"No, not for you. It's me. It's not safe for me," Ilfair said. Anxiety was evident in his furrowed brow and his heart was beating so hard that its throbbing could be heard in his voice and breathing.

Halloch's face and posture softened, and he took in a breath to speak but was cut off as Ilfair abruptly continued.

"It's... the symbols... they are... *on* me." It was like saying it out loud made the horror of it more palpable. As he said it, he extended his right arm and pushed up his tunic sleeve, revealing the image.

"Oh, merciful Mercial," Halloch said.

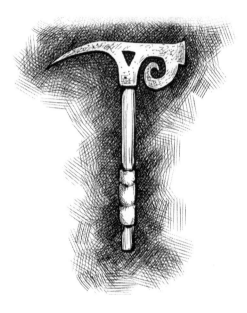

CHAPTER 31

HALLOCH'S PLAN

*From within and beneath the Spirelight, the devout of Ullumair, his
Mythals, prayed for the knowledge to defend themselves from the raids of
the Feraliths. They were shown how to forge weapons, armor, and other
items from Amberglass. The Mythals fused this holy glass from the sands
in Ullumair's ancient footprints using the secrets of flames, fueled by
whale oil. Further, they did learn the ways of sound and light, which
could be used against the dark silence of the Feraliths.
—from the Athenomancer archives*

A
s Halloch moved around the desk, Ilfair stiffened. He stood
and moved away from Halloch.

"Oh, be calm son," Halloch froze where he stood. "I
mean only to look more closely at your arm. How can I set you at
ease?"

Asking that is a good start, Ilfair thought, and his posture relaxed
a bit.

"Tell me what it is in your mind to do to me?" Ilfair asked.

"My god son, to help you, of course!" he exclaimed. "To help
you," he repeated more quietly. Halloch exhaled and his arms
relaxed to his sides; he turned a bit to show pity for Ilfair.

Ilfair grew calmer but had to work hard to bring himself under control. Calming the knot in his stomach, the images in his head, the lump in his throat, and the water in his eyes.

"Take your time, Ilfair." Halloch shifted his weight to his back leg to remove any feeling of imposition in his posture.

Without speaking, Ilfair sat back down in the chair and looked at his feet for a moment before shifting his gaze to regard Halloch.

Likewise, silently, Halloch took a step forward and kneeled beside Ilfair. He took Ilfair's left hand in his and pressed the tunic sleeve up to look at the mark. "My god," he said under his breath.

He looked up at Ilfair and said, "Now, again, please tell me. What happened?" He paused. Sensing persisting reticence from Ilfair, he added, frustration sneaking into his tone, "By mercy and grace, son, you *can* trust me."

Ilfair told him everything. Almost everything. He told him about the ascension to the moon and within, about the rift, the ancient temple in the glacier, and about the lighthouse and Abby and her necklace, and even about the alcoves under the lighthouse and the various items he had collected along the way. He only left out the map and the Aberithic parasites inside him that he learned of from Abby. *Eventually, perhaps*, he thought. He needed to see how this played out to share that bit of information.

"You poor creature," Halloch said at the end.

Ilfair cringed. *That is what I called Abby*, he thought.

He took a deep breath and added, "And now I have very little coin left. And you said it would take you days to find out what this is. I feel like I should just run home while I still can."

"That won't be necessary. And I don't think it would help, even if you did," Halloch said matter-of-factly. "You can't run from this, the touch of a godsmark; or a witchmark for that matter. Being touched by either will follow you wherever you go, I fear."

"Touched?" he asked, pointedly. This was exactly what Ilfair had feared. That he would be considered insane or tainted by evil spirits. He had seen those who had been put in the asylum temples of Illinir labeled as such for much less than what he had just shared.

"No. No, not like that. Poor choice of words. My apologies," Halloch quickly corrected. "Chosen would be the better term. It's not entirely unheard of, this type of thing, but I have never seen something so, well, I don't even know what to call it. Acute?"

"What do I do?" Ilfair asked simply.

He had known what to do up to this point. Survival and the goal of Graywater had been enough. Now he was here and had no idea what to do next. He was at the mercy of Halloch. Just then he noticed that two more red-ribboned scrolls had shown up from the water squirrels, *watermunks*, he thought to himself. The name made him smile, *a smile quite out of place*, he thought, and the curve of his grin dropped. In any event, he noticed that Halloch had ignored the documents. He was totally consumed with attending Ilfair. That gave him some hope.

"Patience, Ilfair. Have patience. I don't know what to do about the mark on your arm yet. Please, give me time." He stood and walked over to his desk. "But let's get that necklace off of you. Maybe we can find out what it is if you are to ever put that back on."

Halloch opened a drawer and produced a kris knife with a handle shaped like a fish or water snake with iridescent scales. The blade was pure iron with inlays of some type of bone, probably whale, though Ilfair could not be certain.

"Lean forward, son," he directed. "This will surely sever the braid, particularly one of witch construction."

Ilfair did as he was asked. Halloch spoke words; Ilfair could not make them out, but he heard a call to the deity Mercial, and then the necklace was cut free of Ilfair. The sound was like a beetle being crushed and his flesh felt ice cold where the braid had been in contact with his skin. It felt good to have it off. He felt better. It was a small thing, but it was something and he hung some hope on the ease with which Halloch had done what he could not do. He had tried to remove it in many ways, all of which had failed.

Halloch tossed the thing on his desk. He sighed as he looked at it for a moment.

"Thank you," Ilfair said, still not calling him by the familiar.

"Of course," Halloch grimaced, almost a smile but not quite. "Wait here."

He walked to the door, opened it, and closed it behind him. Ilfair could hear ascending footfalls. Moments later, he could hear faint talking from the other side of the door, but it was distant. *Most likely one floor up*, he thought. One of the voices was softer and higher. *Embrey*, he thought with a deep breath. A few minutes later, he heard two sets of footfalls coming back down.

CHAPTER 32
ASHHAVEN

The Mythals lived beneath the watchtower in homes built into the wall of the Keening Cliffs. From the Spirelight tower they would descend to the wall of Harrowfell to rebuke Feralith raids. Their weapons and armor of glass canceled the Feralith's spiralore; their ways of light and sound countering the Feraliths tactics of darkness and silence.
—from the Athenomancer archives

The door opened and Halloch and his ward-acolyte Embrey entered.

"Embrey will take care of you from here, at least until I return. I will be in contact with you as soon as I can figure out something to tell you. Until then, you will have a home with us. Our brothers of Laifell have space in the Arborhaven chapels in the groves. They are simple quarters, but they are warm and there is food and water." Halloch said.

"Come, Ilfair," Embrey said.

Ilfair stood. He was fuzzy-headed at this point with everything that had happened, and so he went quietly over to Embrey. She put her hand on his shoulder and directed him out of the room.

Ilfair stopped suddenly and turned. "Thank you, Elder," he said to Halloch, reverting to his formal tendency.

"Of course. Now go and rest. I will find you later." Halloch smiled as he said this. With that, Embrey and Ilfair left the room and closed the door behind.

Ilfair followed Embrey up the stairs and out of the temple. They each walked down the short steps and followed the path, which led into the grove.

Embrey turned and, while walking slowly backwards, spoke. "There is no room in the Leviathan, it's completely full with the staff and innerworkings for maintaining the waterworks here in Winters Haven. But we have a cooperative arrangement with the clerics of Laifell." Embrey continued without prompting.

"You see, the water from the Leviathan feeds the groves that were planted and maintained by the clerics of Laifell. And, while they have clergy for maintaining the bridges and trees in the city, they have more space to grow into and have added extra space to help needful souls. Halloch seems to think you qualify. I agree."

She smiled, turned, and pointed to one of a few steep-roofed wooden buildings. Each was covered in fall leaves and sat just beyond the grove in front of them. "They have enough room for you in the small abbeys, we call them the Arborhavens or Arborhomes. There are a few within the two groves."

"Is it okay for me to stay there? I mean, they are Laifell, not Mercial, right?" Ilfair asked, concern and confusion in his voice.

Embrey stopped and looked at him sympathetically. "As I mentioned, the temples of Laifell and Mercial work together for the betterment of the city. We call it a binary. Elder Graywater is the highest-ranking priest here in this temple binary and is on the Council of Lords here in Winters Haven. He is in regular contact with Elder Blackstaff, the archpriest of Laifell, and so the priests of Laifell here near the Leviathan take Graywater's lead. I actually serve both temples. I am an acolyte of both. I may pick one temple over the other someday, but I'm still young. That can wait," she smiled at Ilfair. "You shouldn't worry about it, though. If Halloch says it's good, all will follow. And you've had quite the time of it recently, so let's just find you some space to rest."

Ilfair nodded, vacantly. *It's like the Circle of Eights in Overmoor; the temple union of Ulmaith and Iroin*, he thought. He kept the thought to himself, though, and instead said only, "Yes. Okay." He was too tired to say more.

"I will get you a spot out of the way. Someplace quiet. Follow me." Embrey said.

She led Ilfair through the grove, crunching over leaves. Ilfair noticed the grace with which she moved. She had a slight form, like him, though slightly shorter, but he could tell that, beneath the priestly garments, she was lithe and svelte. He guessed that she, like him, would make a good deep runner.

And she had been kind up to now, as had Elder Graywater, for which he was both glad and impressed. But at that moment he was completely disoriented. She had been right: he needed rest and quiet.

Earlier in the day, when he had been waiting to meet with Elder Graywater, he had noticed only one narrow house. But now, as they walked, Embrey pointed out a few of them, maybe five or so. As they passed each, Embrey had told him the name, given for a type of tree; Aspenhaven, Elmhome, and so forth. The one they finally entered, the largest it seemed to Ilfair, was named Ashhaven.

They passed into its narrow hall, sparsely adorned, through an open door. There were a few priests busy in the hall tending to various items and a few people, perhaps needy or sick villagers. There were tall windows, which ran the full height of the walls, nearly touching the floor and ceiling, to the left and right. There was a hearth in the center of the hall in front of them; stones and decorative vines encircled the hearth and lined the walls up to the high-pitched ceiling. There was a door into another room at the right corner of the back wall, *probably leading to the kitchen*, Ilfair guessed, following the signals from his olfactory senses.

Without speaking, Embrey led Ilfair through the hall to a wooden stairwell that started in the back left of the hall and ran up the back wall, ending high above the kitchen door at an opening in the ceiling.

She started up the stairs. "There is a private space up here for the clergy. It's actually quite close to my quarters. Come," she said as she paused on the stairs and turned to him.

She continued up the stairs and Ilfair followed. They reached the end of the stairwell and came out onto a landing that turned them to the left, the floor being the ceiling of the hall through which they had just passed. It was a bit like being in the attic of his home in Eightowns, only larger. Much larger.

They walked to the center of the hall and turned left again. There were two windows, one behind and one in front, at each end of the hall. Numerous additional small windows lined the top of the pointed ceiling. The top of the roof was nestled in the canopy of the grove and let in fingers of light from outside.

There were ten doors along the hall, five on each side.

"I am here," Embrey said, pointing to the first door to the right. She walked quickly down to the second to last room on the left. "You will be here," she said, pointing to the door. "The acolyte of Mercial who quartered here has recently moved to another temple, the main one for Laifell, Oakhaven. It's across Winters Haven and is led by Elder Blackstaff, near the southeastern wall. It's a promotion for him, though no one says it is so. At least not out loud. In any event, you can use his old space."

She opened the door and showed him in. The room was small. There was a bed—a cot, really—to the right. Under the cot was a chest, *for clothing storage*, he guessed. The wall opposite the door was slanted steeply, being the top of the roof. There was a long four-paned rectangular window on it, the sill littered on the outside with colorful leaves. The room was bright from the speckled light that leaked in, though it was a bit drafty. A cup rested on the inside ledge of the window. To the left there was a small table and chair with parchment, ink, and quill, as well as two books and a plate with dates, figs, cheese, and bread.

Ilfair stood and stared at the space. "Is it ok?" Embrey asked quizzically.

"Oh, yes. Yes, of course. I am sorry, I didn't mean to be rude. I'm just..." Ilfair drifted off mid-sentence as he entered and set his pack down. He sat in the chair and looked back at Embrey. "It's perfect. Truly, thank you. I don't know what else to say."

She smiled again, radiantly, seeming genuinely pleased. "You don't need to say anything. Eat, drink, and rest. There are extra blankets under the cot. I will let the others know you are here. If you need anything and can't find me, just ask any of the clergy. They will help if they can. Now I will leave you to your privacy." She bowed again slightly and backed out of the room and pulled the door to.

Ilfair lay on the cot and looked out the window. His mind was reeling still, and images of blackness still lingered but were tolerable. It seemed that even the Leechkin were tired. He was hungry and thirsty, but was more exhausted than either. He looked out the window and let his mind wander. Soon he was sleeping, having not even bothered to close the door fully. Evidently, he felt safe and was glad of it.

CHAPTER 33
A(NOTHER) BAD NIGHT

*As with the mortals on Erlan, war raged with the moon: a war between
gods, a Chaos War. Feralzmoon struggled and grew and, in response,
Ullumair grew. His shell forever spiraled outward to contain
Feralzmoon's madness. The Aberiths, too, did attempt to destroy
Ullumair's shell to release their champion-god, Feralzmoon. But just as
Ullumair denied Feralzmoon, the Ullumyths denied the Aberiths.*
—from the Athenomancer archives

This time Ilfair knew it was a dream. It was dark in the
room where he found himself, lit only by a few candles on
the far side of the room. The candles were on either side
of her. He stood near the stairs as he had the last time he was in
Abby's lighthouse. Something shiny and black sat behind her, stirring but a little.

Abby touched the shiny black shell with her left hand, and it
shifted slightly. She was looking down at it and whispering. He
couldn't hear what she was saying. She was holding something in
her right hand, but he couldn't see what.

"Oh, Ilfair," she sighed. "I see you took off my gift."

"Why are you doing this to me?" Ilfair skipped over all the

other questions and asked the one question. Her legionvoice still put him on edge and drew forth black eels behind his eyes and ears, but he still mustered frustration and anger in his voice.

"Doing what?" she said with faux innocence.

"Just leave me alone!" he said with his whole body, his frustration finally vented, black eels writhing behind his eyes.

"Oh, you don't mean that. You need my help," she said the first sentence with sarcasm and the second with dire seriousness. The flickering candles created jittery shadows on her paper-white face.

"You call this help?" Ilfair asked, exasperation in his voice. His hesitancy lost in his anger; he took a step forward into the room.

"Oh, you are getting bold, aren't you? And yes, I do. And I will continue to help you until you succeed in your task." She leaned back and stroked the thing at her side as her legionvoice echoed in the cylindrical cavity that was the top room of the tower.

Ilfair hung his head. "Please... just stop," he said this quietly to himself. He tried to will himself to wake but he couldn't.

"I'm sorry, Ilfair. This isn't really any fun for me either. Well, okay, that's a lie. It is a little fun," she paused and, when Ilfair did not react, added, "I want you to meet my new friend."

"Friend?" Ilfair asked in disbelief. "I can't believe you have any friends."

"Well, yes, we made a new friend after you left. We, Ixo and I, just finished him." She laughed, but it was unclear to Ilfair what was funny.

Perhaps noting his confusion, she added, "Made a new friend, Ilfair. Get it? *Made* it," again she laughed.

She leaned forward to reveal what she was holding in her right arm, making clear the play on words, which to her was mirthful. It was a doll. But it was no ordinary doll. It looked like a shrunken, desiccated, white-skinned version of Ilfair. And about its neck was Ilfair's necklace.

"My god, what...?" Ilfair's heart sank as much as it raced. It hurt him to see his mother's necklace used in such a way.

"See here?" She looked down at her own work. "It's you! And, while Ixo and I helped to make it, the necklace you gave me is what makes it really seem like a real friend, almost like it's alive. Don't you think?" She was looking down at Ixo now with that terrifying, face-splitting grin on her face.

"Why would you do such a thing?" Ilfair shook his head and closed his eyes, again wishing he could wake up.

"You thought that you could be rid of me when you took off my gift? But really you have only put yourself at greater risk. My necklace really was charmed for protection," she said with dire seriousness. Ilfair was astounded at how varied her legionvoice could be, varying from playful and childlike to serious, dark, and full. It was the same with her smile, which could split her face and turn her instantly into a truly unearthly horror.

"I don't believe you. I don't." Ilfair said, looking down and shaking his head.

"I'm offended. But don't worry, I don't hold a grudge. Well, okay, that's a lie, too," she sighed and continued.

"You're a monster, Abby," Ilfair said flatly, deflated from the horrible reality of it all.

"I know. Isn't it great?" Abby said and sighed.

"No," Ilfair said very quietly, mostly to himself.

"Anyway..." she said sarcastically. She rolled her overly large, almond-shaped eyes, dragging out the word to bridge the space. "Now, with my new friend, Mr. Ilfair I'm calling him, we can talk now whenever we like. We just ask Mr. Ilfair where you are, and he tells us! Now we never have to be alone. Doesn't that sound great?" She paused and stared at him seriously and with what felt to Ilfair like malice.

"Now get out of my sight," she said angrily. She turned and dismissed him with a nonchalant flourish of her hand.

Ilfair awoke lying in his bed. He didn't move for many moments. He just lay there and stared at the ceiling. It was still dark outside. He eventually sat up and lit a candle, just for the company of the flame. The images of Abby and the parasites still swam in his vision. He counted and breathed and, as the images receded, he lay back down on his bed. He kept the candle going and turned on his side to face it. He stared at the candle and focused on watching the flame and the wax-cooled shapes that dripped and formed on the table. The candle extinguished itself just a little after sunrise.

He heard footsteps and voices, both in the hall and downstairs, and even some noise from the city outside through his window. The last of the birds that were still around this late in the fall flitted about, quietly for the most part, on the tree branches outside his window. And there was the occasional squirrel. It made him think of Halloch, and though it could have, it did not make him feel much better.

He did not move all day. He just lay there. He did not eat. He barely shifted in the bed. He just thought. And as he thought on his situation, he only felt worse. As the sun set, he heard his father's voice in his head, calming the itching eels. He remembered what his father had always said. It came in different colorful forms, but it boiled down to the same thing. With that thought in mind, he stood up and left his room.

He walked down the hall and listened for a moment at Embrey's door. She was not there. He walked downstairs and out of Ashhaven. He saw Embrey approaching from the groves.

"Ilfair?" Embrey called to him and waved as she approached. When she was close enough, she asked, "How are you feeling?"

"A little better," he said honestly. "Now," he added after thinking for a moment.

"Good. That's good," she said simply, a smile on her face.

Ilfair smiled back, albeit somewhat forced. He shuffled his feet a bit in the fall leaves and then spoke. "This waiting is... um... proving difficult. Is there something I can do to be useful to take my mind off of... all of this, well, me?" he asked, gesturing to his forearm.

"Oh, of course. With Elder Graywater looking into your gods-mark, I could use help. And it's something below ground, so you would be perfect for that, right? Did I hear correctly that you have some experience in that area?" she smiled as she asked, tilting her head to the side. He noticed she had a habit of doing that. It was disarming and effective. He liked it.

"Yes, I do. Quite a lot, in fact," he responded boldly and with some pride. "Though in the mountains, not below cities," he said, adding the clarification as a way to walk back the boldness and potential arrogance of his initial statement.

"I am sure you will find these engineered underground water-ways much easier to deal with than the wild ones. Come, let's get something to eat and I will tell you about it." she had a look in her eyes, like she knew something he didn't. She turned and looked over her shoulder and nodded her head for him to follow.

They went into Ashhaven and collected some items to eat and drink from the pantry and reservoir. He felt better in her presence already. They sat by the hearth on the wooden floor of the Arborhome. Ilfair listened as Embrey explained the task.

"Our waterworkers have let us know that the portcullis of the main outflowing under-city waterway is partially blocked. This can cause very serious problems if it goes unaddressed. The waterways and works of the city require constant care," she said, pausing to eat.

Taking the cue to ask a question, Ilfair spoke. "Where is it located?"

She finished her bite and, after swallowing, answered, "It exits in the city at the very northwest corner of Winters Haven, just south of the north edge of the wall and north of the port. Elder

Graywater usually deals with this particular area, as this area sometimes attracts wildlife, mostly from the sea, but occasionally from the air as well."

Ilfair gave an expression to suggest he needed further clarification.

"The hole in the cliff face looks sort of like a cave," she added, in evident response to his expression.

"Oh," Ilfair said, not contributing much to the discussion, he noticed somewhat uncomfortably. He felt suddenly self-conscious for no reason he could identify. *My curse*, he thought as he considered his chronic feelings of social awkwardness.

Embrey's expression suggested to Ilfair that she sensed his anxiety. With Ilfair's unspoken gratitude, she spoke again. "In any case, with Halloch out, this task falls to me to handle. I had planned to take one other from the faith with me, just out of caution. Can I count you in their stead?" she asked playfully, with a bit of challenge embedded in the tone.

Ilfair actually smiled at this, earnestly; the first in a while. "Oh," he chuckled once, "Of course. Most definitely."

Embrey smiled and stood, took down the last of her water, and had a final bite of fig. She threw the uneaten bits of food into the hearth. "Fantastic. Ok, I have other duties I must attend to before bed so I should go. But how about I find you at sunrise tomorrow here by the hearth and then we go? Good?"

Ilfair nodded and stood with Embrey. "Yes, good. And thank you. I'm looking forward to it. Thank you, Embrey."

Ilfair had to admit, he *was* looking forward to it. He watched Embrey depart then turned back to the hearth and sat down on the wood floor. He absorbed the goings on around him, watching the clerics of Laifell and the occasional cleric of Mercial tend to various duties and people. He exchanged the occasional nod or pleasantry.

Soon, he noticed that the light in the room was from only the hearth and the activity in the room had dwindled noticeably. He grabbed a bit more from the pantry and headed to his room. He found it difficult to go to bed that night, but not due to his various dilemmas. He was looking forward to the morning, anticipating it even.

His father had been right. By taking his focus away from himself and directing it outward, he managed to feel less anxious and neurotic.

When he looked back on this moment in the future, he would wonder why it had not occurred to him to write to his father. But that is sometimes the way of it when dealing with trauma, the focus is on your own misery, and you forget to remember the misery of others. Either way, he was happy to lay awake and think about what the next day would bring.

He finally fell asleep, smiling for the first time in a long time.

CHAPTER 34

THE GRAYWATER COLLECTION

Over the years, just as Mythal and Feralith fell on Erlan, so too did Ullumyth and Aberith succumb to the ravages of the Chaos War within Umbral. From the mixture of the fallen below Ullumair and Feralzmoon, the new gods were born, given new divine life by the energies.
—from the Athenomancer archives

Halloch strode with purpose, east toward the town center on Graywater Lane. He left the alabaster Leviathan Temple and the groves about the Arborhavens behind him. The cobblestone lane had been named after his ancestors. He always felt humbled, like he was walking in the shadow of his family name, when he walked down Graywater Lane. He quickened his stride and soon he could see his destination, the Aelinth Tower, in the distance. The sun had still not risen. He would be there before the sun was full above the Godskeeps, which formed the northeastern horizon.

Normally the tower, which housed all the documents of note in the city, opened at dawn, as was the custom of the clerics of Aelinth, the goddess of light. He, however, being an elder of the city, could gain entry at any hour, and he was impatient this morning to begin his research. He had left Embrey in charge of the waterworks in his absence, but she could not handle that alone for long. He would need to get this figured out quickly, for everyone's sake.

He walked through the dark mists of the market square and crossed the east-west leg of the crisscrossing double bridge, the Rivercross Bridge. On the other side, he passed the windowless white cube that was Kindrid Hall. The white-clad Knights of Kindrid who guarded the doors did not speak, they only bowed to him quietly as he passed. He nodded back to them, in acknowledgement of their deference to him and their honoring of tradition. He took the cobblestone path as it curved south and ended at the Aelinth Tower.

He walked directly up the three steps to the elevated door just above the base of the tower and produced a key from the chain that hung about his neck. He unlocked and opened one of the pair of glass doors at the base of the tower. The glass doors had only the slightest amount of metal framing, made of colorful braised metal. They were impossibly sturdy, despite their delicate glass construction.

He made his way into the large entry hall of the tower. At the center of the marble-white room was a large circular desk of dark wood with a hole in its center. Within the hour the clergy and scribes of Aelinth would be busy within this main hall and monitoring activity throughout the library from that very desk. He remembered Ilfair's transcription of the symbols on his arm. Truly the young man could be a scribe for the clergy of Aelinth. And a notable one at that.

He passed quickly by the desk at the room's center to the stairwell on the side opposite the doorway through which he had entered. He strode up the white stairs with purpose. The marble construction of the flight of steps was inlaid with glass and braised metal. He took them in haste, two at a time, passing the numerous windows along the height of the tower. He could have seen, as he went spiraling clockwise up the tower, the beauty of the entire panorama of the city.

But he was distracted. His mind was full of the potential implications of the runes. He had no idea what they were. And for some reason that he couldn't quite place, he had an ominous feeling that if he failed to decipher them there could be dire consequences for the young man... if not for the realm.

Focusing his attention back to the stairs in front of him, he passed floor after floor full of books, shelves, worship halls, offices, art, and numerous other curios until he reached his destination. On the eleventh floor, some three hundred feet up, was the tower library's Graywater Hall. Only the quarters and observatory of the Archpriestess of Aelinth was higher on the tower. The hall was very quiet, and he was thus permitted to study in peace.

His family kept their entire collection, spanning many generations, in the Graywater Hall. Dozens of generations worth of books, art, parchments, relics, and other curiosities. He crossed the carpet runner that ran between the shelves and headed straight to the desk between the map drawers at the back of the room.

He turned the desk chair around, sat, and caught his breath. He thought for many minutes about what he had learned from Ilfair. He decided that, since the moon featured so prominently, even divinely, in Ilfair's message, he would start there. For the next several hours he collected up and scoured over everything he could find in the collection that had anything to do with the moon.

He had worked without eating. It was on into the middle of the afternoon when Lady Miralinth Starscribe arrived in her formal Archpriestess white and black regalia, indicative of the order of Aelinth. Her name meant in the ancient tongue she who reflects the light, or she who reflects the goddess of light. For generations her family, the Starscribes, had followed the goddess of light, and Miralinth had dutifully followed suit.

Halloch, whose name meant he who makes the water his home, had known Mira, as her close friends called her, for decades. He liked his name well enough, but as far as he was concerned her name was beautiful. And, in his eyes everything about her was, well, perfect. She found him exhausted and consternated, seated at the desk covered in a mountain of documents and relics, resting his furrowed brow in his hands.

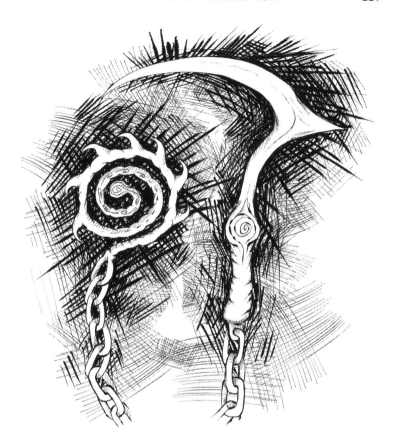

CHAPTER 35

MIRA'S HELP

Some of the new gods derived more from Ullumair and others more from Feralzmoon, but all were simultaneously of both. To this day, depending on the balance of that admixture, they are called Ullic or Ferric deities. These new gods saw the value of both chaos and order. In their eyes, the stalemate between the ancient ones was the only stable solution.
—from the Athenomancer archives

"Dearest Halloch, it's good to see you," Miralinth said with a smile on her face and mirth in her voice. After a short moment, she added. "Whatever are you up to?"

"And you as well, Mistress Starscribe," Halloch replied, looking up and sighing.

"Mistress? Oh, please, not that title. It makes me feel old... Elder Graywater," she added the latter bit of the sentence with mirth and a cockeyed grin and tilted head.

"Of course, but you carry the title with such grace, Mira," he said with all honesty, using the familiar to be respectful of her request.

"I was told that you were up here early this morning. And when

I heard you were still here, I thought I would bring you some black tea and see what you could possibly be up to for so long. What could take one as brilliant as you so long, buried in all this dusty parchment as you are." Mira came to the other side of the table and handed him one of the two cups of hot black tea she was carrying.

Halloch looked up to her and nodded his gratitude as he accepted one of the cups. He took a swallow of the tea, felt the warmth, and exhaled a sigh. "Yes, I needed that. Thank you. I had forgotten to eat." He set the cup down next to him and returned his attention to the scatterings on the desk.

"I rather guessed that, knowing you as I do for as long as I have," she paused, looking down on him from over his right shoulder before turning her attention to Halloch's parchments. "What exactly has you so engrossed?" Mira again queried, but more poignantly.

"A young man brought a strange symbol to my attention. He transcribed it from the original location where it was found," he pulled Ilfair's parchment out from the table scatterings to show her. "He brought it here to me to identify."

Halloch could see somewhat now the origin of the boy's story. Until he knew the whole of it, he wasn't sure he wanted to make Ilfair's scenario public knowledge either. He trusted Mira of course, but stories like this had a way of spreading of their own volition and he did not want her to have to deal with any consequences he did not yet foresee. He had been friends with Mira for decades, she would understand if he needed to clarify things later. He hoped.

"The transcription is beautiful," Mira noted.

"I told him the same. Mentioned to him that he might make a good scribe. Sounds like you agree?" Halloch was glad to move on from the misdirection and back to the symbols themselves. He felt lucky that Mira did not ask where the symbol was found. It would have been a reasonable question. It made him wonder if she suspected there was more but trusted him enough to not press him until he was ready to say more.

"I do agree. He shows a talent at the level of one instructed as an acolyte of Aelinth." She held the symbol up close and pulled her spectacles up to look closely at it. The wrinkles on her skin were more noticeable now as she concentrated, Halloch noted. She was beautiful, though. One of those women who just becomes more graceful and alluring with age. She tucked some of her impossibly raven-black hair behind her left ear and turned to Halloch. "So, what do you think?" she asked.

"Well, I've looked through what I daresay is every relevant book in my family's collection and I am happy to say that I have found at least something of interest. Two engravings in particular have my interest. Each have symbols like on the young man's... parchment." He had almost said arm. He was glad to have caught himself.

He continued. "One is in this book," he pulled the book over the glass engraving in front of him. "This is a text of one of the ancient authors of the moon goddess Umbral. It's normal enough. Talks about phases of the moon, tides, mental illness, and whatnot." He turned a few pages as he spoke about the works. Then he stopped on a loose page in the book.

"But this image here," he pointed to a detailed engraving of the moon, "has writing on it that I cannot read, but they look to be labels for different parts of the moon. They look strikingly similar to the boy's."

He handed the parchment to Mira. As she inspected it, he added, "Except his symbols are arrayed in a spiral." He reached up and pointed to the parchment and made a spiraling motion with his hand behind the lettering on the document. "These are written top to bottom and left to right. In the more normal fashion."

Halloch paused. Mira looked down, saying only "And?" encouraging Halloch to continue.

In reply, Halloch pushed the book away, revealing the Amberglass beneath. "I also found this. An engraving on glass from my family's collection of relics from ancient Harrowfell. My god only knows how it has survived. But it's similar to the engraving in the book. Pictures of the moon, one pristine and the other marked as you would see today through the looking glass at the top of this tower. No book to describe what it's all about, but the symbols are again everywhere. Though, again, not spiraled. That part, the spiraling that is, and of course what the symbols mean is still quite a mystery." Halloch paused, took a deep breath, and leaned back. He looked up to Mira, who eyed him intently, and continued.

"Currently I am trying to feel encouraged but am honestly at a bit of a loss as to where to go from here." Halloch leaned forward, took the teacup from the desk, and drank again. "Again, thank you for this tea."

"Of course, Halloch dear," she put her left hand on his right shoulder.

He looked up at her. "So, I have this," he gestured to the table, "but I am not sure I am much closer to knowing what *this* is. I'm still no closer to being able to interpret the boy's symbol and the Umbral text gives no clues on how to translate it or where it comes from."

"Well, you have come to the right place, almost. For if anyone can read it, it would be our Athenomancer." Mira added.

"The Athenomancer?" Halloch asked "But Ao'faer resides in the temple on the Kindledcrest Isles."

"That is why I said *almost* the right place. He is not here, but at least I am and know well enough to point you in the right direction," she said with a smile.

"But I thought he was just a steward of old relics in the Atheneum Tower," Halloch said, shaking his head and furrowing his brow.

"Oh, he is that. But not only," Mira said. "The Atheneum Tower there, like this one, is full of recorded knowledge, but of a more ancient and, as your ancestors knew, sensitive and sacred variety. And the line of Athenomancers have maintained the ability to read such ancient texts. It's part of their duty. They must choose an ascetic and monastic life to bear the Everburning Mantle, but they gain much by so doing. Their home becomes the Atheneum and their family, indeed their life, becomes the books."

Halloch raised his eyebrows, a bit embarrassed. "All of that? Truly?"

"Yes." Mira answered matter-of-factly.

"How did I not know this?" Halloch responded with self-deprecation.

"Well, dearest Halloch, none of us can know everything. And you are quite busy with maintaining the Leviathan Temple, the entire city waterworks, the sick, and, with the clerics and Black-staffs of Laifell, all the roads and many of the public buildings." Mira spoke with earnestness, indeed no hint of other meaning crept into her tone.

"You are kind, Mira," Halloch said smiling.

"It is not mere kindness, Halloch," she said, her posture and face relaxing, radiating respect for the man she had known for so many years.

"The Graywater, Blackstaff, and Whitehaven families have made this city what it is, built it from the bottom up, starting with the waterways and foundations engineered by your ancestors. The Starscribe family is proud to advise the great Winters Haven families. We have been free to make knowing things our concern because you and the other great families have made that possible. You don't know about the details of the Atheneum? Well, I wouldn't have a hope of running even just one floor of the Leviathan."

Halloch smiled. "We are as much in your debt as you are in ours. But you are right, I do get lost in my many duties. It seems that in my duties to the present I have lost touch with some of the wisdom of the past," he again drank.

"I am happy and honored to rely on your advice yet again. One of these days I will remember to come to you sooner. Maybe I just enjoy looking through my family's collection too much."

"Quite understandably. It is remarkable." She looked around.

"But you are right," Halloch said, interrupting the reverie, "there is much for me to get back to. I've left Acolyte Embrey too burdened. She is quite capable, but she cannot be two places at once. I should get back to her, back to my temple." He began to rise. "So, it's clear then, yes? I will ferry these with the boy and Embrey to the Athenomancer to see what more can be gleaned."

"Yes. I will arrange passage for you on the Orca. Jona, youngest son of the Gaffspells, is our regular ferryman to the Athenomancer these days. I can send word ahead so he can be prepared for passage to the Kindledcrest Isles in the morning?" Mira added in questioning concurrence.

"Clear headed as usual, dear Mira. Yes, please, that would be most welcome," Halloch added, genuinely impressed with Mira's reliably lucid thinking.

"Can I convince you to join me for a repast? I could have this reorganized for you," she gestured to the mess he had made of the collection at Graywater Hall, "to buy you some extra time. They could also package your two findings and deliver them to Embrey at the Leviathan Temple. If you are okay with that, of course," she asked.

Halloch noted how Mira had read his mind to send Embrey to the Atheneum with Ilfair. "Of course, I trust you to do that better than I would trust myself. I would make an even more disorganized mess of the whole of it, the collection, and the packaging of the findings, I daresay." He felt a little bad about the misdirection from earlier at this last comment. But he could cover for that later, he was confident.

"And yes, something to eat sounds great," he smiled. He was in fact very hungry.

Halloch rose and stood in the space that Mira had just vacated. He turned and looked out the window. "The view from here is spectacular." The orange light of the setting sun made brilliant the features of the city and had turned the hall a warm and inviting amber color.

Miralinth, without looking away from Halloch, smiled and said, "Yes, it is."

They exited the room together and started down the stairs. Halloch's deep rich voice and Mira's refined noble tones echoed comfortably through the tower as the two descended.

CHAPTER 36
THE CLIFF WATERWAY

*The new gods decided to flee the Chaos War, relying on the continued
stalemate between the ancient gods. They fled Umbral, leaving twelve
new craters on the lower surface of Umbral, and landed along the length
of the Godskeep Mountains, earning the mountains their moniker.*
—from the Athenomancer archives

Ilfair woke a bit before dawn, but not before Embrey. He was
still lying in bed when he heard a gentle knock at his door.
"Ilfair?" came a soft voice through the door.

"Yes, I'm awake," he called back. He smiled to himself and
added in his head, *dad*. It reminded him of being a child and of
home. He felt a pang of homesickness, a slithering black eel chased
that feeling away quickly.

Embrey cracked the door open and spoke through the opening.
"Get ready and meet me downstairs. I will ready some food for us,"
Embrey said equally softly but more clearly through the opened
door. She padded away quietly down the hall. He heard her grace-
fully navigate the stairs. He could see her gliding over the wood
floors in his head. She had a memorable grace about her demeanor
and movement.

Ilfair cast the sheet aside and sat, then stood up. He stretched his body and rubbed his face then donned his Amberglass shirt, his pants, and boots. He pulled on his pack, looped his spiralhammer over his belt loop, and pulled over the sliipmare cloak. He shrugged his shoulders to get everything settled properly and pulled the door open and, upon his leaving, closed it behind him and headed downstairs. His footfalls, while graceful, seemed loud to him after hearing Embrey's. He tried to be quieter, thinking of the others still sleeping.

Despite the quiet of the early morning, others must have been up earlier since the fire in the hearth was going and appeared to have been going for some time. Embrey was standing with her back to him. She must not have been able to hear him over the fire. As he approached her, he said, "Good morning, Embrey." It felt easy.

She turned and smiled. "Good morning, sleepy sea serpent. Nice of you to join me," she handed him some bread and cheese. "Get your waterskin filled and stuff a bit of extra bread in your pack for later. We should eat and walk."

Ilfair nodded and did as he was instructed. While he did so, Embrey grabbed a few digging spades and strapped them to her pack, which she then pulled on. She was dressed differently today. She looked more like him, dark and heavy clothing suited for hard physical work.

She turned and faced him. "Ready?" she asked cheerily as she adjusted her spade-laden pack.

Ilfair nodded. "Yes."

They left the hall, leaving the Arborhavens behind, and passed through the grove, the Leviathan Temple to their right. Ilfair walked just a hair behind Embrey so he could follow her lead but still talk to her easily if that should prove necessary.

As they crossed the bridge and set foot on the street proper,

Embrey, still looking forward, said bluntly without preamble, "Ilfair. It's an odd name. What does it mean?"

She had a way about her that made him feel at ease and not offended. "Um, well, I don't know," he eventually replied.

"Didn't your parents tell you?" she pressed further.

"My father never did. I thought maybe it had something to do with the god Illinir as there was a plague in my village when I was a boy. But I never asked. And my father never offered." Ilfair explained.

"You say your father... what about your mother?"

"Um, my mother passed away when I was a baby. Maybe she would have told me, but I don't know," Ilfair said quietly, Leechkin stirring.

"Oh, merciful Mercial, I am sorry Ilfair," Embrey said, sincere sadness in her voice.

"It's okay, Embrey. I never knew her, so it's not a sharp pain. Of course, I do wonder sometimes, but it's just a curiosity in my head. It makes me feel weird, like I should feel sad, but its more just a questioning feeling about what could have been. My father was very kind to me and told me of her often. I am grateful, he was a good man, but I was just a very quiet child and I suppose he was just letting me be. I could have come to him, but never did," Ilfair was shocked at how much he had shared in that moment. He felt calm around Embrey, he realized only in this moment just *how* at ease he felt.

"Oh, okay. Well, I'm glad of that for you," Embrey said with genuine sentiment in her tone.

"I plan to remedy that if... well, when... I can get back to him," Ilfair said.

"Yes. It will be when, of course." She looked at him and smiled.

They were heading west on some road or other and he could see the cliff ahead. They would reach the end of the road soon. He could see a black wrought fence in the distance.

"You know, we could have a correspondence sent to Overmoor for you. It could be there quite quickly by Osprey. Perhaps you could put your father at greater ease to let him know you have arrived here safely?" she ended the statement with a questioning tone. "Could it make it to them from Overmoor somehow?"

"Oh, that is a good and kind thought. And yes, there is a message courier between Overmoor and the surrounding Eightowns. It would make it to them within a day or two of arriving in Overmoor," Ilfair quickly continued, wishing to change the topic away from himself, though he did resolve to write the letter upon returning to Ashhaven. "And what about you? What does Embrey mean?"

"Ha, yes, well, it means, rather embarrassingly, the young life or the young light. A bit dramatic I think," Embrey said with a smile.

"I like it. It fits you. Was it your mother or father that named you thusly?" Ilfair added, turning to face her, squinting against the rising sunlight.

He noticed in that moment that what he had to force with the young waitress at the inn and the shopkeeper in the tannery came without effort with Embrey. He felt emotion, though guarded, with her and the Leechkin were kept at bay by just a little extra effort, which was not detracted noticeably from his ability to hold conversation. *At least I think*, Ilfair wondered.

"Well, both I guess. I never really asked, but my mother and father always did things together, so I would guess naming me was no different." She furrowed her brow and looked up and to the left as she said this, gesturing questioningly with her hands low by her side.

Ilfair rejoined. "As I understand from my father, he and my mother were the same. Always working from the same cloth as they say in my village," Ilfair shared, uncharacteristically open.

"In fact, yes." Embrey responded.

It was quiet for a few minutes. They had left the houses and shops behind. There was just the river to their right and, to their left, large, spaced-out buildings. For storage, Ilfair guessed, but of what he had no idea and, to retain the silence he enjoyed so much, he did not ask.

Eventually they reached the iron gate. Embrey produced a key from a chain about her neck. The key looked like the symbol of Mercial, and the wavy features fit into the keyhole on the gate, which was adorned with various aquatic flowing forms.

Embrey pulled the gate open. She looked at Ilfair, "Come ahead of me. I will close and lock the gate behind us. We wouldn't want anyone to run afoul of the cliff edge."

Ilfair again did as was requested and saw immediately what Embrey meant. "Oh, yes," he said simply with raised eyebrows, looking over the cliff edge at the steep and long drop to the Moonsong Sea below. It reminded him of the descent to the beach from the caverns below Abby's tower, though much shorter in this case.

"Watch your footing on the ladder, the iron can get slick from the sea mists," Embrey gestured to the rungs embedded into the cliff face.

Ilfair turned his back to the water and faced Embrey and made his way down the ladder to the landing some fifty feet below. She was right, the rungs were cold and slick. He was accustomed to that thought from deeprunning in the iron mines. He heard Embrey close and lock the gate and then watched her begin to make her way down the ladder as well.

From the landing, just to the north, Ilfair could see the river they had followed fall over the cliff to the ocean below. Far in the opposite direction, to the south, he could see the ships at the city's port located in a short natural reprieve in the cliff wall. There were at least two other waterfalls too, past the port, where the cliff wall again rose sharply.

Ilfair heard Embrey's footfalls on the landing behind him, and he turned to regard her with a small smile.

"Excuse me... and careful of the ledge," she said, moving by him. She guided him gently with her hands to prevent either from stumbling.

Ilfair looked down to his feet as he stepped back. There was a short wall behind him, maybe hip high. With the ladder now behind him, the cliff wall to his left, and the sea to his right, Ilfair could see an opening in the cliff wall in front of him. Embrey stepped down into some ankle-high water in front of a black wrought iron gate that covered an opening.

"Come, Ilfair, this is our task. Not glamorous by any means, but necessary. The portcullis and drain are partially blocked, and the water is backing up. If we don't clear it out it will eventually be completely blocked and then we will have real problems as the water backs up into buildings. Not good," she made a face at this last point.

Ilfair stepped down into the water in front of the portcullis with Embrey. He could see what had happened. Some large debris had become lodged in the bars of the gate and had slowly collected more and more debris so that now the opening, large as it was, slightly bigger around than he was tall, was nearly halfway obscured.

"I see. Yes, that would be a problem. What should we do with the debris? Just pitch it over?" Ilfair asked.

"Let's break it up into smaller pieces and let the filter here do its job," she pointed to her right, just before the end of the landing. "The Graywater family, out of respect to Mercial, built this long filter full of black rock that runs down to the sea. It filters out the sludge and toxins from the water before it flows out into the sea. Practically speaking, we don't want the fish we consume eating our runoff."

"Amazing," Ilfair said, quickly inspecting the massive drain-like porous black rock filled structure. He noticed a couple more similar structures on the cliff face further off, along with one more massive waterfall. They had similar marvels of engineering in and about Overmoor for dealing with all the water of the Sliipmoors. But this was different. Where Overmoor was engineered out of the land, this was, by contrast, integrated into the land.

"Even more so when you consider how many generations ago it was built," Embrey looked at the black rocks. She put her hands on her hips, cocked her head, and sighed. "Let's get to it," she said. "It's probably a few hours of work and it would be nice to finish before high sun," Embrey said as she donned black leather working gloves and retrieved one of her spades.

"Good enough," Ilfair said, donning gloves and producing his spiralhammer from his belt loop. *And my fair skin and eyes couldn't agree more. It's so bright here,* he thought.

They worked diligently and quietly for some time. As they made progress, and the day grew brighter, they removed much of the debris from the portcullis. As the day warmed, their breath grew less visible, and beads of sweat appeared on their brows.

"How did you end up doing this? I mean joining the priest-hoods?" Ilfair dared to ask.

"Well, my parents had great plans for me, but I felt a calling to serve the city. I couldn't think of a better way to do that than serving the Arborhalls and the Leviathan; Laifell and Mercial," she said.

"That's laudable. What did your parents want you to do?" Ilfair asked.

Without looking up Embrey said, "Well, I am a daughter of the Whitehaven family, so they wanted me to be a noble. So, I guess mostly nothing," she laughed.

Ilfair stopped working and stared. "Wow."

Embrey stopped working and looked up to meet Ilfair's gaze. "It's nothing to be so impressed by. I didn't do anything to earn your amazement. My mother is a daughter of the Starscribe family, and my father is a son of the Whitehaven family. That's it." She paused for punctuation.

"I want to earn my nobility... and I love my city. If I were to ever take any of the authority my noble birth affords me, I would like to be able to wield it with gratitude, respect, and humility... and wisdom. So, I chose to serve at the Leviathan and the Arborhavens under Elder Graywater. Even that choice is something that most don't get by birth. Elder Graywater is a great man, and I am blessed to serve under him. I want to learn everything I can. And I also get mentorship from Elder Blackstaff of Laifell. If you want to know how this city works and what its people need, you want to know what they know," she finished the monologue with a seriousness, a furrowed brow, and a downward gaze.

"Well, I am not less impressed now," Ilfair said with a smile.

"You know, I never thought of it, but it is nice that my Starscribe and Whitehaven family lineages don't overlap with the Blackstaff and Graywater lineages. It's nice to not wonder, or at least wonder less, if you are being treated differently because of your lineages. If I served within the Cube or at the Aelinth Tower, that would most certainly be the case. The Whitehavens and Starscribes have formed the leadership for the clergy of Kindrid and Aelinth for as long as there has been a Winters Haven," she hadn't stopped working while she talked.

"You remind me of my father," he smiled and nodded. He noticed Embrey stiffen. He could not decide why, and, fearing that he had made her uncomfortable, he decided to pick up his spiral-hammer and get back to work. After some moments, Ilfair got the courage to speak again.

"What do you think about me slipping through here and getting on the other side of the debris? We will have more room to work then, and we can attack it from both sides," Ilfair suggested.

Embrey nodded, appearing happy to have conversation again,

especially on a new subject. "Excellent idea. Can you fit between the bars?"

Ilfair set his tools on the other side of the gate and turned sideways, making himself thin, and slid between the bars.

"Ha-ha! Impressive!" Embrey smiled.

Ilfair reached to pick up his tools and looked up and smiled, not sure whether to be embarrassed or proud. "Thanks. I do that often in the mines. Some of the miners called me Roach," he paused, seeing Embrey's expression. "I don't mind it. They mean it as a compliment. The men of the mines give everyone nicknames like that. It's like a rite of passage."

"Oh," Embrey said simply. Her half-smile made him wonder if she found the moniker insulting or endearing.

Ilfair crawled over the loose debris and found himself in mid-thigh-high water on the other side. He noticed to his left a couple more of the watermunks he had seen carrying colored ribbons into Halloch's office. He also saw a collection of colored ribbons clumped together in an alcove hewn into the tunnel well, just inside the entrance to the tunnel. All the ribbons were blank. So, the watermunks just milled about since they had no tasks to perform.

Absently, he started the work of clearing by using the pick to pull the debris apart. He pulled it towards himself as he walked backwards, slowly, deeper into the underground waterway. He felt, oddly, more comfortable here than he did out there. He was used to this type of close quarters work and did not have the steep exposure behind him.

Also, it gave him a break from feeling the pressure of thinking of things to say.

As they continued to make progress, the water level lowered, and the origin of the blockage finally revealed itself. A small clump of black rock with bits of wood connected by some white strand-like material, like spider webs, had become wedged in the grating.

Ilfair looked up through the bars and tapped them with his spiralhammer to get Embrey's attention. He waited till Embrey made eye contact with him. "Let me get this?" Ilfair asked, pointed at the black rock agglomeration. "This is my specialty."

"Be my guest," Embrey laughed, wiping sweat from her brow, and leaned back against her spade. They were both sweaty despite the cold wet wind from the late fall Moonsong Sea.

Ilfair, using each side of the spiralhammer in turn, made quick work of the blockage. While Embrey moved the debris toward the filter, Ilfair, on a hunch, turned to look down the waterway. He could see some additional loose rock down the waterway some twenty-five feet or so in. He suspected this was the origin of the material that had ultimately blocked the grating. If it was not addressed, Ilfair suspected the blockage would recur sooner rather than later.

"Should I get that as well?" Ilfair said, pointing down the tunnel to the black, rock-strewn debris.

"Get what?" Embrey asked.

Ilfair forgot she did not have his shadowsight and therefore could not see down the waterway. Especially from out there, where it would have been difficult for even him to see.

"Some more loose rock. I can already see smaller bits of it breaking off and coming towards the grating. It's further down the tunnel," he explained.

"Yes, please do. I will finish cleaning the filter out here. Call out if you need me," Embrey turned as she spoke, moving over to the filter.

Ilfair walked down the waterway. His feet were protected, but the water splashed under his footfalls, wetting his lower leg up to his mid-calf. He could feel the cold of the water and the frigid weight of it made the going slower.

The underground waterway was almost perfectly cylindrical. Seams from the many thousands of black bricks, which had been used to engineer the tunnel, glistened with moisture. The debris stood out clearly against the perfectly arrayed blocks. In fact, as Ilfair approached he could see that a hole had been made in the side of the wall, half above and half below the waterline in the tunnel. The rock fragments seemed to be scattered radially out from the hole in the wall.

Ilfair walked over and investigated the hole. There was a shiny black hemisphere inside. It writhed slowly. Ilfair took a step back and raised his spiralhammer instinctively. With horror, Ilfair stared as the sphere bloomed open. Two black eyes on a white circle looked out at him.

"Dreaming again, boy?" Abby asked.

CHAPTER 37

DOWN THE TUNNEL

The emergence of the new gods was named the Twelve Tears of Umbral by the Ashfallen. With the ancient gods silent, the Ashfallen immediately recognized the divinity of the Twelve Tears and their prayers to the mountains were answered by the twelve new gods.
—from the Athenomancer archives

"No, no, no... no," Ilfair panicked, black eels blossoming in his head. *This can't be*, he thought.

"No, you say?" Abby responded quizzically. She began to shed the shiny black bloom like a cast-off skin.

"I dare say you are right. This is no dream."

With that the writhing shell dissolved behind her, falling into the water. She now stood at the opening of the hole, water up to just below her knees. She smiled and, after a few heartbeats, two millipede-like creatures burst forth from behind her, water erupting around them as they emerged. The two creatures rushed across the ground, their millions of tiny legs propelling them smoothly across the watery ground, and spiraled up Ilfair's legs.

Ilfair cried out.

"What's that?" Embrey yelled back. "Ilfair?" she repeated after a beat of silence.

Ilfair fell back, seated in the water with his back against the wall opposite the hole, arms up guarding his neck and face. Ilfair had dropped the hammer. The lamprey-like mouths of the worms tried to work to his neck. The creatures looked like those from the temple, like the Leechkin too, but smaller and with more legs.

His mind rushed with images of black eel-like creatures, their white eyes flared crossly. Ilfair grabbed at the legs of one of the creatures. With panic-fueled strength he ripped a handful of feet from it. The two creatures were all over him and he could not tell one from the other, he just grabbed and ripped. Black ichor covered him. It seemed as though it were enough deterrence, as the creatures rushed off of him and slithered rapidly down the tunnel, further under the city. With them gone, he could see Embrey standing over him, black ichor dripping from her spade, a light flaring from the necklace at her chest.

She knelt down to his level, kneeling in the fetid water.

"Are you ok?" she asked, panting, and concerned.

"I... think so," his heart was racing and he tried to get control of his thoughts, filled with horrors as they were. His hands were shaking as he tried to clear the ichor off them. "What were those?" he asked.

"I don't know. I'm sorry, Ilfair. I should not have let you go in alone. Sometimes creatures make homes of these cliff caves. Graywater has warned me of this. I just forgot... I didn't think. I'm sorry," she was clearly upset.

"It's okay. I'm okay," he said, looking at her. "It will be okay."

She looked back at him, attentively. "Ilfair, your eyes. What is...?" With a quick movement of her left hand, she deftly moved the small light, which dangled down by her waist. She lifted it between their now-close faces. The waves of the symbol of Mercial

WINTERS HAVEN

she held in her hand seemed to wave with blue light. Ilfair shielded his eyes. While shielded, they shifted back to how they had been before, adjusting to the light. He lowered his hand and met her attentive stare.

"Yes, my eyes are a bit odd. In the dark my eyes change, just like your eyes do. Except the color of my pupils change rather than just getting larger. It's a birth defect that runs on my mother's side. Most people never notice," Ilfair tried to explain, quickly lying. His eyes had once been normal, before he had gotten sick as a child. Before the Aberith's invasion, he now knew. *My gods, I hate all this lying*, he thought amidst the Leechkin. If they had mouths like men, he could swear that they would be grinning at his disquiet.

"That is, uh, peculiar," she furrowed her brow and slowly stood. She took a breath and looked as if she wanted to press the topic further, but instead offered her hand. "I've seen stranger things... let's get out of here, shall we?" it wasn't clear to Ilfair if Embrey believed the lie, but she at least did not seem overly concerned. It relaxed him, and the Leechkin blossoming in his head receded.

Ilfair took her hand and pulled himself up. He looked around and could see no signs of Abby. As they exited the tunnel, Embrey continued to glance at Ilfair sideways. At the exit to the tunnel, she made a note on one of the ribbons. A watermunk dutifully and rapidly absconded with the ribbon down the tunnel. They exited the tunnel hastily thereafter and climbed the ladder.

On the walk back to the Arborhalls, Ilfair asked again, "What were those things? They looked like giant millipedes. But with teeth," he tried to laugh at the last comment, but it didn't sound very mirthful. And, truth be told, it wasn't that which scared him. It was Abby... again. And he was pretty sure he wasn't dreaming. Had she really been there?

"Yeah, I don't know. We will need to get the Kindrid guard in there after those. Elder Graywater can tell us what action is best taken next. But I would guess we don't need those making more in there," she said, putting her hand on his shoulder. "I am glad you are okay. You are okay, right?"

Ilfair nodded. "Yes. My nerves are a bit rattled, but my body has seen worse in the mines."

"Oh, I bet so. You will have to tell me some tales of what you have seen someday," she responded.

Ilfair smiled and nodded. But did not speak. They both seemed to be content to walk back quietly.

When they reached the bridge, Embrey spoke. "I will go to see if Elder Graywater has returned. You should go to Ashhaven and clean up. Make sure nothing is amiss." Embrey paused as if considering whether to say more. At length she said, "Perhaps you could work on the letter to your father," she opened her mouth to say more, but instead just closed her eyes, nodded, and turned to leave.

Embrey's words were prophetic. Upon reaching his room, Ilfair stripped out of his wet clothes. He took off his gloves first and then his boots, shirt, cloak, and pants. He dried off with the linens under the cot. He scrubbed the mud and muck from his body. He would need to bathe himself and his clothes again. He guessed that could be handled here somewhere.

As he scrubbed his hands, he noticed that he could not remove the black from the tips of the fingers on his right hand. The hand that had ripped the legs from the creatures.

He looked closely at them and could see black-blue veins trail off before the first knuckle. His hand had been covered by the glove so it couldn't be the ichor.

He stared at it for a moment more. He touched the black tips of his fingers with his other hand. They felt like smooth black callouses. And they were on the same hand as the arm which bore the godsmark. Then he spoke aloud, staring at his hand. "Oh my god. Now what?"

To take his mind off this new oddity, he decided to heed

Embrey's suggestion. He found parchment in the small desk by the bed and recovered the quill and ink from his pack and sat down to compose a letter to his father. He thought for many moments. "What do I say?" he asked the parchment. *This is not my strong suit,* he thought, when the parchment failed to respond.

Short and simple... and honest... he decided.

Father,

I cannot possibly explain to you in this letter what has happened to me. But do not worry, I am well and safe. By a quite bizarre and circuitous path, I have found myself in Winters Haven in the care of the Elder of Mercial. I will find my way back to you soon and explain everything.

Before closing I want to say to you something I have not often thought to share, though I realize now that I have always thought it. And that is that I am grateful for you and all you have done for me. I am a blessed child, despite everything, and that is because of you. I will see you soon and we shall embrace and be father and son and, in a way, it will be for the first time.

I will explain everything when I see you.

Emotions began to get the better of Ilfair, encouraged by the Leechkin in his head, so he closed the letter.

With love and gratitude, your son, Ilfair

Ilfair studied the letter for many moments. The letter was awkward and somewhat confusing and unclear. He considered throwing it away and starting fresh, but he simply couldn't decide in what way he could improve it. Furthermore, he was tired and wasn't sure he had the energy to try again.

He decided to leave it and bed down for the night. He would look at it again in the morning. Perhaps it would be clearer if the letter was what it needed to be then. That had often worked with drawings he had done as a younger man. Only with the fresh eyes of morning could he decide on the quality of his work.

Yes, in the morning it will be clear, he thought. In that moment, the blackness of his fingertips began to creep back into his mind. He forced the thought from his mind. He busied his mind by counting up and down to and from eight. *Just like in the rift. That's strange*, were his last thoughts of the day.

CHAPTER 38

JONA GAFFSPELL

The impact of the new gods on the Godskeeps created massive craters within which they did dwell. The energy from the new gods created all manner of mythical creatures about these craters, being both light and dark in spirit. The Godskeeps to this day are considered hallowed, magical, and dangerous. The Ashfallen do not journey there.
—from the Athenomancer archives

T lfair walked down the cobblestone street, the main east-west thoroughfare in the city. He had learned it was named after Halloch's family. As he walked his feet crunched on the fall leaves that littered Graywater Lane. He pulled his sliipmare cloak close against the chill morning wind, which came up the street from the sea.

He had used the lane multiple times now. He had taken it when he arrived to get to the Diving Osprey, or at least to the road that led there. He had taken it the next day to the city center to get his quill and ink, and had taken it to get to the Leviathan Temple and then, again indirectly, with Embrey to get to the cliff wall the day prior.

Now he was on a new part of the lane. They were south of the city square and the temple, and the street had turned slightly southwest toward the sea. And it was descending now, rather steeply actually. He could see the port out in front of him.

He was accompanied by Halloch and Embrey. The two had exchanged pleasantries when they had met at the bridge outside of the Arborhalls and the Leviathan Temple earlier that morning. Ilfair had not spoken, standing slightly behind Embrey, instead only exchanging a brief glance with Halloch.

Embrey and Halloch continued to talk as they walked, but Ilfair remained silent, continuing to remain sheepishly a stride behind the pair. He thought he heard them discussing something about the things that had attacked him in the waterway. He decided to fall a little further behind, so their conversation became a nondescript white noise. Ilfair's mind was a blur of the events of the last two days, particularly the day before, and he was sure he did not want to learn more about that at the moment.

Mercifully, he had an uneventful night's rest. The next morning he had managed to get his person and belongings cleaned. Including picking out some sort of disgusting aquatic ticks from the hair on his sliipmare cloak. Again, miraculously, the Amberglass shirt had managed to stay pristinely clean.

After caring for his hygiene, he had reviewed the note of the night before. It was a simple but adequate note he had decided. He had more to say, of course, but wanted to say it in person. He had given the letter, wrapped in a white ribbon with his father's name on it, to Embrey, who had given it another of the Laifell clergy.

Off to an osprey, he had thought.

It would fly to Overmoor from the Leviathan, he had learned, and land at the binary of Ulmaith and Iroin. The followers of the gods of knowledge and invention acted as, among other things, couriers between the cities. The temple to Iroin and Ulmaith in Overmoor was impressive. Ilfair had seen the imposing structure before, an iron obelisk surrounded by a ring of white cylindrical buildings. It sat

atop a hill in the center of Overmoor, which acted as a major hub of
activity in the city of Overmoor. The Circle of Eights it was called. It
was led by the Thirteen, priests of Ulmaith and Iroin. It was a bit like
Laifell and Mercial in Winters Haven, Ilfair had come to understand.

Embrey had returned then, from the letter exchange, and they
had partaken in some food together. It was still early in the
morning when they had finished their meal. Embrey then had
escorted him to Halloch's office. It was what he had learned there
that filled his thoughts as he walked down the lane behind them.

Evidently, Elder Graywater had learned that the symbols on
Ilfair's arm could be translated by someone called the Athenomancer on an island two days away by ship. So, here he was again,
frustratingly on his way to somewhere else to meet someone else
with the promise of answers.

But at least he was not alone. While he was a little disappointed that Halloch had not translated the symbols, he was trying
to focus on the positives. First of all, no one had noticed the marks
on his fingertips. Embrey had not asked more about his eyes. He
had not needed to reveal anything about his visits from Abby. And
he was going to be accompanied to the island by Embrey.

He liked and trusted her and, while he tended to prefer to keep
to himself, he was glad to have some company, having been almost
entirely alone for the last few weeks. And now that he was in a less
predictable scenario compared to his life in Fayrest, he found it was
an advantage to not have to rely entirely on his own devices to
solve every problem.

He looked up from his leaf-shuffling reverie to notice his
surroundings. As when he had come close to the cliff edge during
his task with Embrey the day prior, he noticed the buildings here
were larger and more widely spaced. The difference was the area
here was bustling with activity and smelled of, not surprisingly,
dead sea life. Heavy lumber and fish were being unloaded from

boats, both large and small, by men and women in large and colorful heavy coats to protect against the wet cold.

He saw the port proper was within a few hundred feet. He had never been on the ocean before and now that it was imminent, he felt a bit of eel-invoking trepidation.

As though he could feel an unspoken uneasiness radiating from Ilfair, Halloch turned and regarded him with a smile and put a hand to Ilfair's shoulder.

As they continued walking, Halloch spoke. "That's our ship there," Halloch pointed off to the right. "The Orca."

There were eight long piers. At the end of the shortest of the eight, farthest to the north to his right, was the boat to which Halloch referred. It was one of the smaller boats, but it looked sturdy.

Halloch continued, "The Orca is a whaling boat, which is where it gets its name. Its captain, Jona Gaffspell, is pretty well known, almost famous in his own way. He's quite the whaler. Less well known is that the Aelinth temple has used the Gaffspell family for generations to transport goods regularly to the Athenomancers. Or, at least, somewhat regularly. Actually, I don't know how often they do it, if I'm honest. But they do, I've been told. As I said, that bit is not widely circulated or known, so I would ask that you not go spreading that around."

Ilfair nodded, as it was clear to him that he was not talking to Embrey.

"Regardless, the Gaffspell family is respected... and trusted," Ilfair felt Halloch had added the last bit to try to ease his mind. It worked somewhat.

Ilfair didn't speak, just gave an uneasy smile and another nod. Halloch and Embrey both put a hand on each of Ilfair's shoulders, one of hearty encouragement from Halloch and one of gentle concern from Embrey. They both helped, but the positive emotions they brought forth caused the black eels to stir with annoyance. Ilfair frowned.

They dodged the throng of humanity working in front of the docks. Once they made it to the dock and were walking its narrow wooden length toward the boat, they could see the boat and crew more clearly. Two men were working the deck of the boat in preparation for departure, Ilfair guessed, as he really had no clue what was involved in such an endeavor. A large man stood on the pier, directing the two ship hands.

He turned and, seeing Halloch, raised his right hand and called out, "Halloch! Well met!"

Halloch called back, "You as well, Captain Gaffspell."

Halloch turned to Ilfair and whispered, "Some of the ship hands down here call him Jona the Whale. But I don't recommend you do so. He's a sweet man, but with a sailor's temper and a large man's strength," he winked and smiled.

Embrey laughed and said, "Elder, don't be cruel!"

Ilfair couldn't suppress a smile. He had to admit he liked Halloch Graywater. He understood why Embrey felt so privileged to be in the shadow of his tutelage.

The captain was massive, *The Whale indeed*, he thought. Jona was dressed entirely in black with a crimson cloak that flapped in the breeze. The insignia of the boat, an Orca, was emblazoned on his chest. He held a red handled gaff in his left hand, the gaff head was dark and pointed to the sky.

The man had short sandy brown hair and a curly red beard with no mustache. He had boyish features, and his skin was smooth and slightly freckled across the nose.

They arrived at the boat. "Captain Gaffspell... Jona. It's good to see you again. I trust Lady Starscribe told you we were coming," it looked to Ilfair as though that was indeed the case. The pleasantry was followed by Jona and Halloch grasping each other's forearms in a masculine greeting common on the docks.

"Aye, she did. And tell me she did that my cargo should be these two young ones?" His statement was made with a questioning tone and a big smile. His voice was higher than Ilfair had expected, and friendlier too. He had expected a gruff salty character, but he really had no idea why. Jona was tall, although only slightly taller than he was wide. When he looked down at them his neck disappeared under his chin.

"Don't worry, young ones. I will keep ye safe. I've been doing this for a long time. And I am good at my job if I do say so myself!" He paused and puffed his chest out a bit. "Plus, if we sink, ye can always just ride back on me!" He laughed loudly at his own joke.

He boarded the Orca. The gangplank bowed under his weight as he moved to the dock. He moved his considerable self out of the way and gestured for Ilfair and Embrey to board.

Ilfair had been unsure about Jona at first, but the large man's easy demeanor and self-deprecation calmed him. *These are good people*, Ilfair thought, an easiness filling him.

CHAPTER 39

THE ORCA

The evolution of the Ashfallen on Erlan mirrored the Chaos War within Umbral. Within the moon, the order and chaos division of Ullumair and Feralzmoon fell to the union of the two in the form of the new gods. While on Erlan, during the same time, the Ashfallen of Aberron and Harrowfell, like the new gods, had grown weary of the loss of life born of constant conflict. They were beginning to understand the value of a balance of order and chaos. This was looked upon kindly by the new gods.
—from the Athenomancer archives

"Let us get ye on board you two. It's best if we leave soon. The seas are most dangerous near the rocky coast and are calmest early in the morning. We don't want that sunlight hitting us until we are a league or so out, do we now?" Jona shook his head and chuckled at the silly question.

Ilfair had no idea about any matter nautical, but nodded as if he did. Jona laughed knowingly. He was bow-legged and moved slowly, almost ponderously around them over to Halloch. As they boarded, Ilfair and Embrey could hear the two men talking but couldn't make out what they were saying.

Jona turned and called out to them, "Head ye below decks and find a bunk."

Ilfair and Embrey walked across the black wood deck under the crimson-and-white sail and found the stairwell down to the rowing galley. The ceiling was low down here and there were benches and oars with ports and windows. The oars lay on the benches and the oar ports were closed. The windows were covered with wavy glass. Toward the front of the galley was what Ilfair assumed were the captain's quarters, flanked by two other doors, which were likely the deckhand's quarters.

Beyond the benches were three more doors. One led to a privy and the remaining pair to quarters. These tiny rooms, each with a cot, were Embrey and Ilfair's destinations. They each dropped their packs in their respective rooms and hurried back up to the deck, the captain's deckhands passing them on the stairwell.

Emerging onto the deck, Ilfair and Embrey saw Jona walking the gangplank, it bowed under his weight. The ship shifted slightly when he stepped on deck. He turned and disconnected the gangplank. He groaned as he rose back up to stand. He reached his gaff out and used it to push the boat away from the dock.

Halloch stood on the dock and waved as they drifted away, his hair and coat rippling in the ocean wind. "Farewell, you two."

Embrey called back, "We will see you soon."

Jona added a simple, "Aye. Indeed. Don't ye worry, Halloch!"

Ilfair was quiet.

Once the boat was clear of the dock, the oars emerged from the side of the boat and hastened the boat out to sea. Ilfair had seen Winters Haven from the north a few days before. Now he was seeing it from the west, from the sea. It was a remarkable city from both vantage points; the sheer cliffs, the three waterfalls plummeting over the cliffs, the black rock filters. As they got further away, the Leviathan Temple, Kindrid's cube, the Aelinth Tower, and some of the Laifell Oakgaards and Oakhaven Temple came into view.

Ilfair watched the sun come up behind Winters Haven. He remained quiet and watched the sun rise from the undulating deck. He turned and watched Jona work. Embrey had returned below decks, so it was just him and Jona. Occasionally, Jona would make eye contact with Ilfair between barking orders to the rowers below him. Ilfair turned away to look out to sea to avoid feeling awkward. Unfortunately, he found the ensuing silence no less awkward.

What was more, Ilfair felt worse than useless and was sure he would only be in the way. His element was on the earth, and they were undoubtedly not on the earth.

He spoke to calm his feelings and break the awkwardness, loud enough to be heard over the sea, "So, it's two days to the Athenomancer?"

"Aye. It is. Just a day beyond and slightly north of the lumbering outpost on the Hearken Isles. We will be able to see it from the ship tomorrow, early," Jona responded in his lilting voice.

"Oh," Ilfair said. He couldn't think of anything else to say.

Embrey emerged from below and came over to Ilfair, "Are you ok?" she asked. Ilfair guessed that she could hear the awkwardness from below.

"I am. Just tired. I'm not used to talking so much," he smiled a grimacing smile.

"Aye, I know the feeling," Jona replied as he continued his duties.

The coastline was vanishing, so there wasn't much to see but water in all directions now.

"I think I will head below deck. Is that okay, Captain Jona?" Ilfair asked, not sure if he needed to ask or not.

"Of course, lad. Grab some bread from my cabin. And some water. Good to keep something in your belly. Helps with the seasickness," he said over his shoulder.

He did as he was asked, nodding to Embrey and Jona as he went below deck. He found the food and water in the captain's cabin. The captain had a board mounted to the wall behind his desk. The board displayed various whale teeth with the type of creature written in elaborate script below. The desk had various navigation tools and maps laid out across its surface.

He inspected the implements for a moment but soon hastened his way out of the room. He knew the deckhands had seen him enter the room and he did not want to be rude by staying too long.

He found his way to his room, passing the deckhands who were rowing in silence, save the sounds of their exertion. He noticed that only two of the three hands were rowing. He guessed that they must take turns. It would be two days to row to the island, he now knew, and they would need rest. He guessed one of them must be in their quarters resting. The sails could not be used as they rowed against the wind, which blew directly in their face, coming out of the cold reaches of the northwest. He sat on his cot and just looked out the window and thought. He could hear the muffled voices and footfalls from Jona and Embrey on the deck above.

He gnawed on the bread and pulled some liquid from the waterskin. He nodded off. He must have slept for hours, for when he woke, he saw the sun was nearly set in the northwest, its orange mass slowly and beautifully sinking into the Moonsong Sea.

He was happy to be alone, so he stayed in his room. Eventually, he heard Embrey come downstairs. He could see her shadow creep under his door as if she meant to knock. But she turned and entered her small cabin.

He waited a little bit and then very quietly left his room to go above to sit on the deck. He wanted to continue to avoid conversation. He could hear Jona and one of the shipmates talking in one of the cabins as he approached the stairs. They must have come down from the deck. The deck would be empty then.

Perfect, he thought. He went up the stairs and out onto the deck and sat near the front of the boat, leaning his back against the railing.

He looked up at Umbral, the moon, and the stars, half fearing the moon would crack open again and spill out some thin black screaming god of madness. But it didn't. He sighed and shook his head.

It was cold and the north-westerly wind was biting. He pulled the sliipmare cloak about himself and sat cross-legged, staring up. He sat there for many hours. He thought of the dead priest he had taken the cloak from. He prayed a thanks to Oever, the god of the dead, for the gift of the cloak from the long-dead man. He absently made the spiral gesture over his heart as a part of the prayer. *The spiral*, Ilfair thought, *it's everywhere: the symbol to Illinir, the gesture to Oever, the shape of Abby's tower, the breathing colors on the spiralhammer, and who knows what else*. His father had said that it came down from the ancient gods. *But why?* he thought.

He sighed. He knew he could not sleep, so he thought to just try to enjoy the view and have the cold wind help keep him alert. He was very preoccupied with the imminent meeting with the Athenomancer, and he had no interest in dreaming tonight. His mind was a flooded mess.

In that moment, since it looked like he would have hours of solitude, the idea of intentionally evoking the black eels into his thoughts occurred to him. He hadn't had a chance to practice his isolation training since arriving in Winters Haven. The separation exercises he had practiced on the walk to the city had helped and he wanted—no, needed—to continue them.

He allowed the flooded mess of his mind to deteriorate to a more anxious state and, predictably, the Leechkin eagerly stirred. Again, he held the symbol of the god Faid to his chest and closed his eyes.

The last time he had tried this, on the hills leading to Winters Haven, he had imagined the shadows of an obelisk hiding the

Leechkin from his sight. He had used the obelisk and shadow in reverence to the god Faid; it was, after all, the god's holy symbol.

This time, in addition to the shadows of the obelisk, Ilfair imagined a large rift, like the one he had awoken at the bottom of, opening up under the black writhing eels. The whispers from the eels raised to more cacophonous protest as they slid down into the rift. For a moment the noises from them grew more distant. But eventually they just clawed up the sides of the rift, each crawling over the other to escape the rift and shadows.

Ilfair opened his eyes, watering. *Well, that worked better,* he thought. But it wasn't quite enough to keep the Leechkin trapped, separated from his conscious thoughts. He breathed deeply for many moments, eventually calming the whispering, writhing eels.

As he calmed, he watched the moon slowly move across the sky. He released the symbol to Faid from his grip and allowed it to dangle. *Useless thing,* he thought, but quickly purged such blasphemy from his head, fearing the Aberithic thoughts might find a permanent home there, within such malignant nihilism.

Many hours passed. He guessed it was just shy of midnight. Jona emerged onto the deck, which startled him. He wondered if he had perhaps nodded off, as he should not have been startled. Jona nodded to Ilfair.

"Good morning, young man," he laughed. He seemed as awake as he had when they met. "Well, morning by the time anyway... beautiful night," he added somewhat ironically. He laughed for some reason that Ilfair didn't quite understand. There wasn't anything particularly funny about what he had said. But it was a friendly laugh and pleasant to hear.

"It is. Aye," Ilfair replied, lying and trying to mimic the phrasing he guessed Jona would have used. He was good at mimicking. He had been doing it his whole life. It was a good way to pass as normal during an Aberithic attack on his mind.

"The Hearken Isles. And a logging ship," Jona said and indicated the direction with a nod of his head.

Ilfair turned and looked west out to sea. By the light of the moon and stars, he could see the northern tip of the Hearken Isles and a bobbing white dot, which must have been the ship.

"We're making good progress," he added. "The rowers are strong. We'll be there before high sun tomorrow."

"Oh. That is good," Ilfair said without looking at Jona. He was happy that they would be there soon.

"Bit nervous, are ye?" Jona asked.

"Yes. A bit," Ilfair replied simply, dropping the mimicry.

"Does ye know why they are called the Hearken Isles?" Jona asked.

Ilfair shook his head. He also did not particularly care at the moment, but he appreciated Jona's efforts to distract him. So he turned to regard Jona, a gesture which he hoped would invite the story.

"The legend goes that the early Ashfallen of Winters Haven were in need of lumber in the long years of the Leechkin Wars. Going east into the foothills of the Godskeeps nearer the Sliipmoors for wood was unwise, to say the least. Leechkin burnings and attacks, aye? And what's more, there weren't much to be had besides, eh? At least not near to Winters Haven, and they needed much lumber... for walls and homes, aye?"

He paused to see if Ilfair was still paying attention. Satisfied that he was, Jona continued.

"Anyway, one of my ancestors, I am most proud to say, Sebastian Gaffspell, had a vision of an island bristling with forests. Long story short, he set out on a small boat with a small crew just like this. He mapped the location and returned with a boat full of lumber he and his hands had cut down with their own axes. Elder Sebastian had left a crazy zealot on a useless, if not deadly, journey and returned a hero. A hero, I say. Aye, a hero," Jona puffed with genuine pride. Ilfair wondered how many times he had told this story. Many, he guessed.

"Elder Seb said the vision had come to him from Hearken, the god of harmony. So, they naturally became known as the Hearken Isles. Those isles saved Winters Haven and many lives in the Leechkin Wars," he became somber at that last statement.

Jona brightened back up quickly, though, irrepressibly. *Ebullient as ever*, Ilfair thought.

He added, "And would ye believe this is the very ship he used? Ye sit on a legendary craft my boy! What do ye think about that tale, eh?"

"Most impressive," his tone may not have adequately conveyed it, but Ilfair was impressed, truly. "Very," he added trying to correct the tone to match his true feelings. He even looked down at the ship and touched the deck, imagining what his captain's ancestors must have felt at the time. But he struggled to muster sincerity over his anxiety, try is he did.

"Look, son, I know ye be worried. That's understandable. But Ao'faer is a good man. It'll be ok... if I had to guess anyway," Jona said.

The man's frank honesty lent more credibility to his encouragement. Ilfair appreciated the effort.

"Oh," Ilfair said again, defeat in his tone.

Jona sighed compassionately.

They sat the rest of the morning together in silence, with the moon and the cold wind waning as dawn came.

CHAPTER 40

THE KINDLEDCREST ISLES

*In the Ashfallen armistice of the ensuing years, for reasons unknown, the
silent gods, Aurum and Umbral, moved in the heavens. Aurum grew
more distant in the sky and so Erlan grew colder and the Elderime
Glacier advanced slowly south. Chasing the life from Aberron and
Nihilin. Umbral too did move in the night sky, growing closer to Erlan,
and the Moonsong Sea rose. Harrowfell and the Spirelight emptied in
response.*
—from the Athenomancer archives

A o'faer watched the ship approach from the east, some fifty
miles out. The vessel's broad and narrow features were
backlit by the rising sun. Ao'faer had taken the Mantle of
the Everburning Sphere into his body from the previous Athenomancer over two hundred years ago and he couldn't recall any
instance of the Orca making the trip to the Atheneum Tower out of
cycle.

In fact, the Orca had become somewhat unreliable over the last
few decades, often missing its regular trips. There was always some
reason or other given for not showing up, but it made Ao'faer feel
like he was being forgotten, slowly. Nonetheless, it did not take

much of his considerable intellect and wisdom to glean that something was afoot. Admittedly, his famously intense curiosity was piqued.

He stood from his desk and moved over to one of the many windows on the top floor of the Atheneum Tower. He was some hundreds of feet over the water and, in the foreground to the left and right, he could also see the other Kindledcrest Isles. Some quite large in the near space and others the size of a small pebble in the distance.

The sacred Kindledcrest Isles were each small, his being the largest and at that only a few miles across. They were arrayed in an almost perfect circle. A white column of natural volcanic rock formed a small cylindrical hillock with vertical rock striations at the center of each. Each was a few hundred feet tall.

Centuries ago, a Spirelight Tower, flame alight, had crowned each rock column. An homage to the long-forgotten, save to a few like Ao'faer Lightwarden, god Ullumair. The Mythals claimed the islands sacred, a mortal representation of Ullumair's flaming crown cresting the water to walk the surface of Erlan.

The ancient Mythals of Harrowfell had built towers on the isles and, on the largest and highest northernmost isle, they had built the Atheneum Tower, whose flame still burned and whose Athenomancer still protected its ancient lore. Of the few who remembered such things, fewer still put much stock in that lore, as Ullumair had gone silent centuries ago. But the tradition of the Athenomancer was bound to honor the god, even if the faith and the power of Ullumair were now split among the lesser deities that had come afterward.

Ao'faer put his hand to his chest. His fingers absently traced out symbols over his cloak as he looked out at the ruins of the now-extinguished Spirelights. He sighed. He wondered what the splendor of Ullumair and the Spirelights had been like. The other towers had fallen to ruin long before he had taken on the mantle of

Athenomancer. He knew all about it, of course, but to see it? It must have been glorious.

It moved him to prayer, the thought of it. The priesthood of Aelinth, the goddess of light and knowledge, had adopted the Atheneum Tower and thus the mantle of the Athenomancer over an age ago. The priests of Aelinth prayed to their god, meditated really, in the morning to the sun and in the evening to the moon. Though they did not worship them, they paid homage to the Silent Gods of light, the moon Umbral and the sun Aurum whose radiance Aelinth guided.

Ao'faer slowly ascended the spiral staircase about the whale oil reservoir that fed the flaming glass sphere atop the Atheneum Tower. He had climbed this staircase thousands of times. And, though he still managed it with ease, given youthful vigor by the mantle he wore, the repetition of it made him feel old.

"You were old over a century ago. Hmph," he said, chuckling to himself. He noticed that he had talked to himself more and more as the decades advanced. Isolation had a way of doing that to a man.

He stepped out atop the tower. It was an invigorating feeling. The wind off the sea whipped his white robe with aggressive cold, revealing amber colored clothing underneath. The side of his face and body that faced the flame was hot with the heat that radiated through the glass. Any of the grogginess of morning was quickly removed. He smiled.

He seated himself with the flame to his back and faced the approaching ship and sunrise. He closed his eyes and let his senses open up to the rawness of the deep ocean's morning. He could smell the salt, he could taste the burning whale oil, he could feel the cold wet air raise the flesh on his neck, and he could see Aurum's sunlight through his closed eyelids.

He always began his meditative prayer with his thoughts concentrated on the deep of the ocean. As in the ancient ways of Ullumair, his spirit manifested within a great whale. His soul rose from his body then rapidly dove down the length of the tower. It sped across the ground, hovering just above the surface, and went out to sea. There it dove down, without disturbing the water, deep into the sea. In the black of the fathomless ocean, where only the tiny bioluminescent life provided any light, his essence was drawn to the great beast. His lifeforce merged with the great blue whale, the holiest living creature on the whole of Erlan.

Slowly they rose from the deep, the black giving way to gray. The sky came into view before he breached the surface into the brilliance of the light of Aelinth.

Ao'faer, from within the whale, felt the light wash over him. Aelinth's light, no matter its origin, was holy to Ao'faer: the light of the sun, the light reflected from the moon, the light of the flame, it mattered not. He and at least three Athenomancers prior to him had been of the priesthood of Aelinth, having left active prayer to Ullumair behind. But they, and he, had taken on the Mantle of the Everflame, and thus all the knowledge of all previous Athenomancers were theirs. And so, while he was devoted to Aelinth, there was part of him, perhaps a larger part than he would admit, who longed for the glory of Ullumair. The new gods were glorious to be sure, but they were but a component of the glory that was Ullumair.

This happened to Ao'faer often, these misaligned thoughts. He wondered if the prior Athenomancers had such thoughts. Alas, he could never know, so he refocused on his meditation.

Ao'faer's spirit rose further, cresting the surface. The bulk of the whale then came crashing back down, diving back into the cold, deep ocean. On the top of the tower, Ao'faer still sat with his eyes closed. Two of the lights of Aelinth bathed him, burning flame from behind him and rising before him.

With his eyes closed, he saw through the mind of his spirit, which rose high into the sky, having departed the body of the whale. The creature, which his spirit had just left, disappeared under the waves. He could see the tower to his right and the Orca in the distance beyond the other Kindledcrest Isles.

The sun was now above the Orca at its early morning position. Ao'faer spread his arms on the tower. This allowed his spirit to be filled by the light of the sun and flame, the essence of Aelinth. His spirit felt another source of illumination then, albeit just a pinprick, on the deck of the Orca.

He floated out over the Orca and saw the source. In his spirit form, all life appeared radiant to him, even the wood of the ship had a dull glow. But from the form of a small young man, who stood hunched over on the deck of the Orca, a point of brilliant light radiated, seemingly from his forearm.

What's more, mottled within the young man's normal light was a swirling blackness, something alien within him. On top of the tower, Ao'faer opened his eyes.

"Most curious. This I have not seen before," he said to himself, his voice carried off by the strong ocean squalls.

FROM THE DECK, Ilfair could feel the sun on his back, a welcome warmth against the cold sea. It felt warmer and more calming than he had expected. It almost felt like a large hand on his back. *Curious*, he thought.

"There they are," said Jona. "The Kindledcrest Isles."

Ilfair could see the isles. Eight of them, small in size compared to the Hearken Isles he had seen earlier. Each had a tapered column of white rock protruding from the center, taking up much of the surface of each isle. The columns appeared to be natural, but atop each was a tower, or at least the ruins of one, clearly manmade, like a lighthouse. He could imagine all of the lighthouses lit and could see the origin of the name as the towers and white columns looked like the tines of a crown cresting the water's surface. It reminded him of the top of the Leviathan Temple in Winters Haven. Disturbingly, and undeniably, no matter how hard he tried to put it out of his mind, it also reminded him of Abby's tower.

"That one is our destination," Jona said, gesturing. Ilfair turned around to see him pointing. He followed Jona's direction to the most distant of the isles, the tower atop its white column lit by a massive surging and breathing flame. It was the only one fully intact and the only one lit. The tower was intimidating, and he shivered from an appropriately timed cold, wet wind.

Ilfair felt mild panic and flickering black images whispering within himself.

"The Athenomancer lives there?" he asked, hoping that hearing the answer would help him maintain his calm. It worked... a little.

"Aye. Of course," Jona said with a bit of questioning in his tone, as if to say, "*Who else?*"

Hearing Jona say out loud that the Athenomancer, and not Abby, was the tenant of the tower helped a little. Embrey surprised him with a hand on his shoulder. She spoke.

"Good morning," she said simply. "How are you feeling?"

Hearing her voice helped, calming him further. Her presence had surprised him, but there was no doubt he welcomed it. The simplest things from her had an earnestness in them that always calmed him.

"Um... okay," he said finally.

"We will be there in an hour or thereabouts, eh?" Jona said a knowing smile on his face as he regarded them each in turn.

"Good," Embrey and Ilfair said at the same time with different intentions and tone. Embrey was eager to see the holy site and person. Ilfair had heard her say so to Halloch on the walk to the Orca back in Winters Haven. Ilfair was simply anxious.

The three of them stood there for many moments, regarding their destination. Their reverie was broken by Jona bellowing "Oars, boys!" as they approached the nearest isle. Two of the deckhands navigated about the nearest island. Normally Ilfair would have felt uncomfortable allowing all the work to be done by others, as he had felt at Ashhaven. But he was anxious and preoccupied and still felt completely out of his element on the water. Work to occupy his thoughts would surely have helped, but he was absolutely certain that he would just be in the way. Even Embrey, who he guessed had been on the water before, stayed out of the way.

So Ilfair tried to close his eyes to calm himself, but he could not. He wanted to see the isle, to anticipate the exact instant of their arrival, and to be alert to anything that he might deem alarming.

Embrey, sensing his tension, squeezed his shoulder and leaned in. She spoke so that only he could hear.

"It will be okay," she said, "Master Lightwarden is a pure soul. You can trust him. You will see."

"Thank you. That does help... a little," he looked at her and tried to smile. But it was a weak smile. She smiled back and then they both turned and watched quietly as the craft glided deftly to its destination, guided by the oarsmen and Jona's direction.

Within the hour the Orca passed the second of the Kindledcrest Isles. Off to the starboard side the white column of the isle was more imposing than Ilfair would have guessed from his initial view of it. The Orca passed through the column's shadow, cast by the midday sun riding low above the northern horizon. Ilfair stared up at its bulk, craning his neck to see the top of the column. The ruins of the old tower perched atop the column looked like a broken tooth, hollowed out by time and neglect.

He stared at the column for many minutes. When he redirected his gaze forward, he realized they were now quite close to their destination, the northernmost isle. They approached their destination isle just after high sun, exactly as Jona had predicted. The Atheneum Tower awaited their arrival.

CHAPTER 41

ATHENEUM ISLE

The Ashfallen headed south, to the warmth and high ground beyond the Godskeeps. It was during this migration that the ancient gods Ullumair and Feralzmoon, who had grown quieter over the years, consumed by their Chaos War, went completely silent. Prayers to the ancient gods within the moon were replaced by prayers to the Godskeep Mountains, which marked the boundary between the ancient world and the new.
—from the Athenomancer archives

I lfair stood stiffly on the swaying deck as the Orca made its way toward the northernmost of the Kindledcrest Isles. The Atheneum Tower rose from the white stone that erupted from the isle's center. The spire eclipsed the sun and the boat moved in its shadow. The sleek vessel forced its way through the waves and Ilfair shivered as the wind bore more sea spray over the hull. It was suddenly much colder without Aurum's warmth.

In that moment, perhaps brought on by the chill he felt, Ilfair suddenly felt self-conscious, worried, and scared. He was somehow keenly aware that he was the cause of all of this. The Leechkin in his head seemed to writhe in delight on the cocktail of emotion. The way that he was being treated, or rather transported, like some kind of sick person, brought to his mind a memory from his childhood.

He closed his eyes against the sea spray and wrapped his cloak tightly about himself as he recollected the events. The process of pulling the event through the Leechkin was challenging, but eventually he managed a coherent recollection.

He had visited Overmoor with his father, who was to sell some of his leatherworks there. He had been half the age he was now. They'd stood on the Highmoor Road just outside of Overmoor, his father then a head taller than Ilfair had been.

THE OVERMOOR LANCERS guarded the only break in the iron gate that surrounded the city. They sat atop their sliipmares. The coats of the mares and their leather armor and clothing were a mottled gray and moss green, a camouflage in the Sliipmoors. The tips of their lances glowed with the same magic as the Erlanlights that topped every spire of the gate.

The lights glowed in the heavy fog that had descended as the day had neared its end, as it almost always did. The city beyond the gates lay atop a black rocky ridge. Off to their right in the distance, atop the sloping crest, they could see an iron obelisk surrounded by a collection of shorter white cylindrical buildings.

"What is that?" Ilfair asked, looking up to his father and pointing.

"That is the temple to Iroin, the iron-gray one. The white ones are the temples to Ulmaith. The priests of those temples, the Circle of Eights... they run Overmoor from the temples," his father said, looking down to Ilfair.

"Wow," Ilfair replied, wide eyed.

"Yeah," his father said somewhat dismissively, "C'mon son, they are waving us in."

Ilfair followed his father in through the gate, but his gaze did not leave the temples as they made their way into the city.

The road rose into the city. To their right terraced agricultural land dotted with a few farmsteads led up to the temples. To their left were the homes of the Overmoorians, tightly packed with smoke rising from many chimneys. Little lights were beginning to light within as the day darkened.

"With me, son," his father said, pulling him off the road just before they reached the intersection in the thoroughfare, which permitted one to head to the right up to the temple or to the left down into the city. A wagon rounded the corner, coming uphill out of the homes. It was covered by a canopy dotted with silvers, blues, and reds and pulled by two tall lean black horses.

Again, Ilfair was awestruck. There was something about the caravan and horse and driver that struck him as worthy of reverence. He stared as the wagon moved by. The black-clad driver of the wagon looked down at Ilfair. He was lean and dusky skinned. He had a crescent moon tattoo under his right eye. He wore a white mask of spiraling knotwork that covered the lower half of his face.

"What is *that*?" Ilfair asked, looking up at his father.

"That is an alienist-priest of Faid," his father said somberly. This was the first Ilfair had heard of such a thing. Not long after this experience Ilfair procured his symbol to Faid.

"But why are *they* here?"

"Looks like someone needs their, um, help. Someone's mind is sick," His father spoke more haltingly than usual, pausing to find the most sensitive words he could.

"But..."

"Shh," his father demanded.

Just at that moment the wagon passed them and Ilfair saw a young girl looking out. Their eyes met. The look on the child's face was a combination of fear and exhaustion.

He imagined that was exactly how he looked now. The Orca jerked suddenly and Ilfair had to adjust quickly to keep his balance. The act brought him out of his reverie. *Not seasick, but certainly no sea legs,* Ilfair thought, smirking.

He could see the dock of the Atheneum Isle clearly now from atop the Orca. A figure stood on the deck awaiting their arrival. He cut a sharp contrast in his amber robe against the massive white column.

Ilfair heard the oars being drawn in and turned to see Jona manning a paddle to direct the Orca smoothly toward the dock. The hull of the ship dragged against the sand of the beach and one of the ship hands sprung from the deck of the Orca to the pier, rope in hand. He pulled the light but sturdy ship to the side of the dock and tied it off on a post.

Ilfair stood on the Orca as it undulated on the waves. He intently regarded the man who stood on the shore, just off the deck. His heavy amber robe rippled in the wind, revealing his ornate white clothing underneath, lined with runes and symbols. He clasped a staff in both hands, its end planted in the wet sand. Ripples of water lapped at the staff and the man's thin leather boots.

The staff he held had a tentacle spiraled about its length. The tentacle was multi-hued, prismatic like that of the inside of an abalone shell. The tentacle wrapped about an elliptical glass bauble at the top, and a flame flickered inside. The man's face and bearing reminded him somewhat of Halloch, for he was neither a small nor frail man. He was surely older than Halloch, that much showed clearly, but he did not stand as one who needed a staff to lean upon.

The man, this Athenomancer, called out over the noise of the wind and sea, "Well met, dearest Jona! It's been too long. Welcome back!" there was a hint of sadness, or perhaps loneliness, in his exclamations.

Jona nimbly—for his size at least—hopped to the dock, its boards flexing beneath his bulk. He strode with purpose toward the Athenomancer, a huge grin on his sparsely haired face.

"Aye! Ye as well, Ao'faer," Jona said as he grasped the extended forearm of the Athenomancer. They each rested their other hands on the opposite shoulder, a common physical greeting of men in Ilfair's experience, especially strong men.

They relaxed their embrace. "Gods, if ye don't bear warmth in this bitter wind, Ao'faer. That Everburning Mantle still doing the trick I see," Jona's right hand slid down to over Ao'faer's heart.

"Ever so, dearest Jona. Until my time comes," he smiled and winked at Jona. "So, what brings you? Out of cycle, that is."

Jona chuckled. "I know ye well enough to know ye already be knowing that."

"I do at that. Just trying to be polite," Ao'faer chuckled and he turned to regard Ilfair, who was now standing on the dock. Ilfair, flanked by Embrey, looked down to the deck.

The two men turned and walked toward them. "We brought more besides the lad. Extra stores for ye... since we were coming anyway," Jona said, turning to talk to Ao'faer as they approached. Ilfair felt it was intended to distract from him, to some use at that.

"Couldn't hurt, eh?" Jona added.

"No indeed, and I thank you for it," he smiled. "But it's this slight lad, and the lass as well, actually, that I need to attend to I would guess."

"Aye. And at the behest of Elder Greywater and Lady Starscribe at that," Jona said, reverence in his tone.

Ao'faer stood over Ilfair, half a head taller. He reached down and grabbed Ilfair's right arm and pushed back the sleeve of his shirt, revealing the mark. Ao'faer seemed a bit brusque to Ilfair, but maybe some of the niceties had been lost living alone for so long.

As the old man eyed the mark, Ilfair could feel the warmth that Jona spoke of. It was a physical heat that simply radiated from the man.

Ao'faer looked up from the symbols and met Ilfair's gaze. Ao'faer grimaced and furrowed his brow.

"Let's get out of this cold, shall we?" he looked past Ilfair to Embrey when he said this. "Some tea? Warm bread?"

"Oh, yes. That sounds nice in fact, very nice," Embrey replied, somewhat surprised to have been addressed.

"Come then... with me," he added before turning and walking away.

Jona gestured with his eyes and a slight nod for them to follow. "We will be here when ye both are ready to leave," Jona explained. Ilfair and Embrey hesitated.

"Coming?" Ao'faer said, looking over his shoulder.

"Go on, now... eh?" Jona encouraged softly, only barely audible, quite uncharacteristically, reflecting some concern for them in his words.

The two trotted to catch up with the Athenomancer.

They followed a path through the low growing plants of the island, which led to stairs hewn into the massive white column at the center of the isle. The stairs meandered up the white wall of stone. Embrey and Ilfair fell behind the Athenomancer, who strode up the stairs without a break or word. There was a metal rail to hold onto and for good reason. The wind whipped aggressively at them, buffeting them with a bitter and salty vigor.

After many minutes, perhaps an hour, they crested the top of the column. There they saw the Atheneum Tower. Just as had been the case with Abby's Spirelight, a spiraling covered walkway led to the base of the tower. It continued up the length of the tower, which ended in twisting white fingers that gripped the glass covered light at the top. The covered walkway was fully intact here, unlike on the mainland, and when the wind blew past the entryway it emitted a deep resonant barely audible hum. Walking through the tunnel Ilfair could feel as much as hear the hum.

"Do you feel that?" Ilfair whispered to Embrey.

"Yeah. It feels... good," she said, pausing to find the right word.

They walked through the tunnel, gradually gaining elevation until they reached the entry to the tower, marked by a wooden door of deep blue. Passing through the door, a glass spiral staircase awaited. Embrey let out an exhausted noise between breaths. And Ilfair did not disagree. His legs and lungs had just recovered from the column, only to be faced with more stairs.

Ao'faer chucked. "Come now... surely..." he had a glimmer to his gaze, and he didn't need to finish his sentence. He did pause though. Ilfair wondered if his incredible ageless energy was somehow connected to the warmth he radiated or the Mantle of the Everflame that Jona had mentioned. Ilfair took the opportunity to rest with silent gratitude.

He watched Ao'faer, who looked up. Ilfair and Embrey followed the Athenomancer's gaze to regard the murals that lined the height of the interior of the tower. Ilfair had seen something like it before in the Spirelight, but here the murals had not been defaced.

"Beautiful," Embrey said.

Murals spiraled up the white walls: gods and whales, flames and oceans, the sun and the moon. On one half was what must have been a god, crowned with a spiraling horn, standing upon black earth. The form wept under a dark moonlit sky. On the other side the same form stood, arms reaching to the sun, on a verdant land. The tip of the horned crown was alight with flame and the sea behind the deity was alive with breaching whales.

Chimes of glass and whale bone dangled from the bottom of the lowest floor of the tower above, some hundred feet up at least. They made gentle noises as the wind leaked through the drafty windows. This beauty had been marred in the Spirelight by time without a tending care and, more likely, the malice of Abby.

"Almost there, young ones," Ao'faer said as he started up the stairs again, his footfalls echoing in the expanse of the tower. Ilfair noticed the light that radiated from his footfalls, just as he had seen in the Spirelight.

Some minutes later they crested the lowest floor revealing a cylindrical room with barren wooden floors. The sweet smell of ambergris filled the room like in the caverns below the Spirelight. The walls were lined, top to bottom, with books or, in places, loose parchment spilling out onto the floor. The only space on the wall not filled by books was the occasional break for a window or sconce. Many of the sconces burned with what looked like whale oil, likely producing the pleasant odor, but not the unpleasant side effect of smoke.

There was a place to exit the stairwell, but they pressed on. The stairwell plunged upward through the center of the room. The next room was the same. As was the next and the next after that.

"What is all this?" Ilfair finally asked. He paused on the stairs, both to rest and to look more intently at the books.

Ao'faer looked down, the light from his staff casting long shadows on his face from his angular nose. "This is the largest collection of information in the entirety of the realm of Erlan. Collected for ages, it contains everything worth knowing. It is the divine knowledge. It is the heart, mind, and soul of the Atheneum Tower. And I know every word of every book here," with that he continued his way up. His tone had been more serious than it had been up to now.

They passed a few more of these levels, perhaps a dozen or more, Ilfair guessed, before entering Ao'faer's quarters.

CHAPTER 42

AN ATHENOMANCER'S ANSWERS

The displaced Ashfallen founded three cities south of the barrier formed by the Godskeep Mountains. Iilhi was founded first, in the eastern Alrasun Desert, by those who fled Aberron and the Nihilin Temple via the Umbervale Pass. Winters Haven was founded next by the Ashfallen who fled Harrowfell and the Spirelight along the coast of Moonsong Sea. The waypoint city of Overmoor was founded many years later.
—from the Athenomancer archives

B y contrast to the lower floors, Ao'faer's quarters had just a few shelves worth of books. Its wooden floors were less barren than the others with the expected living amenities: carpets, paintings, bedding, a few desks, and a stove. Then there were the unexpected items: a strange cylinder on the far side of the room and the oil reservoir for the light above. The vessel dominated the room and was encircled by a large desk with numerous chairs. The desk had a small break for access to a stairwell up to the top of the tower.

Another striking difference from the lower floors was that almost everywhere along the perimeter wall of the room was covered by glass windows, letting the mid-afternoon sun stream in brightly. And it was warmer than the other rooms, likely owing to the preponderance of windows and, of course, the flame above. It was draftier than the library levels, but the warmth of the flame above made up for the chill, wet wind.

It was a comfortable room, both in feel and look. And of course, there was the view. A glorious panorama of the sea and other isles; the scope of it—the tower and the sea—made Ilfair feel small.

"Sit. Please," Ao'faer gestured to the chairs nearest them, at the front part of the large circular desk, which was brightly lit by the sun moving low across the afternoon sky. The chairs were made of what looked like large ash tree stumps. The desk was a massive slab of something that looked like quartz. Runes and symbols were engraved everywhere over its surface. In fact, there were sigils everywhere in the room.

"Not that one," Ao'faer said to Embrey. "That one is mine," he grinned. "I'm a man of very old habits."

It was clear that the chair to which he referred was more worn. Embrey chose the chair next to it, leaving the worn chair between her and where Ilfair had chosen to sit. They both looked at each other, clearly wondering if this arrangement had been planned by their host.

"Here, as promised." Ao'faer had disappeared over toward the stove, which was now burning—or had always been, Ilfair could not recall—and had returned with a tray that he placed on the table. On it was some type of warm sweet bread and black tea.

"Eat. Drink," he sat in the chair between them. "And then, Ilfair, why don't you tell me why you are here? In your own words."

He looked at Ilfair and then Embrey, and then back to Ilfair.

"Don't you already know?" Ilfair asked plainly, hoping to avoid answering.

"Aye, I do. But I want to hear it from you," Ao'faer said. There was no hint of malice or sarcasm in his voice.

"Well, the simple answer I guess is that Elder Graywater and

Lady Starscribe think you can help me," Ilfair said, continuing to be obtuse. The climb had given him something physical to focus on, but the question had brought him back to reality quickly and not pleasantly. He felt something dislodge inside him and felt tears welling and a lump forming in his throat, and the unpleasant images began to spiral and murmur. Suddenly, more words burst forth.

"Something has happened to me. Something terrible, I think. Maybe, at least. I know where I am, but I am lost in every other way. I want to go home but I fear I cannot hide from this thing, whatever it is," he produced the underside of his right arm, shoving his sleeve up to his elbow. "And what's worse, this thing is but a part of what's wrong with me," he paused and looked up at Ao'faer.

Embrey looked on intently, concerned, but said nothing.

"I have seen much, young man. And I see your intentions. You are not as lost, or as bad off for that matter, as you might think. We will get you sorted. You will see." Ao'faer said cryptically.

The confusing nature of the response jarred Ilfair back into his mind and calmed his emotions. He nodded.

"Good. And what of you?" Ao'faer turned to Embrey.

"Halloch sent me with Ilfair, to help, and to bring these." Embrey produced the two documents that Halloch had found on the mainland tower of Aelinth.

"I see." Ao'faer took the book and the glass plate from Embrey. He regarded them each in turn briefly and set them on the table. The light from his staff, which was leant against the table, made the glass glow a warm amber. "Well, I do thank you for that, dear Embrey," he smiled and looked at her. "But I think there may be divine providence at play here. Your purpose will soon be revealed, Bearer of Young Life and Light."

Embrey said nothing, looking somewhat stunned.

Ao'faer turned back to Ilfair. They could not see, as Ao'faer could, the brilliant light behind the mark on Ilfair's arm.

"Fear not, young Ilfair, you have not been marked, but rather chosen. The light I see behind your symbols is nothing to fear."

"But what does that mean?" Ilfair asked, his tone heavy with exhaustion. This was more or less what Halloch had said, and while he was even more impressed with Ao'faer, he was frustrated with the continued vagueness of the information he was getting.

"It means you have a divine purpose. You have been chosen," turning and regarding Embrey, Ao'faer added, "As have you, dearest. Your presence here is not by chance, nor was your meeting."

Embrey looked surprised and inhaled to speak, but Ao'faer continued before she could.

"I can read your symbol plainly enough, so let me do so now, please," he looked at the symbol for many moments. Ilfair began to speak. "Stay silent," Ao'faer said curtly.

Ao'faer gasped and then, moments later, mumbled to himself, too low to understand but awe evident on his face. Fearful thoughts, along with the scratching of Leechkin, began to form in Ilfair's mind.

With a sigh, Ao'faer stood. He moved across the room and disappeared down the stairs. Embrey and Ilfair watched him go and then stared at each other, silently waiting and listening to the moving footfalls below.

"It will be okay, Ilfair," Embrey said quietly, she could evidently sense Ilfair's anxiety.

Ilfair looked at her and smiled in a way that said, *thank you, but you can't possibly know that.* Ao'faer returned a few minutes later with a few books under his arm, an intense look on his face.

"Let us start here," he opened one of the tomes and pointed to an engraving. "This is much like one of the images found in the more modern text on the moon, Umbral, that Halloch sent with you, Embrey."

"This engraving, like Halloch's, shows both the ancient and modern moon. Few remember, perhaps only I in fact, that the ancient moon was occupied by Ullumair, as a prison for himself and Feralzmoon and their Ullumyths and Aberiths. He cast them all high to protect us, his children, from the primal chaos of Feralzmoon; The Great Sacrifice of Ullumair. Or what we thought was the Great Sacrifice, it turns out. And for us to have nearly forgotten. So shameful," he grimaced and shook his head. It was unclear to whom he was speaking.

He continued. "This is why the Feraliths and the Mythals, the ancient followers of Feralzmoon and Ullumair, directed their prayers to the moon." He looked up to see that the two still followed. With that confirmation he continued. "Each prayed to their own god for their own reasons: the Feraliths in search of redemption for Feralzmoon, the Mythals to provide strength to Ullumair, their father. They did so for ages, to support their gods during the Chaos War that raged within the moon." He moved his finger over to the pockmarked moon.

"This persisted for ages. Then, rather suddenly, the ancient gods went silent. Around the same time, Aurum and Umbral moved in the sky, and the great Elderime Glacier and Moonsong Sea stirred, driving the Ashfallen south of the Godskeep Mountains. The new gods began to appear to the Ashfallen, emerging south of the Godskeeps, as if they had been waiting for them," he sighed and added, "But no one knows that for sure. Not even the line of Athenomancers."

He opened another book and pointed to a pantheon of deities, arrayed on either side of a great divide represented by a rift in the ground. One side of the rift was labeled Ullic, the other Feric. The gods Ilfair knew were represented there, some under the Ullic label, and some under the Feric. Some were nearer the rift and others farther away.

Ao'faer continued. "Anyway... everyone thought Ullumair and Feralzmoon dead, each killed by the other in the Chaos War. Alas, it appears it was not so. The symbols on your arm are a message from

Ullumair. They are proof that he has endured!" Ao'faer's brow and voice raised, and he looked and gestured toward the sea outside the tower, his faith impassioning him.

"Ullumair?" Ilfair interrupted. "But Abby said it was Feralz-moon's doing."

"Abby?" Embrey asked.

"That poor creature," Ao'faer said. "She was long ago completely corrupted by the essence of Feralzmoon, the Aberiths. She is naught but lies. It is truly a misfortune that it appears you crossed paths with her. More likely, she sought you out or lured you to her."

"You pity her. How? And how do you know who she is?" Anger was audible in Ilfair's words.

"Of course I know who she is, and how she came to be for that matter. It is my job to know. And of course I pity her. She was only a girl. And I pity you as well for being touched by her and the Aberiths. For Abby though, unlike you, only the Aberithic corruption really remains. By the way, you have forgotten to ask how I have known many things. But never mind that for now," he looked intently at Ilfair, seriousness radiating from his deep-set eyes.

"Now quiet yourselves again, both of you, and allow me to finish," he paused for effect.

"As I was saying, most thought the ancient gods were dead. But now, thanks to Ullumair's glory resplendent on your arm, we, or at least I, now know better. All this time he has continued his sacrifice for us. Holding Feralzmoon inside a spiraling shell of his very body. But now even that fails. Entropy cannot be held at bay for all time, not even by the glory of Ullumair," he stopped and looked in turn at each of them. "That is where you come in young Ilfair."

Ilfair started to speak, "I have more to say," Ao'faer interrupted. "Ullumair knows he will fail soon and if that happens Feralzmoon would be unleashed on the realm. Our new gods would be no match for his primal chaos. It would be the end." Ao'faer shook his head. It looked like tears were forming in his eyes. He closed them for a moment and brought his passion under control before continuing.

"Ullumair has a plan to save us from this doom. Again, it is the glory of his sacrifice. Instead of containing Feralzmoon, he means to absorb him, ending both himself and Feralzmoon and in the process create a new being. He means for this to happen at the new moon of the next spring, the Dawn of Life moon." He eyed Embrey with intent when he said this. "By that time, you two must have completed the task he has laid out for you."

Ilfair meant to speak again, and Ao'faer tried to stop him, but Ilfair would not be denied his question.

"But why me?"

"That is clear to me. Ullumair feels kindred to you. For you have lived your whole life containing the mortal variant of the divine chaos he has contained for ages," he touched Ilfair's shoulder. "Furthermore, your very essence, a spiral of life and Aberiths, is unique. It will be like a beacon to him. He will need to find you, in the end, among all the myriad life of Erlan. You will see," he said. He paused and added, "He and I are truly sorry you have had to live your life with the Aberithic infection."

"What?" Embrey said. "Why didn't you tell me, Ilfair? I could see something in your eyes. Is that why?"

"I'm sorry, Embrey. I was afraid. I still am. I have kept this a secret from everyone my whole life. Even my father. You two are the only ones who know," he paused, considering, "Well, and Abby. How could I tell anyone such a thing?"

"I understand Ilfair," Embrey said.

"Of course you do, dear one," Ao'faer smiled. "You are not alone anymore Ilfair. You needn't do this on your own. And the purity and strength of you to be able to contain this? Truly impressive and clearly the reason Ullumair has chosen you," Ao'faer grimaced.

"Surely someone else would be better suited for such a task?" Ilfair blurted.

"Do you mean to question, the father of the gods? I suggest not, young one," Ao'faer replied.

"But what about you? You are the Athenomancer for godssake, surely suggesting you do this would be no offense to the gods," Ilfair reasoned.

"And you are so powerful and knowledgeable. For mercy's sake, your name title means wielder of knowledge," Embrey added, seeming to agree by referring to the ancient meaning of the Athenomancer name.

"Such flattery. I thank you for that, but it was not me that Ullumair named. And, in any event, it cannot be me, child. Remember, Ilfair, you will be the beacon holding the vessel the nascent entity seeks. All will be clear later," Ao'faer replied.

"But why send me away from my home?" Ilfair asked further.

"At this I can only guess, but I believe that to be Feralzmoon's doing. You see this pattern of writing in these books?" he pointed to yet another book. "This is the Mythic script of Ullumair, it is written left to right, top to bottom. Now consider this book, this is the Feric script," he pointed to a black book coated in obsidian shards. "See it grouped in haphazard spirals? I think Feralzmoon tried to destroy you and the message, taking advantage of the distraction when Ullumair redirected some of his energy to contact you. I think you were saved by Ullumair. Message scrambled, your body dislocated, but still legible, at least to me... and you're still alive."

He looked at them both and, seeing understanding on their faces, paused. Ilfair remembered seeing the same spiraled groupings in some of the books in the temple back at the glacier. Some of the pieces were beginning to fall into place in his mind.

"What does he have to do?" Embrey asked.

"Ilfair must carry a vessel to the Asiil Temple in Iilhi to contain the child of the union of the ancient gods, Feralzmoon and Ullumair. Mnemylith is to be its name. The name reflecting deference to the Ferric Aberiths and the Ullic Ullumyths and in reverence to its purpose—memory. It shall be neither man nor woman; mortal nor god; chaos nor order. It shall be an immortal vessel of unbiased knowledge, a chronicler of knowledge, a living memory of all things and all times. This child will bring forth all the knowledge of the ancients to the realms and will mark the beginning of an Age of Knowledge. Without this continuity of knowledge, we will end ourselves as the ancient truths are forgotten and erode all we have built. Rather than a ravenous devourer in the form of Feralzmoon, it would be the slow erosion of lost knowledge. But a death of all we have built all the same."

"What vessel? I can't do this! I don't even know the way to Iilhi!" Ilfair said tensely, his anxiety growing, eels stirring and whispering.

"Calm yourself, Ilfair," Ao'faer raised his hands.

Embrey crossed the distance between them and touched his shoulder.

"I will not calm myself! How could I have something to do with such a thing... with such a task? Let the gods handle such business and leave me alone!" He was breathing fast now, images spiraling in his eyes and screeching in his ears. Embrey withdrew her hand. "Surely if this child is born and there is no vessel, it will manage, it comes from gods for heaven's sake."

"I do not think so, Ilfair. Ullumair would not request it if it were not needed," Ao'faer ran his fingers through his thick gray-and-black hair, standing before Ilfair directly now. "And Ilfair, think on it: if Ullumair can combine with Feralzmoon and walk among us, could Mnemylith perhaps not help you be rid of your Aberithic parasites, or even perhaps absorb them as he did? Or maybe he could heal you or mentor you."

Ilfair looked up to Ao'faer at this and met his gaze, trying to see if he was being manipulated by the old man. He did not think he was.

Ilfair calmed. "Yes. Maybe there is a hope in this for me, too. But it's just so much... it feels beyond me..." Ilfair trailed off at that.

"You will handle it as we all handle things that seem beyond us, one footfall at a time. Do not look at Orizon, Aurum, or Umbral, but rather at the path on Erlan at your feet," he paused and looked at Ilfair with love.

Ao'faer closed his eyes and shook his head. "So, let us begin with the vessel. It shall be of my making, but I will need your help," he stood up and held his shoulders back and sighed. "And you will find your way to Iilhi, you made it here, didn't you? And you will have Embrey's help, and others, of course." He smiled at her. She looked back straight-faced, brows raised in concern, but more solid and steadfast than she had been up to now, Ilfair noted.

"And what of you? Will you also come with us?" Embrey asked.

"I will come with you, of course," he smiled weakly. "But that is enough for now. You need to rest, and I need to read and think more. Try not to worry. I will write everything down and work everything out for you. Everything will be goodness, by the will of Ullumair, the father of Aelinth and Mercial."

Ao'faer set a place for them to sleep on the library floor below his quarters. Embrey did not know that Ilfair could see in the dark. So, she did not know that he could see the concern on her face as she lay awake. It calmed him to know she cared so much for him. He imagined her concern as a comforting shield. He hid behind that mental safeguard, ignoring the swirling mess of dark eels: the confusion and emotion. Ensconced in that warm keep, mercifully, he fell asleep quickly.

CHAPTER 43

THE NEXT MORNING

Taking advantage of the armistice which continued during the migration south of the Godskeeps, the settlers of Iilhi and Winters Haven forged a peace. This cooperation led to the settlement of the waypoint city of Overmoor; a gothic marvel rising out of the Sliipmoors.
—*from the Athenomancer archives*

Ilfair woke the next morning, the sun, through a window, shone on his face. Embrey was seated on the stairwell at the center of the room, watching him. She smiled and he returned a half smile.

"Good morning, sleepy sea serpent," she said, using the same awkward phrase she had used in Ashhaven. "You slept as the dead."

"I imagine the dead feel better than I did... and do," Ilfair said, in an uncommon moment of emotional honesty.

"I can imagine," she paused, rose, and crossed the room. "I'm sorry, Ilfair. I can't imagine what you must be dealing with."

"It's okay," he lied. "It's not your fault," he added after a moment.

"I know," she reached her hand out to help him stand. "Ao'faer is waiting for us."

Ilfair took her hand and stood. They walked together over to the stairwell and walked up.

On the way up Embrey said, "You know, Ao'faer was right."

"I suppose so, yes," Ilfair said and then realized he didn't know what Embrey was referring to, so he stopped on the stairs and added, "About what?"

"You don't have to do this alone. I will help you. And Halloch will too. And my family," she said simply, stopping just above him on the stairwell. She had turned to look down to him.

And with her words, he was undone. It was as though hearing the words *help* and *family* released a valve on dammed up emotions. And it was her voice as well. To Ilfair, it was the very sound of kindness, like a beautiful song that could bring forth emotions in the most stoic heart.

At that Ilfair collapsed on the stairs and cried silently, only his spasming shoulders revealed his state to Embrey. At the thought of all that companionship, everything that had built up over the last few weeks—nay his whole life—rushed forth and exploded out as tears and snot and chest-wracking sobs. He didn't even try to stop the whispering black hoard from filling his head.

He felt Embrey's soft touch and her head on his shoulder. Then he heard footfalls and felt Ao'faer's heavy hand hauling him up.

"Come now, son, come now. Come on now, all things pass," he straightened Ilfair up and Embrey grasped Ilfair's arm and hand with both of her hands until he calmed a little.

They guided him the rest of the way up the stairs. Ao'faer returned Ilfair wordlessly to the same chair he had occupied the night before. Embrey hastened away and returned with equal haste, bearing food and drink.

"Have some food. Drink. You will feel better," Embrey said.

After a few bites of food Ilfair did feel better. The three of them

were silent for many moments, Ilfair and Ao'faer seated and
Embrey standing just behind and to the left of Ilfair. Eventually,
Ao'faer sighed, stood, and spoke.

"Come with me, you two," Ao'faer said. And then, with some
abruptness, he turned and walked up the stairs.

Ilfair and Embrey followed somberly. From atop the tower the
vista was breathtaking even with the sourness of everyone's mood
and with half of the view blocked by the glass-enclosed flame.
Ao'faer was on the other side of the sphere already, on its southern
side. Ilfair and Embrey joined him.

"Look there," he said, pointing to a small satellite island off the
southern shore of their island. It wasn't a proper island, just a part
of their island really with a low point in between that was overwhelmed by the sea.

"Ilfair, I need you to retrieve something from there for me. Do
you see that small abbey on the north shore of the satellite isle?" he
looked at Ilfair, who nodded once.

"Good. Take the small boat there, it's guided by a chain
between the two shores. Take the stairs down at the center of the
abbey. I need you to retrieve something from the Whalefall there. I
need the tusk of the juvenile narwhal in the Whalefall at the
bottom. Take this," he handed him an amulet made of a glass
sphere with a small piece of whale bone inside. Ao'faer could see
the confusion on Ilfair and Embrey's faces.

"Ah, sometimes I forget what is obvious and what is not. The
Whalefall is a graveyard just below and to the west of the abbey. It
was a sacred site to the followers of Ullumair. It resides under the
sea just to the west of the small isle. The great beasts were drawn,
at the ebb of their lives, to come to rest at the holiness of these
isles and the Atheneum Tower. The ancient Mythals tended the
graveyard for ages. The Athenomancers carried on this tradition,
even though the whales no longer come with the same regularity
they once did. The amulet will let you move around there safely

and light your way. Clear?" Embrey and Ilfair looked at each other.

"Yes," Ilfair said. His expression showed that, while it was clear, it was also hard to comprehend how all of that was possible.

"So..." Ao'faer paused and looked intently at Ilfair, "have you accepted your choosing?"

"I don't know," he said simply, the rims of his eyes still red.

"Well, think more on it. And it will do you good to have something physical and different to do while you think. I daresay you will find it hard to fret while you are at this task. You will see why soon enough." Ao'faer smiled.

"Yes. I agree. I hope," Ilfair added and managed a half smile.

"And what of me?" Embrey asked.

He turned to look at her and said, "I will need your help preparing for Ilfair's return. We have some work to do and there is much I need to tell you so you can tell your mentors."

"When you get back, Ilfair, Embrey and I will have everything you need ready and you can be off with dear Jona, who waits for you below." He nodded over to the eastern shore where the Orca was still docked.

"You know, in all these years, Jona has never been up here. Can you believe that? It is quite a view after all," he looked at them both. Paused and smiled.

After a second, they all laughed out loud for many seconds. It felt good.

CHAPTER 44

THE WHALEFALL

The bravest Ashfallen of Iilhi and Winters Haven engineered the outpost
fort of Overmoor out of the Sliipmoors. They engineered the land to raise
the Highmoor Road between the three cities. But their disturbance of the
Sliipmoors awakened the Leechkin, heretofore hidden descendants of the
Aberiths. Thus began the Leechkin Wars, which would rage for years.
—from the Athenomancer archives

T lfair descended from the top of the tower via the glass staircase. He emerged from its spiraling base and set foot on the white stone column upon which the Atheneum rested. Leaving as he had arrived, he crossed the flat top of the stone column and took the rock-hewn staircase down to the scrub-covered sand of the island. At each stage of this journey, he took a moment to look back and up. Stunned at how small each of the structures—the stone column and the tower—made him feel. Each loomed over him ominously as he rounded the southwestern side of the rock column. The feeling of smallness they invoked matched his feelings concerning his current circumstance.

He sighed and turned back toward the sea. Back and to his left he saw the Orca docked, undulating with the waves. No one was visible there above deck. Forward and to his right he could see the small boat chained to the beach and the small islet just beyond. The path in front of him split, leading to the two ships such as they were. He walked the path to the right. The briars of the scrub brush clawed at his clothes where it had overgrown the path, this was obviously the path less taken. The sand yielded under his feet and made the walking more arduous than he would have expected. His thick boots left deep impressions in the sand.

Soon the sand hardened, moistening as he approached the beach. His shadow stretched across the beach, its blackness stark against the sunlit sand. Just as the sand was bright with sunlight, so too did the sea sparkle. He squinted against all the brightness. He pulled up the cowl on his sliipmare cloak to shadow his eyes.

He splashed through the shallow saltwater for the few steps it took to get to the boat and unhooked the metal clasp from a post buried deep in the sand. He pushed the boat with a bit of a run and hopped aboard as it drifted out to sea, breaking through the small waves. The chain clattered as it slid wetly through an iron ring on the starboard side of the boat.

Ilfair sat and grabbed the chain and pulled hand-over-hand. The boat moved easily through the water as he pulled.

Just then, as he focused on his hands, he realized that the black veins on the tips of the fingers of his right hand had grown worse. They had grown darker and now stretched further up his fingers. He guessed it might have happened that morning on the stairs, when his emotions had gotten the better of him and his mind had rushed with what he now knew were Aberithic insinuations of some kind. Now he noticed that the areas marked by the darkest blackness on the tips of his fingers now also gleamed with the shine of a polished stone. A quick touch with his other hand revealed a hardness; a toughness, almost like a callous with the associated reduction in sensitivity.

He sighed and was glad to be alone. He liked Embrey, and

Ao'faer for that matter, but he was glad to only deal with his own mind and his own problems. He thought of what the Atheno-mancer had said as he had looked at his fingertips. Maybe this Mnemylith, this union of the ancient gods, could help him. Even if he could not be rid of his infection, perhaps this new entity could be the mentor he needed.

"Ha. What a thought," Ilfair said to himself. Laughing at the idea of being mentored by a god, or whatever it was. "Absurd," he added, shaking his head.

In the meantime, he had begun to consider whether this Ao'faer could do the same. He was coming along after all and Iilhi was far, farther than the distance between Winters Haven and Overmoor.

As he considered all these options, he realized that the hull of the small boat was dragging on sand. He looked up and saw he had reached the small island. He had passed the league or so almost completely lost in his own thoughts. He was breathing hard from the work and his hands were sore and wet, but he had hardly noticed.

All just as well, Ilfair thought as he hooked the boat to the post at the end of the chain and disembarked. This island was tiny. He would have been able to see all the way across the island but for a black, rocky hillock at its center. It was only perhaps thirty or so yards away. There was no path to speak of, so Ilfair forged his way with some difficulty through the clingy flora. The vegetation here, like the mother island, was often thorny and clawing. Again, he was glad of his durable attire.

Happy to reach the rocky outcropping, he quickly scrambled up its wet black face, its jagged surface full of foot and handholds. He summited the outcropping with little difficulty, as it was only perhaps five or so times as high as he was tall.

From the top, he could see in front of him a circular white wall decorated by ancient runes. He recognized them from the books

Ao'faer had shown him as the language of the Mythals. He could see clearly now too that they looked like the symbols on his arm. *That is comforting... I think... I hope,* he thought. He walked around the wall to the western side. There he found an arched entryway. The arches were sculpted to look like two breaching whales, their tails at the ground of the entryway and their heads coming together at the top.

Inside, the walls were similarly decorated. There was no roof to the structure, Ilfair noticed.

"At least not anymore," he said, looking up to the clouds.

The structure housed only a stairwell, which disappeared into a pit. *Not another one,* he thought. Nonetheless, wasting no time, he descended the stairwell. The sconces on the walls were extinguished, but it was no matter to Ilfair as his eyes adjusted to the environment, inverting to permit his lightless sight.

The stairs were hewn from the rock for many dozens of feet of descent. Eventually the man-made rock stairs gave way to a steeply descending cavern. Here Ilfair felt at home, sighing, almost smiling. Rough footholds had been cut in the floor of the steep descent. In their absence, one would simply have slid to the end of the slick-floored cave, wherever that was.

Ilfair followed the cave. He knew he was moving below the shoreline and was moving toward the beach. The descent was more rapid than the movement toward the shore, but nonetheless, eventually he reached the end of the cave.

Impossibly, he was staring out onto the sea floor through another whale-adorned archway just like the one at the entrance above. The water was held at bay at the threshold of the door by some barrier of divine magic. Ao'faer had explained this before he had departed, but seeing it now was still beautiful, inspiring, and a bit intimidating—more than he could have ever pictured in his mind. It was like a window of water looking into the sea.

He squatted down and looked up. He could see beyond the

doorway to the top of the sea. Everything down here was now dimly lit by the sun above, filtering and wavering through the water. As Ao'faer had instructed, Ilfair grabbed the amulet in his hand and walked toward the doorway of water before him.

The amulet flared in his hand and as he approached the door, the water yielded to him, pushed away as if he were covered by a sphere. He continued, although with some hesitation, until he was all the way outside the door, fully in the sea. It took a few moments for the feeling of discomfort to abate, but dealing with disquieting circumstances was something to which Ilfair had become quite accustomed. He allowed himself that needed time, feeling his feet sink into the ground, which, having been covered by water only moments before, was really just muck.

With his senses adjusted, he set off in the direction Ao'faer had prescribed. All around him were alien sights, as he moved through this underground grove of whale bones. Many of the whale bones towered over him or were long and wide enough for him to walk on or between for many strides.

He could see off to his left the ribs and tale of the great blue whale that Ao'faer had mentioned. Monuments and manicured paths with coral-covered walls were everywhere. The contrast of the white bones and the bright coral was stunning.

Ilfair recalled Ao'faer's instructions. *Follow the tail and walk through the ribs along the spine and find the small narwhal in the skull of the great blue whale.* Evidently, a mother whale had laid her dead calf to rest in the head of the great beast.

Ilfair made his way to the skull of the great fallen whale. Water dripped down from the coral-encrusted bones as his air pocket moved through the sacred grove. Crustaceans flitted out of the air pocket when he occasionally crossed paths with them. As he moved, a fish fell to the ground next to his feet, flopping and gasping. He quickly moved on, allowing it to dart off, its silver skin catching the light.

Ilfair walked by the spinal bones of the neck and entered the massive skull. He could see that he was but the size of the eye socket. Right between where the whale's eyes would have been, just as Ao'faer had said, was the skeleton of a juvenile narwhal. It was probably twice the length of the massive skull, but it had been laid to rest in a u-shape so that its horn lay parallel with its own tail. It faced him.

Evidently, this young Narwhal was deformed, and its tusk was actually two tusks, twisted about one another. The likeness of the two tusks to the crown of Ullumair was undeniable. As such, this young whale skeleton had always stuck with Ao'faer, or so he had told Ilfair. And now, for some reason that Ilfair still could not figure, Ao'faer wanted the horn of the young dead narwhal.

He knelt down on his haunches and pressed his hands down into the muck to grip around the horn. He worked a bit on the tusk, twisting and pulling to get it free of the skull.

The entire length of the tusk was about the length of his forearm, perhaps a little longer. He stood to leave and felt a pang of Aberith-laced emotion. He turned back to the skeleton. He knelt in front of the ancient skull of the juvenile narwhal. He placed his hand between the eyes of the still-wet skull. He closed his eyes and spoke to the gods, particularly Oever, the god of death, and Mercial. He gave them his thanks and asked for forgiveness for what he felt could best be described as grave desecration, Ao'faer-directed or not. He wasn't sure that it mattered, but it made him feel a little less like the most despicable type of thief. "My thanks, and apologies, little one," he said. Then he stood, sighed, and turned to leave.

He made his way quickly back to the archway. As he entered the cave, he noticed how differently it smelled, rich with the earthy smell of clay and roots instead of the overwhelming smell of salt and seaweed in the sea. Somehow, he had not noticed when entering the grove, but now it was very noticeable. He noticed his nose and eyes adjusting as he made his way through the cavern and up the rock-hewn stairs. He exited the sacred rune-covered Whalefall Temple through the whale-adored archway. His eyes adjusted quickly to the light, and he noticed that the amulet was dim again.

It was much later now, and the sun was growing amber as it descended in the northwestern sky. It was getting much colder now, and the wind whipped through his cloak. He pulled it tight against the wet wind and pulled his hood up again. It helped.

He wanted to get across the water while there was still light, so he hastened his trip to the boat, breaking into a trot where possible. Upon reaching the boat he decided to lash the narwhal horn to his pack, in place of carrying it by hand as he had up to that moment. It stuck up just slightly above his head and he could feel its presence behind him.

As he pulled his way back, his hands ached with the cold wetness of the chilling air. He thought about the horn to take his mind off the discomfort. He was eager to learn its purpose and that eagerness—and the hunger in his belly—propelled him across the water, up the path, column, and stairs of the Atheneum Tower. Ao'faer had been right. This activity, the beauty of the Whalefall and the sacrifice of the baby whale, had created an enthusiasm and sense of purpose in him for his task that sitting and thinking could not have done.

I have accepted my choosing, he thought.

CHAPTER 45

WAITING FOR ILFAIR

The ancient Mythals of the Spirelight were given the secrets of navigation through their prayers to Ullumair. They became great mariners and explored the vastness of their Father's home, the Moonsong Sea. Their greatest accomplishment was the discovery of a ring of eight small, white rock islands. These isles resembled the points of a white crown emerging from the sea. The Mythals built great flaming Spirelight Towers upon each and named them the Kindledcrest Isles in honor of Ullumair's crown. The greatest of these, the Atheneum Tower, was built on the northernmost isle.

—from the Athenomancer archives

Embrey and Ao'faer stayed behind on the top of the tower until they saw Ilfair exit the spiraling entrance of the Atheneum and begin his descent of the column.

"He will be gone till about sunset if I guess his endurance correctly. He is a strong, if slight, lad," Ao'faer commented.

"I have seen as much as well," Ember agreed. "He has endured so much already and shows very little sign of fading. And in his own quiet way he is very concerned about others, mostly about not being a burden."

"Growing up as he has, I suppose that could make some sense," Ao'faer said, looking back down at the dot that was Ilfair disappearing over the white stone column's cliff edge.

"Perhaps," Embrey frowned, unsure about all of it. She breathed and straightened up. "So, why did you want me to stay behind?"

"You are clever. I can tell you perceive my duplicitous motives," he smiled for a moment and then continued. "Of course, I could use some help preparing some items, but that honestly won't take that long. What I really want to discuss with you is the rest of the message on Ilfair's arm. Perhaps you can help me with delivering the rest of the message to him. Walk with me?" Ao'faer gestured with his body and, seeing agreement from Embrey, started toward the tower stairs.

They descended the stairs quietly. When they entered the room, Ao'faer continued. "The message to Ilfair contains numerous specific details, some of which are somewhat, um, disturbing."

"More disturbing than what we have already heard from you?" Embrey said, concern in her voice and on her face.

"Yes, in their own way. Surely the scope of the message is intimidating, but some of the specific tasks that lay before you will be challenging. I am thinking of two things in particular," he paused.

"Okay," Embrey said, prompting him to continue.

"First, you will want to be careful who you tell about this. I would recommend keeping it to known and trusted confidants. Ilfair is not completely unwarranted in his fear that he may be viewed as mad by the unfaithful or cursed as heretical by the faithful to the new gods," Ao'faer looked at Embrey and declined his head to accentuate his seriousness, his staff casting dark shadows across his face.

"That makes sense and should be easy enough to do. Very few know about this at the moment. Even Halloch was intentionally opaque, even with Lady Starscribe." Embrey looked a little side-ways at Ao'faer as she said this, belying curiosity about what else concerned him.

"Just be careful with the information," he added.

"I will. We will, I'm sure," she corrected herself. "Surely that isn't the worst of it."

"It isn't. My other main concern is that a sacrifice is required both at the beginning and the end of this divine undertaking," he moved across the room toward a silver drum. "Could you bring me some of the contents of that container by the window there?" He pointed to another drum, this one was made of glass and contained a white sand-like substance.

"Of course," Embrey said. As she walked, seemingly stunned and overwhelmed by the scope of Ao'faer's words, she prompted him to continue, "What sacrifice?"

"At the completion of this task you, I mean Ilfair, will need to sacrifice a creature of the deep earth. This creature will not be, um, cooperative. It is of the Aberiths. So, it's more of a slaying, really... rather than a sacrificing. It will not be easy," he placed the glass end of his staff below the silver drum, mumbled a few words Embrey could not make out, and a flame kindled below the drum. The flame was white, like the sunlight, like the flame within the sphere atop Ao'faer's staff, not yellowed like that of a normal flame.

"Ilfair is no warrior, Ao'faer," Embrey said skeptically as she crossed the distance between them, carrying a container of the sand. "And neither am I."

"I know. That is what we are doing now. Perhaps with our help you both can complete the task despite that fact," he took the sand and poured it into the silver drum. "You will see. Another container full ought to do it... please," Ao'faer looked down into the drum as he spoke.

Embrey responded to the request and retrieved more sand from the drum. As she walked back to Ao'faer she asked, "How are we helping?"

"Before I get to that, allow me to explain a bit more about what I think is going on here," he paused, rhetorically.

"Okay." Embrey said perfunctorily.

"The message on Ilfair contains many details but omits others. But, based on these details, I think there are many important things to ensure will happen. You will be the better of the two of you to keep this clear as Ilfair has much to keep in check in his mind. It's best we keep his tasks simpler until, and if, he is able to get his mind fully sorted." Ao'faer paused again.

"Of course. That is completely understandable. And I mean no disrespect to Ilfair in saying so," Embrey added as she crossed with another container of the white sand.

"Oh, neither do I! Please don't misunderstand. I have great respect for the lad, how could I not? He was chosen by the father of the gods after all." He accepted the next container of sand from Embrey and poured it into the silver cylinder.

Embrey looked into the cylinder with Ao'faer. It still just looked like sand. "What is this?" she asked simply.

"This is purified earth from the mainland temple where Ullumair first walked on land. It is touched by the divine. A fire kindled by the Everflame can melt it," he explained as he looked up at the flame at the top of his staff.

"It is how the stairs were formed. The first Athenomancer was a master forger with such glass. He made the stairs ages ago. They are unbreakable and it will not permit the passage of those with ill-intent in their heart," Ao'faer explained further.

"Incredible, truly," Embrey said with an admiration in her voice that Ao'faer only ever heard in the young.

"Yes. It was... and is. What I seek to do is but a tiny deed by comparison. I'm afraid glass forgers of his quality have been lost to time. But I do retain enough of the talent to create some simple objects." He walked to the southern area of the round room and returned with a dark silvery cylinder. The object was entwined by an iridescent tentacle ending with a receptacle designed to hold another similar cylinder. Spirals extended off to the sides of the opening.

"What is that?" Embrey asked.

"It is a holy symbol of Ullumair. It was, ages ago, the handle of the morning bell-star of the great Mythal Chorister. It has resided here for years, being repurposed as a holy symbol rather than as part of a weapon used against the Aberiths and Feraliths. It used to accept a chain connected to a spiked bell shaped like two intertwining whales. Now it accepts a candle. Much nicer, yes... and quieter. Ao'faer turned the object over in his hand so Embrey could see the details.

"What are you going to do with it?" she asked.

"Let's just say it will be returning to its more ancient function," he paused, regarding the handle intently, but continued before Embrey could speak. "You will see soon enough. But Ilfair is almost back, I can hear him on the stone stairwell outside." He paused, letting the silence fill the room.

"I hear nothing," Embrey said after a moment.

"I know. I want you to understand some of my suspicions based on what I learned from the message and my reading the night you arrived. I think the process that will bring Mnemylith to us combines aspects typically associated with both Ullumair and Feralzmoon. I think this is intended to ease the merger for Ullumair, or Mnemylith, depending on to whom you are referring."

"What do you mean?" Embrey interrupted.

"I mean everything about how this is coordinated and who is involved is intentional. And the intention is to help Ullumair succeed. Yes?" he paused and looked at Embrey, whose intent expression bade Ao'faer continue.

"You see, the bearer is Ilfair. And he is Ashfallen and Aberith, a mortal version of Ullumair's condition in a way. The vessel I will make is of the sun and light and earth and water, as you will see. These are aspects of Ullumair and Feralzmoon both. It should be placed in water deep in the dark of the earth near a temple of Faid, the god of shadow, in Iilhi on a new moon. Again, aspects of Ullumair and Feralzmoon," he paused again and looked at Embrey, who nodded.

Ao'faer continued. "So, mortal and Aberith, sun and moon, light and dark, water and earth; each aspects of Ullumair and Feralzmoon, in turn. And, as you will soon and hopefully ultimately see, whale and Aberith. I believe that all of these aspects will be important to this working correctly. Some of this is explicit in the message, some is not. But it is my belief. Does it seem sound to you?" he asked Embrey earnestly without pausing for her response.

"But Embrey, Ilfair is the key. He is the mirror on Erlan of Ullumair's struggle within the moon. And the message is clear on this point. He will be like an antenna. The nascent Mnemylith will be drawn to his signature like a moth to the flame. He will be like the song of Ullumair to Aurum. Mnemylith will be drawn to it when it is blind like the newly born. Am I being clear?"

"Yes. If I fully comprehend, that is. I am humbled." Embrey replied in matched earnestness.

"Me as well." Ao'faer responded simply. "Ilfair must be near the vessel when the time comes, or Mnemylith will be lost."

At that moment, Ilfair entered the quarters, breathing heavily. He eyed them each, paused and said simply. "I found it."

He pulled off his pack and unlashed the white spiraling horn.

CHAPTER 46

THE VESSELS

The line of Athenomancers were the guardians of the great Atheneum
Tower. The line was made by the passage of the Everburning Mantle,
which carried with it all the life and knowledge of the line of
Athenomancers. The mantle also protected the Athenomancer from the
ravages of time and disease, granting them long life. At the eventual end
of their time, each Athenomancer would pass the mantle and knowledge
on to an apprentice who had been selected from the most adept of the
Mythals who resided in the neighboring Spirelights.
—from the Athenomancer archives

Ilfair eyed Embrey and Ao'faer curiously upon entering Ao'faer's quarters. "Did I interrupt something?"

"No, of course not," Ao'faer paused. "So, you found it?" he asked rhetorically as, clearly, he could see the horn. "Excellent," Ao'faer said, answering his own question without waiting for a response. He crossed the room, meeting Ilfair halfway as he rounded the large stone table.

Silently, with only Ao'faer's gestures guiding him, Ilfair understood what to do and handed over the horn. Ao'faer fitted the root of the narwhal spire into the holy symbol.

"Oh, most excellent. This will do perfectly. It's as if it was meant to be," he beamed with pleasure. "Ilfair, please take off your cloak and let me see your right arm," Ao'faer instructed.

Ilfair complied, if not without an expression of confusion, which was matched by Embrey.

"I could use my own strands, but this seems more appropriate." He used a small hook, which he produced from one of the pockets of his amber robe, and drew many long Amberglass threads from the sleeve on the shirt Ilfair had found beneath the Spirelight. Ao'faer wrapped the threads about the holy symbol. "These are virtually unbreakable, you know?" he said as he looked quickly over to Ilfair before looking back to his work.

"Um, okay. That does sound useful," Ilfair said, trying to use sarcasm to mask his feelings of smallness.

"Oh, it is. Embrey can explain more to you later."

Ilfair looked at Embrey who just shrugged, apparently having no idea at that moment to what Ao'faer was referring.

"But what are you..." Embrey began, but Ao'faer stopped her with a raised hand and a click of his tongue.

Ao'faer worked intently and with haste, wrapping the threads around and around the symbol and the lower quarter of the horn until they were both well covered. He left two long leads and, taking one in each hand, pulled them apart so that the holy symbol and horn were suspended in front of him, horn pointing down.

He brought it over to the cylinder and lifted it above and slowly lowered the ensemble down into the cylinder. He wrapped the threads around two eyelets on the opening of the cylinder.

"Now we wait a bit. How about something to eat and drink? Maybe you can tell us about the Whalefall?" Ao'faer made his way to the teapot and produced more of the sweet bread from the day before.

They all sat around the table as they had when they had first arrived.

Embrey, clearly still fixated on the comment about the shirt, tried again. "Athenomancer, what exactly is it I should tell Ilfair about the shirt?"

"Oh, I thought that would have been obvious," Ao'faer stated somewhat bluntly. The comment stung Embrey, but she said nothing, permitting Ao'faer to continue. "The threads of the shirt were made in the same way that the stairwell was made. They are divine fibers, forged and woven by the Mythals, the ancient priests of Ullumair. They are light but stronger than wrought iron. You will see more later. In the meantime, tell of us Whalefall!" Ao'faer took a bite of bread and a drink from his tea.

They talked of Ilfair's visit to the Whalefall grove. Ao'faer and Embrey talked of their discussions in Ilfair's absence, sharing most everything except the confrontation with one of the children of Feralzmoon who awaited Ilfair on the journey.

After the conversation and the repast, Ao'faer produced a bundle of scrolls from his robe and handed them to Embrey. "I have written down some important things you will need. You will need to first go to the Circle of Eights temple of Ulmaith and Iroin in Overmoor. You should see the ecclesiarch Inafeign Umberhallen." Ao'faer unrolled the parchment. Among numerous sketches and notes, there was an array of numbers.

"The only thing I was not able to determine was the meaning behind these numbers. The followers of Ulmaith are like the quantitative equivalent of the knowledge focus of the Aelinth temple in Winters Haven. Where the temple of Aelinth focuses on light and beauty, Ulmaith focuses on rigor and practicality. There is simply nowhere else in the realm that knows more than The Thirteen of the Circle of Eights. Last I checked, Inafeign was the master of numbers there. Present this scroll to him. He will help you," Ao'faer completed. "You've heard of them, yes, Ilfair?"

"I have. He is on the ruling council of Overmoor. All of Eightowns know them. But aren't you coming with us? I thought you said you were coming with us?" Ilfair asked, slight panic in his tone.

"Hm. Yes, I did. And I am. I think the item is complete now."

Ao'faer stood and walked over to the silver drum. He pushed the sleeves of his robe up and muttered something Ilfair could not make out. The Athenomancer's arms seemed to drip with liquid, a moist sheen visible thereupon. He reached down into the silver drum and worked his arms on what must have been the contents of the drum. This continued for a few minutes until at last he stopped.

"There," he said, marking what must have been the completion of his efforts.

He removed his arms from the drum and used his hands to strip a glossy substance from his arms.

He loosened the strings and pulled the horn from the container. "Ah, yes. Perfect," Ao'faer admired his work.

The horn had been bent over upon itself, reducing the length by half. Further, the bone had been worked to contain points and edges. Both the horn and hilt shone with an iridescent gleam, covered by a thick layer of the divine glass of Ullumair. The glass formed a curved keen edge along one edge of the length of the horn, like the blade of a curved dagger.

"This will do quite nicely for you. The Athenomancers always thought there was some purpose to this particular young whale's horn. It's actually two horns twisted about each other. It looks exactly as the horn atop Ullumair's crown. It was always foretold that it would have divine purpose. And, just as Aurum heeded Ullumair's call, so too will you be able to call Aurum's light to this blade."

He wrapped the remaining thread about the hilt and tied it off. He handed it to Ilfair, who took it in his right hand. "I have formed it into the shape of a kukri blade. It was a common blade of the Feraliths. I think it should be of both Ullumair and Feralzmoon."

"This looks like a weapon. What in godsname would I do with this?" Ilfair asked, looking confused.

There was only silence in response. Ao'faer glanced quickly over at Embrey. Ilfair followed his gaze and looked over at her as well. She remained impassive, although conspicuously so, which caused Ilfair some concern.

"Wait. What is going on here?" Ilfair asked, deepening his tone with seriousness, looking more at Embrey than Ao'faer.

Embrey went to speak, moving slightly toward him, but Ao'faer interrupted. "Soon enough, Ilfair. Let me prepare just one more thing."

Ao'faer took his robe off and sat in his chair. "Come close you two."

Ao'faer laid his staff across his lap and looked at the pair. "Embrey, remember that I said two sacrifices were needed? One at the end and the other..."

"At the beginning," she completed, understanding dawning on her.

"Wait, what is going on? What are you two talking about? What sacrifices?" Ilfair said, hurriedly.

Ao'faer disconnected the oval glass from the end of his staff, the yellow flame still flickering inside. He then unbuttoned his shirt and removed his left arm from the sleeve revealing his chest on the left side. Where his left pectoral should have been, there was a hole. In that hole was a bright white light, housed in a porous bone-like shell.

"That is the Mantle of the Athenomancer, which contains The Everflame." he held the glass bauble from his staff up to his chest and the white bone-covered flame entered the glass sphere. The yellow flame of the staff danced around the white globe that floated in the center of the glass. Its presence displaced the yellow flame, which now orbited about the white sphere like a small sun.

"When it was my time to pass on the mantle, I would give this to my apprentice who would become the next Athenomancer. The divine Everflame would protect the new Athenomancer from the ravages of time and pass on all the knowledge of the Athenomancers past as well as all manner of other advantages besides. It would seem that I am to be the penultimate Athenomancer. This will be the vessel for Mnemylith, who shall be The One Athenomancer forever forward."

"But you said you were coming," Ilfair said, voice trailing off. He looked at Embrey. Tears were forming in her eyes. "But..."

"I am coming, Ilfair. I am in the vessel. I and all who have come before me," Ao'faer smiled. But he already seemed less radiant, an ashen grayness that had not been there moments before now shadowed his countenance.

"But that isn't what you made me think," Ilfair said, sounding betrayed.

"I am sorry, Ilfair, truly I am. I would have loved to help you in the way that you wanted. But I am bound by the message just as you are. It is very clear," Ao'faer's voice was already weakening.

"This isn't right. Why didn't you tell me?" Ilfair asked.

"I told you what I thought would be best at the time. Perhaps I erred. It was so much for you to take in and you had already been through so much. I did my best. Please do not remember me as deceptive. You must succeed, Ilfair. Please, don't waver," he looked at Ilfair intensely. Tears were forming in Ilfair's eyes, and he could hear Embrey's quiet sobs.

"I won't," Ilfair said after a moment of quiet.

"And Embrey, please don't let this place be forgotten," Ao'faer asked.

Embrey simply nodded, apparently not wanting to try to speak.

"Don't be sad. I have had my time and much more. I will be with my brothers and my gods. Now it is your time," he stood and set the vessel on the chair. He looked out of the window and down at the Orca.

"Tell Jona he was right. It is cold," Ao'faer slumped back down into the chair and was gone. The life and light, gone from him.

Embrey went quietly over to him and touched him. Ilfair heard her whisper something, most likely a prayer of passing from Mercial.

Ilfair just stood there stunned. He walked over to the vessel and took its warmth in his hands. He hoped that it would make him feel better. It did not.

"Embrey..." Ilfair tried to think of what to say exactly, something appropriate for the moment. "Help me," was all he managed.

Embrey stood from kneeling by Ao'faer and came over to Ilfair.

She wrapped her arms around him. They stood there, Embrey holding Ilfair, and he holding the vessel that glowed between them. They watched the sun set as Ao'faer's body slowly turned to dust.

CHAPTER 47

THE ORCA'S RETURN

*Though separated by the sea, even the line of Athenomancers were
affected by the great migration and the eventual silencing of the ancient
gods. The support sent to the isles waned during the migration. The
Spirelights, save the Atheneum Tower, eventually came to ruin. The crop
of apprentices was decimated as the Spirelights all came to ruin. Upon
the founding of Winters Haven, the support of the Athenomancer and
the great Atheneum Tower resumed. The apprentices, but one at a time,
were provided by the priests of the goddess of light, Aelinth. The support
of the towers fell to the priests of the god of the sea, Mercial. In this way
the line of Athenomancers was retained. However, the line of
Athenomancers still risks being broken as the ancient world wanes.
—from the Athenomancer archives*

Ilfair and Embrey slept on the floor below the
Athenomancer's quarters as they had the night before. They
did not know what to do with Ao'faer's ashes and both
silently agreed not to be in their presence for the night. The next
morning they rose early and silently collected their belongings.
Embrey found a vessel for Ao'faer's ashes and put them in a pack
with their other belongings.

"We should take these to Halloch," Embrey paused, then added, "Or Lady Starscribe."

They then descended the tower and the stone column in silence.

When they reached the split in the path Embrey paused and spoke. "I would like to see Whalefall someday."

Ilfair nodded somberly but did not speak. They started off to their left toward the Orca together.

"I think we should not speak of Ao'faer to Jona," Embrey said when they neared the Orca.

Again, Ilfair nodded and remained silent, battling whispering black images in his head. Judging by her expression, Ilfair guessed Embrey could tell as much.

"I will tell Halloch. He will know how best to handle it," Embrey seemed to be talking as much to herself as to Ilfair. Perhaps working through things out loud.

Hearing their footfalls on the deck, Jona emerged from the belly of the Orca. They were quite near the boat when he set foot on the deck. He greeted them with his customary smile and wave and addressed them both.

"How fare thee this morn?"

"Well enough. And you?" Embrey said with forced cheer.

Ilfair simply nodded quickly and gave a tight-lipped smile.

"Good, good. So, we are off then, eh? Ye got what ye needed?" Jona asked.

"Yes," they both said, almost together.

Embrey added, "We did. We got what we needed. Thank you. We are grateful to you, Captain Gaffspell."

"No need to thank me. Always a pleasure to assist the great families," there was only earnestness in his oddly high-pitched voice.

"Alright boys! We're off!" Jona bellowed, breaking the calm of the morning. Stirring below deck was followed by a bustle of activity above and below.

"Jona, allow us to be out of you and your men's way. Yes?" Embrey said.

"Of course, lass. Of course," Jona said, pausing his work on the deck ropes to address her eye-to-eye.

Embrey and Ilfair disappeared below deck, and both quietly went to their quarters.

Ilfair sat in his room on his bed and watched through the small circular window as the Orca moved out to sea. In a few minutes he took the small glass vessel, slightly smaller than his head, from off the bed next to him and eyed it closely. He thought that Embrey had had it. In fact, he was sure of it. He closed his eyes, turned his head slightly to the side, and grimaced. Had she dropped it off in his room without him knowing?

"She must have," he said, but he simply couldn't remember. It was an odd thing to forget. And it was such a short time ago. He really must have been in his head the whole way to the Orca, to not recall that at all was strange. It made him worry for a moment. He was punished for that by whispering, white-eyed ebony-skinned eels, so he quickly put it aside and returned his attention to the vessel.

He felt the warmth through the glass and watched the lights within it for many minutes. Looking closely now, he could see that the glass, which had looked to have small imperfections riddled throughout its surface, was in fact instead covered with symbols.

"More symbols," Ilfair said. He sighed and put the vessel back.

He lay back on his bed, hands behind his head, and stared at the ceiling. His mind raced with the reality of his circumstances. He felt Aberithic fingers pressing at his thoughts as his feelings dipped toward depression again.

He shook his head and said "*No*" to himself. He again closed his eyes and held the symbol to Faid. He imagined *himself* this time as the obelisk, as the shadowcaster, casting the shadow on the protesting black eels. He opened the rift under the eels. This time though, in a moment of divine inspiration, he imagined the shadow he cast as a physical thing. In his mind the shadow was a *thing* with weight the eels could not bear and a solidity his sight could not penetrate.

And with that, the eels were gone, at least for a moment. In his exuberance of success his solid shadow faltered, and the moment passed. The eels burst through cracks that spit the shadow chaotically. He opened his eyes and stood, his mind somewhere between hope and despair.

He realized, at that moment, that he had to become so practiced at this exercise that he could do so without concentrating. Like a bard and his instrument, thoughtlessly playing it so he can sing. In that way he could endure stresses and continue to function normally without having to pull himself aside from life to meditate himself to calmness. He would need to *be* the shadowcaster, not become it.

He left the room, intending to go to the deck for air and space to consider his thoughts. But instead paused at Embrey's door. Quite to his surprise, he knocked on the door. "Embrey?" he said quietly.

"Yes?" she said through the door.

"Can I come in?" Ilfair asked. He heard her walking to the door before he had finished his question. The door pulled open and she gestured him in with a nod of her head and a downcast gaze.

Ilfair walked past her and leaned against the corner of the room near the window, trying to get as much space as he could in the tiny quarters.

Embrey sat back on her cot and looked up at him.

"What are you doing?" Ilfair asked, with no real intention behind it.

"I am looking through Ao'faer's scrolls. I want to understand everything as best as I can... before we are back," she gestured to the scattering of scrolls on her cot.

"Oh. Thank you. That is good of you. I hadn't even thought about that yet," Ilfair said, guardedly.

"It puts my mind at ease. It makes me feel useful. Like I have some control," Embrey replied first with a scoff and then, to cover the undesirable cynicism, with a smile.

Many thoughts entered Ilfair's head, about powerlessness in particular, and he wanted to give them voice. But he did not. He simply said, "Thank you," again and moved to leave the room.

"Are you okay, Ilfair? I know I keep asking that. I just... I don't know, want to help, I guess," Embrey asked as he moved.

"Yes. Yes, I am okay. And I understand how you are feeling. But really, I am okay, all things considered. I just want to get some air. I will leave you to your scrolls. That's important," he said and paused to regard her. He wasn't lying to her, but he wasn't exactly telling the truth either. His head was such a mess he wondered if he would even know the truth of how he was feeling.

Instead of expressing this Ilfair simply added. "And again, thank you. I will ask you about them. But later, please. If that's okay."

"Of course, Ilfair," Embrey stood and opened the door for Ilfair and watched him depart her quarters.

Halfway down the hall, Ilfair turned. "You are helping, Embrey," Ilfair paused and, seeing confusion on Embrey's face, he added, "You asked if you were helping. You are." He smiled sincerely and then he turned and walked the rest of the way out.

The rest of the day passed quietly, little else of note being said or done. Ilfair sat quietly on the deck with the occasional word exchanged with Jona or a deckhand, much as he had on the way to the island. The Orca glided quickly across the water, the sail filled by the same wind that had resisted them the previous days.

Embrey spent the remainder of the day studying the scrolls and annotating them. They all gathered for food as the sun set. They talked only of trivialities, all sensing something of import was hanging overhead but never giving it breath.

Afterward, Ilfair resumed his position, standing at the foredeck looking towards the coast in the distance, where Winters Haven awaited. They would arrive there sometime in the night. The trip was quicker back from the islands, as the currents favored the southeastern direction of travel.

As the sun set behind them, Ilfair heard Embrey coming up behind him. In a moment she was beside him. He turned his head to the right to regard her.

"Hi," Embrey said.

"Hello," Ilfair replied.

After many moments of silence Ilfair added, "I am glad you are with me. No... lucky. I am lucky that you are with me."

Embrey did not speak but took his right hand in her left. Ilfair wondered if she felt the toughness of his fingertips. If she did, she did not speak of it. Ilfair felt a warmth radiate from her hand. At first, he stiffened at her touch, but the warmth calmed him. And best of all, he did not feel the need to speak. He was happy, if only for that moment. And it was a calm happiness, which called no emotional eels to his mind.

They stood there for many moments, watching their shadows lengthen on the sea, pointing the way home to Winters Haven, just visible in the distance.

"I would have gone, you know? Even had you chosen otherwise," Embrey said, breaking the silence.

"I know," Ilfair said, looking up to meet her gaze with a timid smile and a knowing nod.

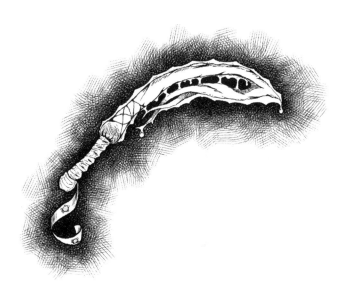

EPILOGUE
GOODBYE ABBY (FOR NOW)

Ilfair slept that night, unlike on the boat ride out to the island. But he regretted it the next morning, for with the sleep came dreams.

He tossed and moaned quietly in his cot as he slept. As far as his mind knew, he was floating above the mainland now, just east of Winters Haven, looking down onto the Sliipmoors. The High-moor Road that connected Winters Haven, Overmoor, and Iilhi cut a path through it. But something was wrong.

The sky was gray, and the moon was cracked in the sky. To his left, Feralzmoon, who was himself the size of Gray Peak, was ravaging the Godskeep Mountains, casting clawed-up mountains of earth about erratically. Some of the castings left Erlan entirely, others fell back to Erlan leaving devastating craters upon their impact. Fires raged on the ridge where Overmoor was perched. Behind him, Winters Haven was gone, evidently pulled out to sea by the raging colossal waves. He could not see Iilhi from here, but he was not hopeful about its condition.

He descended then, down into the moors. Closer and closer he came to the surface until he could see thousands of Leechkin squirm and swarm about in the moors. Amidst the hordes he could see a figure walking in circles on top of circles on a patch of dry land.

His feet set down just in front of the path that the man had walked into the ground. At first, he was distracted by the undulating mass of Leechkin all about him. That is, until the figure, a form he could see more clearly now, approached him. The dust and darkness of the blasted land had, until now, mostly obscured the man.

Ilfair was not surprised to see his face when he got close enough. He stopped and looked at his doppelganger. The man was clearly him, but clearly not as well. The man's right eye was milky-white and, where his flesh was visible, the right half of his body was freckled with black chitin. His form was rail thin and his face gaunt. Ilfair reached out to touch the man's face.

Abby stepped out from behind the body, holding the doll of Ilfair to her chest with her left arm. Ixo's chitinous bulk was visible behind her. "I haven't forgotten about you, Ilfair."

Ilfair just closed his eyes, tilted his head up and sighed, exhausted by Abby's harassment.

"Don't you like what you may become?" Abby asked.

"What is the point of this Abby?" Ilfair asked curtly and with evident exhaustion.

"Oh, it's just a bit of fun. Don't be so sensitive."

"Fun?" Ilfair scoffed.

"Well, okay. Really I'm just trying to help. In my own way. This is really good information for you! This is what will happen if you fail—to you and to Erlan." Abby gestured with her arm.

"Goodnight, Abby. See you again soon I would guess," Ilfair smiled.

"But...!" Abby tried to protest.

Regardless, Ilfair opened his eyes and sat up in his bed. He could hear Abby's last words echo in his head. He lay there and allowed his heart to calm and the images in his head to subside. In a few moments he was calm.

"Better," he said, giving breath to his thoughts. He rested calmly, though he did not sleep, for the remainder of the night as the Orca made its way to Winters Haven.

As he watched the city grow on the horizon, shadowy footfalls cast by a bright sun, filled his mind and a deep voice filled his ears. The dark voice echoed down from above the footfalls.

"Better indeed," it said. Ilfair did not know it, but Faid, the god of shadows, had spoken to him.

Made in the USA
Columbia, SC
25 January 2025

52614711R00205